BATTLE
FOR THE
SHADOW
PRINCE

BATTLE

FOR THE

SHADOW

PRINCE

GENEVIEVE JACK

USA TODAY BESTSELLING AUTHOR

Battle for the Shadow Prince: A Bargain with the Shadow Prince Book 2

Copyright © 2024 Carpe Luna PublishingPublished by Carpe Luna, Ltd., Bloomington, IL 61704

This book is a work of fiction. Names, characters, places, and incidents are either products of the author's imagination or used fictitiously. Any resemblance to actual events, locales, or persons, living or dead, is entirely coincidental.

All rights reserved. No part of this publication can be reproduced or transmitted in any form or by any means, electronic or mechanical, without permission in writing from the author or publisher.

FIRST EDITION: Dec 2024

eISBN: 978-1-962757-15-7

ISBN: 978-1-962757-16-4

Cover art: Karen Dimmick / ArcaneCovers.com

V2.2

About This Book

To save my monster, I must become a monster.

Roll the dice.
Choose a challenge.
Try not to die.

Winner take all.

My shadow prince was wrested from my arms and dragged through a portal, and I don't know who took him or why. Damien showed me my power as a woman and as a mage, and he means everything to me. He built me back up after my ex tore me down. And now he's gone.

I'll stop at nothing to free him, but when I learn the vampire queen is responsible, things get complicated. The subterranean city of Night Haven isn't accessible by humans, and even the most powerful magical creatures in my life won't dare challenge the vicious and bloodthirsty Valeska.

Everyone tells me there's nothing I can do, that I'm not strong enough to free him. They tell me to give up. But I'd rather die than live a life without my mate. So there's only one thing I can do. To save my monster, I must become one too.

I

BLOOD & BINDING

DAMIEN

I lose my grip on Eloise's fingers, and dread consumes me. Not again. The Gowdies captured me once with their dark magic. To do it again now, after everything, after Eloise, it's too cruel to fathom. I will kill them. I will kill them all.

As a shade, I'm usually soothed by the darkness, but the shadows I command are gone, magically stripped away to leave nothing but a void. I fall and fall and fall. Eloise's expression of anguish grows smaller, more distant, as the black throat of the portal constricts, swallowing me. I roar as it closes completely, cutting off the channel between us. All that's left is nothingness and pain and loss. Until I drop into a blinding ring of conjured sunlight. My wings flare and my talons itch to tear through as many Gowdie witches as possible. I won't allow them to bleed and bind me this time. Not again.

"Welcome back to the palace of Night Haven, Damien. It's been far too long."

That's not a Gowdie voice that pierces the blinding light but one from my nightmares. *Fuck.* How… how did she find out so quickly?

"Valeska." The vampire queen's name leaves my mouth on a hiss. My wings spread defensively until the tips singe against the bright circle containing me. I retract them with a wince. That's pure sunlight. We're underground in Night Haven, but this is the real thing. No vampire can wield this kind of magic. She has help. Powerful help.

"Damien." The slight tip of her head conveys the greeting. "Allow me to introduce you to my new friends." She gestures toward two humans to our right, twins. The exceptionally tall and narrow Korean men have spiky, blond-tipped hair and high-collared dusters embroidered with a sun sigil over the left breast. "This is Tae and Lang of the Kim family of witches. I'm sure you've already guessed that their family's keyspell is sun wielding."

Shit. Powerful help indeed. Sun wielding is rare. The Gowdies needed a coven of witches and a full ritual to summon me from Tenebris. These two did it without breaking a sweat.

"I thought witches were forbidden in Night Haven?" I say dryly.

Valeska's tall, shiny boots clack on the stone just outside the reach of the light. Although sunlight weakens me, it can kill her. At least there is that. She can't touch me without breaking the magic that binds me, and if she breaks the spell for any reason, for any length of time, my shadows will slaughter every being in this room, including her.

"I make the law here, Damien. You'd do well not to forget that." Her words snap like a whip. "I have to admit I hesitated to employ their help, given our general distrust of each other as a species, but when Lazarus explained how the Gowdies captured you, I realized the beings who could bind you would also be the only ones strong enough to free you, and as it so happens, the Kim family owes me a favor."

I clench my jaw as she paces around the walls of light, studying me as her blood-red fingertips drum on her biceps. She knows. Somehow she's learned I'm free of the Gowdie curse. A low growl percolates in my chest, and I search the boundary for vulnerabilities. Even though the light keeps me from using my shadows, if I can charge through the beams, escape is possible.

"Don't try it," she snarls, presuming what I plan to do. "I promise you the Kims will not allow you to leave this room without my permission."

"And when will that be?" I grit out. I position myself at the exact center of the symbol, where the light is only a mild irritation.

Her nostrils flare. A vampire's sense of smell is unparalleled. There's no doubt what she's picking up in this enclosed space. Eloise. We had sex not ten minutes ago. I am covered in her. I dig my talons into my palms as my protective instincts rage.

"Imagine my surprise when I engaged the Kims to break your Gowdie curse only for them to discover via their private network that someone had already broken it!" She bares her teeth. "What luck. I'm sure it would've been only a matter of time before you shared the happy news with me. I've made it known to you twice now that I need a consort and you are my first choice."

"Let me out and we can discuss it," I say calmly. One shadow is all I need.

She huffs. "Oh, Damien, don't take me for a fool. The stench of human sex coming off you carries the unmistakable musk of bonding. You've already mated someone. Didn't take you long to find a willing partner. Not surprising considering your power, although I am shocked you chose a human." Her gaze hollows, turning impossibly darker and even more soulless. "They are so incredibly breakable."

Every part of me longs to knock Valeska's head off her body. Mentioning the vulnerability of my mate is meant to be a threat, and it takes all I have in me to suppress my murderous response. But I must suppress it. Valeska is deadly in her own right but weakened by sunlight—my only chance at freedom is convincing her to release me. That won't happen if she suspects I intend to kill her.

"Why have you brought me here, Valeska? What do you want from me?"

"You know what I want."

"I won't be your consort." Even vampires have rules and limitations. I will never voluntarily agree to Valeska's plan. If she tries to force me, I'll either escape or kill her the second she frees me. She wants to use me as both protection and a weapon, but as long as I have free will, she can't let me out of this cage. I'm useless to her in here. The only way she can control me is to bind me. If she *could* force a mating bond, my instincts would compel me to protect her. Not only could I not kill her, but no matter how much I wanted to, it would be almost impossible for me to avoid executing her commands. Mated shades, like mated vampires, serve their mates.

Vampire tradition, though, forbids taking a mate without their consent. Mating is more than sex; it's binding by blood and old magic. As queen, Valeska could ignore that prohibition and force a mating bond on me. She'd likely even escape any reproach for it. But she can't ignore that I am already mated. A vessel can only hold so much, and mine is full. My biology will not allow me to have sex, let alone mate another as long as Eloise is alive.

Which is why I must proceed with caution. The last thing I want is for Valeska to target Eloise. The queen absolutely cannot know my mate's identity. The second she does, she'll send the finest soldiers from her army to kill her. I can't let that happen. Maybe I can distract her. "I'll be returning to my homeworld as soon as I find a witch who can open the rift. I'm the wrong choice for you."

"That would be counterproductive, Damien. You're needed here. I find your specific talents to be exactly what I'm looking for in a mate and consort."

Yeah, the ability to serve as her combination blood bag and watchdog makes me the ideal companion. Only problem is I hate the bitch, and the idea of spending a single night in her bed, let alone hundreds, turns my stomach. I'd rather fall on my blade. "Not interested."

"Maybe you just need the proper motivation. Who is it I smell on you? Who is this human woman you've mated?"

I say nothing. I'll die before I offer a single thing about her.

"Who is she?" Her shrill voice echoes off stone.

I glare at her from my prison of light.

Our eyes lock, and I don't mask my hatred for her.

She releases a frustrated hiss. "Conjure the woman!" she commands the Kims.

Tae exchanges a worried glance with his brother. "If you have a vial of her blood, we can attempt it once we've rested."

"Of course I don't have her blood. Use his. He must have drunk from her."

Lang swallows hard, then bows. "Your Majesty, it isn't possible. While he is surrounded by light, he is mortal. If her blood remains in his system, its magical properties are, unfortunately, destroyed and therefore useless to us."

The way Valeska's lips peel off her teeth removes any pretense of humanity from her visage. She's an animal. An unholy demon.

"Bring the scribe!" the queen commands.

The sound of footsteps heralds Lazarus's arrival. Armed guards escort my friend and confidant into the room. His conformation is even worse than normal, his skin ashen and papery, as if he's underfed. The guards thrust him forward, his oversized nocturnal eyes blinking against the bright light that surrounds me. "My queen?"

"Is there a spell in that vast pile of books you keep that the Kims can use to conjure Damien's mate? Something in the lost-or-forgotten-magic section, perhaps?"

Lazarus frowns, his bulbous eyes seeking mine for a fraction of a second before he rushes forth an answer. "No, my queen. It is impossible without her blood."

I grimace. In all my years of friendship with the scribe, he's never called something impossible. There's always more research to do. Finding lost magic is his specialty.

Valeska's scowl turns murderous. She knows he's

lying. "How can you be sure, scribe, unless you check every book?" She bares her fangs. "Guards, escort Lazarus back to the stacks and keep him there until he finds a way to be more… helpful."

"Yes, my queen." One guard bows, then takes Lazarus roughly by the arm and drags him from the room.

Valeska redirects her rage-filled glare at me. "Who. Is. She? Tell me now and I will show mercy."

Mercy, my ass. Eloise poses a problem for Valeska, and she knows it.

"Who is the woman?" she demands again.

I flash a wicked, taunting grin. "Come to me through the sunlight, Valeska, and I'll whisper her name in your ear."

The vampire queen paces around my cell, wringing her hands. She's frustrated. This plan of hers won't work and she knows it.

"Tell me her name."

"Free me and I will." *Right before I slice your head from your shoulders.*

Valeska laughs, and the sound is like shattering icicles. Frigid. Brittle. Heartless. "I'm afraid that won't be possible, Damien. You see, I may not be able to mate you or take you as my consort under the circumstances, but I am within my power to keep you as my political prisoner for as long as necessary."

"Political prisoner?"

"Yes. You've admitted to me you herald from a different world, a different kingdom. How do I know you haven't been spying on Night Haven the entire time you've been living among my vampires, taking advantage of our hospitality?"

"That's bullshit and you know it."

She shakes her head. "One way or another, you'll remain at my side. Give me your mate's name and your living conditions will be far more comfortable."

"I will never give up her name." I growl, baring my teeth.

She turns toward the Kims. "Please escort our guest to the cell we've prepared."

Tae lowers himself into a crouch and circles his forearms at the elbow, hands clutching invisible spheres. I'm temporarily blinded by a flash of light that stings my skin. Weakness and fatigue settle on me like a disease, and I stagger forward just as the symbol dissipates.

Immediately I attempt to escape through the network of shadows, but my power fizzles, and it doesn't take long for me to understand why. My wrists are bound in front of me in cuffs of pure sunlight. All my energy drains away. My knees wobble with the effort to remain standing.

Valeska flashes an evil grin. I cringe when she crosses to me and brings her blood-red lips close to my ear. "In time you'll beg to be my mate."

My teeth grind even as my bones ache where the light shines through my skin. My voice holds every ounce of hatred I feel for her as I respond. "Don't. Bet. On. It."

2

NUCLEAR WINTER

ELOISE

Damien slips through my fingers and I scream.

"No. No. No!" My love, my mate, disappears through the dark portal. With no hesitation, I leap, throwing myself toward the closing maw of darkness. It's a stupid thing to do. I have no idea what's on the other side of that portal. But I don't care. I just want him back.

But it's no use. Like a fish only drawn to one bait, the spell is selective. I pass right through it, ending up splayed on the floor of the attic, the wind knocked out of me. Pressure builds in my chest, clogs my throat like a fist, until it finally bursts out in an agonizing wail. He's gone. He's really gone. And the worst part is, my best friend or her family took him.

I will kill the witch responsible for this. I don't care who it is. I won't stop until their blood coats my skin. The only reason I know my heart hasn't been torn from my chest is it's hammering against my sternum like a prisoner trying to break through their cell wall. A fiery whirlwind of fury is building within me. I plant one foot and then the other under me.

Only then do I hear the low rumble in the room, like stomping feet on the bleachers in high school. All the books in my parents' magical library are vibrating on their shelves, snapping their covers like rabid dogs. Pages rustle. Paper shreds rain to the chalkboard floor like confetti.

Something deep within me quiets at the sound. My skin buzzes with arcane energy. Each book tingles along my skin, as if invisible whiskers grow from my flesh and attach to their spines. I sense each of them. One lifts from its shelf and flies across the room, circles my head like a bird.

Another person might watch this display with wonder or awe. Maybe fear. All I feel is frustration. There is power here. There is power in me. But I haven't the slightest clue how to use it to get Damien back.

Experiencing magic isn't exactly new to me, but experiencing it alone, in the attic of Harcourt Manor, still is. Memories of the night I killed my abusive ex Tony rush to mind. Technically, he killed me first, choked me to death in my mother's art studio downstairs. I descended into the underworld, where I saw the souls of my parents and grandparents living in an alternate version of Harcourt. They told me the tattoo on my back was a keyspell. Within me lives the power to open portals between worlds. With my parents' help, I mustered the strength to stab Tony with my palette knife. At that moment, my mother's sculpture came to life and killed him. Well, we both killed him. I knocked him off-balance with a well-positioned kick, and her tower of blades sliced through his torso and ended him.

Since then I've suspected that my house, Harcourt Manor, is some kind of conduit for spiritual energy. I hesitate to use the word *haunted*. It's a loaded word with a negative connotation, and whatever is here with me is benevolent. Considering my great-grandfather was a spiritualist and claimed to speak to the dead during the séance parties he threw here in the twenties, it isn't actually surprising that the place would be home to a few spirits.

Oddly though, I never believed in the supernatural until I met Damien and found out that my best friend Maeve is a witch. Turns out my parents were witches too, when they were alive. Before I was born, they practiced with a coven that used dragon's blood to imbue its members with magical powers—the same dragon's blood that still flows through my veins.

Fisting my hands, I shuffle across the attic, madly searching for my phone. I dig in the pockets of my clothing, still strewn across the floor from when I made love to Damien. Above my head, the flapping books return to their shelves like trained birds landing on their perches.

Maeve was supposed to help me navigate my parents' magic. As a witch, she's the only one I know who can help me distill the overwhelming amount of information in this attic. Now… if she's responsible in any way… Dark thoughts fill my head as I pull the phone from the pocket of my leggings and dial her number with trembling fingers.

She answers on the second ring. "What's up?"

"Bring him back. Bring him back now!" I shout. I'm

shaking with rage. My eyes burn with it. My tears evaporate in the heat of my fury. And that's not all. Red haze has moved in around me, and ash falls like spindrift. I smell smoke and sulfur.

"Bring who back?" Maeve asks.

Her confusion multiplies my fury. How can she not know? The entire world should know. The world should stop.

"El, what's going on?"

The genuine concern in her voice sinks in a fraction, turning my skin cold. "You must know. You have to know."

My accusations dissolve into silence.

I check the connection, about to ask if she's still there, when she speaks again. "It's almost two in the morning, El. I have no idea what you're talking about. Take a deep breath and tell me what happened."

"Damien is gone," The words scrape up my throat, which is already raw from screaming. "He was taken in a cage of light. He told me… He said only a witch with his blood could do that. Who could wield a spell like that, huh?" My words fall heavy with accusation. Tears sting my eyes again as I add, "Your family just couldn't let him remain free, could they?"

"When did this happen?" Now she sounds positively baffled.

"About five minutes ago."

"Eloise, it wasn't me. I've been in a bathtub with a glass of wine and a book. I was about to go to bed when you called." My phone dings and it's a selfie of her in her pj's.

My thoughts scramble. "Someone in your family then."

"It's possible," she says softly. "If it's true, I'll free him, I promise. Everyone agreed to leave him alone, El. I haven't heard a peep about any plans to get him back."

"You honestly weren't aware of this?" Tears finally start to fall, fueled by the relief that my best friend didn't betray me. But that relief is short-lived. If the Gowdies didn't abduct Damien, who did?

"I swear on the Earth and the goddess who created it," Maeve says. "I don't even think it's possible. His blood is no longer in our possession. No one kept it because no one believed he'd ever be free of the candle."

"Shit. But if it's not you, then who? Fuck, I have to find him, Maeve. I have to." My knees give out, and I slump to the floor, rubbing a growing ache in my chest. "It feels like my heart is ripping in two. It's racing and, oh God, everything hurts. I'm dying. I'm *dying*."

"Take a deep breath." I hear Maeve draw air in and out. Eventually I follow along. In two, three, four. Out two, three, four. We do it together again and again. Somehow it helps.

Maeve is the first to speak again. "I have no personal experience with this, but I think what you're feeling is the mating bond. Mates aren't supposed to be separated. It's a good sign you can feel that in your chest. As long as you can sense the bond, you know he's still alive."

I blow out another breath, cling to that. He's still alive. He's still alive.

Maeve speaks up again. "I'm going to help. I'll go now and ask my family. I'll come see you first thing tomorrow with what I find out. We will get to the bottom of this, okay?"

"Okay." My voice cracks.

"I love you, Eloise. We'll find him."

A lump forms in my throat, and I remain silent as she ends the call.

What now? I bury my face in my hands, a new wave of hopelessness blowing through me like an arctic wind. If it's not the Gowdies, who could it be? If it's not them, where can we even start to look for him?

I turn toward my mother's grimoire, the one where I found the spell to send Damien home. I still don't understand my family's magic. I came up here for the first time yesterday. I didn't even know this room existed until my parents told me about it during the vision I had when Tony almost killed me. The message they passed on during my near-death experience was a simple one: find their journals. Everything I needed to know would be in them. In the end, this book had found me—literally dropped onto the end table next to the reading chair in the corner of my attic. The book opened itself for me, its pages flipping to my family's keyspell, one meant to open a portal between worlds. I intended to use it to send Damien home to Tenebris.

But Damien refused to go without me.

He loves me too much to leave me.

He promised to wait for me.

A sick feeling swirls in my stomach. We deserve better than this. We deserve more time.

I snatch my sweatshirt off the floor and pull it over my head. My eyes sweep the room in all directions. Maybe there's something in my parents' grimoire to help find Damien. I grab the book and start thumbing through the pages, but all the words run together.

I'm no witch. Even the spell to send Damien home was risky, and I only tried it because the book seemed to be encouraging me in that direction. I didn't actually know what I was doing. I followed the instructions like a recipe. All of this, it's like it's written in a different language. Some of these spells have ingredients I've never even heard of. What the hell is elecampane? Even finding the right spell seems impossible. It's not like the spells are cross-indexed. I'll have to go through each one.

My vision starts to blur, and I wipe my eyes again.

Everything I know about myself, everything that makes me *me*, started in this house. The Harcourt name is a crucial part of my identity, a linchpin into who I am. Finding out that my parents and grandmother kept this room from me my entire life, kept this power from me, makes me feel like a hermit crab in search of a new shell. Everything that was my security, my safety, is gone, and in its place is this mystery, this living library of magical information that seems hopelessly beyond my full under-standing.

I slam the grimoire closed and start to sob again, Damien's loss crashing back into me like a returning wave. Deep, wrenching sobs come from a place within me so dark I never knew it existed until now. I'm exhausted. Grief over my grandmother's recent death springs up within me like a sleeping wolf whose tail I've stepped on. It compounds with memories of losing my parents. My grief is a growing thing, the memory of one rattling free memories of them all, layer by interlocking layer. Suddenly I'm achingly lonely. So lonely I'd call Maeve back if I didn't think she needed her phone to investigate Damien's disappearance.

A tingle brushes the back of my neck like someone straightening my collar. I whirl, but there's no one there.

The room, however, is now drenched in the creeping red haze. I rub my eyes, wondering if it's from crying, but it doesn't go away. It's like the entire attic is awash in smoky red light. The scent of rosewater fills my nose. My grandmother's soap. I blink again, and she's standing there, a worried expression on her face.

"Grams?" It's like she's a newsprint version of herself. Grayscale with silver eyes and dark, pinprick pupils. Unlike the last time I saw her, when cancer had left her bald and frail, she's round cheeked and her sleek curls frame her face. She smiles warmly at me, and all the air vacates my lungs. I reach for her. "I miss you so much."

She reaches back. Her lips move but there's no sound. Hand on her heart, she shakes her head and mouths something again.

"I-I don't understand!" I want to touch her, hug her, but when I try to approach, the space between us seems to widen. The red flickers. And then she's gone. So is the snowing ash. The scent of burning. The crimson haze.

"Grams!" I raise my hand and reach for the place she just was, but my fingers pass through nothing but air. The attic is quiet as freshly fallen snow. I can't even feel the buzz of the books anymore.

For a moment I just breathe, and then I can't move fast enough. I pull on my leggings and race down the stairs, barely stopping for my jacket and boots. Pushing out the back door, I ignore the cold night air and sprint straight back to the family cemetery, stopping only when I reach my grandmother's grave. My tears are streaming again.

"Grams?"

I wait, praying her ghost will show herself again, that maybe, if I'm closer to her remains, I'll be able to hear what she has to say. But the only sound is my breath. The only scent is that of fallen leaves and pine, not rosewater. And the world is awash in silvery-blue moonlight. Not a hint of red.

I fall to my knees. Last time I was here, Damien arrived to gather me into his arms and carry me inside. I wait and wait, but no one comes to save me. I'm ice-cold. Shivering. Still, I wait until I can't feel my fingers or toes.

A rustle to my right catches my attention and I search the woods, still hoping that somehow it could be Damien or Gram's spirit. But as I focus on the sound, the outline of a narrow nose and long ears comes into view and then the body of a fox. It takes a few steps toward me, the white of its chest showing in the darkness, the moon painting it in silver tones like a phantom. Our eyes meet. It looks thin. Too thin.

"Are you hungry?" I ask softly. "Do you want something to eat?"

It waits, ears twitching. I rise, suddenly consumed with the need to feed this poor creature, my grief temporarily shoved aside. I hurry into the house, pull a bowl from the cupboard, and load it with some leftover rotisserie chicken and a cut-up apple. I fill another bowl with water and leave them both on my back stoop.

I don't see the fox when I set the bowls down, but after I'm back inside, it's only a minute before I catch the little phantom creeping from the woods again and feasting on my offering. "My little phantom out of nowhere," I mutter, wiping tears that feel hot against my cool skin.

The sky lightens above the feeding fox, and a wave of fatigue makes my head throb. Feeling defeated, I climb the stairs and collapse into bed.

3

QUEEN'S GAMBIT

DAMIEN

If my hate for Valeska were a visible thing, the dimly lit passageway the guards lead me down would brim with tearing claws and snapping teeth. I burn with hatred for her and the Kims, whose magic binds my wrists. Sunlight cuffs. I scoff. Even the dark elves of Willowgulch hadn't developed such enchantments.

Valeska trails behind me, surrounded by her guards. I can't see her back there, but I can hear her, those godsforsaken boots of hers clacking on the stone.

The guards steer me through a door, into a strange, circular room. At its center is a simple bed with a crude wooden canopy. The guards force my weakened mortal body to sit on the thin mattress, the sun-charged cuffs on my wrists draining every ounce of my energy. I'm still naked and in my battle form, what Eloise calls my monster form. I'm too big for this bed, but at least I have my horns, wings, talons, and fangs. With the right opening, I'll turn these vampire scum into ground meat.

When the guards part, Valeska is there, standing just beyond my reach. Her gaze flicks over me, frowning at my taloned fingers.

"Normally this is an execution chamber," she says, her gold eyes drifting upward. I raise my chin and find an unobstructed view of the stars. The chamber has no ceiling. Like any evil queen worth her crown, Valeska has banished me to her dungeon. And in Night Haven, a subterranean kingdom where sunlight is the deadliest consequence she can bestow, the tower is a stone silo open to the sky some two hundred feet up. "The walls cast shadows as the sun moves across the horizon, slowly executing any vampire I trap here when it reaches its apex." Her pointed red nail arcs through the air until it points straight up. "They tell me most vampires throw themselves into the sun rather than wait for the inevitable. In any case, I've never bothered with a bed before. No other prisoner has survived here long enough to use one."

"How kind of you." I layer on the sarcasm, thick as poison-laced honey. She ignores me. "And the canopy? Isn't the point for me to bake in the sun?" I hold up my wrists, still bound in the cuffs.

She tips a crooked smile. "You pose a problem for me, Damien. You are no vampire, and the sun won't kill you. Then again, we both know your death has never been my goal. If you are to be useful to me, I need you alive and I need you strong."

My wings twitch with annoyance. "Then why am I still wearing the cuffs?"

"You know why. Tell me her name, and I will spare you any further discomfort."

"Not happening."

"I thought that might be your answer. I'm not sure if I'm disappointed or impressed at the level of loyalty you have for the human. In any case, it's only a matter of time until you break."

For the first time, I meet her gaze directly. It almost kills me to speak to her with respect, but I try it. The simplest way to get out of this is if she lets me go. "You're better than this, Valeska. A powerful queen such as yourself doesn't need me. There are warriors in your guard who would kill to serve by your side. Fuck, there are other shades besides me, ones who aren't mated."

She snorts. "No vampire warrior can walk in the sun, Damien. They can't sustain me with their blood. A vampire can't fly. And as for the two other shades on this planet, you know that neither are within my reach. If I used the spell I used on you to call Cassius or Morpheus, I'd be declaring war against the covens who protect them. As much as I have enjoyed growing this hive, without you by my side, even my armies would struggle against such foes. You pose no such risk. You are mine."

"I am not."

"Are you so apt to forget that you are a citizen of Night Haven? You are sworn to serve your queen."

"Serve you, not mate you."

She lifts her chin an inch. "I think your stay here will give you plenty of time to reconsider."

My mortal stomach chooses that moment to growl, a soft sound but impossible for a vampire to miss.

Valeska's full red lips twitch and then widen into a wicked grin. "Hungry, Damien?"

In fact, I'm starving. I haven't eaten since the small amount of Eloise's blood I drank before my capture. I was too eager to get to her tonight and didn't bother to hunt first. The light has drained my reserves. I glare at her. She knows I'm hungry. I won't give her the satisfaction of admitting it.

She moves closer, stopping only when her knees touch mine. Close enough that if the sun-wielder magic did not weaken me, I'd punch through her rib cage and crush her heart with my bare fist. Unfortunately, in my current state, trying something like that would be suicide. As long as I'm wearing the cuffs, I'm mortal. As long as sunlight touches my skin, she's stronger, faster, and way more durable.

All I can do is load my eyes with hatred, let her see just how much I want to kill her.

She bends forward, offering her neck. I think about thrusting my cuffs against her face, but the Kims have designed them to only shine where they touch my skin. The little damage I'd do from what escapes the edge would only serve to piss her off.

"Drink from me, Damien. I can smell your hunger like the stench of rotting leaves. The sun is rising. I promise you, it will be a hellishly long day to face on an empty stomach."

Despite myself, my gaze drops to her throat. The scent of her blood, earthy and spiced, meets my nose. But unlike Eloise, unlike the animals on whom I feed or the humans at Marabella's, Valeska has no pulse. No beating heart. I don't know exactly what animates vampires, but they are constructed more of magic than living flesh.

Valeska has tasted my blood. It's how she called me here. But I have never sampled hers. Blood exchange by supernatural creatures is dangerous. She can't force me to mate her, but a blood bond is almost as bad. I could end up craving her blood. I could end up handing her some of my precious control. I have no interest in potentially blood-bonding to any magical being, especially not her.

I swallow, and my throat feels like sandpaper, hot and dry and far too tight. I peel my tongue from the roof of my mouth before rasping, "I wouldn't drink your blood if it was the only thing standing between me and the afterlife."

She lashes out and slaps me. Pain explodes through my cheek and jaw. I curse and lift my cuffed hands to my face. My fingers come away bloody. Bitch got me with her claws.

Behind her, the night gives way to silvery dawn. Thank the goddess.

The guards retreat toward the door, skin already steaming, but Valeska stays and bares her teeth. "What you fail to understand, Damien, is that my blood *is* the only thing between you and the afterlife." She whirls and exits in a blur of silver, leaving me alone with the Kims.

The twin witches press their backs together and spread their hands, each one performing that strange conjuring motion, their long, lean bodies tangling like two battling cranes. A pulse of power travels through me and slams into the stone. The walls of the silo glow as bright as my former cage. Everything shines but the floor.

Oh fucking hell.

The Kim's drop their hands, and with a flick of Lang's wrist, my cuffs are gone. And then so are they.

I'm left sitting on the bed. The sky overhead brightens with streaks of color. Sunrise. The last time I saw one, I was watching Tony's body burn and lost track of time. Now I enjoy it the best I can in my mortal state.

Weakness weighs me down, and I'm tempted to curl up on the too-small bed, but resting won't bring me any closer to escaping. I must escape. Eloise is in danger. If Valeska pulls the right strings, talks to the right people, it's possible she could discover her identity without my help. I picture her in her room, in her bed. Vulnerable.

Mine.

I will get back to her even if I have to kill Valeska with my bare hands to do it.

As I move to stand, the mattress lifts from the base of the bed. I lift it higher and slide underneath, creating a wedge of shade. It's not big enough to entirely encompass me, but it's enough to provide a refreshing break from the unyielding light. Enough to give me time to think. After three long breaths, I hoist it off the bed and use it to partially shelter myself as I walk the periphery of the silo, scanning the stone for vulnerabilities.

I make it three times around before my exposed skin blisters. I'm forced back to the bed and the sliver of useless shade it affords me. And then I can fight sleep no more.

4

COFFEE & QUESTIONS

ELOISE

Soft light shines through the gauzy curtains of my bedroom window, and for a few blissful seconds, I'm lost in the peaceful nothingness between sleep and wakefulness. And then I remember. Damien is gone. Grams is dead. I'm not sure if I can trust the Gowdies even though I want to believe Maeve that she had nothing to do with Damien's capture.

Am I alone in the world like Van Gogh's *Girl in White in the Woods*?

Three loud knocks come from the first floor, and then the doorbell rings. I scrunch my forehead. Was it the light that woke me or the knocking?

Ungracefully, I roll out of bed, feeling sluggish and heavy, like I'm carrying the weight of the sky on my back, but at the same time my chest feels hollowed out. An ice cream scoop has shucked out my innards, and someone has replaced them with lead. Somehow I manage to slip on my pink bathrobe and trudge down the steps. Rubbing my face, still sore from crying, I unlock the door. Maeve stands on my stoop, red-eyed and even paler than usual.

"It wasn't a Gowdie," she blurts defensively.

Over a decade of friendship, I've learned all her tells. She's not lying. I grab her hand and pull her inside. As I'm closing the door, I notice a man with a yellow vest on a cherry picker, doing something with the lines that run across our driveway.

"Are you having problems with your power?" Maeve asks. "I had to drive around a Dominion Energy van to get in here."

Stifling a yawn, I reach out and flip a switch. The foyer light comes on. "Working fine."

Her dark eyes rove over me. "Did you just wake up?" she asks incredulously.

"Yeah." I tuck my mop of unbrushed hair behind my ears. "I only got to sleep just before dawn."

She gives me an empathetic look, shaking her head. "I'm so sorry you're going through this, El."

And just like that the lump is back in my throat and I'm fighting tears. "What did you find out about Damien?"

She intertwines her fingers in front of her hips. "I spent most of the night and morning calling every Gowdie witch in my family. No one has Damien. Believe me, if they were lying, I'd know. We're a close-knit group. We don't keep secrets from each other."

I give her a skeptical look. Doesn't everyone have secrets?

"I tried to lie to my parents about your freeing Damien, and a flock of wrens barraged my window until I fessed up. Our magic keeps us honest. Believe me, whoever did that spell wasn't a Gowdie."

A breath leaves my lungs, but any relief I feel is replaced quickly by a new anxiety. "If it wasn't your family, who else could it be?"

She shrugs. "Who else had his blood?"

I shake my head slowly. The truth is, I have no idea. I both feel like I know Damien better than anyone in my life and also don't know him at all. I know he hunted animals on my property for food. But he never shared with me where, exactly, he sleeps during the day. All I know is he called it Night Haven, it's underground, and I can't go there.

"What other missions did he do for your family before he came to me?"

"Nothing where he'd leave *his* blood behind," she says darkly. "Damien was good at what he did and rarely made mistakes."

I sigh. "Then I have no idea. Come on. I'll make coffee." I trudge in the direction of the kitchen.

"Are you okay?" Maeve asks from behind me.

I glare at her over my shoulder.

"I mean, I know you're not okay. But it's almost two in the afternoon. I've never known you to sleep this late, especially during a crisis."

I come to a halt just outside the kitchen, my eyes drifting to the clock on the wall. "Oh my God. I had no idea it was this late."

"It's reasonable you'd be run-down after everything. It's understandable. You need the sleep." She places a palm on my forehead.

"I'm not sick." I nudge her hand aside. "Unless you

count heartsickness. Breakfast blend or dark roast?" I pull up short when I see a full pot in my coffee machine. I reach out tentatively. The carafe is hot to the touch. The scent of fresh-brewed beans meets my nose.

"Looks like you already brewed a pot," Maeve says, brow furrowing with concern.

"I don't remember making this." I stare and stare at the pot. It's fresh. I definitely washed this pot out last night. Someone made coffee this morning, and it wasn't me.

Maeve frowns. "Do you think you made it in your sleep? I read an article about people on Ambien doing all sorts of crazy things in their sleep."

"I'm not on Ambien."

"But in your heightened emotional state… Maybe…"

I sigh. What other explanation is there? "Right. That makes sense. Weird though." I open the cupboard and retrieve two cups. Only after I pour the coffees do I realize the mugs I picked were two of Grams's favorites. One is pink with white kitten paw prints and says PAW-SITIVE VIBES ONLY. The other is covered in red roses and says OLD GARDENERS NEVER DIE, THEY JUST SPADE AWAY.

I smile, thinking of her as I bring them to the table and offer both to Maeve so she can pick. She's taken a seat where my Grams used to sit. As always, she's wearing all black like the gothest goth that ever gothed. She even takes her coffee black. The two silly mugs rest in front of her like kindergarteners at a field trip to the morgue.

I manage a half smile when she chooses the pink one.

She shrugs. "I like cats. Thinking of getting one."

I reach into the fridge for the cream and pause as the scent of my Grams's rosewater soap fills my nose. My hand starts to tremble, and I hurry to set the cream down on the table.

"El? What's going on? All the color just drained from your face." She leaps out of her chair and takes me by the shoulders, easing me into my seat. "Are you okay?"

"Did you… smell my grandmother's rosewater soap just now? Like she was here?"

Her dark eyes narrow behind her glasses. "No. All I smell is coffee."

I straighten, allowing my eyes to drift around the kitchen. "I don't think I made this coffee."

Maeve's brow furrows. "Then who did?"

"I think it was Grams."

"Grams is dead, El." She reaches across the table to squeeze my arm. "She's gone."

I stare into my mug. "Yeah, but, um, I saw her last night, in my attic." The last syllable rises as if I'm asking a question rather than sharing an experience. I follow it up with a nervous lift of my brows.

"You saw your Grams here last night?"

"Well, her ghost. She was gray and white, sort of translucent, with silver eyes and pinprick pupils. She was trying to tell me something. I reached for her but—"

Maeve holds up a hand. "Whoa, whoa, whoa. You actually saw your grandmother's ghost in the attic last night? You're sure this wasn't like a dream or a hallucination?"

I nod. "She appeared when I was really upset." I give her a brief rundown of what happened in the attic and then about visiting her grave.

"And you didn't see her again?"

"No. I waited on her grave. Only came in when a fox caught my eye at the edge of the woods. That reminds me.

I need to put out food again today. It looked like it was starving."

Other than the twitch of one of her eyelids, Maeve doesn't react, just picks up her black coffee and takes a sip. "So… do you think your Grams is, like, haunting you?"

I shake my head. "No. Definitely not, at least not in a bad way. I think she was trying to comfort me. And it only happened when the room changed color."

She arches an inquisitive eyebrow.

"Everything turned hazy and swirled with crimson, like I was on a stage with a red light and a smoke machine." I drum my fingers on the side of my mug. "When Tony was choking me and I saw my parents in the underworld, it looked the same. Smelled the same too. Like the world was on fire."

"Fuck, Eloise, that's a lot to take in."

"Yeah."

She lowers her voice and leans forward. "Does it freak you out a little? You haven't had much experience with stuff like this."

I snort. "No more than learning my best friend is a witch and the man I love shifts into a horned beast with wings? No. At this point I've learned to roll with it. It's comforting, to be honest. I wish she'd come back." I look down at my coffee. "Actually, maybe she did. I think she made me this."

We stare at each other for a few minutes while we both process it all. I take another sip. The coffee is exactly how Grams used to make it. Just a little on the strong side. I fight back another round of tears. If Grams is here and watching, I know for damn sure she wouldn't want me wasting my time crying for her. She always wanted me to be happy. If she were here, she'd tell me to keep going and to control what I could control.

After a few deep breaths, I ask, "I have to get Damien back, Maeve. I need him. How do we find out who took him?" I dig my hands into my hair and rest my elbows on the table.

She swallows, leaning back in her chair. "I might be able to track him using magic if you have some of his blood."

"Unfortunately, I don't make it a habit of storing people's blood."

"What about during, um, sex?" she asks awkwardly, her nose wrinkling. "Did you drink from him?"

I think back and then shake my head. "No. He drank from me though."

She scratches behind her ear. "Fuck—it's his blood we need. I'm afraid magic is out. That's the only way I know to track a shade."

My head pounds. I bury my face in my hands.

"Hey, have you eaten anything yet? You look really pale. Let me make you some toast." I hear Maeve move behind me. The rustle of the bread bag. The spring-loaded arm of our ancient toaster.

"There has to be a way," I say softly, lowering my hands. "Do you know anything about how he spent his time when he wasn't with me?"

"Only that he lived among vampires when he wasn't working for us."

Vampires. What do I know about vampires? "What about Morpheus?"

Maeve seems to tense at the name. "What about him?"

"Damien told me he's also a shade and his bar, Bad Witches' Club, caters to supernaturals. Maybe he knows something."

"Morpheus isn't someone I'd ever consider to be intentionally helpful."

I pivot in my chair so I can see her face. "Why not? He seemed nice enough the night I met him. He remembered my mother."

She groans. "He did seem to have a soft spot for you." Her eyes narrow. "Just so you know, that reaction wasn't exactly typical. He's usually quite the hard-ass. And—"

"And?"

"Well, my ancestors are the ones responsible for opening the rift that brought him here and for binding Damien for centuries. Morpheus isn't exactly a fan of my family."

"Oh. Right." My shoulders slump. I must be tired not to have thought of that. Of course there's animosity between the two. Only, Maeve is my only way into Bad Witches' Club. I can't ask Morpheus for help without her. And I'm convinced he's my best chance to locate Damien.

Maeve's hand lands on my back. "I'm not saying no, Eloise. The Gowdies and the Caspians are allies. As a member of the Caspian triune, Morpheus has to take an audience with me if I request one. I'm just not sure he'll be receptive to helping us."

"Even with your history, surely he has a soft spot for Damien. They're both shades from the same world after all."

"True."

"Morpheus must hear rumors in his position. We have to try."

She sighs. "It's not as if we have anyplace better to start."

A spark of hope ignites deep within my chest.

Maeve gives a resigned shrug. "Yeah, all right. We'll go as soon as the sun sets."

"Why wait?" I ask, hating the long delay. "I thought he could walk in the sun?"

"Yes. As a shade, Morpheus can daywalk, and being a part of a triune allows him to do so while preserving all of his powers." The toast pops up, startling us both. "But he's also a club owner who serves vampires who can't. He's been up all night. I, for one, have no intention of waking him up in the middle of the day to ask him to do us a favor."

"Right. We want him in a good mood."

She scrapes some butter over the toast before sliding the plate in front of me. "I'm not sure Morpheus has ever been in a *good* mood. Let's just hope he's in a generous one."

I ponder that over a bite, silently praying that tonight we'll have answers.

5

BAD WITCHES' CLUB

ELOISE

Bad Witches' Club is a nightclub for supernatural beings living among humans. It's themed after all the dark characters from well-known stories and fairy tales, each section enchanted with magical ambience. The last time I was here, I had an uncomfortable run-in with the freezing temperatures of Narnia's white-witch section. That visit changed everything.

Only a few months ago, I didn't know witches were even real, let alone vampires and shifters, but they are, and apparently they like to party like the rest of us. I ordered Damien to bring me here to investigate Gold Weaver before we discovered Tony was using the magazine as a front to counterfeit and launder money. Then, I hadn't a clue what I was in for. This time, when Maeve uses her special gold key to let me into the stark white room with the bare bulb swinging from the center of the ceiling, I'm already facing the wall we'll walk through to get inside even before she relocks the door.

"Take a deep breath," she says without even looking my way, as if she can smell my anxiety. "It's going to be okay. We'll figure this out."

"Right. Morpheus has to know something." Blowing out a deep breath, I step through the enchanted barrier and am welcomed by the steady thump of house music. Before me, an enormous mural of an evil queen, her crown tipping back with her laugh, greets me. She's my mother's design. How could I have ever missed the sharp details that are the hallmark of her art? But then, I never suspected Mom could be a witch. "Looking back, there were signs," I say absently as Maeve sidles up to me. "Like how she stood so close to the edge of the cliffs behind our house and how her hair looked freshly brushed even when the wind blew it every which way."

"And your father could make anything grow. His landscaping business performed miracles."

"Miracles," I parrot. I can't help it. The idea that my parents were magical, my mother a witch by birth and my father made one by drinking dragon's blood, still seems unreal to me.

"We should go. I made an appointment, but Morpheus won't wait around if we're late."

I take one last look at my mother's mural and follow Maeve.

Morpheus's office is in the back, the Hansel and Gretel section. Here the tables and chairs are all made to look like candy with peppermint stools and licorice railings. A trail of lacquered breadcrumbs is the hallmark of the walkway. The bar is decorated like the witch's sugar-windowed cottage with a mural of the witch herself on the back wall, complete with an open, bloodstained oven. I catch a couple of vampires in the corner, making out atop a sofa designed to look like a pile of bones.

Maeve nudges me toward an unmarked door in the wall. She knocks three times, and it opens for us from the inside. We enter a surprisingly mundane office where Morpheus types vigorously on a sleek silver desktop Mac.

"Have a seat," he rumbles without looking at us. The vibe reminds me of opening an account at my local bank. There are definite bank vibes in this office. Bank sounds.

I slowly sink into one of two GUBI meeting chairs across from him—again, very bank-like. Morpheus is an older-looking shade, an odd thing considering the creatures are immortal for all intents and purposes. Yes, they can be killed if they're exposed to sunlight first, but Damien told me they otherwise don't age. Also, now that I've seen Damien in his monster form—black-skinned, leather-winged, with talons and fangs—I know that the image I'm looking at is an illusion. So I wonder at Morpheus's choice of appearance. A scar runs through his right eyebrow down to his upper lip. His skin is sallow, his dark eyes beady as a rat's. If I've understood Damien correctly, he could make himself attractive by human standards if he chose to, but instead, he looks like this.

But when he turns those dark eyes on Maeve, I get it. I squirm in my seat at the intensity coming off him. Morpheus doesn't want to be attractive. He wants to be intimidating. And he is. When his attention shifts to me, my palms instantly start to sweat.

"Ms. Harcourt!" His brow lifts as if he's surprised to see me, and his entire face softens. "A pleasure to see the daughter of Diana Harcourt once again. Is this about getting you your own key? Maeve should have told you the front desk can handle that request."

"No. Not that," I say quickly. "Damien was taken. We need your help."

Maeve shoots me a stern look like I've made a grave error. I don't understand why until Morpheus leans back in his chair and laces his fingers over his waist. His previously warm smile morphs into something far more chilling. He glares at Maeve, eyes burning with repugnance. "Do the Gowdies wish to enlist the triune's help in returning their guard dog?"

Shit. Now I understand why Maeve was hesitant to come here. Morpheus loathes her. His expression is dripping with barely restrained malice.

"No," Maeve says. "But—"

"Then I'm afraid I can't help you. Show yourself out." Morpheus turns back to his computer.

I open my mouth. "No... No..." I raise both hands. "This isn't about her family at all. He's my—"

Maeve stomps on my foot. *Oww.*

"What Eloise means to say is he was her friend. We know you have a connection to Damien, and he's missing. We are afraid something nefarious has happened to him. We were wondering if you'd heard anything about his disappearance."

"Right," I chime in. "You must be as concerned for him as we are. Damien told me you both come from the same world... Tenebris, right? Along with..." I try to remember the name of the third shade that was caught up in the Gowdies' spell.

"Cassius," Morpheus supplies flatly.

I nod once. "You have a history together."

He waves a hand dismissively. "That was a long time ago."

I scoot to the edge of my chair and lean across the desk. "He sacrificed himself for you. He bore the Gowdie curse for centuries so you and Cassius could be free."

Morpheus studies me. "You seem to know a lot about the situation, Ms. Harcourt. How exactly does this have anything to do with you?"

"They're friends," Maeve interjects.

Morpheus rolls his eyes.

"I'm the one who freed him from the candle's hold," I interject.

The room plunges into a sudden and complete silence.

"*You* freed him?" Morpheus finally says, leveling a stare as if I've suddenly become far more interesting to him. His nostrils flare and he leans in, studying me. I swallow hard, edging away until my back hits the chair, my hands gripping the armrests. Have I said the wrong thing again? "I heard he'd been freed but not how. Perhaps you have more of your mother in you than I assumed, Ms. Harcourt, to be powerful enough to break a Gowdie curse."

Maeve shifts, her fingers tapping nervously against her thigh. "How exactly did you come to find out that our binding spell was broken, Morpheus?" she asks, drawing the heat of his attention back on herself.

Morpheus's nostrils flare on a deep inhale. His eyes don't stray from me as he answers. "Your Aunt Hildie. She was in here the other night, drunk on dragon fruit martinis. I overheard her tell that ancient friend of hers—"

"Hazel?"

"The one with the hearing aid. I assure you, every vampire in the building heard the news."

"Oh *fuck*." Maeve's curved fingers come to rest against her temple.

"What?" My gaze darts between her and Morpheus, my stomach contracting like it knows something I don't. "Why are you saying *fuck*? Vampires wouldn't want Damien, right? What would they gain, taking him from me? It has to be a family of witches, doesn't it?"

Morpheus's nostrils flare again. In the time it takes a chill to travel the length of my spine, he's standing beside me, the tip of his nose mere centimeters from my carotid. "You are his mate." Not a question. Out of the corner of my eye, all I see is fang.

"Yes." My voice is breathless from fear.

"Oh fuck, indeed," he drawls.

I shiver at the way he's looking at me.

"Morpheus," Maeve says, the name holding a note of warning.

"Relax, Gowdie. I'm not crazy enough to lay a hand on another shade's mate." We both stare at him unblinkingly as he returns to his chair, his gait as steady and smooth as a flowing river. "I normally do not feel obligated to alleviate someone of their ignorance, but you are right about one thing—Damien and I have a history. You are correct, Ms. Harcourt, that I owe him for what he did the night we came through the rift. Even beyond that, it is a grave sin against our gods to separate mates. So let me fill you both in on circumstances that normally do not concern your kind. The vampire queen of Night Haven is in need of a consort, and she's had her eye on Damien for years."

"Night Haven." I remember Maeve and Damien using

the name of the place, but I otherwise know nothing about it. I certainly don't remember Damien ever mentioning a vampire queen.

"That's the subterranean city where the vampire covens of this area reside. Damien is a citizen," Morpheus explains.

"Oh?"

"Damien never took the queen's advances seriously because he was bound by the Gowdie curse. The queen would never take a consort charmed to obey a witch's orders over her own. But if she knew his curse was broken, she'd want him for herself. As Ms. Gowdie can confirm, a shade is a very powerful weapon to have at your command."

I rub my palms on my thighs. "You're saying this vampire queen took him? But I thought the spell had to be performed by witches?"

Morpheus scoffs. "I don't *think* she took him, Ms. Harcourt. I know. Everyone knows. The queen wanted him, and she has him. How she managed it, I haven't a clue. But she has him. Only, she encountered an unexpected complication."

"He was already mated to Eloise." Maeve squeezes her eyes closed behind her glasses with a silent wince.

"Already mated," Morpheus confirms, rubbing his chin.

"If you know where he is, why are we here? Where is Night Haven? Can you get him back?" I look between the two of them, waiting for someone to suggest next steps.

Maeve chews her lip.

"Oh, should you tell her, or can I?" Morpheus deadpans.

"I will." Maeve turns in her chair to face me. "The queen wants a shade as her consort. She captured Damien. But to force him to be her consort, she first has to gain control of him by forcing him to be her mate. Vampires and shades mate for life. Neither can take more than one mate. The queen was probably shocked as shit to find out Damien's cherry had already been popped."

"Okay." I blink twice. "Then why hasn't she let him go? He's useless to her."

"He's only useless to her while his mate is still alive." Maeve says the words slowly, as if she's speaking to a small child, and I'm thankful for that because my mind does not want to pick up what she's laying down.

I feel my brows cram together. "She plans to…"

"Kill you," Maeve fills in. "She needs to kill you in order to force him to be her mate and consort."

"All right." I pull myself together. "But if she wants me dead, why hasn't she come for me yet?"

Morpheus leans forward in his chair, resting his chin in a nest of his fingers. "That's the delicious part. No one knows who you are, Ms. Harcourt. The queen can smell the mating scent on him, just as I can smell it on you, but Damien has refused so far to give up your name. Just yesterday she offered a reward for any vampire who could unmask your identity."

A bounty on my head. And now Morpheus knows. *Shit.* A chill skims along my spine, and I tamp down a growing flare of panic. For a second I just stare at him, swallowing repeatedly while I get ahold of my emotions. A meltdown right now won't help anyone, especially not Damien. The vampire queen doesn't know who I am.

Damien hasn't told her. Even Morpheus didn't know until now. And that's the only reason I'm still alive.

I burst out laughing, and they both look at me like I've fallen off my rocker. "Of course she has. It's been almost a week since someone tried to kill me. I'm overdue!"

Morpheus exchanges a glance with Maeve. "Is she all right?"

Maeve nods. "Just give her a minute."

Eventually I wind down and catch my breath. "So what happens next?"

Maeve locks eyes with Morpheus. "The Gowdies and Caspians have been allies for centuries. But if you do a single thing to put Eloise at risk, I will consider it an act of war."

His lids lower. "You'd do well to remember that we do not respond to threats, Ms. Gowdie. However, in this case, I have no desire to help the queen. She has already amassed far more power than any of the supernatural communities are comfortable with. If she succeeds in mating Damien and forcing him to become her consort, she'll be unstoppable. A shade bound to his mate by blood will protect her at all costs. He'll obey her direct commands. He will be her deadliest weapon. It is imperative that Ms. Harcourt's identity remain a secret."

"If that's the case, why not rescue him!" I say, popping out of my chair. "With the power of the triune, you could have him home before nightfall."

Morpheus growls. "Sit down."

I'm raging mad that he hasn't already rescued his friend, but reluctantly I lower myself back into my chair.

The shade glares at me. "While I respect and admire Damien, unfortunately, crossing the vampire queen is akin to declaring war on Night Haven. I'm sorry for your loss, Ms. Harcourt, but that isn't a battle my triune is willing to fight. I'll keep your identity as his mate a secret, and I'd advise you to do the same, but that is all I can do for you."

I glare at him right back, folding my arms in front of my chest. "Fine. At least tell me where this Night Haven is. We can go."

He looks confused for a beat, darting a glance between Maeve and me, then snorts. "I can never tell when you humans are making a joke."

"I'm serious."

He folds his hands on his desk. "As a favor to Damien, I won't share the location of Night Haven with you. And now I have truly paid my debt to him, for you and Ms. Gowdie, if she was dumb enough to help you, would be dead the moment you set foot in Valeska's territory, if not for being his mate then because you are human and would make a delicious meal."

I look him dead in the eye, my voice low as I say, "But we have to do something." I'm so angry it feels like my skin might split like a dried husk to make room for all the fire in my veins.

"I am sorry," he says, and this time there is no humor in his voice, only sorrow. "I cared for your mother, and Damien is a friend. I'd like to help you. But take it from a warrior far more experienced in the ways of war than yourself. You do not want to pick a fight with the queen of Night Haven. She's a vicious, heartless psychopath. The worst of her species. She will lie, cheat, steal, or kill to get what she wants. Damien is a warrior and a very powerful shade. He's faced worse than this in our world and survived. My advice to you is to lie low, allow Valeska to grow tired of looking for you, and trust that Damien will solve the problem of his freedom in time."

Like he did with the candle? I stand again and stare down my nose at him. "There's no doubt in my mind that Damien is strong enough to survive anything the queen throws at him on his own," I say firmly. "But even the strongest among us need saving sometimes. That's why we have friends and mates, so that we don't have to face our enemies alone."

Morpheus's expression softens, even his scar becoming less pronounced, his eyes dulling with memories he doesn't share, ghosts from a past spent in another world if I had to guess. "The only way he'll truly be alone is if he loses you. Don't make him suffer that fate."

Maeve stands and takes my hand, tugging me toward the door. "Thank you, Morpheus. We appreciate your time and your silence."

He bows his head and turns back to his work. I allow Maeve to guide me from the club, a lump lodged deep in my throat.

6

OLD FAMILY RECIPE

ELOISE

I stomp into Harcourt Manor with Maeve frustratingly quiet behind me. She hasn't said a word the entire ride home and asked that I wait until we got here to discuss everything. She said she needed time to process what we'd learned. But I've had enough of waiting. I confront her the moment we're inside.

"What if we offer Valeska a trade? Like we find something else she wants and give it to her if she frees Damien? If that doesn't work, maybe we can find the third shade, Cassius. Just because Morpheus won't risk his own hide to help his friend doesn't mean Cassius won't."

When she doesn't answer right away, I march to the kitchen and grab a bowl from the cupboard. I dig in the fridge and find some deli meat, berries, and leftover vegetable medley. I dump it all in the bowl.

"What's that for?" Maeve asks as I nudge past her.

"Phantom. The fox I saw last night. I never fed him

this morning. At least I think it's a him. It could be a her. I don't know. I didn't get close enough to check." I rub my aching head and make a point of easing my heavy footsteps as I reach the back door. Quietly I open it and scan the backyard, looking for the critter. When I don't see the fox, I set the bowl down and snag the empty water dish.

The thunk of Maeve's moto boots follows me to the kitchen. I yank up the handle on the faucet and fill the bowl, then smack it down again. When I turn around, still fuming, Maeve is blocking the way out.

"What are our next steps?" I ask, meeting her eyes. "How do we get him back?"

She brushes her thick fringe of black bangs to the side and blinks at me through the square frames of her glasses. "I think Morpheus is right. There's nothing we can do."

I set the water dish down on the table. "What the fuck, Maeve?"

"You can't win against the vampire queen, Eloise!" Her voice is raised, stern even, like a mother's voice. "I've heard stories about Valeska since I was a child. Believe me when I say her reputation is well-earned. She slaughtered every rival to rise to her position and has been slowly absorbing covens into her hive ever since, some by force, some by intimidation. Valeska is a ruthless killer from a long bloodline of ruthless killers. Aside from the fact that I can't get involved without dooming the entire Gowdie family to a war against the vampires, we can't take any action without risking exposing your identity. Even if we developed your magical abilities, it would take a lifetime for us to get you strong enough to defend yourself against her. And it's not just her you'd be up against if anyone found out you were his mate. She has the Night Haven military at her command and hundreds of allies across the East Coast."

I huff. "I can't beat her in a fight. So what? I'm the fucking key. My sigil can take me anywhere. If I can find out where he is, I can reach him using the symbol, then bring him back the same way."

Maeve scoffs, shaking her head. "You have no idea if you can do that. From what you've shared with me, you have only the narrowest understanding of what your sigil is capable of and are completely unpracticed in its use."

"I can learn!" I hold my hands out to my sides, my heart pumping harder. "Why am I the only one who thinks rescuing Damien is a priority?" I seethe. "Weren't you going to give me magic lessons? This seems like a great time to start."

"And what if you succeed in reaching him using the keyspell? Do you think the queen has Damien somewhere no one is watching him? Do you honestly think you'll be able to sneak into a vampire dungeon without detection and somehow have enough magic left and everything you need to reperform the spell from scratch to get you both back? I doubt it. Considering how powerful Damien is, she likely has him guarded around the clock. But even if you made it there and somehow succeeded in bringing him back, they would see you and they would come for you. The only thing protecting you right now is that Damien refuses to reveal your identity. We were stupid even to share it with Morpheus. One slip of the tongue and that's it. You are dead."

Pressure builds inside my head, my eyes burning, but I have no tears left to shed. I spread my hands out to her.

"Why can't you understand that half of my soul has been severed from me? I can't live like this."

The tension in her jaw eases, and she moves closer to me. She rests a supportive hand on my shoulder. "Oh El... Damien is powerful. Really powerful. He'll get *himself* out of this. All you have to do is give him time. I guarantee he's planning his escape right now."

I bury my face in my hands and rub my eyes with my fingers. "Damien may be immortal and have all the time in the world to free himself. I'm not." I grab the water dish and shove past her, striding for the back door. This time I see Phantom watching me from the woods. I slowly place the water dish down, then make a kissing noise. Ducking back inside, I watch through the window for a second before Maeve's voice carries down the hall.

"Eloise, I know you're frustrated, but try to be clear minded about this."

I push off the window, mind reeling, and march into the parlor just as the grandfather clock strikes midnight. I wait for the last gong before whirling around to face Maeve, my hands on my hips. "If I could just talk with him... Somehow know that he's okay—"

A loud thunk like someone is pounding on the wall interrupts my thoughts. We both look toward the gallery wall as my grandfather's photos tilt askew. Another thunk comes. Bits of white dust fall from the ceiling. *Thunk... thunk... THUNK!* The metal grid over the air register pops off, screws shooting across the room and clattering to the floor. The grill drops to the carpet. We both stare at it, then at each other, our brows rising. She seems as baffled as I am. Until a tinny, flapping sound has us looking up toward the vent again. A purple book flies from the gaping hole in the wall and hurls itself into my arms, followed by a plume of dust.

I catch the tome against my gut with an *oomph* and take a few steps back to find my balance.

"Is that…?" Maeve's red lips twitch with a nervous smile.

I flip the book over, noting the familiar key on the cover. "My parents' grimoire."

I hold it out to show her and gasp when the pages start to flip fast enough to blow back my hair. They fall open about three-quarters from the end. Maeve approaches, glancing between me and the book.

"Hitch and Cast, a spell to find lost loved ones," I read aloud. "This potion allows the drinker to cast themselves into another's dreams while anchoring themselves in the present."

"It says you'll be able to communicate with your target lucidly, as if you're actually there." Maeve reads over my shoulder.

"I can use this to talk to Damien—find out how I can help him!" I run my finger down the list of ingredients. "Do you know where I can find silver sand root?"

"I think I have some at home. Actually, I have most of these things."

"You do? Can we get them now? How long do you think it will take to brew?"

She holds up a hand. "Not long, but it will have to wait until morning."

"Why?" My question comes out with a sharp edge, and I can't miss the way she winces at my tone.

"Chill out, El. I'll help you, okay, but you need to take a beat."

I squeeze my eyes shut. "I'm just ready to come out of my skin."

"I know." She rubs my back supportively. "We have to wait until morning because shades sleep during the day, and he has to be asleep for you to enter his dreams."

I take a deep breath and blow it out slowly, feeling like a fool. Of course she's right. And this is why she's been acting like she has. I'm in such pain that I can't think clearly. "Oh my God, Maeve. I'm sorry. I—"

"It's okay. I've never experienced a mating bond, but I've read about them. I knew when you decided to mate with Damien that there would be consequences."

"So did I," I say. "And I would have been fine with them if he hadn't been taken."

She shakes her head. "This isn't me saying I told you so, El. This is me letting you know I'll help you. I'm going to go back to the office and clear tomorrow's schedule. I'll be here in the morning to brew the Hitch and Cast potion."

I set the open grimoire down on the sofa and give her a long hug. When she pulls back, she looks at the vent again and then up at the ceiling, then back to me.

I shrug.

"If you see Grams again while I'm gone, say hello from me."

7

GARDEN OF DREAMS

DAMIEN

"Drink from me," Valeska orders.

It's still dark, but dawn isn't far off. Too bad the stars that shine through the open roof of the silo don't bring me any peace. I'm back in the sunlight cuffs, sitting on the bed. Valeska grips the back of my head with her nails and presses her wrist to my lips.

It's tempting. My tongue is a leather stump. My head throbs. It's been twenty-four hours baking in this silo with its sunlight walls and open dome. How have I survived? My blood grits through my veins like shards of broken glass. One bite. Just a nip and Valeska's blood could sustain me, perhaps even make me strong enough to find a way out of this mess. As it is, I am dying. My body, made mortal by the sunlight, is starving, growing weaker by the minute.

"Drink!" she orders again, and this time she raises her wrist to her mouth and scores the skin with her own teeth. The scent of fresh blood hits me square in the face, my nostrils flaring and my fangs extending. My lips tremble, and I have to close my eyes to keep from striking.

Just a taste, comes a voice at the back of my head. No one will know. No one would blame you anyway for drinking the blood in your current state.

But then I hear my father's voice, the king's voice. "Beware food or drink offered by your enemy. At best, it is meant to make you dependent. At worst, it is drugged to make you compliant. Nothing good comes from accepting sustenance from one who would kill or enslave you."

He knew better than anyone. He'd earned that wisdom. Captured by the dark elves of Willowgulch, he'd been poisoned by sunlight magic and kept so weak that he couldn't even stand by the time we recovered him. Once he was home, Father rarely talked about those days, but the only way to hold a shade is by light. He'd lived through what I am going through now. If he could survive, so can I.

I turn my head to the side.

"You stubborn fool," she hisses, then slaps me across the cheek. Pain explodes through my eye and jaw, her vampire strength so much more than mine with my wrists bound in sunlight.

I open my eyes and glare up at her with all the hate I can load into a stare.

I will die before she gets a single clue from me about my mate's identity.

She bares her teeth. "Fucking pigheaded fool." She seethes. "I will break you. Mark my words." She spits on me, and it slides down the side of my face. And then she's gone, and I'm left with the Kims again as the sky lightens above us.

I study the twins. Tae and Lang look like hell. Dark crescents stain the skin under their eyes. As they perform that strange magical dance they did at the end of last night again, I notice this time that it takes both of them to complete it. My cuffs fade away, replaced by the steady glow of the silo walls. Hmm. Keeping this place lit up like a Christmas tree must cost them a heavy toll of magic. I speculate that one of them must be awake at all times to keep the lights on. I doubt they could make this happen passively.

My lips crack with my smile. If the magic containing me takes two witches to maintain, all I have to do is kill one of them to free myself. I might not be strong enough to overpower Valeska in the state I'm in, but a witch? Maybe.

The Kims wobble as they exit my cell, and my smile grows wider. No, they can't keep this up forever. Hell, if I survive long enough, one of them might magically burn out without me doing anything. A few minutes in the darkness and I'm gone, never to return.

Until that happens, there's nothing I can do but conserve my strength. I've inspected every inch of this cell, and there is no weakness to exploit. I'll have to find another way.

I wedge myself under the mattress again, easing as far into the shade as possible. Shutting my eyes and turning my face away from the burning light, I try to forget the raging pain along the parts of me exposed to the sun. Sleep is even more important in this mortal, starving body. With measured breaths, I will my muscles to relax until my mind floats on the dark river toward unconsciousness.

Blackness gives way to the deep green of a shaded garden. The bright moon of Tenebris, oversized on the horizon, shines in the sky above me. The sweet, heady scent of trailing veritas, a vine from my world with neon-violet, orchidlike flowers, grows along the trellis behind me. I sit up from the stone bench I'm lying on, run my hands through my hair. That's when I realize my horns, talons, and wings are gone. I'm in my corse form, my polite form, the way we often appeared in the kingdom during times of peace.

It's been years since I've dreamed of this garden. I rise and turn toward the castle with its white marble spires and stained-glass windows. I wonder if it still looks like this, like I remember, or if the dark elves have breached our boundaries and leveled it. I wonder if my parents and siblings are still alive and if my younger brother Brahm crawled into a bottle permanently after I left. I wonder if my sister Karyl was married off to another kingdom that could offer security. I frown at the memories. It was a lifetime ago. Lifetimes. Everything must be different now, after so many centuries.

"Damien?"

I whirl to find Eloise standing among the night-blooming roses and midnight lilies. "And just like that, a good dream becomes a great one," I mumble to myself, thanking every god in the Darklands for this even if it isn't real. I rake my gaze down her long-sleeved T-shirt and jeans. Focusing, I picture a sheer white kimono, held in place by a silk bow.

Her clothing transforms effortlessly. *Fuck*, she's even

more beautiful than I remember, her red curls wild past her shoulders, the darker flesh around the tips of her breasts visible through the robe. At my command, candelabras appear around the garden, outfitted with red candles that flicker in the moonlight.

Now *this* is a dream worth having.

She looks down at herself, her lips parting in an expression that falls just short of a smile. Isn't that always the way with my little bird, always flying from trouble straight into my arms. No doubt that big heart of hers has been her downfall again. What tragedy will my mind produce to bring her to me this time? She's already mine, but I'll play. I'll enjoy every minute of it.

"Damien," she says, reaching for me. "I don't know how long we have."

I swagger toward her, a cool night breeze surrounding us with the scent of roses. Our eyes meet, and I see her breath catch in her throat. Slowly I trail two fingers along her full bottom lip, her jaw, the pulse of her left artery. Down, down, lower. Between her breasts where the sleek edge of the robe wraps silkily around the edge of my fingers along with the weight and warmth of her breasts.

Her chin lifts on a throaty moan, her lids growing heavy. "Oh my God, I forgot how overwhelming it feels to be near you," she says softly. "But we need to talk." She grabs the sides of my face like she's trying to get my attention.

I don't want to talk, and this is my dream. I capture her mouth with my own, circling her waist with my hands. My tongue explores the map of her mouth, her teeth, her tongue, the inside of her cheeks, ignoring her tiny protests. There isn't a single part of her I don't want to taste.

With a leisurely tug, I unfasten her belt, and the robe parts between us.

"Damien..." she protests breathlessly.

Palming the back of her head, I massage the base of her skull, carefully calibrating my touch to the intensity that makes her breath draw lazily into her lungs and the naked front of her body stretch against me. I move my kisses to her ear, her throat, carefully kindling the fire within her. Her spine is a string of pearls. I drag my touch along one mound, then the next. Slowly, seductively.

"Oh my God, you feel so good. But listen, I need to... I need to..." Her hands are in my hair, her breath against my chest. She's smaller than me, my little bird, but I don't mind bending to her height. Wouldn't mind falling to my knees and tasting her. My hands smooth over her ass, gently coaxing her feet apart. Her breath catches.

"Damien, please, listen to me. *Please.*" Something in her voice gives me pause, dream or not, and I draw back to look at her. Fuck, the peaks of her full breasts are clearly visible through the gauzy fabric and the robe is open, giving me a delectable view of warm, naked flesh from the hollow of her throat to her glistening sex.

A possessive growl rumbles in my chest. My cock throbs to be inside her, but I'm distracted by a sound. A persistent ticking fills the garden. I search for the source.

"Damien," she says again, and there's a note of exasperation in her voice. The ticking grows louder. There! I spot the grandfather clock from Eloise's parlor at the edge of the walkway. My eyes narrow at the annoyance, and I try to send it away in the same way I changed Eloise's clothes and lit the candles, but it persists.

"This doesn't belong," I whisper, my throat suddenly as raspy and dry as it is in real life.

"It's me." Eloise grabs me by the face again, looking desperate now. "I drank a potion to journey into your dream. I'm here. This is really me."

I shuffle away from her. Is this some kind of trick by the Kims? Some new torture? Now they're using my mind against me.

She holds out her hand. "I've been doing everything in my power to get you back. I even went to see Morpheus."

"Morpheus?" My mind scrambles for an explanation. "What cursed magic is this?" I look around myself. "If this is a trick, I will never give up her name. Not even in my dreams."

"It's not a trick." She brings a hand to her sternum. "Morpheus told me the vampire queen took you, but he won't help me get you back. Where are you? How can I help get you out?" Her eyes line with silver.

Is it possible this is really happening? I have no experience with astral projection, but all my senses tell me that Eloise is with me. Her body, her scent, it's too familiar. Too perfect. She moves closer. I jerk back.

Her brow furrows. "It's me, Eloise." Her hand flattens against her bare chest, then presses against mine, right over my heart. "Oh God, Damien, I've missed you so much. I found the spell in my parents' grimoire. Maeve helped me with the ingredients." She gestures behind her. "The grandfather clock is my anchor so that I can find my way back to the parlor. I don't know how long this will last. You need to tell me how we can help you."

"Eloise?" No one in Valeska's camp would know about the parlor or the clock or her real name. Even if they'd discovered her identity, they couldn't reproduce her in my mind like this. Her soft curves, her luscious pomegranate-and-narcissus scent.

Her eyes widen. "Yes! It's me."

"My mate." I draw her into my arms again, hugging her to me as my eyes burn with an onslaught of emotions. Longing, fear for her safety, desperation to get back to her, love, need. I can't sort them all.

My mouth finds hers again, but she cuts the kiss short. "I don't want to stop, but I have to know where to find you. Tell me. I'll… I'll find help to come for you."

"Come for me?" When I realize she's serious, I take her by the shoulders, scowling at the thought. "No, little bird. You must not come for me under any circumstances."

"Little bird?" She releases a sharp breath, the line between her brows growing more pronounced. "What happened to calling me little dragon?"

"When the sky is as large as the universe, even dragons look like little birds against it."

"I freed you, Damien. I killed Tony. I… I have magic. I just need help or maybe the right spell—"

"No!" I say firmly. "I know you are powerful, my mate. The strongest woman I've ever met. But your power will not save you against Valeska. She has an entire hive of vampires at her mercy. You will never reach me alive if you try. Do you understand that?"

She shoves out of my grip, her expression souring with mounting rage. "I can if you tell me where you are! I'll use the key. I'll pass through the underworld and come to you. The same symbol can bring us back."

I squeeze my eyes closed. It's tempting to ask her to try the spell. The thought of having her in my arms again in real life fills me with deep yearning. Only, it's pure fantasy. She'd never make it back out. Nothing, absolutely nothing, trumps a shade's instinct to protect their mate. No matter how seductive the idea of a possible escape is, I won't risk Eloise for anything, even my freedom.

"Once you were with me, you'd have to redraw the symbol and offer it blood." I extend my hands, appealing to her sense of reason. "Even if you were strong enough to perform the spell twice in a short time, you'd never get the chance to open the way home. I am heavily guarded, always surrounded by vampires at night and witches during the day."

"Witches?" Her face tightens. "Who? Maybe Maeve can do something on our end."

"A family called the Kims. They're sun wielders. That's why I haven't returned to you. They keep me caged in sunlight at all times."

Her face tightens and her lips start to tremble. "The Kims. I'll tell her. But there must be something more. I won't accept that there is nothing I can do to help you. What about your friend Cassius?"

My brow lifts at the sound of Cassius's name. If anyone *could* help me, it would be him, but I don't want Eloise doing anything that might alert Valeska to her identity. She's already risked far too much visiting with Morpheus, and if I didn't trust the shade more than almost anyone, I'd be telling her to run and hide right now.

I take a deep breath and stroke her hair back from her

face. "You have the most beautiful heart and the purest soul, little bird. Do you ever think of yourself first?"

"All the time. That's why I take care of the people I love, because they mean the most to me."

I laugh softly and draw her into my arms again. I press my lips to the top of her head. Is the ticking growing louder? Or do I only now realize this is no ordinary dream and our time together could end at any moment? I can't lie to my mate, and I've already shared more information about my predicament than I wish for her to know. My only hope is to distract her. "Can you guess where we are now? Here, in my dream?"

The question serves its purpose, and at least for the moment she gives up on her quest for information. She turns around, taking in the flowers, the trees, the stone benches partially covered in blooming vines.

"I've never seen anything like this. I don't recognize any of these plants aside from the roses, although I've never seen ones this color before." She cradles an amethyst bud in her palm.

"Careful of the thorns. They hurt just as much as the ones in your garden. Perceptive of you to notice about the flowers. Roses are one of the few varieties that are the same on Tenebris as on Earth, although they're more frequently purple where I come from."

She releases the flower and walks the periphery of my dreamscape. "It's beautiful." She whirls back to me, a ghost of a smile breaking through her former stormy expression. "This is what your world looks like? What you dressed like there?" She gestures toward my royal garb, black pants and a wrapped tunic.

I look down at myself. "It is when I'm not in battle. This form is considered more socially appropriate, or you might say diplomatic. As for the garden, this is the one behind the castle where I was raised. At least how I remember it. When I was summoned to Earth by the Gowdies, we were at war. I have no idea how much of this place remains." I approach her from behind and wrap an arm around her shoulders. Drawing her back to my front, I point toward the sky.

"A supermoon." She sighs. "It's beautiful."

"No. That's how the moon looks every day on Tenebris."

"Don't you mean every night?" She rests her soft curls against me.

"No. This is day here. Our galaxy works differently than yours."

She looks again at the amethyst roses and reaches out to run a finger along the petals. "I don't have time for a lecture on the astronomy of Tenebris." She turns in my arms to face me, sighing heavily. "I pray I have the chance to see your world in person someday, but after what happened, I regret not going with you when I had the chance."

I nuzzle the side of her face. "You weren't ready. You were right to want to stay and practice your magic."

"A lot of good it's doing me if I can't use it to get you back."

I brush my lips along her ear, inhale the scent of her hair. "Give me time. I'll find my way home to you."

The clock chimes. "We don't have much time."

The beat of her heart grows louder, her fear and yearning bringing her blood to the surface of her skin. I run my nose along the side of her neck. "There is one thing you can do for me."

"What? Anything."

"I need your blood. It will make me stronger and increase my chances of freeing myself."

Without hesitation, she sweeps her red curls over her shoulder, offering her vein. "Will it work? We're inside a dream. Is my blood anything more than thoughts?"

I turn her to face me. "I don't know. I'm not familiar with this magic. But I can smell your blood. You feel real."

"Then take it." She waits, head tipped, the warm skin of her throat exposed like a dish of cream.

I lower my lips to her flesh and breathe her in. "Do you think I'll simply strike, little bird, and take your blood like I would a goat's? Oh no. You are too delicious a meal not to savor."

Her pulse ratchets faster, and a sensuous shiver travels the length of her body. I brush a knuckle between her breasts and over her navel. Her breath stutters. When my fingers reach the apex of her thighs, I find her drenched. My erection turns valiantly hard. Gods, the feel of her slick folds makes my cock drool to be inside her. I'm hungry, starving for her blood, but if I'm going to take her vein, I'm going to do it while I'm in her and she's screaming my name.

She moans into my mouth as I dip my fingers inside her, cupping her sweet pussy and massaging the underside of her clit. I bend lower, my tongue finding her breast, sucking the tight nub. I bite gently until I hear her gasp.

The clock ticks louder. "The clock. We're running out of time," she whispers breathlessly.

"Then I'll need you to come faster." I drop to my knees and replace my fingers with my tongue, sucking and licking, eating her like the starving man I am. The taste of her almost makes me weep. Her chest flushes, her nipples hard pearls that I take between my fingers.

Her pleasure sweeps through her hard and fast as a clap of thunder. She cries out, gripping my shoulders as if I'm the only thing holding her to the earth. But I'm already on my feet, my clothes gone as fast as I can think it. I lift her, dragging her up my body. Her soft curves meld against all my hard edges as her legs wrap around my hips.

I'm at her entrance, her slick need welcoming me inside, and I can't hold myself back any longer. My foot finds purchase on the bench and I unleash myself on her, filling her again and again with sharp, quick thrusts. She cries out as another orgasm seizes her. I support her back as she arches over the bench and I run my palm along her sternum until my fingers wrap gently around her throat.

Mine.

Her pulse thrums against my fingers. Warm. Alive.

Mine.

With her body sheathing me, I'm on the verge of ecstasy.

I pull her flush against my chest, enjoying how each of my thrusts makes her breasts swell between us. "You're mine, little bird," I say against her throat.

"Yours," she answers, her voice laden with promise.

And then I strike.

My fangs sink into her throat. This might be a dream, but her blood is thick and warm and real. It is all the heavens of all the worlds wrapped into one. I swallow her down, the taste, the power she feeds into my veins pushing me over the edge. I empty myself inside her, gulping down what she so freely gives me even as her body constricts around me, her hips grinding, driving me deeper.

The clock ticks again, louder, and then stops. Our eyes meet, hers wide and desperate.

"I love you, little bird. I will find a way back to you."

She and the clock fade like blown smoke.

I wake under the mattress, the light sizzling against my exposed skin. A warrior never weeps. Tears are a waste of energy. But I gnash my teeth at the loss of her, burying my wail in the filthy fabric. Only when I gain control again do I notice a change.

I'm no longer hungry.

Eloise might have been a dream, but my body tells me her blood was real enough. The question is, will it be enough to gain the upper hand against Valeska.

8

COLD REASON

ELOISE

"Wake up! Jesus Christ, Eloise, don't do this to me! Wake the hell up!"

Maeve's voice is shrill in my ears as I jolt awake and draw a deep, gasping inhale. "What are you doing? Put me back. Put me back in."

I sit up on the green velvet sofa in my parlor and reach for the mason jar we used for the potion. It's empty. I already drank it all. My head spins like I'm tipsy.

"No way!" Maeve grabs the jar from my hands. "All the blood's drained from your face, and I couldn't find your pulse a second ago. What the hell happened in there? I thought I was going to lose you!"

I shiver, registering for the first time that the room is icy cold. I grab the crocheted blanket I keep on the end of the couch and wrap it around me.

"Your teeth are chattering." She presses her palm to my forehead. "God, you're freezing."

"Turn up the heat. We should start a fire." My voice sounds weak, and I'm thirsty as hell.

"The temperature is just fine. It's your body that isn't working. Can you make it to the kitchen? You need to move and eat something hot."

I grumble in protest but allow her to help me to my feet. "It feels like I have the flu."

With her help, I hobble down the hall and into the kitchen, where she sits me down at the table and digs in my cupboard. "Chicken noodle or Italian wedding?"

"Italian wedding."

She pulls down the jar and dumps it into a saucepan. "Now start talking."

I hug myself, fighting the urge to lay my head on the table. "It worked. I saw him. We were together."

"Did you see where she's keeping him?"

"No. We were in his dream—a garden behind his castle in Stygarde." I can't hold my head up. I fold my arms on the table and rest my head on top.

"How did he look?"

"You mean does he look beat up or like they're torturing him?"

She nods.

"Not in the dream. He looked the same as always. But..."

"But?"

I rub my face. "I think she's starving him. He took my blood, and it was like the night we met. Like he would have kept drinking if the anchor hadn't pulled me out of the dream. And now that I think about it, his voice sounded gritty, like his throat was dry."

Maeve stops stirring and stares at me. "You let him

take your blood on the astral plane? No wonder you looked so pale."

"He was hungry. He said it would help strengthen him to face Valeska."

"I get that, but listen, on the astral plane you don't have actual blood. You exist there as energy. Magical energy. When he drinks from you, it might taste like blood to him, and it might nourish him, but he's draining your energy and your magic. He could kill you if he takes too much."

"Same as blood then."

She rubs her eye behind her glasses. "No… No… When Damien drinks your blood in real life he can hear your heart slow and feel you struggle. Clues he's learned to listen to over hundreds of years living among humans tell him when to stop. But in his dream, his reality is created by his mind. He might not recognize your cues of distress if you even have any on that plane."

"Oh. That explains some things." I close my eyes just for a second.

I wake to Maeve shaking me by the shoulder and sliding the hot soup in front of me. I wipe drool from the corner of my mouth. She watches me as I try to lift the spoon and my hand shakes so hard all the soup falls off it. With an exasperated sigh, she takes it from me. Carefully, she feeds me like a child. Our eyes meet through her glasses, and hers are unusually glossy.

"I'm sorry if I scared you," I say softly between bites. "You've been such a good friend to me through all this. Thank you. Thank you for everything. I don't know what I'd do without you, really."

She glances down at the soup. "You had no pulse."

"I'm sorry."

She nods. Smiles a little. "I forgive you. Magic can be a bitch. You're new. You'll learn."

"I'll be more careful next time."

"Next time?" Her spine straightens and her chin tucks.

"Next time. If his plan doesn't work, I have to go back in."

Maeve feeds me another spoonful. "What exactly did he tell you? You were in his dream for over an hour."

"He confirmed the vampire queen has him. He confirmed I can't use the keyspell to come for him because he's watched all the time and is being held in a cage of sunlight by witches. Oh, Maeve, he said it was the Kim family who captured him. They're sun wielders. Have you heard of them?"

She winces. "Unfortunately, I have. The Kims are mercenaries. They're hired magic. They're who you call when you have a dirty job to do and you don't have a shade bound to a candle to do it for you."

I squint at her. "Sun wielders? Really?" When I think of mercenaries, I think of weapons or explosives, not a warm sunny day.

"One Kim acting alone could give you second-degree burns over all your exposed skin in under three minutes. Two Kims working together could fry your skin completely off your body in that amount of time. With three or more, they could cut you in half with the strength of the beam they could produce."

"Fuck."

"The Kims are not good people. Even so, vampires and witches don't normally work together. Rumor has it that the senior Kim has a terrible gambling problem. It could be as simple as money. Valeska must have something over them if they're working for her."

I swallow. "Do you think there's anything we can do aboveground to influence them to abandon the project?"

She squirms. "I doubt it. I can't imagine Valeska makes it easy for her allies to break their agreements."

"But we could try right? I mean, what good is all this money I'm supposedly getting from Tony's estate if I can't use it? Can we try to buy them off?"

She frowns. "I think it would take more than you have, unfortunately. Valeska is quite wealthy. Not to mention, the amount you'll end up inheriting from Tony's estate is far from settled. The probate court is still working on dividing his assets. He had a will, but it was made years before he married you and didn't include everything. I haven't seen the proposed breakdown yet from our financial team. I suspect you'll get something but not everything."

"Fair enough. I wasn't expecting anything." I shrug. "Honestly, I'll be relieved when it's over. I don't want any connection to Tony or his family."

She nods. "That's what I thought you'd say, and that's how I plan to proceed on this. I'll only involve you if we need a decision." She stands. "Which reminds me, I have a stack of work at the office that desperately requires my attention."

"Sorry." I wince. "I've been taking up way too much of your time lately."

She hugs me. "You'd do the same for me."

Our eyes meet again. "I would."

She starts for the door and I follow. "Um, Maeve, you

will help me go back again if he's not able to free himself, right?"

She stops at the door and squeezes the bridge of her nose. "One week. I want you to wait at least one full week before trying again. You should be completely recovered by then."

I smile and nod. It feels like forever, but Damien looked strong in his dream. Remembering the feel of his arms around me causes some of the tension in my shoulders to drain away. Maybe all he needs is more time to free himself. "Thanks, Maeve."

She gives me a supportive nod. "See you after work for magic lessons."

I beam at her. "You're still going to teach me?"

She laughs. "Yeah. Is it too much to hope it will keep you out of trouble? Just so you know, I never want to find myself in Morpheus's office again."

"I think it will help me take my mind off Damien while he's finding a way home," I say softly.

She smiles. "That's the spirit."

I let her out the front door and return to my soup.

Five minutes later, the doorbell rings. I rise to unlock it. "Did you forget some—"

A man in a suit stands on my stoop. "Eloise Harcourt?"

I take another hard look at the guy. Short brown hair, a bit too much scruff, a suit that looks like it came off the rack at a warehouse store. I wonder what he's selling. Must be desperate to travel all the way out here. "Can I help you?"

He pulls a wallet from his pocket and opens it to show me a badge. "Branson Fuller, FBI. Can I ask you a few questions about your late husband Tony Denardi?"

Not a salesman. Anxiety shoots through me, and I shift nervously on my feet. When it comes to Tony, there's the truth and then there's what the world thinks is the truth. If the FBI is involved, I can only guess that something somewhere isn't adding up. I rummage through my exhausted mind for what's safe to say to this man.

"Um, why?" I swallow and press a hand to my chest. "It's still such a shock to me how they found him."

He slides his badge back into his pocket. "Right. Shocking," he mumbles. "That's why I'm here. Just covering all my bases. Do you mind?" He gestures inside and gives me a warm smile. "It should only take a few minutes."

I consider telling him to talk to my lawyer, but that sounds like something a guilty person would say. *You're innocent,* I think. *Act like it.* "Sure. Come on in."

I walk him into the parlor without thinking. He frowns at the thick path of dust and the fallen vent screen that I still haven't screwed back into the wall.

"Ignore that. Haven't had a chance to fix it." I take a seat in the lion's-head rocker and gesture toward the couch.

He sits. "Tell me about your relationship with Tony."

I huff. That doesn't sound like covering his bases. "You're going to have to be more specific."

"How long were you married?"

"Two years."

"But you recently filed for divorce."

"No. He filed. But I'd recently left him after he hit me."

Agent Fuller shifts in his seat. "He hit you?"

"Yes. Tony was physically abusive. I moved out to

escape the abuse, and he filed for divorce when I wouldn't move back in with him. It was his way of punishing me."

"But the divorce was never finalized."

"No." I tuck my hair behind my ears. "My lawyer told me they found him dead on a boat with some other men. That's how I found out." I shake my head.

"What does Gold Weaver mean to you?"

I shrug, adding a few blank blinks. "Nothing."

"Genesis Corp?"

I shake my head. "Never heard of it." I've never enjoyed lying, but I'm capable of it. It saved my life with Tony.

"Hmm." He pulls out a small notebook and jots something down. "Are you aware that Tony was involved in a money-laundering operation?"

I don't have to feign surprise. It comes naturally at his bluntness about the crime. "No! What kind of money laundering?"

"Strange you weren't aware considering a key part of his operation happened under this house."

My jaw drops. And now I'm regretting not calling Maeve before letting this guy inside. "Under my house?" I laugh in a way that sounds a little unhinged. "You're mistaken. I'll take you down to the basement right now, Agent Fuller. There's nothing down there but old furniture and canning jars."

He sits up straighter. "Not in your basement, Ms. Harcourt. *Under* the house."

We stare at each other for a beat. I make my face as blank as possible.

"Are you aware that there are caverns under your home?" he asks, sounding a bit frustrated now.

I shrug a shoulder. "There are caverns everywhere in these cliffs. I can only assume."

"Do you know they are accessible from the river?"

"I wasn't aware."

"Did you have anything to do with Tony's death?"

I snort. The secret to a good lie is believing, however momentarily, that what you're saying is true. My mind flashes back to my mom's sculpture. Technically, I was not the thing that caused his death. "No. I didn't kill Tony. Why would I? We were separated. I was days away from a divorce settlement. I didn't want Tony dead. I just wanted my life back."

"Hmm." He toys with the edge of his cuff. "Can you explain why you were the named beneficiary on the operational accounts of Gold Weaver, Inc.?"

I blink at him. "Sorry? What are you talking about?"

"You are the named beneficiary on the Gold Weaver accounts."

"That doesn't make any sense. I didn't know it existed until now."

His eyes crinkle, and he slants me a skeptical, cynical smile. "That's weird, because we found a man who identified you as someone he's seen poking around an old warehouse in Richmond that used to be a Gold Weaver printing operation just weeks before Tony was murdered on the river very close to here."

Fuck. The homeless man? How? He never knew my name, which means Fuller must have shown him a picture. He must've already suspected me. Of course he suspected me. My name was listed as a beneficiary on the Gold Weaver account! My fingers ache, and I realize I have the arms of the rocker in a death grip. I stretch them, then rub my sweaty palms on my thighs. "Agent Fuller, I don't know anything about any of this. I think I'd better call my lawyer before we go any further. I feel like there are things you know that I don't."

With a throaty grunt, he stands. "I think that's a good idea, Ms. Harcourt. It seems that Tony had an unusual connection to accounts in the Caymans and a printing operation here. Interesting, don't you think? I have to believe that those closest to Tony are disappointed that so much of his wealth and capital will be transferred to you, considering you were so close to breaking ties before he died. Stay safe, Ms. Harcourt."

With a slight tip of his head in lieu of goodbye, he rises and lets himself out. As soon as he's gone, I pick up the phone and call Maeve.

9

DEAD MAN WALKING

DAMIEN

Pain is manageable. Eventually the mind blocks out the sensation, disassociates to a better place. The body grows numb. My better place is Eloise. I replay our dream encounter again and again. I fixate on the taste of her blood.

Night falls over the silo. I tip the bed on its side and lie in the pool of shade created by the frame. I still can't go anywhere. I'm still surrounded by light on all sides. But for a blissful time, the pain stops. I rest under a canopy of light-fringed stars and just breathe.

Only then do I realize the damage my prison has caused. Even with the partial protection of the bed and mattress, even with the gift of Eloise's blood, the light has burned a small hole through the webbing of my right wing. Now that I'm in the shade, it's already healing.

I wince when the sound of two sets of perfectly synced footsteps fills the silo. There's whispering and then Tae's face appears over the canopy of the bed. A second later, power blows through me. The cuffs are back. The walls grow dim. It takes all my strength to stand from my fort of shadows and rise to my full height.

Valeska enters the silo and crosses to stand next to the two Kims. I meet the vampire queen's deadly gaze.

"We will speak now," Valeska commands. As always, she possesses a rare dark beauty. No one would deny it. Her brown skin is smooth as marble, flawless under the black silk dress she wears. Her ebony hair falls in waves around her shoulders, and she blinks golden-amber eyes at me that put off their own light. But Valeska is bright in the way of a poisonous spider—I know better than to be fooled by the colors she displays to draw prey into her web.

"Talk then," I croak through my parched throat.

She laughs cruelly. "Oh, Damien, you've looked better."

I say nothing. She wants a response. She wants lively banter. I am a toy whose buttons she's pushed, and she expects a reaction. Negative or positive doesn't matter. Whether I beg for mercy or fight for freedom or pretend to be interested in her, any response feeds her ego and makes me her entertainment.

I am no plaything.

Perfectly silent, I stare past her at the wall, willing my body to heal, thinking about the gift of Eloise's blood in my veins.

Valeska digs her nails into my lower jaw and turns my face toward her. "Look at me when I'm talking to you."

I do, but I keep all emotion from showing. The look I give her is flat, soulless. I might as well be dead. *Tire of me. Set me free.*

"Poor baby. Look at your wing." She tsks, running her fingers over the webbing and probing the wound painfully. It is healing, but slowly, and her rough handling draws blood. She licks it from her fingertips before stepping in close to me. The front of her dress brushes my bare chest. "I bet you're hungry now," she whispers into my ear.

I am hungry, and the scent of her blood makes my throat burn with need. Instinctively, I bring my lips close to the vein in her neck, but I don't strike. Indisputably, I need more blood than what I consumed from Eloise to fully heal. But I am far from hungry enough to even consider drinking Valeska's.

"Go ahead," she whispers. "Drink of me. I know you want to. You need to."

Only my eyes move as I spot Tae and Lang an arm's length behind her. They appear even more drained than before. Tae's head is bobbing like he can hardly hold it up.

I brush my lips over Valeska's vein.

"That's right," she coos. "You need blood. There's no reason to fight it."

"Blood," I concede. And then I stab my talons into her gut as hard as my mortal arms are capable of. I toss her aside, her blood staining my hands. She cries out, but I'm already in motion. I kick Tae in the gut, knocking him down, while at the same time I loop my cuffed wrists around Lang's neck and sink my teeth into his carotid. Blood sprays across my shoulder, and his screams turn into a gurgle as I drink as fast as my body will draw blood. He's the stronger of the twins. If I can take him out first, Tae should be an easy second target. Lang's heart slows. His eyes roll back in his head.

A groan comes from Valeska's direction. I did a number on her, tearing open her abdominal cavity, but she won't be down for long.

Out of the corner of my eye, I see Tae struggling to get his feet back under him. He finally succeeds and starts to circle his arms. Fuck. I stab Lang in the gut, wishing I was free of the cuffs and could simply tear his head off. With what little energy I have left, I toss Lang aside and barrel into his brother, disrupting the spell. I might not be strong enough to tear him in two, but I'm strong enough to drink.

My fangs sink in.

My cuffs sputter as Tae's heartbeat slows. Just as I thought. Kill the Kims and I kill the magic. Almost there.

A curse comes from behind me, and before I can swallow my next gulp, I'm lifted above the vampire queen's head and thrown. I hit the stone of the far wall. Bones crunch. My teeth clack together. I end up on my side on the ground, gasping for breath through fractured ribs. The fucking cuffs glow brighter. What energy I gained from the blood I guzzled drains away once more.

Valeska appears beside me in a blink, emanating pure rage. "You dare challenge me?" she shrieks down at my broken form. "You impudent shade!"

She kicks me in the side, and I grunt as my ribs crunch. She bares her teeth. Finally the reaction she was after, evidence of my suffering.

"You fucking imbecile," she hisses, bringing her face close to my ear. Her fingers constrict around my throat. "It's only a matter of time. Maybe not today, maybe not tomorrow, but you will tell me her name. And then you will be mine."

I turn my face away from her, refusing her another moment of my attention. I'm too weak to rise to my feet. Out of the corner of my eye, I see Tae helping Lang to stand, their glowing hands touching each other's wounds. Fuck me. They're healing each other.

"You should know I've put a price on her head," Valeska says through a wicked grin. "Ten million for anyone who can identify her. I'm willing to bet it won't be long until a vampire comes forward. Why, I've even hung flyers at Bad Witches' Club. Every supernatural on the Eastern Seaboard is searching for the truth."

A growl tears through my throat, but I'm still too weak to do a thing about it. Valeska rolls me onto my back and rests her boot on my chest. Her dress is torn, but underneath, she's already healed.

"She's as good as dead anyway. Mating a human." She shakes her head. "What does she have? Fifty years? Seventy? What's the difference if I accelerate the process? You must know that becoming my mate and consort is inevitable. I have chosen you and I will make it happen. All that's left for you to decide is how much pain you'll suffer first."

Now I meet her gaze and let my absolute certainty fill my unblinking stare. "I can think of no greater pain than becoming your consort."

She seethes, then removes her boot from my chest only to kick me again. More bones crunch. She leaves me writhing. Just as she's passing through the door to my cell, she orders, "Take the bed."

No! But a team of guards rush in, and the bed, the mattress, any break from the endless sun, is gone. The Kims raise their hands and sluggishly perform the spell.

The cuffs fade. The walls begin to glow. I cry out when pain consumes me as if she's set me on fire. I crawl to the center of the silo, the pain in my back and ribs ratcheting up with my movement. I roll into a ball, covering myself with my wings.

And pray to all the gods in this world and my own for Eloise's safety.

IO

THE HAUNTING OF HARCOURT

ELOISE

"This is just a really basic exercise to get you in touch with the elements. We all start here when we come into our power." Maeve removes a silky purple scarf and drapes it across the coffee table, then sets a white candle in front of me, a small white bowl, a white plate, and a white flowerpot full of dirt. "Every spell boils down to elemental roots. Before you can master the spells in the books and journals upstairs, you'll need to figure out how your personal brand of magic translates into mastery of the elements."

"Got it." It's late, half past eleven, but after I called and dumped on her about my visit from Fuller, she had a long day ahead of her before we could meet for magic lessons. I make a mental note that I need to buy Maeve the biggest bouquet of goth flowers imaginable.

"What's with all the white?"

She grins. "You can get this set in different colors:

pink, blue or white. Black wasn't an option because of the risk of evil interference, blah, blah, blah. This went with my monochromatic aesthetic." She laughs. "Besides, it's the combination of all colors of light. Makes sense that it might help beginners key into their natural vibration. The really important thing is that all the dishes are the same color so that we're not unconsciously influencing a proclivity toward a specific element."

"The candle is fire, the flowerpot earth… What's the plate and the bowl?"

"Oh." She reaches into her bag for her water bottle and pours an inch into the bowl, then sets a feather on the plate. "There. Water and air. Technically there's a fifth element we can try—metal—but it's a difficult magic to work with even for those who come from metal-aligned families. We usually don't practice it until we've mastered the others."

I scooch to the edge of the green sofa and square my shoulders. This is starting to feel like a test. Tests usually don't bother me. I was always good at school. But I've never felt the pressure I do right now to get it right. Damien's life could be at stake. "What should I try first?"

"When you broke Damien's curse, you tossed the candle into the fire. You also saw red and ash when you spoke to your parents and grandma. If your magic comes from dragon's blood, I have to think fire will be easiest for you."

I glance at the candle. "So what do I do?"

"Gently ease your intention for the candle to light over the wick." Gracefully, she sweeps her hand from her heart toward the candle like it's the easiest, most natural thing to produce flame from thin air.

Narrowing my eyes, I grit my teeth and glare at the wick, repeating *burn, burn, burn* in my head.

"Now you look like you need an enema." Maeve laughs wickedly.

"Hey!"

"You're not trying to start a fire with your mind," she says through her smile. "Magic is in you. In the deepest part of you. Blood pulses through your veins, but magic pulses through your spirit."

I tip my head to the side and quirk my lip. "How simple. I just direct the pulse of my spirit at the wick." It's ridiculous. I give her a dismissive snort.

"It is simple once you feel it." Fire springs to life on the wick. She spreads her hands and smiles. "Easy peasy."

"Did you— How did you do that?" I ask breathlessly. "You didn't even look at it."

She rests her black nails over her heart. "Think of yourself standing in the center of a spider's web. Each strand of the web connects you to everything else. One silky thread leads from you to that wick. Don't concentrate on the wick with your mind. Go inside yourself to the vibration in your core and pluck the string."

Inner vibration. I search for it. Feel for it. Close my eyes and wait for it to appear. I've got nothing. "What did you find out about Agent Fuller?" I ask to distract us both from the fact that I'm not getting this at all.

She sighs. "Really? You want to talk about him now?"

"Hey, I'm working on it. I can multitask."

She leans back in her seat. "I confirmed that the FBI found the cavern under your house, which was, um, decorated with the blood of three men, all with mob ties. One of them was Tony."

"Decorated?"

"Damien made a mess and didn't clean it up."

I shudder.

"They found partially burned bills on the boat with his body and matching bills on a barge in the Atlantic. The captain of that vessel was still alive, and they learned from him that his destination was the Caymans and that he drove for Genesis Corp."

"You got Fuller to admit all that to you?"

She snorts. "No. I have a cousin on the inside."

"What does any of that have to do with me?"

She adjusts her glasses on her face. "They also found copies of *Echo Mills Today* down there and put together that the paper matches what the counterfeit bills were printed on *Echo Mills* that's published by Gold Weaver, which was owned and run by Tony under a pseudonym. My office was notified on your behalf this afternoon that you are the beneficiary on those Gold Weaver operating accounts, and there are millions in there, El. It doesn't look good. Fuller knew before I did."

I gape at her. "Why? The man was divorcing me, taking me to court to not only make sure I didn't get a red cent but also to take this house. Why on earth would he list me as a beneficiary on one of his company's accounts?"

She shakes her head. "The company involved in a money-laundering scheme under your house? I'm pretty sure he meant to frame you if things went south."

"Fuck me!"

"Exactly. That's what he was trying to do. His family members were listed on all the other financial assets, but the Denardi name is suspiciously absent from Gold

Weaver. I think he planned to have you take the fall in the event he was ever caught."

"Agent Fuller made it sound like he suspected me in Tony's murder too."

"You are inheriting a ton of money because of the death of a man… a man you were divorcing. Money from a company the FBI believes is a front for a money-laundering operation that was happening under your house. You're a suspect."

"Fucking fantastic." I huff and flop back on the couch.

"There's something else."

I frown at her.

"I don't know how you got on those accounts, but I suspect the Denardi family will want to talk to you about it."

"Fuller said essentially the same thing when he was trying to get me to talk. *Fuuuuuck.* The last thing I need right now is trouble with the mob too. Can't I just refuse the inheritance? Tell the bank there's been some mistake. Give it to someone else."

"That's actually a good idea. You absolutely have the right to do that."

"Fine. Do that. I don't want it. I don't need it after what Grams left me."

"It's probably the safest way. Makes me sick though. After everything Tony put you through, you deserve that money and more."

I bob my knee. The last thing I need is something else to worry about. I have enough stress in my life trying to get Damien back. Tension rises in my muscles, and I rub the place where my neck meets my shoulder. It feels like my brain is boiling. Sweat breaks out on my brow.

"What if Agent Fuller arrests me? Or one of Tony's pissed-off relatives stabs me in a back alley?"

"When are you ever in a back alley?"

"I don't know! But it happens. People are stabbed. Honestly, it doesn't have to be an alley. It could be in my own foyer, for God's sake. I'm alone out here most of the day. I can't deal with this right now, Maeve. I need to focus on helping Damien come home." The grandfather clock strikes twelve. With each gong, my heart pounds harder. My chest aches like my heart is caught in a steel trap. "Damn, it feels like I'm having a panic attack." I rub over my sternum.

"I'm here. Just breathe through it." Maeve rubs my back.

"No. It's not in my heart. It's..." I look toward the grandfather clock. I feel a steady, buzzing tug like an electrified string attached to my rib is attached to the clock. "I think I can feel the clock."

Maeve's eyes flash excitedly. "That must be your magical anchor. Some witches have them. Usually it's a talisman or a ring, but this makes sense considering this house has always been your spiritual center. This is good. You chose the clock as your anchor when you journeyed into Damien's dream."

I focus again on the candle. Red haze creeps into the room, and ash floats like snow from the ceiling. "Can you see that?"

"See what?"

"The red is back."

She shakes her head. "Go with it, El. Light the candle."

A man appears by the fireplace in denim overalls. A tall man with graying hair and a straight, muscular frame you only get from hard work. He turns, and his eyes glow silver from a face the color of newsprint. His entire body is black and white and slightly transparent, just like my Grams was in the attic. But I recognize him right away from his pictures on the gallery wall.

"Grandpa Harcourt?" He's actually my great-grandfather and has been dead since before I was born.

"Henry Harcourt is here, in this room?" Maeve asks.

I nod. "He's smiling at me from beside the fireplace."

"Light the candle, Eloise," Maeve says breathlessly, her eyes so wide I can see the whites around her pupils. When I look at her, away from the red, black, and white of where my great-grandfather stands, her skin is radiant even though she's dressed all in black and the green sofa behind her is vibrant. She's like a breath of life in a room where death looms.

"Can you help me light the flame?" I ask the ghost.

He holds up a finger. Turning to the fireplace, he reaches through the wall. My mother appears, grayscale, just as he is, eyes twinkling silver. She walks straight up to me.

"My mom is here," I say softly, tears falling. "I miss you, Mom."

She mouths I love you, but I can't hear anything. Then she points at the wick. I concentrate on it again but feel a warm tingle enter my side where my mother stands. I grunt as a second web, exactly like the one between me and the clock, forms between me and the wick. There's a chiff and the candle glows to life.

"We did it!" I yell, looking between my mother and Maeve.

"We?" Maeve asks.

"My mom helped me. She's right here." I look back up at her but she's moved away. Silently, she points at the candle and mouths something. "I think she wants me to try on my own."

Maeve blows out the candle, but I can still feel the web. I look at my mom and feel the vibration deep within, the one I felt when she was beside me, and I think down it, *fire*. The wick ignites. I laugh and clap for myself.

"Good work," Eloise says. "Goddess, I can feel your power, but it's so, so different than anything I've ever felt before. A completely different vibration."

"I sense the web strands you were talking about now, but until my mother helped me, I could only sense the one to the clock. I'm on my own now though, and it's still there."

Maeve grins. "Spiritual training wheels," she mutters.

"Huh?"

"The spirits of your ancestors are teaching you how to connect to your power through them. Should we test it?"

I nod vigorously, excited to try again.

"Float the feather, Eloise."

I glance at the feather and try to call up the web. It comes, but instead of rising, the feather starts to smoke. I pull back and look to my mother, who is smiling and shaking her ghostly head. She comes close again and waves her hand near my brow. The web forms again, only not from my side, but from an area between my eyes. I feed energy down the vibration, and the feather floats toward the ceiling.

Maeve squeals. "You did it! Was that with or without her help?"

"With. Let me try it again without." I nod, and my

mother recedes toward the fireplace. I find the thread again. It's harder this time, like the feather weighs more, but I lift it.

"That's so good, El! Goddess, it took me so long to master two."

I grunt and the feather floats down to the plate. A sharp pain cuts through my skull and I grab my head, squeezing my eyes shut. "Oww. Fuck."

Maeve's hand is rubbing my back again. "Shhh. That's all for tonight. I'm afraid we overdid it." She shoves a tissue into my hand. I don't understand why until warm liquid oozes out my nose. Blood.

I lean my head back on the couch. The red haze is gone, as are the ghosts of my family members. "Shit, I feel like crap," I say around the Kleenex. "And it's cold as fuck in here."

Maeve grabs the afghan off the back of the couch and wraps it around me. "You're drained again. I'll make you some of Aunt Hildie's tea." She grabs a tea bag from her purse and heads for the kitchen.

I watch her go, suddenly sleepy. The parlor tilts and then the lights go out.

II

PRACTICE MAKES POLTERGEIST

ELOISE

The next night, Maeve is back again with her Little Miss Witch starter kit as I've come to call it. We set up in the parlor as we did the night before.

"If you start feeling cold or your head hurts, we'll stop," she promises.

"I slept twelve hours last night after drinking the tea you made me. I'm ready. Let's do this." Like last night, the candle, feather, bowl of water, and pot of earth challenge me from their sectors on the purple silk.

"Let's warm up by lighting the candle," Maeve suggests.

I snort. "You make it sound like I'm readying myself for a workout."

"You are. Using magic is like using a muscle. You grow your abilities with practice."

Sitting up straighter, I concentrate on the candle,

trying to find the web again. But I can't reproduce the vibration from the night before. Until the ticking of the grandfather clock reminds me to anchor. I shift my intent to the clock, and the web rises between me and it.

"What did you just do?" Maeve asks. "I felt your power bubble into being."

"I connected to the clock. I wasn't able to form the web directly to the candle but now…" I cast out toward the wick and it ignites. I turn my attention to the feather, and it floats into my hand and then back again.

"Interesting." Maeve frowns.

"You sound disappointed. Hey, I did it."

She shifts. "It's just yesterday, I thought your connection to your anchor was so you could channel your ancestors. I didn't realize it was also the source of your power. It poses a challenge. It's not like you can carry the grandfather clock everywhere you go. If we can't move your anchor into something more portable, it's possible you may only be able to practice your magic in this house."

I sigh. "Terrific. As long as I never leave my house, I'll be a force of nature."

She laughs. "We'll do some research in that attic library of yours and see if there's a spell to change the anchor. For now, if you feel okay, try to swirl the water in the bowl."

I turn my focus on the water but can't seem to connect to it. That is until the room turns red and my father appears in front of the fireplace. I grin. "My dad's here."

Daddy smiles, and my heart swells. I miss him so much. His silver eyes twinkle at me.

"Can you teach me how to move the water?"

He approaches me on the opposite side as my mother did, and I feel his energy flow into me. A hair-thin web appears between me and the water. He twirls his finger, and I picture that movement in my mind. The water circles in the bowl.

"Good," Maeve says. "Now the pot. If you're feeling strong enough."

I am. The vibration of my father's energy, so much slower and more even than my mother's, flows through me. I watch in wonder as a thread forms between me and the pot. And then a green shoot rises in the center of the earth. Two leaves sprout from a scrawny stem.

"Wow, Eloise, you really are—"

Passing out is inevitable. At some point of practicing magic, my body just gives up and my head hits the sofa cushions. But each day I've been able to do more. By Friday night, after Maeve revives me once again, I'm feeling pretty good about what I've learned and my rate of improvement. We sit at the kitchen table, scarfing pizza from Echo Mills' one and only pizza place, Slice of Home, and I already feel stronger, like I could try again. I know I'm recovering more quickly than before and definitely am able to do more on my own without the help of the spirits who come to train me.

"I think the pizza has gotten better since we were kids," I say around the bite in my mouth.

"Yeah, it only took them twenty years to get the crust right." Maeve sinks her teeth into another slice.

"So…" I sip my iced tea and swallow. "I'm a medium, I guess." The question of how to define my magic has popped up before in my head. Am I a witch like my mother and father? A spiritualist like my great-grandfather? A magical mutt?

Maeve snorts. "You are far more than a medium, Eloise. I think we've completely misunderstood your sigil up until now."

"How so?"

"Your parents told you your sigil was a key. We assumed they meant that it unlocked a portal to the underworld, which it did. We focused on the portal part, not the underworld part."

"Right."

"You can, presumably, transport yourself and, again presumably, transport others to the underworld and then jump from the underworld to anywhere else. But maybe we've been viewing your sigil too narrowly. Maybe that's just one way you can use it."

"You think there's more?"

She takes my hands. "I think your real power is in channeling magic from beings in the underworld and using it as your own. Think about it like this. You are the key, not to a portal but to a doorway, and as long as you hold that door open, you can allow what's on the other side through. Your family members are the easiest for you because they want to help you. But potentially you could tap into the power of any dead witch or wizard if you practiced long enough. And if I'm right, the name for your brand of power is spirit magic."

"Spirit magic?"

"Yes. I'll be honest, I'm a little out of my element here.

The Gowdies, we animate things. Nothing we work with includes souls. I'm not sure exactly how it works. It could be the clock or the house itself that allows the spirits to interact with you, but it seems more likely to me that you yourself hold the power and are simple using the clock as an anchor or a brace to support all that magic coming though from the other side. And if that's the case, we should be able to move your anchor so that you can practice magic outside these walls. In fact, I think we should try practicing somewhere else."

I take a deep breath and let it out slowly. "I'm certainly willing to try." I try to wrap my head around everything she just told me. It's a lot but not altogether surprising. "Maeve, I think you're right about unlocking the passage, but I wonder if maybe it's, like, always open when I'm here."

"Why would you say that?

"I, um, recently learned that my ancestors have been more involved in my life than I originally thought."

"What do you mean?"

I point at the spider plant hanging over the sink. "I have never watered that plant."

Slowly she stands up and touches the soil. Her brow peaks. "It's wet."

I nod. "Also, I thought my grandmother had hired landscapers to tend the yard. Well, she had, but they stopped after she died because they were doing it on a volunteer basis to help her. I didn't realize they'd stopped until I ran into the owner at the grocery store and he asked if I'd consider using him again. Someone has been maintaining the grounds, Maeve, and it isn't me."

"Shit. And they didn't start doing all that until you moved in here."

"I think… it didn't start until the day the eye of the dragon opened."

She squints at me.

"There's this painting of a dragon on my mother's art studio door. The eye was closed when I moved in. After I mated Damien, it opened. I think being with him awakened something in me, something dormant."

She adjusts her glasses on her face. "So your house is haunted by your ancestors, and something about you, and perhaps your relationship with Damien, allowed them to cross over. I can think of worse things."

I smile. "Honestly, it's been comforting. Nothing scary has happened. Every encounter I've had with the spirit world has been benevolent. I like to see them."

Maeve squeezes my hand. "This is good, El. It feels natural to you because it is. You were born for this. This magic is yours."

A warm feeling blossoms deep in my chest.

She grabs her purse and slings it over her shoulder. "I wish I could stay, but—"

"No, I get it. You've been so helpful."

"Tomorrow at my place to try your magic outside of Harcourt?"

"It will have to wait until Sunday," I say. "I need your help with the Hitch and Cast spell again tomorrow."

Maeve frowns. "I thought we agreed to take a break and see if Damien could free himself."

I frown. "You said a week. It's been a week. He's not here. I need to go back in and make sure he's okay."

"You're his mate. You would know if he wasn't."

I press my hand to my gut. "I do feel the bond stretched thin like before. I guess that means he's alive, but I've had this awful feeling in the pit of my stomach that something is wrong. How could it not be if he still hasn't managed to escape?"

The sigh she gives is way overdramatic. "Fine. But for the record, I don't like it. You need to be really careful right now. You're in a vulnerable position with your magic."

"Damien would never hurt me."

"He just almost killed you last time," she mumbles, glancing at her watch.

I bite my tongue to keep from saying something snarky. Technically it's true, but it was an accident. "It won't happen again," I promise.

"Right." She chews her lip. "Tomorrow is Saturday. Let's do it in the afternoon again. That's when he's most likely to be asleep. On that note, considering I need to be back here in twelve hours, I'd better get out of here."

"Thanks. You're the best."

"I am!" she says through a smile. "You're lucky to have me."

We both laugh and hug goodbye.

After she leaves, I bring a bowl of pizza crusts, fruit, and leftover beef from the fridge out to feed Phantom. Tonight he's waiting for me. I sit on the back stoop and watch as he comes straight to the bowl beside me and starts eating. He looks like he's put on some weight, but I notice now, with him so close and within the circle of light from the house, that he's an old fox. His face is peppered with white, his eyes are rheumy, and there's a concerning lump on his ribs.

I frown. Phantom is a wild creature, not a pet. I don't try to touch him or anything. I understand that nature will take its course. But before I go in for the night, I make sure his water dish is full, and I leave a warm blanket next to it.

12

CRACKED EARTH

ELOISE

The next afternoon when the doorbell rings, I rush to let Maeve in so we can get started on the spell to journey into Damien's dreams. The feeling in the pit of my stomach that something is seriously wrong is exceptionally bad today. I know Damien is strong and powerful, but everyone needs help sometimes. Everyone else might be willing to wait and see, but he's my mate. If all I can do is offer him my energy, that's what I'm going to do.

But when I throw open the door, it's not Maeve there but a man who looks disturbingly familiar. His chocolate-colored waves curl against the collar of his dress shirt, just a little too long, and his aquiline nose is a replica of Tony's. Fear spikes through my system. I try to slam the door but he charges through, drawing a gun from the back of his waistband once he's inside and kicking the door closed.

"Relax. I just wanna talk," he says.

He's not pointing the gun *at* me but toward the corner of the room, his opposite hand clasping the wrist of the hand holding the gun. It's the stance one might take in church or at a solemn event. Relaxed and polite. That's what the body language conveys.

But his finger is still on the trigger.

It's a posture Tony would take. At once decorous while harboring barely contained violence. His shoulders shrug beneath a tailored suit jacket the color of money.

I back up a step.

"Stay where you are, Eloise. I don't need a tour. We can do this right here."

I've never met this man, but his resemblance to Tony is too close to be a coincidence. "Who are you?"

"Jared Denardi."

"Jared…" I don't remember him.

"We've never met. I've only recently returned to the area with my cousin's passing. I'm sorry for your loss, by the way. Tony was a good man."

Is he fucking kidding me? I look at my feet and force my face to remain impassive. "My condolences to you and your family. Tony and I were separated, but I wished him no ill will."

"That's good to hear, Eloise, because my family needs your help rectifying a simple misunderstanding."

"What's that?"

Jared's eyes crinkle at the corners. "Some friends of ours at the bank notified us that you refused the money you were owed from Gold Weaver. We need you to change your mind about that. Take the money."

I flinch. Of all the things I expected him to say, that

was not on the list. "Why? I don't want Tony's money. You keep it."

He rocks back on his heels, the nose of his gun twitching slightly. He pulls a frown that somehow comes off as threatening as well as disappointed. "Yeah? Well, neither does the Denardi family. You refuse that money and it goes back to Tony's estate and then to us. That's unacceptable. This whole operation happening under your house has drawn the wrong kind of attention. The Denardis want nothing to do with it, understand? Your name was on those accounts because Tony loved you and wanted you to have it. You were his wife. You were aware of his affairs. You deserve it." His sleazy, disingenuous tone is one I remember Tony using far too well.

"No, actually," I say, heart hammering, "I had no idea what Tony was doing and was never involved with any of it. I don't want the money. Donate it to charity."

He raises his chin and stares down his nose at me. An exasperated sigh leaves his lungs. "That's not what's going to happen, Eloise. You will accept that money."

"Or what?" I try to sound brave but my voice shakes. I can't take my eyes off the gun.

"Or your estate will receive the money," he says softly through his teeth.

My *estate*. Like after I'm dead. "And what happens if I take the money?"

"Then we'll be in touch. Our family has an excellent accountant and financial advisor who can show you exactly what to do with it."

"While I'm fending off the FBI."

He shrugs. "If you weren't involved as you say, I

predict you'll slide right out from between their greasy fingers."

"Are you suggesting I grease those fingers?"

He shrugs again. "You'll have plenty of money to do so if you accept what's coming to you. A year from now, they'll give up this investigation and you'll be golden."

Right. If golden means entangled with the mob. I have to get this guy out of my house. "Fine. I'll talk to my lawyer," I say, trying to appease him.

It seems to work because he nods appreciatively. "You do that."

The doorbell rings. Maeve.

"Are you expecting company?" He glances over his shoulder at the door.

"It might be Agent Fuller." It's a lie but one that has the desired effect.

His eyes narrow and he side-eyes the door, slipping the gun into the back of his waistband and covering it with his jacket. "We're done here. For now. Back door?"

More than happy to spare Maeve a run-in with Jared, I point him toward the rear of the house and wait until I hear the back door close behind him before I let her in.

Maeve steps into the foyer, waving a hand in front of her face. "Goddess, is that Axe body spray? My eyes are burning."

"Tony's cousin."

"Jesus fucking Christ. I suspected something was up when I saw the Maserati in your driveway." She points a thumb over her shoulder. I move the curtains aside on the sidelight window, and we watch his car back down the drive. "Let me guess. We were right. Tony made you beneficiary to screw you and insulate his family if anything happened to him, and that was the family making sure you stay screwed."

"Appears so. I'm sure he didn't expect to die. He certainly didn't think I was capable of hurting him. He didn't think enough of me for that. I think it was just one more insurance policy."

Maeve snorts. "I think being part of a mob family probably comes with inherent risks and you get really good at defensive measures." She runs her fingers along the strap of her bag. "So what do you want to do? Do you want me to rescind your rejection of the inheritance?"

I raise my chin, steeling my spine. "No."

Her brows shoot up. "No?"

I share a dark laugh with her. "I know they can come for me. They will come for me if I reject it. But things won't be easier if I take the money. That won't be the end. He said if I took it, they'd be in touch to advise me how to use it. They'd still want to control it. Control me. I'll be damned if I make the mistake of tying myself to the Denardi family again."

She frowns. "But if you don't, they will try to kill you. You know too much."

I scrub my face. "Yeah."

"You seem distressingly unconcerned with your possible death."

I hug my middle and look her in the eye. "I'm too worried about Damien to have any room for concern about anything else."

"Have you given any additional thought to a security system?"

"Like the Denardis haven't run up against one of those before." I look toward the ceiling. "I don't think any system I could buy for this place would be enough to keep me safe. But you know what would?"

"Hmm?"

"Damien."

She snorts. "You have a one-track mind."

"Only when it matters."

"All righty then. Let's get started."

"Why does it have to smell so bad?" I tip the green sludge into my mouth and force myself to swallow the bitter concoction.

"It's the belladonna. It's poisonous and wants you to know it," Maeve says. "But whoever wrote this spell did call for a refreshing squeeze of lemon for flavor." She turns the book toward me, and I read in my father's handwriting *for flavor* in the margin.

"It tastes even more like ass this time than last time."

"I think the first time you were so worried about what would happen when you drank it, you would have downed the ingredients without a blender."

"Thanks for not letting me do that."

She chuckles. "No problem. What are witchy friends for? It's just one of the many ways I've kept you alive recently."

"I'm not actually *trying* to die. There just seems to be so many things that want to kill me. I mean, between hiding my identity from the vampire queen, dodging the mob, and trying not to die from overusing my magic."

"It's practically a full-time job." She grins and places a hand on mine as I start to drift. "Be careful this time with letting him take your blood. Remember that you're in his head, inside his thoughts—he can't tell if he's taking too much. I'll be here if something goes wrong."

"Thanks, Maeve," I say sleepily. My eyes blink, then blink again. "You're a good friend."

The next second, I'm standing in a silo. Weird. Is this Damien's dream? Bright light blinds me. I try to shade my eyes, but the light is coming from the walls, the sky, every direction but the floor. It's like I'm in a room of mirrors.

Hands cupped around slitted eyes, I search for Damien, but there's only a rock at the center of this room. He's not here. Wait, is that even possible? I must be inside *someone's* dream.

The ticking of the grandfather clock has me turning back toward the anchor, wondering what went wrong. Whose head am I in? I crack my neck, already sweating, and walk toward the boulder while I figure out what to do next.

The ground is packed earth, parched and cracked without even a weed to break its monotony. I reach the ashen boulder at the center of the silo and lean against it. Odd—the texture is almost rubbery, and the sides are peppered with shallow holes like the rock has taken a few bullets. I run my hand along the bumpy ridge along the top, then over the sides. I retract my fingers with a gasp when they touch something that feels like ribs.

I shift back onto my feet. "Oh my God."

I want to be wrong, but when I walk around the stone and see horns and a tuft of hair on one end, I almost gag. This is Damien! He's in his monster form, curled in on himself, shading as much of his flesh with his wings as he can. All of his exposed skin, usually the deep black of a shadow, is now chalky and the color of concrete.

Frantically, I pull the oversized tunic I'm wearing off and hold it over his head. With some repositioning, I'm able to shade about a quarter of him. Not enough. Fuck, is he even alive? He must be. The ache in my chest I've come to associate with the bond is still there. Besides, I couldn't be in this nightmare if he wasn't.

"Damien? Damien."

He moves ever so slowly, unwinding his wings from around his body as if every inch of movement hurts like hell. How could it not when flakes of his flesh fall away like ash with every fraction gained? When he's finally able to turn his face to look at me, I can't suppress a gasp. He's wrecked. More dead than alive. His once-beautiful mane of hair is thin and greasy. His eyes are red-rimmed and bloodshot, and his face— God, his features look like he was carved from pale marble.

"Eloise," he rasps.

"Is this where she's keeping you? Are you dreaming about where you really are?" His eyes roll toward my throat. I need to feed him, but first I have to get him out of here, at least temporarily. "Can you picture the garden again? Picture somewhere safe?"

He raises a hand to my cheek and slowly, as if each grain of thought costs him something, the silo fades and I'm huddled over his sitting form in a dark forest. I help him lean back against a tree, tossing my sweater aside. I'm in a sports bra and leggings. It will be easier for him to get to my throat like this. He stares up at the moon and stars, breathing deeply.

"You need my blood." I kneel in front of him. "Maeve

says it's my magic you're taking, but it should be able to keep you alive."

But he doesn't move toward me, just shakes his head.

"Let me die," he whispers. I can hardly hear him. He's not even looking at me. He stares up at the stars as if he'd rather be somewhere else. Maybe something else.

"What's that?" I must have misheard him.

Now his eyes drift to mine, and my stomach clenches at how empty they are. He's looking directly at me as he says loud and clear, "You need to let me die."

For a second I wait for what he said to make sense. It doesn't.

"No!" My eyes pool with gathering tears.

His head rolls forward, and he stares at the ground.

"What has she done to you?" When he doesn't answer, I say, "I'm not letting you give up. You'll take my blood and tell me where to find Cassius and where Valeska is holding you. We'll come for you. My blood will see you through." When he doesn't look at me, I grab his chin and turn his head until he does.

Finally he focuses on my face, but when I hold my wrist to his lips, he pushes it away.

"I haven't eaten anything since the last time we were together. I'll drain you dry. Can't you see that I'm close to death? A few more days and I'll be gone. You'll be free of our bond. Find another mate. Live your life." His large, dark eyes droop. His mane is stringy, and even his horns seem duller than the last time I saw him in this form. God, the sun has burned holes in his wings. He must be in so much pain.

Something clamps around my heart and squeezes. If Damien is talking about me moving on, he is truly suicidal. No shade gives up his mate so easily. "No," I say firmly. Loudly. "You're not giving up. You're my mate. Fight for me."

He groans and closes his eyes. It takes effort, but I lean him forward enough for me to step behind his back. He's big in his monster form, and I find myself standing with my back against the tree and his back against my hips and torso. He's sitting, slumping, but his horns reach past my shoulders. I wrap my arm around his head and bring my wrist to his mouth. He places a kiss on my pulse with cracked, dry lips but doesn't strike.

I whimper at the sight of him, beaten down and suffering. I will kill Valeska for this. The sound of the ticking clock grows stronger in my ears. "I will never give up on you, Damien. I will find a way to get you out of there. You are my mate. I will not move on. There is no one else for me. If you go, I will go too."

He growls. "Don't say such things, little bird. Your eventual happiness is my only light. I can no longer endure. I will die tonight."

"No. You won't. You won't because you're going to drink my blood."

"No." He turns his head away.

"I'm coming to Night Haven," I say through my teeth. "I'm finding a way and I'm getting you out of there."

Now he moves. With one twist and sweep of his arm, he has me on my back at the base of the tree, his taloned hand wrapped around my throat. "What did I tell you, little bird? You are not to come near Night Haven."

I gaze up at him, shifting under him to wrap my legs around his hips. He settles between my thighs with a moan. "You can't stop me. What you can do is tell me how to get there so that I won't have to put myself in danger finding out."

He squeezes my throat ever so slightly. "You will not, little bird. Stay with Maeve. Stay safe."

I lift my hips to grind against him. "I will not give up on you, Damien. Never. I know the queen is dangerous and my coming for you is foolhardy, but I can't let you go. Not any more than you could let me go if I were in here."

He shakes his head, his red-rimmed eyes meeting mine. "I would stop at nothing."

"I will stop at nothing."

He growls and climbs off me, seeming to realize that he's in his monster form in this dream. He spreads his wings. They're riddled with holes where the sun has burned through them, and I can't stop my gasp. With a wince of concentration, they're gone. He shifts into his human form, dapper and attractive again. I wonder how much energy it costs him. "You don't understand. As your mate, I am your protector. Keeping you away from Night Haven is the only way I can do that."

I sigh. "Right now I think it's you who needs my protection. It's you who needs rescuing."

He hisses and draws back like I've offended him deeply.

I hold up my hands. "Don't you see that you *are* protecting me by saving yourself? If I lose you, my life will be nothing."

He stands straighter.

"I can find a way to get you out. We will survive this."

"Give me time. I will escape and come to you," he promises, but I can hear the skepticism in his voice. Even he knows that he won't get out without help.

The clock chimes. It's now or never. I need to convince him to tell me how to find Cassius. "Fine," I say, and he sighs in relief. "Tell me where to find Cassius, and I will go to him and ask for his help rather than come myself."

Damien frowns but seems to contemplate this for a minute. "Cassius is my nearest and dearest friend."

"Then he's sure to help," I say. "Please…"

"He may." Damien grinds his teeth, seeming to come to terms with the idea. "If he can't, he will protect you. I trust him."

I nod. "Where can I find him? I'll go to him. I'll tell him what's happened."

"If he doesn't know by now, he suspects." Damien moves closer, his expression growing resolute. He wants me to let it go, to leave it alone. Visiting Cassius digs me in deeper, but I can tell that this friend is our last hope.

"Where?" I demand again.

"Chicago. 111 E Bellevue."

I make a note of it. I'll fly out as soon as possible.

"Thank you." I close the space between us and wrap my arms around him. He nuzzles my ear, my hair, my neck. His lips brush over my vein. "Drink," I urge. "You need to survive until he can get to you."

I hear him swallow. It's a rough, hungry sound. "Eloise…"

"Yes?"

"I'm sorry." He strikes hard and fast. I melt against him as he drinks. His rhythmic gulps of my blood soothe me. He needs it more than I do. And as always, the act makes pleasure bloom in my core. The tips of my breasts harden to taut peaks and, an ache blooms low in my belly. But before I can act on my desire, fatigue overcomes me and it's his arms holding me up instead of my legs. I slump, but he keeps drinking.

"Damien." I slap his shoulder. "Stop. That's enough."

He growls like an animal and sinks his teeth in deeper.

"Stop!" I say again, and this time I'm begging. My chest hurts and dark spots are circling. If I'm feeling that in a dream, what must my physical body be going through?

Damien clamps his arms around my shoulders and gulps and gulps and gulps. So weak… My head rolls back on my shoulders, and I spot my anchor through heavy lids. Feeling the strong web between me and it, I reach my hand out toward it.

Darkness closes in as the clock rushes toward me. Rushes straight toward my hand.

I come awake with a gasp the moment I touch it. Maeve's hands are pressing into my bare chest. She stops when I drag in a lungful of air. She's straddling me, tears raining down her cheeks and falling on my chest. Her lipstick is smeared. I wipe my mouth with the back of my hand, and it comes away red.

She climbs off me, wiping under her glasses. "That's the last time, Eloise. Do you hear me? Never again. *Never. Again.*"

I3

FLIES TO HONEY

DAMIEN

Once again, I've taken too much from Eloise. I wanted to stop, but as severely deprived as this body is, I could not resist what she so freely offered. I emerge from the dream, still curled in a ball as I was before, holding tight to the memory of the clock taking her home. She is alive. I did not kill her. I did *not* kill her.

I draw in a deep breath, her blood coursing through my veins like cool water.

Only then do I feel something in my hands. Soft fabric skims between my fingers. My wicked smart and resourceful little dragon has succeeded in passing a gift to me through the astral plane, a gift almost as valuable as her blood. A gift that could mean my salvation.

I use my claw to split the black cotton tunic, then sit back on my haunches, using my horns and my hands to shade myself. It's not large enough to completely cover me, but it helps significantly. The color of the skin on my arms darkens. I rest, and I wait.

Hours pass. Maybe days. I grow hungry again, but I have no way of telling how long I've been here, baking in the sun. My mind plays tricks on me, alternating between sleep and waking on no particular schedule. When I dream, I dream of Eloise, but not like before. Not like the times she was truly in my arms. These dreams are replays of the moments we've already had together. Such a short time. Too few days have I been blessed to have her in my life. Still, I would sacrifice anything for more.

"What is that?" I hear Valeska's shrill voice from a distance.

"I do not know, Your Majesty." One of the Kims. "But if it is enchanted, it may interfere with our cuffing spell."

"One of you must go and retrieve it."

A faint mumble. Some sort of explanation from the Kims, too soft for me to hear. They don't know what Eloise's shirt is or how it got in here. I can only speculate that the witches are too smart to enter my cell, knowing that the cloth in my hands could shelter me from their magic. Valeska's growl signifies she does not like their answer. "Bring me a human! A feeder. Anyone who can walk in the light."

Minutes later, I hear a man's voice. A human voice. One of Valeska's human donors I assume.

"Just walk in and retrieve it?" he asks.

I gather myself beneath the shirt, channeling all my newfound strength into my legs. Footsteps. Human. A throat clearing. The corner of the black fabric lifts.

He screams as I snatch him by the waist and drag him

to me, sinking my teeth into his neck and draining him dry as fast as I can swallow. More yelling to my left. More footsteps. I tear the dead man's leg from his body and rip his femur from his flesh. Growing to my full height, I wear the shirt over my horns like a hood, protecting my eyes from the blinding light as I swing the bone like a club. The light burns my arms, my legs, my hands, but I swing at another's head and watch his skull cave in. The door is open. I lock eyes with Valeska in the shadows on the other side, my legs chewing up the space between us even as the energy is sapped from my body by the ceaseless light.

Swing. Pop. Another human crumples to the stone.

"Now! Chain him now!"

One of the Kims, Lang, steps in front of the queen. The twins can't get close enough to me to place the cuffs, but he forms a lasso of light and hurls it toward me. I dodge but it encircles my wrist, the one attached to the hand holding the bone. Once he has me, the lights in the walls go out. As I suspected, the twin's magic isn't strong enough to power both.

The cuff on my right wrist drains me, and the femur I'm wielding drops from my grip. But the light isn't as strong as before, not as instant. I yank and twist, trying to free myself from the binding. The Kims are tired. This is my chance to free myself.

Tae circles his hands, focused on my free arm, his fingers contorted, stacked one on top of the other. I don't give him the chance to finish his spell—I lunge for him, dragging Lang with me. My talons stab into his forehead and shred through half his face and then his chest and abdomen. Blood and entrails pour onto the ground between us. Tae's screams turn to gurgles. I leap over his body.

Valeska's shrill voice echoes in the silo. I can see she wants to take me down with her own two hands, but Lang's lasso of light swings around me before she has the chance. Yeah, bitch, come for me. Lang's little trick will cut you in half. When she hesitates, I rush her, using my remaining power to throw Lang forward, stretching the light out around her and then dropping low to pull the glowing cord like a snare.

I'm too slow. She dodges the light and appears behind me, knocking me flat with a kick that lands with a painful crunch. Her knee digs into my back, and in the next second, my wrists are bound.

I rage at my failure. My roar tears through the night.

Only then does Valeska flip me over. With her boot on my chest, her eyes scan the human carnage littering the stone cell. She grimaces when she sees Tae.

"Impressive." She bends over to run her hand along my chest. I try to jerk away, but with my hands bound behind my injured back, I can't move far. "I was especially enthralled by the way you mercilessly tore through three helpless humans to try to escape your bonds. Bludgeoned with their friend's own femur. Goddess, Damien, you truly are the warrior I need at my side."

A growl rumbles in my chest, and I bare my teeth at her. Never. I will never be hers.

"Yes," she purrs, her gaze raking over me from above. She pulls an exaggerated pout. "You hate me. But what people don't understand about hate, Damien, is that it is an equally strong emotion as love. Both are fueled by passion. Hate me long enough and you might find you can't live without me." She leans forward and licks a spray of blood from my chest.

I turn my head away in disgust but am helpless to stop her. "Don't. Touch. Me."

She laughs and immediately drags her fingers down my chest again. "You don't want me to touch you? Poor baby. You see, I think you've grown too comfortable in this frying pan, and frankly, I'm tired of having you where I can't enjoy you."

She grabs my nipple and squeezes. I grind my teeth against the pain but also the humiliation of it.

"There is a saying among humans that one catches more flies with honey than with vinegar." Her red lips come sickeningly close to my ear, and her palm flattens against my sternum. I refuse to look at her, but her breath skates across my cheek as she says, "I think you've had enough vinegar, Damien. From now on, you'll have nothing but honey from me. Honey until you tell me her name. So much honey she may not want you anymore when I'm through with you."

If I could break into shadow, I would. As it is, my skin wants to climb off my body to escape her touch.

Guards rush forward and pull me roughly to my feet.

"Take him to my chambers and bind him to the bed."

I thought I was ready to die, but only now do I feel true terror. More than I've felt thinking I might burn or starve to death in this silo. More than I experienced telling Eloise to move on without me.

Death is simple.

I have a feeling what Valeska has in store for me now will be far from it.

I4

CANDY & SHADOWS

ELOISE

I can't blame Maeve for being angry. I'm the first person she's ever performed CPR on, and I'm lucky she didn't crack my ribs.

"I'm so sorry. I tried to stop him. I did." I pull the afghan tighter around my shoulders and take another sip of healing tea from the mug she fixed for me. Then I give her a quick explanation of what happened in the dream, but it doesn't seem to placate her. When she crosses her arms, I notice a slight tremble in her fingers.

"Never again." She shakes her head. "I believe you. But you must realize how dangerous this is now."

I run a hand down my face. "Yes. But he's dying, Maeve. That cell she's keeping him in, it's torture. He's my mate, and he told me to let him die. He wanted me to move on without him. I couldn't allow him to give up on himself or us. I had to do something. My blood was all I had to give." Without intending to, I've raised my voice. I shrink back with a sigh. "I couldn't help it."

Maeve chews her lip. "I'm sorry. I do understand why you did it, but I hope you understand why I can never help you again with this spell. I've watched you die now. Twice." Her voice pulls thin at the end, and she swallows hard. "I just can't."

I nod. "I understand." I draw her into a hug until the tightness in her shoulders eases. "The best part is I won't need you to."

She sits back in her chair. "Why not?"

"He told me how to find Cassius. I'm going to go to Chicago and convince him to help us. He isn't beholden to a triune like Morpheus is, and Damien told me he's his closest friend. I'm sure when he hears what condition Damien is in, he'll do whatever it takes to free him."

She frowns and adjusts her glasses. "When are you going to go?"

"Right away. I'll try to get a ticket for tonight or tomorrow."

"I wish I could offer to go with you, but my caseload is out of control. And I still need to follow up on your rejection of your inheritance. The account manager keeps pushing back on my notices. I'm going to have to escalate things."

I wonder if it's a good thing that Maeve can't go to Chicago, considering everything that happened today and all the hours she's put in training me. She'd burn herself out helping me if I asked and never complain. That's why I think she needs a break from me. I've asked a lot of her lately. Too much.

I owe her one. More than one. At least one for every time she's saved my ass.

"I'll be fine on my own," I promise. "Cassius is Damien's most trusted friend. He told me in his dream that he trusts him to protect me. I won't be in any danger. I'll text you all the details after we meet."

She nods and gathers her things into her arms. "I should go. You need to rest and recharge, and I need to work. I'll see you when you get back?"

"Absolutely."

I show her out, giving her one last hug before opening my laptop and searching for flights.

My stomach churns as I stand on the porch in front of 111 E Bellevue, the handle of my rolling carry-on bag in hand. It's twilight, and I'm bundled in my puffer jacket against a bitter Midwestern cold snap. A trio of children dressed as witches walks down the sidewalk toward me, pumpkin baskets swinging from their elbows. Halloween. I've been so busy and distracted with surviving, I'd lost track of the date until I boarded the plane and spotted a pumpkin broach on the flight attendant. How is it already October 31st?

"Trick or treat," the three sing in unison from the bottom of the stairs. Shit, I'm standing outside the door. They probably think I live here.

"Um…" I dig in my purse for some candy. I might have some mints or something. I find Purell. "Hand sanitizer?" I ask them, holding it up.

All three tuck their chins in and mumble, "No, thanks,"

as they start for the open iron gate and their waiting parents.

The door to the house behind me opens. "How about Heath bars?"

I turn around to see a sophisticated black man in a turtleneck and slacks holding out a bucket of full-size candy bars. The girls squeal in delight, rushing up the flight of stairs to us to each take one and politely say thank you. Once they're gone, the man's warm caramel-colored eyes fall on me. Those eyes. They're different from Damien's but still appear lit from within, a characteristic I've learned is common in both shades and vampires.

"Cassius?" I ask.

"You must be Eloise." His soft smile is welcoming but also confusing. We've never met.

"How do you know who I am?"

He gives a warm laugh. "Damien is normally a male of few words, but he was positively chatty when it came to talking about you. I've seen your picture."

"Trick or treat!" A group of six boys, all dressed as Marvel characters, pushes past me to get to the candy. The parents wave to us, and we wave back.

Once they're out of earshot, I whisper, "Damien's in trouble. Is there somewhere we can talk privately?"

He nods and opens the door wider to reveal a foyer with ecru walls and a vase of white flowers at its center. I walk inside and he locks up behind us, turning off the porch light. "We'd better move to the back of the house." He points his chin toward the living room and the hall beyond. "If they see lights on, they'll keep ringing."

"You live here? Aboveground?" I'd assumed he'd live like Damien did.

He tips his head toward the street. "I like the families in this neighborhood, human and otherwise. The windows are coated with a film that blocks out the UV light, and my bedroom has curtains. It's a comfortable existence and one financed by the vampire coven I serve."

He leads me toward the back of the house, turning off lights as he goes. I follow him, rolling my bag behind me, through a perfectly appointed living room and a white marble kitchen with top-end appliances. We stop in a cozy sitting area that ends in a wall of windows with a set of French doors. I find myself enchanted by the charming outdoor living space beyond, canopied in strings of white lights and a brick fireplace warmed by a roaring fire.

"You've come a long way," he says from behind me.

At the sound of his voice, I start and turn around to face him. "I did. I hope you don't mind my showing up like this. Damien gave me your address, but I could find no phone number to let you know I was coming."

"I keep it private. But you're welcome here. Any friend of Damien's is a friend of mine."

My cheeks heat, and I glance at the rug. "I'm more than his friend. I'm his mate."

"Official then?"

I nod. "I'm here because Damien said he thought of you as a brother. He's in trouble. We need your help."

He takes a deep breath, his bright white smile fading slightly. "Damien *is* a brother to me. You came to the right place." He hesitates as if searching for the right words and then breaks again into a welcoming smile. "Where are my manners? Would you like something to drink?"

"Anything is fine." It's not difficult to deduce he's avoiding the part about helping. He hasn't even asked what happened to Damien. I glare at him, wondering how much he already knows.

"Sparkling water?"

I nod, although in truth I feel like I need something stronger. The stress I've been under the past few weeks has given me a permanent ache in my shoulders. I roll them a few times and crack my neck.

He must notice because he says, "Would you like some vodka with that tonic?"

I blow out a fast breath. The truth is I'd love a drink, but as much as Damien trusts Cassius, I don't know him, and this is no time to lower my guard. "No, thanks. I'll take a lime if you have one though."

He gives a low chuckle. "I do."

He moves to the kitchen and starts filling two cut-crystal glasses. I turn back toward the outdoor fireplace and notice a book open on one of the end tables in the seating area.

"We can sit outside if you like," he says. "Might be a little cold for you though. I don't feel it the same way you do. There are blankets."

I am drawn to the lovely space with its potted plants and blooming chrysanthemums, but he's right, I'm only now beginning to warm up from the walk over. I nod toward the open book and furrow my brow. "I hope I didn't interrupt your reading."

He appears beside me, although I don't hear him coming, and hands me one of the drinks. "On Halloween? I would have been interrupted either way. Truth be told, I knew it was only a matter of time until you sought me out. I've felt a disturbance down the shadows for weeks."

"You can feel that something's wrong?"

He takes a sip and stares at the fire crackling outside. "Sometimes. The shadows are like a web—connected, sensitive. Normally I can feel Damien and Morpheus as a soft vibration in the distance. Damien's vibration has been irregular as of late."

"Valeska took him. She's holding him in a silo in Night Haven. She's hired the Kim witches to spell the walls so that he's always in daylight."

His sigh turns into a groan, and he sets down his drink. "Then my worst fears are true. Give me your jacket. This conversation could take a while."

I remove my puffer and hand it to him. He clicks on a lamp and gestures for me to have a seat, then leaves to presumably hang it up. I park my bag and sit, suddenly thankful for the soft armchair. I still haven't fully recovered from being drained by Damien. I flop onto the over-stuffed cushions, my limbs turning to jelly at the first opportunity. My head feels like I'm thinking through cream soup. Maybe I should have asked for coffee instead of sparkling water.

When Cassius returns, my heart gives a tender squeeze. "You move like him," I say, glancing down into my drink. "Smooth, like your joints are just for show."

He laughs, a twinkle sparking in his eyes, and sits across from me. "It's a shade thing. These bodies are more for convenience than anything else."

"Convenience? Don't you mean camouflage? For fitting in among humans?"

"Even on Tenebris, this is our preferred state when we

aren't fighting. Easier to fit around a table. Our horns don't bump into things."

"Right. Damien mentioned something about that to me once." I think back to that first day I entered his dream of the garden and how he'd mentioned that his humanlike form was considered more diplomatic on his planet. I take another sip of my drink and then really look at Cassius.

He has the type of burnt-umber skin that's luminescent, remarkably smooth for a male, without a hint of a beard. His hair is cut short on the sides and back, a little longer on top. But when he shifts to pick up his drink, the movement is lethally fast. From the first moment I met him, I had the impression he was a gentler soul than Morpheus. Now I'm not so sure. My intuition tells me he's kind but also capable. Fair but deadly when he needs to be. He's exactly who I need. I bet he could have Damien out in an afternoon.

"I warned Damien that Valeska wouldn't give up easily." He lifts his drink and swirls the ice around the glass. "He swore she'd move on once she knew about the Gowdie curse, but when the vampire queen wants something, she will not be denied."

"You… suspected this might happen?" It's like taking a blow to the stomach. Damien hadn't so much as mentioned Valeska to me. I had no idea she was a danger.

He nods. "Shades like us are the ultimate weapon to vampire kind. We can both feed from and be fed on by vampires, thrive in the dark but can survive the light, and our control of shadows makes us positively lethal here where their kind has no such power. When we mate, it's for life, and a shade is fiercely loyal to his mate. It's biologically determined. If the queen managed to force Damien to mate her, my brother could not fight the bonding. He'd become her tool, her weapon, until either she or he is slain. She knows this. Knows that if she managed it, he'd be her ultimate protector and assassin. She's already grown Night Haven by swallowing up neighboring covens. With him by her side, no coven in North America would be safe."

A dark pit forms in my middle. I already hated her. Knowing she is a megalomaniac, even to other vampires, only darkens my sense of her. "Then you'll help me free him?"

Cassius takes another drink, this one longer, and scrapes his bottom lip with his teeth. "That is a more complicated question than you as a human could possibly imagine."

"Explain it to me like I'm a toddler," I say with more attitude than necessary.

He leans back in his chair, crossing one ankle over the opposite knee. "By the frustration in your voice, I'm guessing you've already tried Morpheus."

"I have."

"And he refused you."

"He said he couldn't risk starting a war with Valeska. His triune would never agree to it. It would put the entire Caspian line at risk."

Cassius nods. "Alas, I'm afraid I'm in the same boat. I am now the commander of the Lamia coven, the largest vampire coven in the Midwest. The master here is nothing like Valeska. She and her mate are fair and benevolent, but she's also a wise leader. Allowing me to act on Damien's behalf could put her coven at risk. No one,

Eloise, wants to pick a fight with Valeska right now. Her hive is too big and too powerful."

"You say it's too big of a risk, but if Valeska is truly that big and powerful and mating Damien would make her unstoppable, why wouldn't every coven leader band together to make sure that doesn't happen? Isn't doing nothing just as risky?"

"While you might think so, vampire politics is a delicate and complex thing, and that type of strategic cooperation is almost unheard of among them. Vampire covens rarely form alliances. They form armies."

Tears form in my eyes, and suddenly I can't catch my breath. It's like my last hope has been tugged like a rug out from under me. "You're not going to help him, are you?"

"I didn't say that." He shakes his head, face fallen. "I said my master may not allow me to help as long as I hold my current position, and unfortunately, if I leave my current position, I become an option for Valeska. She could slay Damien and target me."

"Fuck." I blow out another breath and throw back the remainder of my drink. "So it's hopeless?"

He holds up one hand. Shakes his head. "What I propose is that you come with me to meet the master of the Lamia coven. Together we can relay the risk that Damien's capture means for her and the Chicago vampires. She and her consort are shrewd when it comes to these matters. It's possible she'll agree to use her political influence to pressure Valeska to give Damien up."

I nod because my throat is too tight to speak. In my heart, I grip the last shreds of hope he's handing me. But Valeska is the only vampire queen I know of. It's hard for me to believe that the Chicago master will be any different. I cough a few times and find my voice. "When can we go?"

He smiles as if he's relieved that I agree to his plan. "Tomorrow night. With it being Halloween, she is otherwise engaged this evening. I will take you to the Star tomorrow night."

"The Star?"

"The Star of Lamia. It's the subterranean world the Chicago vampires call home."

"Is it safe? You should know the queen has a price on my head."

"We will share your identity only when necessary. Once my master knows who you are, her priority will be to protect you, not hand you over."

"Is it safe otherwise? I mean for humans?" Maeve was adamant that visiting Night Haven would be a death sentence.

"It's safe. Our master forbids killing humans. We may feed on them, but we cannot harm them. And I will be there to protect you."

I nod, resigned. All these questions, they are only to help prepare myself. Even if I had to descend into a passageway lined with barbs and broken glass, I'd agree to his plan. He's my last chance at helping Damien. "Okay."

"We'll go at twilight."

I place my empty glass down on the coffee table. "In that case, I should go. I haven't booked a hotel yet."

He stands. "I won't hear of it. You must stay here tonight. Damien would never forgive me if I left you unprotected in the city, especially now that you've shared there's a price on your head. You took an incredible risk coming here alone. This house is warded, and I have plenty of room. I insist."

"Thank you." I sense I can trust Cassius, and not just because he's like a brother to Damien. There's something about the shade that puts me at ease as equally as my meeting with Morpheus disturbed me.

He picks up my bag. "Then allow me to show you to your room. I must report to the Star within the hour, but I'll be back by dawn. Make yourself at home and help yourself to anything in the kitchen. Vampires here don't eat, but as Damien probably shared with you, shades do. You'll find the pantry well stocked."

With only the slightest tug of apprehension about trusting a veritable stranger, I follow the shade upstairs, committed to a plan to descend into a world of vampires tomorrow night.

15

THE VAMPIRE & HER MATE

ELOISE

That night I help myself to a slice of deep-dish pizza Cassius has in his fridge and find a fantasy novel I've been aching to read in his well-appointed study. The doorbell rings every now and then, although I keep the lights at the front of the house off. I don't answer it. Maeve praises me for that bit of wisdom when I text her a play-by-play of what's happened.

Maeve: The last thing you need is to open the door and for some vampire or witch to connect you with the shade. That could get back to Valeska before you even leave Chicago.

Me: Vampires are going to know tomorrow. He's taking me to the Star, which is the Chicago version of Night Haven.

Maeve: Goddess help you. Have I ever told you that you attract danger like honey attracts ants?

Me: I try. I'm thinking of taking up sword swallowing.

Maeve: I'm not worried. On a different subject, can I have your green velvet couch if you die?

Me: You want my couch? You know my great-grandfather picked it out, right?

Maeve: It's vintage.

Maeve: Hey, gotta go. Work stuff.

Me: K. See you in two days.

Maeve: Don't die.

I climb the stairs to the bedroom Cassius showed me with a cup of herbal tea and the book. Each room in Cassius's home is outfitted with blackout curtains, but I leave mine open so I can watch the moon and stars as I fall asleep. There's something comforting about believing that Damien is under the same sky, perhaps gazing at the same moon I am.

My last thought as I drift away is that I have to get him back.

By the time Cassius is ready to take me to the Star the next night, I'm positively vibrating with nervous energy. This has to work. I have nowhere else to turn.

"Relax, Eloise. I can hear your heart pounding from three feet away, and the scent of adrenaline is coming off you in waves." He casts me a critical look as he leads me to the back of a crowded bar, down a narrow set of stairs, to a metal door.

"I'm not sure what you want me to do about either of those things," I whisper.

There's a metal lock but no key. Just a silver panel. I

wonder how we're supposed to get in. A pattern of knocks? Secret password?

"Have you tried deep breathing?" His eyes shift to the side as he presses his thumb to the pad. I hear a click and he opens it for me. A bead of blood forms on his thumb before he sucks it into his mouth, closing the wound.

"The lock samples your blood?" I ask as the heavy door slams shut behind us.

"No one gets in without the blood of a coven member to break the ward, and the spell remembers if there's trouble." His eyes shift to me. "I'm trusting you. Don't make me regret bringing you here. I'm accountable for your actions." He grins as if he's joking, but I sense an element of truth in it.

"I'd never. Just tell me what you want me to do."

We stroll along a hall that descends into a concrete tunnel. "You must be a smart woman, Eloise. Damien would never mate a fool. I'm going to keep this simple. Remain respectful. Give Sabrina exactly what she asks for. She isn't like Valeska. She's a fair master, but she's no pushover. She can be your greatest advocate or your worst nightmare. Don't do anything to make her the latter."

My mouth opens and closes, but no words come out. What does one even say to something like that? My heart lurches and gallops in my chest.

Cassius sighs. "I didn't mean to make you nervous."

I take a few deep breaths and steel my spine. "Why would I be nervous? I'm just in a sealed cavern under the earth with hundreds of creatures that want to eat me."

He chuckles and glances in my direction. "You're holding up well under the circumstances," he murmurs.

A long walk later, we arrive in a massive underground gathering place. I see why it's called the Star now. Tunnels lead from each of the Star's points to this common gathering place. The central area is as large as a football field and teems with vampires coming and going, doing business, exchanging bags of blood, talking and laughing. They stop when I pass, their nostrils flaring, and I flash back to the night in Bad Witches' Club when Jimmy said he could smell me from across the room. Everyone here must know I'm human. They scan me, their oversized eyes catching on my pulse, but the second they notice Cassius at my side, they turn away.

Cassius leads me to the front of the room where a woman I assume is the master sits on a throne on a stage about three feet high. My first impression is that she's gorgeous. Bright red hair falls in loose waves around her creamy complexion and piercing green eyes. Her dress is a darker shade of crimson, silky as a rose petal. It matches exactly the color of her lipstick and the rubies in her tiara. This woman exudes royalty whether or not she uses the title of queen. Like Cassius, one look at her long, muscular arms and legs, the way she moves as gracefully as poured water when she repositions herself in her chair, and my instincts tell me she's lethal. Deep inside, my muscles tense, ready to run. I am in the presence of killers, and she is possibly the deadliest.

And then I see the man standing behind her and understand a new level of intimidation. The apex predator energy coming from the dais isn't restricted to Sabrina. He looms like a gathering storm behind the throne, enormous—easily as big as Damien—and physically intimidating. There's something else. A tiny vibration at the back of my skull tells me he's not a vampire. The way he moves is slower, more humanlike than the vampires around me. Humanlike but definitely not human. I examine him again, trying to figure out what he is. He's blond and his smile is friendly enough, but when our eyes meet, an electric zing travels through me. I look away.

"Who is that behind the master?" I whisper to Cassius.

"Tobias, her mate and consort," he whispers.

"But not a vampire."

"No." Cassius gives a quiet laugh. "But I'm curious, how can you tell with your human senses?"

I swallow. "I'm not sure. Gut feeling."

"Hmm." A line has formed before the throne. "In Lamia coven, royal audience is held once per month. Any vampire can bring their concerns or pleas for help before the master. You came at the perfect time for us to make your request."

I can't hear what the coven master is saying to the vampire at the front of the line, but Sabrina's face is serious, and her lips move like she's having a heated discussion. I assume their voices are outside the detection of my human hearing, because I notice the vampire at the front nodding his head.

I try not to stare, but my gaze keeps darting toward the master's consort. Fuck. All I need is for the master of the Chicago vampire coven to think I'm hot for her mate. I'm not attracted to him. There's just something about him. A pull. I think he feels it too, because we're closer now and out of the corner of my eye, I see him staring at me. His nostrils flare, and then he whispers something into the master's ear.

Only her eyes flick toward me. The rest of her remains focused on the vampire in front of her. It's so fast I barely register it, but I know she's seen me. He's seen me. Her lips thin. Is that a smile? A frown? Annoyance? I can't read the vampire's expression. Moreover, I get the sense she likes it that way. We take another step toward the dais. I grow restless, shifting on my feet. I wipe my sweaty palms on the thighs of my jeans.

"Are you all right?" Cassius asks in a whisper. "I can hear your heart racing. Do you need a human break?"

I shake my head, although I haven't peed since we left the house and the question makes me wonder what kind of facilities are even available down here. "I'm fine. It's nothing." But it's not nothing. It feels like ants are marching on the underside of my skin. "Do you smell that? Like smoked almonds with cinnamon?" I inhale deeply through my nose.

Cassius shakes his head and gives me a strange look. We finally step to the front of the line. I lift my chin, my eyes grazing along the master's stunning red pumps, her exposed leg, the silky fabric of her dress, to her perfectly proportioned face.

"Master Bishop, it is a pleasure to be in your presence once again." Cassius bows, and as soon as I see what he's doing, I bow too.

"Cassius, how many times must I tell you to call me Sabrina? Tobias and I consider you family." Sabrina's eyes shift to me. "But who is this you've brought before us?"

"Eloise Harcourt. Her mate has been taken by the Night Haven coven, and she's here to beseech your assistance in getting him back."

"Your mate is a vampire?" Sabrina asks.

Tobias leans down and whispers something in her ear.

"No," I say, trying not to stutter. "My mate, Damien, is a shade like Cassius. Please. He's being held against his will. I need your help."

Cassius raises a finger. "Damien is a friend from Tenebris. A warrior. He was summoned here through the same rift as me."

Sabrina's brow furrows. "Is he a citizen of Night Haven then, as you and Morpheus once were?"

"Yes," Cassius confirms.

"But he didn't leave when you did to avoid Valeska's attention?" Her voice holds the burn of accusation. Shit. Is she blaming Damien for his own capture? I cringe. Damien would have left if given the chance. I open my mouth to say so, but Cassius shakes his head and does the talking.

"No. But until recently, he was spellbound by witches and was not a viable candidate for her mate. His curse was recently and unexpectedly broken."

Her green eyes spark with interest. "By whom?"

"By Eloise herself. She is human, but magic runs in her ancestry."

"What kind of magic?" Sabrina demands.

Cassius looks toward me.

I'm not sure what to say, so I go with how Maeve defined it. "Spirit magic."

Sabrina frowns, and Tobias again whispers something to her. He's frowning too and studying me with intense interest.

"Bring me her blood," she demands.

What? A bald vampire with a goatee appears beside me, holding a blade and a goblet.

I dart multiple glances toward Cassius. "Is this common?"

He gives me an encouraging nod.

Sabrina clears her throat and levels a hard stare at me. "Before I can help you, Eloise, I need to understand more about you. This is the fastest way." She points a beautifully manicured hand at the goblet.

I hold out my left arm. "Why does it always have to be blood?" I mumble as the bald vampire slices my skin and dribbles the blood into the goblet.

When he's through, he moves to lick the wound, but Cassius has him by the throat before a drop can touch his tongue. "That won't be necessary, Zander."

"I only meant to close the wound."

"I will take care of her." Cassius pulls a handkerchief from the pocket of his uniform and presses it to the small cut. His eyes meet mine. "Hold this."

"You can close it—"

He shakes his head and lowers his voice. "Damien would never allow it."

I nod and press the cloth harder against my wound. He moves back to my side just as Sabrina takes a sip of my blood. She straightens as she swallows, her eyes wildly seeking out Tobias's. She gives him a tight nod. I watch the man drag a deep breath into his lungs and blow it out.

When she turns back to us, the intrigue I know I saw flashing across her face is gone, replaced by a mask of boredom. "I wish I could help you, Eloise, but as Cassius should have told you, relations with Night Haven are already strained. Cassius's defection from the coven has yet to be forgiven. Lamia cannot become involved in a case involving another coven's citizen."

"But… but she's keeping him against his will!" I shut my piehole when Sabrina levels a deadly glare at me.

"I believe you, Ms. Harcourt. There is no doubt in my mind that you've been wronged and are telling the truth about Damien's wishes. Unfortunately, vampire politics is a delicate thing. I can't put the safety of my coven in jeopardy. Not for this."

A lump forms in my throat. All the hope I've clung to when it came to this meeting collapses into a puddle of crushing disappointment.

"Cassius, although we can't help you or your guest, it would be my pleasure of you and Ms. Harcourt would join Tobias and me for cocktails in my quarters before you leave. Your current dress is acceptable."

He bows. "It would be our sincere pleasure. I'll show her back." He takes my elbow and starts leading me toward one of the tunnels. We walk a short distance, but when I'm sure we're alone, I stop. Cassius, to his credit, doesn't try to force me to keep moving.

"Do we have to stay?" I'm trembling. I lean against the wall for support. Disappointment, fear, and hopelessness collide within me. Everything feels heavy. Impossible. Bleak. "I'm not sure how long I can hide my feelings. You might have to watch me break down in front of your master. It won't be pretty. If you knew how close I am to collapsing right now…" I wipe under my stinging eyes, my voice high and tight.

His big hand lands on my shoulder, and his face draws near to mine. I can barely hear his hushed whisper as he says, "Eloise, listen to me carefully. Sabrina and Tobias do not invite others to their table often. It's so rare I can't remember the last time it happened. I think we can presume there's something she wants to tell us in private."

I draw a sharp breath when I realize what he's suggesting. Is it possible that Sabrina might offer a covert solution? I try not to allow hope to inflate within me again, but I can't stop the swelling of my heart. I close my eyes and steady myself. "Thank you, Cassius. Thank you for bringing me here."

He nods and leads me forward once more. We arrive at what could be a bank vault, a massive silver door guarded by a man in uniform.

"Good evening, Paul," Cassius says. "We were invited—"

The portly man coughs into his hand, his thick mustache wriggling with the effort. "They're already inside, waiting for you."

He stands and heaves open the door, which is, in fact, as thick as a bank vault's. I gape in wonder as we enter a spacious, light-filled foyer of what could be a ritzy Chicago penthouse with twelve-foot ceilings and a marble floor. I'm still taking it all in when the door closes and locks behind us. My back is against the wall before I can take my next breath, my shoulders clasped in Tobias's massive hands. The overwhelming scent of cinnamon and almonds hits me again, and I realize it's *him*. He hovers over me, sapphire eyes blazing like an ancient death god ready to take my soul.

His lips peel back from his teeth as he asks, "Why does my brother's blood run through your veins?"

16
UNEXPECTED REUNION

"Wh-what?" I can't find my voice.

Tobias is so close. So overwhelming. Although he isn't hurting me, he could snap me like a twig.

Sabrina appears beside him, her green eyes blazing silvery blue. Her voice is soft as she asks, "What are you? Why do you taste like a dragon but smell like a witch?"

I blink rapidly. My mouth works, but no words come out. I'm too frightened to speak. All my throat muscles clench like they want to run and hide as much as I do. My bladder threatens to empty itself, and I gain control of it just in time. When I try to speak again, my voice sounds frayed.

"Give her space," Cassius says kindly. "She was raised as a human. You're scaring her senseless."

"If she's human, why can't I compel her?" Sabrina

demands, her perfectly manicured hand sweeping through the air as she paces behind Tobias.

"I said she was raised human. I'm sure Eloise will answer all your questions without compulsion. Allow her to breathe. She isn't going anywhere." Cassius places a supportive hand on my shoulder.

Slowly, Sabrina and Tobias back off, and I blow out my held breath. My thoughts whirl. But Cassius catches my eye, gives me a smile and an encouraging nod. As if after all that, I'm supposed to spill my darkest secrets. For fuck's sake, my heart is in my throat and I almost wet myself! Where do I even start?

But with three creatures waiting expectantly, I find the words. These people are my last hope for getting Damien back. It makes no sense for me to hold back the little I know about my heritage or my magic.

"My mother was a witch," I begin. "Descended from the Townsend witches from Oxfordshire, England. My father came from a long line of American spiritualists. When he met my mother, they joined the Order of the Dragon, a small coven outside London. Both drank dragon blood as part of their rituals. My mother drank it while she was pregnant with me. Both she and my father died with the Order's sigil tattooed over their heart. I wear the same sigil on my back." I unzip my puffer jacket, willing to show them, but Tobias holds up his hand.

He snorts. "Order of the Dragon, huh?"

I survey every detail of his reaction, bracing myself for disbelief or a string of follow-up questions.

But he only turns to Sabrina and breaks into laughter. "Nathaniel's going to shit himself."

"Nathaniel?" I ask.

"My brother," Tobias says. "He's the dragon whose blood is running through your veins. Up until recently, he led the Order of the Dragon."

My mouth goes slack. I dart a glance toward Cassius, but even he looks stunned. "You… you're a dragon? I mean a dragon shifter?"

He gives a light chuckle and pulls Sabrina into his side. She smiles warmly at him, transforming from deadly regent to Midwestern wife in a heartbeat. "Yes."

I brace myself on a table in the foyer only to do a double take when the wood groans and I realize that the piece I'm leaning on is old enough to belong in a museum. It looks older even than the furniture in Harcourt. I draw my hand back.

"Please come in." Sabrina gestures toward a glamorously appointed sitting room. "I think we should get to know each other."

I'm not entirely sure I should be as relieved as I am from the change in their demeanors. After all, the door behind me is most definitely still locked, and everyone in this room is capable of killing me. But I go with it, trying to calm my racing heart.

Cassius gently intercepts me before I can sit down. "You mentioned needing the restroom. It's behind you." He gestures toward a hall. In fact, I hadn't mentioned it. He must sense that I'm rattled, and I thank him before making my way to facilities that belong in a high-end hotel. There's a toilet and sink but also a cozy sitting area that I make use of while I collect myself and take stock of my situation.

I've never faced anything like this. Sure, surviving what happened with Tony required courage and cleverness. But he was just a man. Maybe a mobster, but in the end a human man. I am underground in a facility filled with vampires and, my God, a dragon. My life is in the hands of a shade, a monster I've known just over a day. And I do not have Damien or Maeve to back me up this time.

I'm not a stupid woman, but maybe it is stupid that I've put myself in this position. I recognize the risks I'm taking. But without those people, nothing will change. Whatever risks I'm taking now, I'm willing to do far more to get Damien back. I picture him baking in that silo, skin as pale as stone, and I know I am his one and only hope. I know it in my gut.

Damien once killed for me. He would have killed Tony if I'd given him the chance. But he took care of the man Tony sent to murder me and ended the lives of Tony's two cronies before they could retaliate after he died. Even before that, Damien protected me. He helped free me from Tony's hold and made me feel worthy of love and self-respect again. And on a deeper level, a level I can hardly explain, I know he is not just my mate but my one and only true love.

I can't hide in here forever. Quickly I empty my bladder and then stare at myself in the mirror as I wash my hands. "You're strong," I whisper. "You've done magic. You survived Tony. Get your shit together. If they wanted to hurt you, they would've done it already." I splash cold water on my face and steel my spine. Then I join the others.

The room where they've all gathered is truly stunning. Sabrina is playing a baby grand piano that's tucked into a corner—a classical piece—while Cassius partakes in an array of canapés set out on a buffet table at the back of the room. The furniture belongs in Versailles. The chairs are gilded and upholstered in a floral fabric that brings out the red tones in the rich leather sofa and rosewood piano. All of it is anchored by a hand-tied Turkish rug over a polished wood floor. I'm hesitant to even walk on it. If I were to paint this picture, I'd title it *Extravagance*.

Tobias brings me a glass of wine. "I guessed you preferred white."

"White's fine." I have a feeling he did more than guess. He presumed that red would remind me of my blood flowing into the chalice moments ago. It's a small thing but meant to put me at ease. It's thoughtful.

He wanders to Sabrina's side, leaving me alone at the edge of the room. All I want to know is what they're going to do to help rescue the love of my life, but I don't know how to broach the subject. I sip my wine and walk deeper into the room, noticing a painting on the wall that resembles *The Starry Night* by Van Gogh, only painted in reds instead of blues with a silhouette of a couple embracing at its center instead of a village.

"It's what you think it is." Tobias is suddenly beside me, looking up at the painting.

My brows lift and I shrug. "All I was thinking is that it reminds me of a Van Gogh."

Tobias nods. "He painted it. Sabrina's father knew him. It was a gift."

My eyes widen. "Holy shit." This belongs in a museum. It must be worth millions.

"Yeah. Only a handful of individuals have ever seen it."

I glance around the room again, really taking it in. That chair isn't a Louis XVI replica. It's the real thing. And the sideboard doesn't just look like it belongs in Versailles; it's old enough to have potentially been there. The rosewood piano Sabrina's playing is a Steinway with carved legs like I've never seen before. My artist's eye darts to the rest of the art, the sculptures, the furniture. If Harcourt Manor is a time capsule for the early 1900s, this place is an eclectic mixture of decor from the past five hundred years.

"How old is Sabrina's father?" I ask absently.

He snorts. "Very. Old enough to amass quite a collection. We've considered redecorating over the years, but neither of us can stomach giving any of it up. Her father's home is overflowing with it."

I take a sip of the wine, a delicious blend that might be the best I've ever had in my life, and then turn to him. "I'm sorry, but all of this is overwhelming. I just learned shifters were a thing a few weeks ago. And I knew about the dragon blood, but…" I shake my head. "I have so many questions. Are there others like me? Is there someone who can help me learn about the type of magic my parents practiced?"

Tobias frowns. "Unfortunately, I'm not the one to answer that. I'm a dragon, yes, but I don't wield magic in the way my brother Nathaniel does. And he's no longer on this planet."

"Not on the planet?" I parrot softly. It comes out sounding like *what the fuck.*

"He's returned to our home world. I can tell you this though," Tobias continues. "Your blood is both dragon and witch. Dragon blood feeds witch magic. Having both means you have unique potential."

"The only thing I care about is having enough power

to get Damien back." One thought of my mate and I can't play this game any longer. I whirl to face Sabrina and raise my voice over the piano. "Isn't there something you can do? While we're sipping cocktails, Damien is frying in the queen's torture chamber. Can you get him out or not?"

Sabrina stops playing but doesn't remove her fingers from the keyboard. Her eyes snap up to mine, her face an icy, impassive mask. "The piano helps me think," she says. "I need to think because I'm not sure what to do with you, Eloise Harcourt."

Do with me? My gaze darts to Cassius, but he's examining his nails.

Sabrina tilts her head, studying me now. "You and your mate pose one hell of a problem. What I said in the Star is still true. I can't take any official action against Night Haven without putting my people at risk."

I swallow. "What about unofficial action?"

Cassius moves closer, his attention suddenly concentrated on his master.

Sabrina slides her long, graceful fingers from the keys, resting them on the red silk covering her thighs. She ignores my question and continues. "As I was saying, direct conflict with Night Haven puts my coven at risk. But if Valeska succeeds in killing you and takes Damien as her consort, my people are also at risk. Valeska's hunger for power is insatiable. With that kind of advantage, she'll never stop."

She stands and snags her wine off the top of the piano. At least I think it's wine.

"It sounds like a good reason to help me," I say softly.

Everyone in the room stares at me, including Sabrina, her green eyes locked on mine like laser beams.

"Sorry. It just seems like the natural conclusion." I shift awkwardly.

Sabrina sizes me up again. "Our kind is ruled by a council of ancient vampires called the forebears. All covens are. Vampires may be deadly, but we are civilized. We follow a set of laws written over a thousand years ago and enforced by the oldest and strongest of us." She approaches, moving in closer until it feels like I'm standing next to a pacing lion. "If I confront Valeska about Damien, I have three choices. One: I can ask her nicely to hand him over. You must know if I did such a thing, it would only make your mate more valuable to her. Valeska would never willingly part with something she believed was valuable to another master. Two: I could offer to trade for him, but I fear the only thing I have that she wants is Cassius, and as I don't treat my coven members as property and he has no interest in going back, I refuse to do that."

"No. That's not fair to Cassius." I couldn't live with myself.

"Three: I could challenge her for her hive. I can't challenge her for him specifically because he's not my mate or my citizen, but I can challenge her for her power to hold him. It would be a fight to the death and would not be in the best interest of my coven. If I lost, my vampires would be displaced and find themselves under the rule of a tyrant. If I won, I'd become queen of Night Haven while maintaining my place here. Honestly, no one should have that much power. But even if I were willing to take it on, merging Lamia and Night Haven wouldn't benefit my vampires in any way. It's not fair to them."

I release an exasperated breath. "None of this is fair to Damien or to me."

She sighs heavily. "I sense you're a good person, Eloise, and as a vampire in a relationship with a shifter, I personally empathize with your mating bond with the shade. It's unfair what's happened to you. I want to help you."

"But?"

"But I can't fight this battle for you. Even if I were amenable to the idea, the forebears wouldn't like it. The vampire council is already concerned about how Valeska has named herself queen over multiple coven masters. Lamia is the largest coven in the Midwest. Not only would combining the two be completely unmanageable, but the forebears would become involved, and I have strong reasons not to want such a thing. I can't win against her without inviting their scrutiny, but if I lose, I'm dead. And you of all people know why I can't do that to my mate and coven."

I squeeze my eyes shut for a beat. I do understand, but the disappointment is crushing. "Then why am I here? If you can't help me, I need to go and try to find someone else."

She shifts, exchanging glances with Tobias and Cassius. "I asked you here because I have an idea. Well, I might have an idea. Truly it depends on you."

"On me?"

"You said you practice spirit magic. Tell us about your power. I can taste it in your blood but couldn't quite place how it's manifesting."

An idea. I chase the small hope she holds out to me like a carrot on a stick and start from the beginning. I relay everything to Sabrina, from the day I descended into the underworld when Tony killed me to my lessons with Maeve, the red fog, and the ghosts in Harcourt Manor.

Sabrina swallows. "Do you see any spirits now? Here?"

I look around the room. "No, but my magical anchor is in Harcourt Manor. To be honest, I'm not even sure my powers will even work outside my family home. Every time we've tested them somewhere else, I've failed."

"Hmmm." Sabrina swirls her drink. "Your mating to Damien, it's official and binding? Accepted by both parties?"

"Yes."

Cassius clears his throat. "I can confirm. I can sense the mating bond of my kind."

She sets her glass down and moves even closer to me in that fluid way vampires and shades do, until she's right in front of me. Too close. Intimidatingly close. I hold my ground. I swallow. Her eyes flash silvery blue again and meet mine. I blink.

"What are you doing?" I ask.

She smiles, her eyes fading to green again. "Proving once again that I can't influence you, which means neither can Valeska. I can't help you, Eloise, but that doesn't mean you can't help yourself. Are you willing to risk *everything* to get your mate back?"

Beside me, Cassius stills, almost like he's holding his breath.

"Yes. If I knew how to get in and out of Night Haven, I'd already have tried." Even as I say it, I both know it's true and that it would be a suicide mission. From the beginning, everyone I've spoken to has told me there's nothing I can do to get him back. But I'm desperate to hear another opinion.

"There is one way," Sabrina says, "But it could end very badly for both of you."

My heart leaps. "Please. Please tell me. I'll try anything."

"Follow me." When I start after her and Cassius follows, Sabrina raises a palm. "Cassius, stay with Tobias. Eloise and I need some girl time."

He lifts his chin in silent support, and I follow Sabrina from the room. She leads me down a hallway to a closed door with the same type of lock Cassius used to bring me into the Star, a blood lock. When she opens the door and flicks on a chandelier, the scent of ancient books wafts over us. My eyes widen at walls of leather-bound tomes shelved from floor to ceiling in a library worthy of the Beast's castle. There's a desk and chair at the center of everything, but there's nothing on it. I don't think she comes in here much, judging by the layer of dust on everything.

"In vampire tradition, mating is sacrosanct." She searches the shelves, her pointed red nail tapping gently against her chin. "Very specific laws exist for how a mating bond must be made official, how it can be broken, and who can interfere with it." As gracefully as if she were leaping over a puddle, she jumps into the air, snags a book from a shelf no less than ten feet up, and lands softly despite wickedly high heels. Her dress settles back around her legs. The book she holds is massive. As large as her entire torso. But she rests it on the desk as if it weighs nothing and opens it to a table of contents handwritten in a language I don't know.

"What language is that?"

"Vampiric Romanian. It predates the modern version of

the language, but all vampires brought into the royal bloodlines learn it. Valeska can definitely read it, although I doubt she's ever paid any attention to this book in particular. The only reason I've read it is because when you are a vampire mated to a dragon, you become an expert in mating law."

I take a step closer to the book even though the writing on the page means nothing to me.

She flips to the back, her gaze winding down one page and then the next. When she reaches the bottom of the third page, she taps a finger to the margin, her full red lips spreading. When her green eyes meet mine again, her smile is positively wicked. "Yes. There's a way, but it won't be easy."

"I don't care about easy. If there's a way to get Damien back, I'll do it."

She straightens. "Do you remember how I told you that if I challenged Valeska, I couldn't challenge her for Damien but I could challenge her for her hive?"

"I remember." It was only a few minutes ago, but I sense what she's really asking is if I follow her logic. "And I understand."

"Do you? I can't challenge Valeska for Damien, Eloise, because he's not *my* mate or a citizen of *my* coven. But *you,* as his mate, can." She taps the page of the book.

"I can." I stare at her incredulously. "*I. Can.* That's your answer?" I give a bark of a laugh that holds no humor. "I know I said I'd do anything, but how does it help if I'm dead?"

She bites her bottom lip and gives me an impish grin. "But that's the best part. Vampire law has a very special challenge designed to protect valuable mates from being pillaged by stronger vampires. It's called Provocationem Ad Mortem."

"But I'm not a vampire. How exactly is this good news for me?"

"Because this trial is very old and designed to level the playing field between competitors." She turns around and opens a cabinet behind her, drawing forth an ornately carved wooden box with a pattern on the lid that looks as if it's been stained by spattered blood. "Every coven has one of these, although I've never actually seen it used. It's the stuff of legends." She pops the lid to reveal a red velvet lining, three oddly shaped dice that appear to be made of bone, a set of two octagonal mirrors, and a larger rectangular mirror. "You won't fight Valeska directly, Eloise. That would not be a fair fight. You will both complete challenges, side by side, based on old magic—magic designed to test you equally. The box is enchanted to challenge you to the extent of your abilities, but the magic won't assign you a task it deems impossible for you to accomplish."

"So what's this challenge entail?"

"That's the beauty of it. It's different every time. According to the law, your chances are as good as hers. The dice determine who goes first and what the challenges are. It's all detailed in the book." She examines one of the dice. "You both complete the challenges and the box declares a winner once you've finished." She indicates the larger rectangular mirror. "The best of three wins Damien."

"She'll kill me the moment she sees me," I say flatly.

"She can't harm you or Damien once you've challenged her. Not until and unless she wins. The magic will protect you."

"Her winning seems probable," I say.

Sabrina shakes her head. "Maybe not. Three challenges. Each fair and matched to your abilities, Eloise. You'll have a real chance."

"And Valeska has no choice but to participate?"

She nods. "It's vampire law. Once she accepts your challenge, and she *must* accept, you are both magically bound to complete the trials."

"And if I do this, she can't have me killed while I'm competing?"

Sabrina shakes her head. "It's forbidden. And the best part is, you'll be allowed to see Damien. She can't keep him from you while you're participating."

"So all I have to do is go to Night Haven and challenge her? It sounds too easy."

Sabrina's face falls, her hands coupling in front of her hips. "Unfortunately, going to Night Haven and gaining access to the queen to challenge her is not quite as simple as it sounds." She stares, unblinking, at me. "You'll have to gain access to Valeska herself to challenge her. It must be done by you, face-to-face. That means you must not only gain access to Night Haven but stay alive long enough to get the words out in her presence. Night Haven is secured by blood, the same as the Star of Lamia."

"Can Cassius take me?"

She shakes her head. "Too risky. He defected from her coven. They would arrest him, and we'd never see him again. Not fair to him or us."

"Then how do I get in?"

"There's only one sure way to gain safe passage into

Night Haven for a human." Sabrina closes the box and smooths her hands over the top.

"And that is?"

"You were brave to come here. You might not have magic like a witch, but you have courage like a shifter. I see it in you. You'll do what it takes."

I wait. "What will it take, Sabrina?"

She sighs. "You'll have to pose as a human blood donor."

Cassius appears in the open doorway, shaking his head. "I would never question your wisdom, Sabrina, but after tasting her blood, are you sure that's a good idea?"

She folds her arms. "Oh yes. I'm sure of it."

"Damien told me her blood was… different." He frowns.

"It is. The dragon blood in her veins is slightly intoxicating to vampires. Her blood is more though. I only had a drop, but it was like nothing I'd ever tasted. Absolutely delicious. She'll be in high demand."

"She'll be drained before she has a chance to make it to Valeska." Cassius doesn't raise his voice, but it's the strongest statement I've heard him make since we met.

I hold up a hand to interrupt. "Just so we're clear, you're proposing I pose as a blood whore—a human who donates their blood to vampires in exchange for money —until I can get close enough to Valeska to challenge her?"

"Precisely," Sabrina says. "If you go in under the protection of a madam, you'll be safe until you have time enough to plan a way into her presence. And you'll donate to the customers until the next time Valeska appears in public. Perhaps there will be a festival or she'll allow her people to petition the throne as I did today. Then you get close to her and you challenge her."

"And then try to survive the trials," I mumble.

"I can't encourage you to do this," Cassius says, that ever-present smile of his completely gone from his face. "If Damien knew we were even considering selling your blood—"

"Last time I saw Damien in his dream, he was dying. Valeska keeps him inside a tower of sunlight with no shade. He's dehydrated and sunburnt. His skin is as white as a stone." I meet Cassius's eyes. "There are holes in his wings where the sun has burned through."

Cassius inhales through his teeth.

"Damien asked me to let him die. He wanted to set me free. But you know what? The truth is, it doesn't matter what Damien wants or hates or approves of. It's *my* blood and *my* decision. I refuse to give up on him. I refuse to cast him aside. I'm getting him out of there, and if I have to donate a little blood to do that, I will."

Sabrina claps her hands together. "Then the decision is made. I have a feeling about you, Eloise. I predict you'll be back here with your mate someday, celebrating your win."

How I hope that future can be. I am no warrior. I can barely do a single push-up. Just because the challenges are possible for me doesn't mean I'll be able to win them.

"What happens if I don't win?" I ask, suddenly acutely aware that's a possibility.

Sabrina's perfectly manicured hand presses into the space at the base of her throat. "I thought you understood. Provocationem Ad Mortem means challenge to the death. The player who fails dies."

17

PLAYTHING

DAMIEN

After so many weeks baking in Valeska's sun-drenched dungeon, you'd think a soft bed in a dark room would be a relief. Only, the reality I'm living now is far worse. I'd willingly return to the silo if I had a choice.

Valeska has me chained to her bed by the neck. It seems Tae was significantly weakened when I wounded and possibly killed Lang. I don't know if the twin is still alive, but I've only seen Tae since the incident. A collar, it seems, requires far less magic than a silo and offers me no shade or comfort, not even from my own wings. Valeska was smart not to cuff my wrists or ankles. I would chew through my own arm or leg to be free of her at this point. The neck is painful. The neck is degrading. The neck requires suicide by beheading to escape.

I've tried. Thrown my entire weight against the burn in an attempt to snap my own neck. Turns out I'm too weak to even off myself.

No matter, without blood or Eloise's energy, my death will take care of itself. I'm in constant pain now, my stomach trying to eat itself from the inside out, my blood like broken glass in my veins, my tongue a leathery stump, my eyes too dry to open. My head throbs. My heart aches with each laborious thump. I'm always cold.

I no longer can lift myself off the bed. It takes all my strength to twitch a finger. It shouldn't be long now. I'm not afraid to die. In fact, the thought comforts me. I will cross over into the Darklands, triumphant that Eloise's identity died with me. Once I'm gone, Eloise will know. She'll feel it, and then she'll be free. She hasn't entered my dreams again, which must mean she's accepted the truth I conveyed to her at our last meeting. It's time she lets me go.

The soft whine of the door opening meets my ears, and then a sliver of dim light pours in through the crack in my eyelids. The sound of Valeska's heels clacking on the floor draws near. I don't open my eyes or say a word. Maybe I can't anymore. Weakness weighs me down like a lead blanket.

"You're no fun like this, Damien," she says.

I feel her wrist press against my lips but make no move to bite.

"The healers tell me you should already be dead. You have days, maybe hours, until the end if you don't drink. What a waste that would be."

Inside I smile. Not long now.

"The scribes tell me that force-feeding you my blood is a violation of our laws. I can take your blood. I can drain you dry and hasten your death. But to force my blood on you without your consent is considered a violation."

Fingers stroke along my hollowed stomach, across my chest. "Something about blood binding, making victims into zombies, ethical considerations, blah, blah, blah. We're vampires, I told them, not a religious order." She snorts.

I want to cringe, but I don't have the energy. I'm naked, as I have been since the day she captured me, and although she had me bathed when she moved me into her chambers, she has never once offered me the comfort of a covering.

"Can I tell you a secret? I've never been that concerned with the old laws. I really don't think the forebears are relevant any longer. A bunch of ancient vampires who spend their days sleeping in an underground palace halfway around the world don't seem like much of a threat. But what does scare me is losing the faith of my hive, which means I need to give the *illusion* of following those laws."

Her hand skims across my chest, my abdomen. I'm not sure why she bothers. I am dead flesh. Unless the bitch is into necrophilia, I can't possibly be doing it for her.

"Tsk. Tsk. Tsk."

I can't move, can't see where she's looking, but by the lascivious way her fingers graze my hip, I can guess. I will myself to cross from this life into the next, pray to the gods to take me to the Darklands where my kind find their final rest.

"You understand that I can't allow you to die, Damien?"

Despair drills a hole in the center of my being. Starved and foggy, I'm not sure what she has in store for me, only that it is evil and that I will suffer even more than I have already suffered.

When Valeska speaks again into my ear, there is nothing but cruelty in her voice. "I thought with time, you'd grow hungry enough to take my blood. I thought with encouragement, you'd offer up your mate's name. I thought the torture of the light burning your skin and your starvation would break you. But now I see you're too strong for that. That strength was what enticed me to want you from the start. Now I see that I underestimated you. You are a greater prize than I assumed."

Her nails scrape down my shoulder, my side, my hip. I want to run. I want to die. My body refuses to do either.

"The beautiful thing about having you in my chambers, Damien, is no one else knows what happens here. No one can confirm or deny your consent to my blood."

The sound of tearing flesh meets my ears, and then a hand is prying open my lips. I try to fight, but I have nothing left. If she wanted to, she could snap my jaw with one squeeze of her hand.

Blood drips over my tongue, and it at once disgusts me as it elicits an immediate physical response. It's reflexive. My lips fasten over the cut.

Don't swallow. Don't swallow. Don't swallow.

My will is strong but my body is weak.

My throat contracts, and then I'm drinking from my enemy. Drinking blood I'm ashamed to enjoy. Drinking blood that could be my undoing.

"There he is," she coos, petting my hair as I guzzle blood from her wrist. "Things will be so much easier now."

18

TRAINING & PREPARATION

ELOISE

"You don't have to do this, Eloise," Cassius says. "You're human. You can move on. No one would judge you for it. It would be the least foolish thing to do."

Sabrina assigned him to train me in self-defense. I have until the end of the month to ready myself for the challenge. One month to master my magic and find some way to take it with me to Night Haven. Once a month, the madams of the blood brothels of Night Haven emerge from their subterranean enterprises. Past donors who tire of the life or aren't in demand go back to their lives topside. New donors volunteer or are sold into the position by their vampire masters.

Vampires love new blood.

"I'm not abandoning him," I tell Cassius. "If you can't go and Morpheus won't go and it's too risky for my friend Maeve to go, then I'm all that's left. I'm his mate. I'm his way out. I'm doing this."

"You must know that following Sabrina's plan will likely cost you your life. I know your feelings for Damien are strong, as are mine, but you've known him only a short time. If he were here, he'd want you to keep yourself safe. He'd want you to be happy."

All the way home from Chicago, I thought about this. He's not exaggerating the risks. I'll have to become a blood whore to make it into Night Haven, hope and pray that the distinct flavor of my blood doesn't cause a customer to drain me or to accuse me of being a witch. Without calling attention to myself, I'll have to wait until the queen appears in public and then find a way to get close enough to her to challenge her. All without being detected by anyone despite the queen having a price on my head. Then I'll have to hope and pray that the magic of the box and the demands of vampire tradition protect me as I navigate the three trials of the Provocationem Ad Mortem.

Roll the dice.

Choose a challenge.

Try not to die.

It's a fools game. I'm a fool for considering it, all for a man—no, a monster—I've known only a matter of months. But I clear my throat and bare my soul to Cassius because I am that fool, and he deserves to know why. "When I was a little girl, I was loved. Every child should be loved by their family, but the longer I'm alive, the more I see how uncommon it is to have what I had. My parents both loved me unconditionally, and I was happy. I know what love is and what it isn't. I learned firsthand what it isn't from Tony. When my parents were murdered, I learned what it felt like to lose love, to have all the sunshine and gentle breezes stripped from your days. Days of limp sails, gray skies. Dark days. Days that only my grandmother and Maeve kept me alive. Do you know what I've learned from all of it?"

He shakes his head in sober silence.

"Once you know love, you know it's worth dying for. I love Damien. Damien loves me. I know we fell in love quickly and that we haven't known each other very long, but it's like when you see a sprout in the garden. A rose is a rose far before it blooms. I recognize the roots, Cassius, and this relationship is a rare and beautiful species. You're right—Damien would want me to go on without him. He'd want me to stay safe. He wants better for me because he loves me. And unlike Damien, my biology does not restrict me from loving another. But my heart does. I will always know that I had the beginnings of something, a promise so rare that another woman was willing to kill for it. How could I live with myself? How could I move forward as anything but an empty shell, knowing I'd thrown away a chance at something extraordinary, all to settle for something *safe*?"

He glances toward his feet but then challenges me again. "You'd be a woman who survived a terrible loss. An empty shell, maybe at first, but in time, perhaps, something greater."

I scoff. "When I was married to Tony, I survived a life of domestic abuse by hiding who I was and making myself small. All it earned me was a sore jaw and a broken rib. I don't want safe, Cassius. Safe doesn't even exist. I want fair. I want a chance. I want to know I did everything I could."

He smiles, a dimple forming in one cheek. "Damien said you were a warrior at heart."

"He did? When?"

"He came to see me when he first realized he was falling in love with you. He said you'd do anything for the people you loved. I guess he was right."

"He was." I lift my chin another inch.

"Then there's no time to waste. Show me your fighting stance."

I spare him the truth that I'm not entirely sure what a fighting stance is and raise my fists, parting my feet like I imagine a boxer might do.

He shoves my shoulder, and I trip over my own feet. He catches me before I eat the carpet.

He snorts. "We'll work on it."

THE FOLLOWING WEEKS FALL INTO A PATTERN. MAEVE comes to Harcourt directly after work, and we practice magic until around eleven p.m. when Cassius forms from the shadows and takes over with physical training. Progress comes slowly. I can light a candle now, make the water in a glass boil, cause a wind to blow through the room, and sprout a seed without the help of my ancestors. But when we test my magic, my power fades with distance from my anchor, which is still the grandfather clock. I can't manifest a thing once I'm past my driveway. I still need Harcourt Manor to do any of it.

Moving my anchor to something portable is imperative if I want the benefit of my magic in Night Haven, something I can only assume will greatly increase my chances of survival. But when I try to call for the spell I need like before, no book flies into my hands. To make matters worse, when my ancestors appear and I ask them about it, they seem confused by the question. Their mouths move in silent protestations I can't understand.

We spend hours in the attic, combing through books, journals, and notebooks for a way to move my anchor. I've even picked out a gorgeous jade ring that was once my mother's as a new target. We find nothing. When we try to invent our own spell, we fail miserably. Hell, we never designated the grandfather clock in the first place. The clock simply was my anchor from the beginning, from the day we performed the Hitch and Cast spell.

"I'll keep looking," Maeve says as we wrap up our lesson at the end of week three of practice. We're sitting on the floor of the attic within a sea of open books and notebooks.

"I leave for Night Haven next week. I may have to go without it and try to win this thing without any witchy help."

She shakes her head. "I'm not sending you down there without any magic. You practice with Cassius. If there's something here, I'll find it." She reaches behind her and draws another book from her stack.

"You need your sleep." Maeve's been pushing herself too hard lately. Between the office and my training, she doesn't have a minute to herself.

"So do you," she says softly.

I don't have to look in the mirror to know I've got a permanent case of dark circles under my eyes, and my skin is the palest it's ever been. "I'm trying to get used to sleeping during the day. From everything I've read, it takes a few weeks to adjust. All I need to do is stick to it."

"Are you eating?"

I frown. "I'm trying to adjust to that too." I'm too busy training to eat much at night and too tired during the day to make up the calories. I'm lucky to get in one good meal a day.

"Try harder. Your clothes look like they might fall off you." She frowns.

It's true, I haven't been this thin since I left Tony. "It's too long," I mumble, rubbing the ache of our mating bond that never leaves my chest. "Damien is suffering. In one week, he went from being himself in his dream to being suicidal. Who knows what she's doing to him now? I don't want to eat or sleep. I just want him back."

She pulls me into a tight hug. "And the way you're going to do that is to win a challenge against the queen. If you don't eat and don't sleep, you'll be too weak to free him. I know it's hard, but you have to keep yourself strong."

I promise her I'll try harder and then descend the back stairs as Cassius's voice from the parlor carries into the attic. We start with balance and then basic sparring. I know how to throw my weight into a punch with proper form and can now move quickly while maintaining stability. I've done about a million sit-ups and spent more time planking over the past few weeks than I probably have my entire life. But today, when I meet him in the parlor, he thrusts a dagger into my hand.

"Good evening, Eloise. Are you ready to learn knife-fighting techniques?"

"Knives? No swords or guns?" I mean it as a joke. I don't even feel ready for the blade in my hand.

"Guns are almost useless against vampires. And while a sword is works for a quick beheading, they're slower and more awkward to wield, especially for a human. No offense, but any vampire worth their blood would be able to see your intent with a sword the second you pulled it from its scabbard, You'd be blocked and disemboweled mid-swing."

I draw in a deep breath. "All right. So no swords. What do I do with this?"

I immediately flip the dagger over in my hand so that the blade faces upward. He shakes his head and frowns.

"What? I already did something wrong? I just repositioned the knife."

He takes the dagger from me and flips it over, double-sided blade pointing down and back from where I grip the hilt. "When you're in Night Haven, your only hope of slaying a healthy vampire is the element of surprise."

He moves in, pressing the fingers of my fist to my thigh. This close, with him towering above me, it's impossible not to be reminded of Damien. If I closed my eyes, I might imagine he's here. I catch myself inhaling deeply, hoping for his scent, but Cassius's is completely different. White pepper and Egyptian amber. I refocus on the lesson, missing Damien so much my chest aches.

"Pretend the dagger is sheathed at your thigh and I am a vampire moving in to feed. Where do you strike?"

I lift the dagger between us and press my knuckles into his turtleneck-covered torso. "The gut."

He shakes his head. "You can't kill a vampire that way. They'll simply drain you dry, and your blood will heal their injury." He grabs my hand and sweeps the blade between us until the edge presses into the inside of his thigh. "You need to open an artery. That won't kill a vampire, but it may buy you time. There's one here, in the thigh." He sweeps my hand up to the side of his throat. "And here, on either side of the neck. But to kill, you need to go for the heart or the brain. Hit those and you will incapacitate your victim for several minutes. That should be long enough to cut off their head. Never assume a vampire is dead if their heart is still in their chest and their head is still attached to their body."

I gulp. Jesus. Now I'm cutting off heads? "Okay," I drawl, obviously not okay.

"As a blood donor, your best option is to fake romantic interest, pull them in close, and stab them in the heart." He points to the area under his left arm. "Slide it between the ribs."

He wraps my left hand around the back of his neck, moving in like we're embracing. I raise the dagger from my thigh and try to press the tip between his third and fourth ribs. I miss.

"That's too low. If I were a vampire, you'd only piss me off. You'll have to feel your way. You won't be able to see it, and every vampire will be a different height and weight. We'll get there. Let's start with the basics."

He gives me two sheaths to strap to my thighs. Great. I now have two daggers I don't know what to do with. But over the next hour, we go through a set of hooks, thrusts, and slashing movements. I practice over and over—right diagonal, left diagonal, as if I'm drawing an *x* on my opponent, and then straight down like I'm plunging the knife into their chest, dropping to my knees with my entire weight to sink and tear whatever my dagger can reach. Hooking to the head from the left, from the right, slashing on the return. Cassius becomes the world's best practice dummy, turning into shadow the second before my blade makes contact. It's something a vampire can't do, and in no time, I'm sweating fiercely, struggling to maintain a balanced fighting stance while avoiding his intentionally slow counterattacks.

"Remember, you'll have to push hard to break through the rib cage if you hit bone. As hard as you can push. The daggers I'm giving you are the sharpest you can attain in these lands and enchanted by the Lamia coven's witch, but it will still take all your might. It's better if you can slice between the ribs."

"You're giving me enchanted daggers?" I frown. "Will I need such a thing?"

"No one knows, Eloise. But even before you challenge Valeska, you must be able to defend yourself. Night Haven is a dangerous place."

We run through various scenarios. He attacks me from the front, from behind, from the side. He grabs one wrist. Both wrists. He teaches me to kick, to break a hold. We go again and again, the clock in the corner chiming as the hours tick by. Chiming and anchoring me. I might not be exercising my magic, but as I grow tired, I can sense my connection to it, as if it's an invisible hand, steadying me, holding me up, giving me speed, endurance.

"Good!" Cassius yells. "You've got it. Just like that!"

He rushes me, pretending to bite, his teeth grazing the side of my neck. I do as he trained me, pulling him closer and stabbing into his smoky flesh, between where his ribs would be. He re-forms and I slice his femoral and jugular in one sweeping pass between us, then hook into his ear. We go again and again until, despite my exertion, my skin grows icy cold.

He catches my arm. "You're pale and… freezing."

Spots swim in my eyes. "I've overused my magic."

He helps me into the chair near the fire and to sheathe my blades. "I didn't think we were using magic. Is that how you improved so quickly?"

My head is pounding, and I lean it against the back of the chair, closing my eyes. "It just sort of happened."

"Well then, time for a break." He grabs my water bottle off the mantel, his eyes falling on the ventilation grate that's still waiting for me to get the ladder from the garage and reinstall it.

He hands me the bottle and then digs a protein bar out of his bag and tucks it into my hand. "Eat something."

I nod but can't get the wrapper open. I'm too weak.

He grimaces and opens it for me.

I take a bite.

"Would you like me to put that back up for you?" he asks, pointing toward the grill.

I take a deep drink of water. "If it's not too much trouble. There's a ladder in the garage. I just don't trust myself not to bang up the walls with it."

"No need." He grabs the grate and screws, breaking apart into shadow. Black tendrils twist and lift, repositioning the grate on the wall and screwing it in. I stare at it, again wondering why the spell I needed came to me that night after we'd visited Bad Witches' Club but the spell to switch my anchor hasn't come when I've called for it over and over again the past few weeks. Maybe it doesn't exist.

"Thank you," I say when he re-forms next to his black bag.

He holds up a thermos. "Please excuse me. I have not fed, and I'm delighted to say you were more of a challenge tonight than I was expecting."

"Knock yourself out. I think I'm done for the night. Just making it upstairs to bed is going to be a challenge."

"Rest. Hydrate. If we need to, we'll call it an early night." He drinks, staining his lips red with the contents of the thermos. Blood. I concentrate on my water.

"Can I ask you something personal?" I'm suddenly keen to distract myself from the pain in my head and the sight of blood on his lips.

"Of course. I'd like to think we're friends. That seems like something friends would entertain." He gives me one of his bright white smiles.

"We're definitely friends. I really appreciate you helping me. I was just wondering why the turtlenecks?"

"Turtlenecks?" He glances down at himself, then at me.

"I've never seen you wear anything else," I point out. "And I got the impression from Damien that your clothing can look any way you please."

He nods, confirming it. "Saves time," he says softly. "And hides this." He pulls the neck of the sweater down to reveal a jagged, raised scar that travels from above the hollow of his throat toward his left collarbone.

I inhale sharply at the ghastly sight. "That looks brutal. But… couldn't you hide the scar the same way you transform from shade to human form? Damien made it seem like you can look how you wish to look."

He scratches the back of his head. "Damien oversimplified. I suspect he didn't want to overwhelm you with the details of our transmutation. Scars this deep are diffi-cult to hide. I can mask it, but only at a high cost of power that would leave me at a disadvantage in a fight. The same with why we prefer to wear clothing rather than create it as part of our illusion."

I lift an eyebrow. "So Morpheus's scar, the one on his face, it's real?"

He smiles softly. "It is. We earned them at the same time. It was Damien who saved us from the worst of it though. Saved our lives."

"How so?"

He takes a seat on the sofa. "Would you like to hear the story?"

I nod and take another bite of the protein bar. It's chalky but better than nothing.

"Hundreds of years ago, before the three of us were drawn here through the rift, there was a war over the forested territory between the kingdom of Stygarde—the kingdom of the shades—and the kingdom of Willowgulch, where the dark elves rule. Damien's father Malek was captured a year into the war, leaving Damien as the oldest son to rule at the side of his mother, Nyxadora, the queen. As prince regent in his father's absence, he served as supreme military commander of Stygarde's army of warriors, the umbrae."

"Were you and Morpheus soldiers in that army?"

He grunts like he finds the word *soldier* distasteful. "Not a soldier, an umbrae warrior." He taps his chin. "You might consider us similar to samurai in your world, or perhaps Navy SEALs. Each one of us was highly trained, deadly, and powerful, and while we would follow orders as a team, we often accomplished missions independently. One umbrae was as good as an entire legion of soldiers."

"Sorry if I offended you."

"No offense taken. How could you have known?" He sips again from his thermos, his lips coming away red. "Damien devised a system of patrolling the grounds and had made a deal with the witches of Dimhollow to provide Stygarde with wards as well. We'd successfully thwarted every attack on our lands since the king was taken, but Damien refused to give up on getting him back.

"Damien, Morpheus, and I had been friends since our school days and advanced through the ranks together. My mother was a wealthy landowner, and Morpheus's father was Lord of Aendor, the coastal territory of Stygarde and commander of a fleet of ships that was the source of all goods delivered by sea. As such, we'd been aware of each other practically since birth and had aligned ourselves from our first royal ball. He knew he could trust us in a way he couldn't trust his siblings."

"Why couldn't he trust his siblings?" I remember Damien mentioning them but not any animosity between them.

"His sister, Karyl, was still a child at the time, and his younger brother, Brahm, was prone to drinking and debauchery. Damien could never get his mother to consider it, but there were rumors that Brahm was the leak responsible for their father's abduction. A tavern owner told Damien he saw Brahm, so drunk he'd wet himself, whispering with a Rivertoad the night before it happened." I must look sufficiently confused because he explains. "Rivertoads are wanderers. They have no land of their own but live in encampments along the river that borders the mountains. They're not bad people but are as poor as they come. It would be a cruel temptation to give one information so valuable as the location of the king."

He pauses to take another deep drink. "Anyway, he trusted us and so he asked us to help him get his father back. Against every law of the kingdom at the time, we used the shadows, at great personal risk, to find where the elves were holding Malek, a heavily fortified prison called Dhegal Castle. We only made it through their wards at all because Damien had a friend among the witches who agreed to help us. The following night, the three of us staged a rescue. The castle was guarded by elf mages who wielded light magic. They wielded it like swords."

"Lightsabers," I whisper breathlessly.

His eyes crease at the corners. "Not quite as elegant, thank the gods. The plan was to enter from the roof. Elves can't fly, and we'd seen only two guards up there on our reconnaissance missions. We formed from shadow during the darkest night, slit the guard's throats, and descended a spiral staircase to the castle proper. But the elves had a failsafe. At the bottom of the staircase, we found ourselves having to traverse a light-filled passageway. Not only were we rendered mortal, but the magic triggered the arrival of more guards.

"It would have been natural for Damien, as the acting king, to send me and Morpheus forward into battle first. But he never held himself above us or any of the umbrae. He charged into the guards, sword swinging. He'd decapitate one elf only to use its body as a shield against another. Morpheus and I defended his flanks, but we'd never been as skilled with a sword as he was. Morpheus took a hit to the face with a sun-poisoned blade. I took one here." He gestures over the scar at his throat. "When we finally reached the end of the corridor and Damien slew the mage responsible for the light, we all broke into shadow and found Malek. Morpheus slew the mage powering his father's cell, but when Damien entered, his father protested, begged his son for mercy, to kill him. He'd been imprisoned there for a year, starved and tortured. Damien carried him out of there. Both Morpheus and I were still bleeding, but we helped him get Malek to the roof and shadoweave home. Our wounds healed quickly, although the light made them scar. His father's ran deeper. He did recover, but Damien effectively ruled the kingdom until the day we were captured and brought here."

Nothing surprises me about the story. Not that Damien risked his life for his father nor that he refused to use his title to protect himself. I'm not surprised by his competency as a warrior either. But I frown at the fireplace, suddenly swollen with fury.

"I've upset you," Cassius says.

I look at him and shake my head. "It's been over a month since Valeska took Damien. What lengths must she be taking to hold him there?"

His expression turns grave. "If he were dead, we'd know. You'd feel it along your mating bond and I along the shadows."

"But if he's not dead?"

We both stare at each other. Neither of us needs to say it, but I know by the look in his eyes that it's true. By the time I make it to Night Haven, it's very possible that Damien will be as broken as his father was.

19

ON THE INSIDE

DAMIEN

Hell is empty, and all the devils are here. A human wrote that. Shakespeare. I could appreciate *The Tempest* before, but I never so intimately understood the line until now.

"You will not leave this room," Valeska orders me. The taste of her blood still coats my mouth. I hate it. Hate the scent of her that fills my nose. Hate the room where I'm her prisoner.

She glances over at Tae and nods her head. Lang still hasn't shown his face, and I'm pretty sure he's dead based on Tae's general appearance. The witch looks like the walking dead, his eyes red over dark bruises of half-moon flesh. His mouth sags as if he's never known the joy of a smile. And the way he looks at me—if the hate in his eyes were fuel, we'd all go up in flames.

Valeska points at me. "Take it off."

Tae removes the sunlight collar from my neck.

Instantly I break apart into shadow. It feels so good to finally be free of the sun. It's as if every molecule of my existence is charged with pure joy as I slither through the darkness and attempt to leave. But I can't. Every trail of shadow ends at the boundary of the room. I try again and again, until Valeska's laugh echoes around me.

"Enough, Damien. Return to me so we can talk."

My shadows pull together against my will, and I form in front of her, my wings flaring.

"Your other form, Damien. I've had enough of the horns."

Power slams into me, and by my next heartbeat, I'm in my corse form, dressed in casual clothing. I run a hand down my chest. Despair replaces my former elation. "What have you done to me?"

She cracks a wicked smile but doesn't answer me. Instead, she turns to Tae. "Your debt to me is repaid. You may leave."

He gives a shallow bow and storms from the room. The last thing I hear before the door closes is a relieved sigh.

"You killed his brother," Valeska says, brushing a dark wave out of her luminescent amber eyes. "You have not made a friend in the Kim coven, but then friendship isn't even half as useful as fear. He won't hurt you as long as you're with me."

I grit my teeth. "Why can't I leave this room?"

"Because you've had my blood. Twice now actually. Although it's possible you were asleep for the first feeding." She waves a hand through the air dismissively. "In any case, you must obey me. It's my blood keeping you alive. You feel better, don't you?"

Physically I'm stronger, and my injuries from the torture I've endured these past weeks are healing. I'm able to sustain this form and am in little pain. But mentally I loathe the real possibility that I've blood bonded with Valeska.

"This is more than blood," I grit out.

She tips her head. "Hmmm. It's possible the potion I've been taking to increase the bonding effect of my blood is to blame. At any rate, you'll find it difficult to disobey me. Sadly, because the potion's efficacy is untested, you'll have to stay in this room until we settle this mate situation."

"I will kill you," I growl, and I mean it. I grasp for her throat, but when I try to squeeze my fingers, they won't comply.

Her full red lips part into a smile worthy of a lunatic. "No, you won't. You can't. I made sure to enforce that command while you were sleeping. You cannot hurt me as long as my blood is in your veins, and the only blood allowed in this room is in my veins. It's me or nothing, Damien. The more you drink, the tighter our bond."

I shake my head. "Why are you doing this? Let me go," I mutter for the three thousandth time.

"Tell me the name of your mate," she commands.

Eloise's name almost slips from my lips, but I hold it back, shaking violently. "My little bird," I blurt. The magic is satisfied.

"Little bird?" Valeska seethes. "Don't play games with me, Damien. What is her name?"

"My beloved," I bark. I can keep this up all day, although I fear Valeska will get better at phrasing her questions if I do.

Slap! My chin snaps to the side with the force of her

blow. "You will tell me, Damien. Eventually." She stands and heads for the door. "I will expect you to be more compliant in the days to come, my pet. Starting tomorrow, you will accompany me on my visits to the coven masters in this hive, and you will not embarrass me."

"I'm a shade," I say quickly. "I need food other than blood to meet my nutritional needs. If you want me strong and not falling asleep at your side, you need to feed me as you would a human."

"Fine. I'll have Chef bring you the same dishes I serve my human blood donors."

Excellent. Food will be served by someone other than her. Someone who may help me.

She stops at the door, looking annoyed. "Get your shit together. Whether you want to fight me on this mating or not, whether I kill your mate or not, you *will* spend the rest of your days by my side. It's only a matter of time before you give her up, one way or another."

I keep my mouth shut because the last thing I want is for her to change her approach and ask me again about Eloise. But I hold my head in my hands. My body might be healed, but inside, I'm praying I find a way to escape or die before Valeska can force Eloise's identity from me.

20

Nexus

ELOISE

Phantom hasn't been eating his food. I haven't seen the fox in almost a week, and by the looks of the still-full bowl on my stoop, he's moved on from this part of the woods. At least, I want to believe he's moved on and hasn't met a less romantic end. I clean up the bowls and say a silent prayer that wherever the critter is, he's okay.

Later that night, Maeve arrives with a massive oblong roaster in her hands. I open the door for her and she carries it into the kitchen.

"Is that like a cauldron or something?" I ask. "Are we working on potions today?" I'm not against it, but it's hard for me to guess a scenario where brewing a potion would help me during the challenge.

She laughs. "No. It's Thanksgiving! It's a turkey with all the fixings."

When she removes the lid, the scent of roasted bird makes my mouth water. I spot red potatoes, carrots, and green beans too. "That smells so good, but you didn't have to do this. It looks like a lot of work."

She tosses her hot pads onto the counter and turns toward me. "You leave to descend into the vampire city in six days, Eloise. We are going to celebrate Thanksgiving tonight, and when Cassius gets here, he's going to join us. You've worked nonstop for weeks. Tonight you're going to rest, and we're going to celebrate all the things we're thankful for."

My stomach grumbles, and I realize I haven't eaten anything today but a yogurt. "You're the boss," I say through a tight smile. Just the thought of celebrating Thanksgiving with Damien still in that horrible place seems frivolous, but she's clearly gone to a lot of trouble and I need to eat. "If you insist this is part of the training regimen, who am I to argue?"

She grabs me by the shoulders. "Good. You find a knife and a cutting board. I'll get the wine out of the car."

An hour later, I'm stuffed so full of turkey and vegetables I have to lean back in my chair to make room for my stomach. I'm also feeling a bit toasted from the wine. Toasted and sentimental. "I haven't had a meal like this since before Grams died." I look around the kitchen with its pale yellow countertops edged in shiny silver, its mint-green-and-white-painted cabinets, the crocheted sling with its overgrown spider plant, the wall phone with the long coiling cord I used to wrap my fingers in. "This kitchen has seen so many meals. So many Thanksgivings. Thank you for giving me one more before I go."

"It was as much for me as for you." The full truth passes silently between us. We both know this might be our last formal meal together.

"You're the only family I have left, Maeve, and we aren't even related." I sniff, my vision going a bit blurry.

"We're as good as family," she says, swinging her glass through the air until her wine sloshes. "I'm closer to you than any of the Gowdies." She takes a sip and points a black nail at me. "I swear to the goddess, Eloise Harcourt, if you don't win this fucking challenge and return to me, I will find a medium to call up your ghost and slap you with whatever magical element hurts ghosts."

I snort. "You'd never hurt me if I were a ghost. You'd probably send brownies to the underworld for me."

"Probably. I'm such a sucker for you, girlie." She rubs behind her glasses. The tip of her nose is pink. "You know, I'd totally go with you to Night Haven if I wouldn't get us both killed on sight for being a Gowdie witch."

"I know."

"I had an idea though. Maybe I could send you with some Hitch and Cast potion and you can enter my dreams if you needed advice."

I frown. "That would be a great idea if I knew for sure I'd have a stove and the tools to complete the potion, let alone a way to anchor in Night Haven."

She finishes her wine and pours herself another. "Right. Probably not feasible. This anchor thing is the most problematic. Why aren't your ancestors helping you with this?"

We hear the clock strike eleven p.m. in the other room, and the lights flicker. "Cassius is here."

The shade appears in the doorway to the kitchen.

Maeve hands him a glass and fills it with wine. "Happy Thanksgiving."

I look up at him from a face that's grown a bit warm. "I

hope you're game for a night off because I'm not sure I wouldn't stab myself after the amount of wine I've drunk tonight."

In a blur of black, he's across the kitchen and heaping his plate with food. "It's been years since I've had a proper turkey dinner. You wouldn't believe how hard it is to have regular meals when you live and work with vampires."

Maeve flips her black manicured nails through the air. "I thought you shades could subsist on blood."

He gives her a flat look. "And you humans could survive on protein shakes, but it makes for a boring Thanksgiving."

The chorus of their warm laughter fills the space around me.

So much to be thankful for. My gaze catches on the picture of my Grandpa Harcourt on the wall and Grams in her wedding dress, then skates to the pantry. If I open the door, I'll see height markings for my grandfather, my father, and for me, dates and ages in Sharpie on the wood. So many generations, so much time at this table, in this kitchen, inside these walls. If I can take any comfort in it, it's that this too will pass. I will either survive this challenge or I won't. Only time will tell.

Time. "Oh my God. *Time!*" I say, my eyes growing wider.

Maeve and Cassius stop what appears to be a vibrant discussion on the effectiveness of sage in deterring demons and give me their attention.

"What's that?" Maeve asks.

I stand from the table. "Moving the anchor. Maybe it's not about finding the right spell but about performing the intention at the right *time.*"

They both stare at me blankly.

"The night I called Damien using the candle, you told me to perform the ritual exactly at midnight when the veil between the living and the dead was thinnest and my ancestors could help fuel the magic."

"That is the general advice for humans," she says. "I had no idea at the time you could actually communicate with your ancestors."

"I couldn't then. But the spell worked. And then, the night I asked for the Hitch and Cast spell and the book flew down from the attic, that happened right after the clock chimed midnight. And last night, at exactly midnight, I felt anchored as I was sparring with Cassius."

Maeve adjusts her glasses. "But we performed the Hitch and Cast spell during the day."

"And I never chose my anchor. It just was the clock. It was already the clock from when I did the spell in the parlor to call Damien at midnight. It's always been the clock."

"So... you think in order to move it, you have to perform a spell at midnight... and then redirect it? But wouldn't you have to know what spell to use first?"

I look back at the black-and-white photo of my grandfather. "I think at midnight, I need to call my ancestors and ask them for help moving it. They trained me to master the elements. There was no specific spell for lighting the candle or making the seed grow. Maybe this is like that when it comes to spirit magic. There is no spell, I just have to feel it."

Cassius nods approvingly and looks at his watch. "We can find out for sure in thirty-seven minutes."

I put down my wine and reach for my water. I have thirty-seven minutes to sober up.

AT 11:59 P.M., ALL THREE OF US STAND IN THE PARLOR, staring at the grandfather clock. I am not sober. My head is buzzing and I have a case of the giggles. On a positive note, I have no anxiety about trying this.

"Ready?" I ask, although the only person who needs to be ready is me. "Here we go."

"You can do this, El," Maeve says supportively.

Cassius squeezes my shoulder.

The clock starts to chime, and I reach down that spiderweb within me that connects to it. "How do I move my anchor?"

The room flips to red, haze moving in and ash snowing from the sky. I've never had this happen so fast before, with so little effort. My great-grandfather appears near the fireplace again in all his grayscale glory, silver eyes with their hollow pinprick pupils focused on me. Grams and Gramps appear beside him, then my mom and dad.

"Hand me the ring," I say to Maeve.

She grabs the jade ring from the sofa table and plops it in my palm.

"How do I make this my anchor?" I ask my ancestors.

My mother points at the ring and shakes her head. Then she points at the clock and moves her arms as if they were the hands on the clockface. She does it again and again until I get it. "The anchor has to be something that moves. Something animated in some way." I'm not sure how I know that, but I'm sure.

My mother's ghost nods her head vigorously. Grams is beside me, holding out her hand, beckoning me. "Grams wants me to follow her."

All my ancestors turn and follow my grandmother toward the backyard, floating through the wall of the house. I grab my coat and shove my feet into my shoes, then scurry out the back door. They're all heading toward the cemetery, still gesturing for me to follow. It's eerie, seeing the ghosts of my family members stroll toward their graves. It's something I never expected to see.

But when we get there, I understand. Grams points to her grave. Phantom is there, curled beside her headstone.

The fox is dead.

Really dead.

Eyes white and belly swollen with maggots dead.

"Oh no," I say sadly. I cover my mouth and nose with my hands, both from emotion and to block the stench of the dead thing.

Maeve moves in beside me. "Is that the fox you were feeding?"

A heavy weight tugs at my sternum. I press my fist to it and moan. "Something's happening. It feels like..." I can't finish my sentence. It's like I'm tethered to something heavy, something that's arcing around me. For a second I can't breathe. It feels as though it will tear my rib cage out. But once the weight swings into the fox, the tension eases.

My ancestors close in, gathering around the dead animal.

"Eloise, what is happening?" Maeve asks.

"The night stinks of ancient power," Cassius says from somewhere behind us.

Gramps sinks into Phantom's body first, and the fox's milky-white eyes begin to clear. My great-grandfather goes next, and the dull fur starts to warm to a vibrant red. Once my great-grandmother sinks in, Phantom's deflated abdomen fills like a balloon. My parents follow, and more ancestors—ones whose names I do not know, ones I'm sure never lived here but are somehow connected to me through blood—sink in. The red haze in my vision begins to clear as one after another, those black-and-white manifestations blend into the dead fox.

"Something that moves, that can come with me," I mumble. "Something that no one will suspect or be able to take from me."

Grams is the last to slip inside. Phantom climbs to his feet, maggots and a thick dark liquid expelling from his mouth onto her grave. The fox coughs, then shakes itself, blinking and flicking its fluffy red tail, more alive and vibrant than it was the very first day it crawled from the woods.

Beside me, Maeve makes a choking sound.

Phantom jogs closer and sits directly in front of me, his eyes sparkling like someone has replaced them with two priceless emeralds. Maeve and Cassius move to my sides, all of us staring down at the resurrected fox.

"The anchor has moved," I say.

"It's not a ring, but it'll do," Maeve mumbles.

"How the fuck are we going to get this creature into Night Haven," Cassius says.

The fox lifts its chin. "Well, don't just stand there,

darling," Phantom says in Gram's voice. "We're all hungry in here. How about some of that turkey?"

21

TROUBLE

ELOISE

On the morning of November 29, I wake to the alarm I set and throw on joggers and a sweatshirt. It's still dark. I only finished training with Cassius two hours ago, but I force myself to move. I grab the heavy wool blanket I now keep on the bench near the door and hold the door open for Phantom, who silently falls in beside me as we exit the front of the house and cross the yard to the cliffs that overlook the river.

I'm exhausted, but I refuse to miss one of only two sunrises I have left before I leave for Night Haven. No one in their right mind would feel ready to face the vampire queen, especially after only a month of training. Still, a part of me is eager for whatever lies ahead. The ache in my chest that reminds me of my bond with Damien has changed over time from a breath-stealing pain to more of a dull ache. I don't know if that means he's nearing death or his situation has improved. Cassius tells me that most vampires don't know what a dragon smells or tastes like. Tobias's true nature is a secret that has remained contained to the Lamia coven. He doubts, although he can't promise, that anyone in Night Haven will place my scent. As for the taste of my blood, we have no idea how the vampires will react. He's made sure though that I can defend myself if one gets out of hand.

My chances of survival aren't stellar. I've never had a mind for math, and I couldn't begin to guess the odds, but I know they aren't good. I accept that. I'd rather do my best and die trying than spend my life wondering *what if.*

Damien is worth the risk.

I sit cross-legged at the edge of the cliff, wrap the blanket around myself, and watch the sunrise. Phantom sits down beside me, eyes twinkling in the light.

"Don't look so glum, Eloise," the fox says in my grand-mother's voice.

I learned a few nights ago that only I can hear it. To everyone else, Phantom is making animal sounds. Also, just because the fox has my grandmother's voice doesn't mean my grandmother is speaking. The fox contains all my ancestors. I think the fox and my Grams must have had a connection, because when the creature speaks, they always sound like her.

"You have a better chance of surviving this than you think, darling. You are the key. Anything one of us can do, you can channel."

"I'm glad I have all of you. I just wish I knew for sure that I was strong enough to win."

"You're strong enough," Phantom says. "You're a Harcourt. We're made of tough stuff."

I hold up a corner of the blanket, and the fox crawls

under and leans against my side. I wrap both of us up with only our faces showing as light spills over the horizon and color sweeps across the sky like spilled paint. I sigh.

"Do you know what happened to the original Phantom?"

"He's here with us," Phantom says. "He lived a long life. It was his time."

That makes me feel better. "If something goes wrong, I guess I'll be with you too."

Phantom doesn't answer. He's fixated on a scent in the air. Their little leathery nose lifts and wiggles. "I smell trouble."

I look over my shoulder, back toward the house. A fog has formed over the front yard, but I make out a figure walking toward me. As the person draws closer, I see it's a man and then grow certain it's Jared Denardi.

My heart thunders in my throat. I look down at Phantom. "It would be better if he didn't see you." I only mean that the fox should scurry away while I distract Jared, but to my amazement, Phantom blinks out of sight. "Damn. I had no idea you could do that, but it's definitely going to come in handy."

I stagger to my feet, the blanket still over my shoulders, and turn in Jared's direction. Fuck, with everything going on, I forgot about his promise to kill me if I didn't accept the money. It's been weeks since he threatened me, weeks since Maeve refused the money on my behalf. Considering I haven't had a visit from Fuller either, the FBI must be investigating them. Killing me now only complicates things for them, right? But when I see the gun in his hand, I know that's exactly what he intends.

I blink hard, remembering what Cassius taught me about keeping my thoughts from spiraling. I force my breaths to slow. I spread my feet. Find my balance.

"Come with me. We're going for a ride," Jared says from behind the gun.

I raise my hands, a wave of nausea rolling through my gut. All that work, all that training, and one twitch of his finger and I'll be gone, along with the last chance to free Damien. "You don't want to do this, Jared. My lawyer knows who you are. You'll be the prime suspect if something happens to me. It doesn't change anything for your family at all."

He snorts and shakes his head. "You don't know who you're dealing with, do you? You know too much, Eloise. The Denardis don't leave loose ends." The rumble of his voice is laced with arsenic and malice. "Be thankful Fuller's investigation was as thorough as it was or I'd have come around weeks ago. Happy to say, he couldn't make anything stick. I plan to keep it that way."

He takes a step closer.

Beside me, I hear Phantom whisper, "Now would be a great time to practice some of that training, Eloise."

Jared squints. "What the hell was that noise?"

I feel the web between Phantom and me snap into place. "I don't know what you're talking about." I wish I had the daggers Cassius gave me, but I don't. I'm not even dressed. All I have is a blanket.

"You have the elements," Phantom whispers.

Jared swaggers closer. I hold my ground, mere feet from the edge of the cliff and the rushing river below. I lift my hands higher.

"I won't go with you," I sputter.

He takes a deep breath and blows it out. "You'll either get in the passenger's seat of that car"—he points to the Maserati in the driveway, which is barely visible through the fog—"or I'll shoot you here and stow your bleeding bitch ass in the trunk. I'd rather not stain my interior."

The buzz of magic rises in my torso. "You're going to have to shoot me."

He's an arm's length away now. I peek over the edge at the river churning behind me. If I jump, there's no way I'd survive. It's too far of a fall. There's nowhere to go but through Jared.

"Tony always said you were a pain in the ass."

I rush him with a speed only possible because it's fueled by my ancestors, shoving the gun straight up. It goes off with a pop. Whirling, I toss the blanket over his head and gun and then run for the house.

Another gunshot has me diving for the grass.

He's over me in an instant. My heel connects with the gun and it flies out of his hand, skimming across the dew-covered lawn.

"Bitch!"

He dives on top of me, his fingers closing around my throat. The link between Phantom and me goes taut, and then I sense my grandfather's spirit filling my right arm. I slam my fist into Jared's nose, harder than I've ever punched anything in my life. He howls but retaliates with a punch to the side of my head. I block the worst of it and get another blow in. Enough to struggle out from under him and stagger to my feet. I run for the house, but I can't get my feet under me fast enough. A blow hits me between the shoulder blades, knocking my breath from my lungs. Ouch. I go down again, slamming into the cold lawn.

His fingers dig into my arm and he rolls me over, trying to drag me up and toward the car. I stick my leg between his and roll, breaking his balance. As he goes down, I rise up. I attempt to stomp on his balls, but he twists out of the way, right toward the dropped gun. His hand clasps the weapon.

"Fucking bitch. Playtime is over." He levels the gun at my head.

He's between me and the house, so I race for the cliffs, straight into the thickening fog. He can't shoot what he can't see.

"God damn it."

Around me, the fog takes on a red hue and ash snows, smoky and thick. I hear Jared's footsteps behind me, herding me toward the edge of the cliff again. I stop when I can go no farther and turn to face my attacker.

"Use the elements," Phantom prompts.

I reach for the buzz I associate with fire and direct it at Jared's coat. The wool bursts into flame just as he reaches me and the edge.

"What the fuck?" He tries to strip off the coat, but the flames grow higher, engulfing him. He stumbles toward me.

I fake, then duck and weave. With both hands, I shove hard against his back, ignoring the lick of the flames against my skin.

He staggers toward the edge, circling his arms. His hand shoots toward me, snatches my wrist, and then he tumbles over the edge.

"Fuck!" I follow him over, the river racing toward us, his coat still burning as we fall.

"Use the air," Phantom's voice snaps. The vibration inside me engages, and a hard gust of wind answers my call, blowing against me, lifting me. The magic extinguishes Jared's coat but otherwise misses him entirely. My descent slows, but his does not. I grunt as his weight threatens to dislocate my shoulder. But his grip slides down my arm to my open hand, and with a shake of my sweaty palm, he loses purchase.

He falls, his eyes wide with mounting fear, into the rocky river below.

The air pushes me harder, up, up, up, back onto the side of the cliff. Not flying per se but lifting, like I'm carried by a hurricane. I can't even breathe until the gale sets me down and slithers away like a serpent in search of tall grasses.

I peer over the edge, but Jared is gone. The river babbles below, the water holding no rumor of what it knows. But then, his body is likely long gone, washed away. I barely have a chance to feel relieved before black spots circle at the edge of my vision and the familiar hot drip of blood starts under my nose. I raise my fingers to it and the come away red. Damn it! I've overused my magic.

Phantom nudges my knee with their nose. "Better get inside before you pass out."

I nod, snagging the blanket off the ground and wrapping it around my shivering shoulders as I stumble toward the house. It feels like miles before I reach the stoop, but somehow I make it. I'm almost through the door when I spot the problem lurking in my driveway.

Exhausted, I wipe the back of my hand across my bloody face and ask Phantom, "What do I do about his Maserati?"

22

JOURNEY INTO DARKNESS

ELOISE

"We could hot-wire it," Maeve says.

"And drive it where?"

We're standing in the garage, staring at Denardi's Maserati. Earlier, after watching a YouTube video, I figured out how to unlock the gearshift and put the thing into neutral without starting the ignition. The keys, I assume, are in Jared's pocket, somewhere near his dead body, wherever the river carried him. I pulled my Jeep out and used it to nudge the Maserati into my garage, closing it off from the outside world in case Agent Fuller pays me another visit. Then all the adrenaline drained from my body, and I passed out for eight hours. Maeve had to wake me when she got to the house for our usual lesson.

She adjusts her glasses on her nose. "I don't know. Somewhere that isn't associated with you."

I shake my head. "If we move it, we risk someone seeing it."

"There's already the risk that someone saw it when he drove it here. It's not like the tiny town of Echo Mills sees many Maseratis."

I rub my still-aching face. My entire body hurts. Large red welts mar my wrist and upper arm. Half my face is black and blue. Even my back hurts. I lean against the door to the house, barely holding myself up. "Maybe we should just leave it here. I'll be gone after tomorrow anyway."

Maeve turns toward me with a start. "And then you'll be back. You'll go and then come back with Damien. You don't want this car here when you're back." Her eyes are wide, and the words rattle out of her mouth, laden with anxiety. It's the first time Maeve has seemed genuinely shaky about our plan.

"Well, I hope so obviously. But there's always the chance—"

Her phone rings. She holds up one finger and pulls it from her pocket. Her face pales a shade whiter than its usual alabaster. When she lowers the phone, she's shaking her head. "That was my Gowdie informant. The FBI has eyes on your front yard. They saw Jared drive in here but haven't seen him leave. Agent Fuller is coming tomorrow to question you about it."

I close my eyes and groan miserably. "That's the last thing I need, Maeve. Can't you delay him somehow?"

She drums her nails on the screen of her phone. "Oh sure, I'll just call the FBI and tell them the date is inconvenient for you. How's that, pumpkin?" Her voice is soaked in so much sarcasm it almost physically burns.

I fold my arms. "So what do we do with this car?"

Shadows coalesce, and Cassius forms beside us. He takes one look at my face and growls. "What's happened?"

I give him the short version.

He whistles. "As proud as I am that all our training has paid off, I hope Maeve can heal you. It will be hard to convince a blood brothel to take you in this condition."

"Yeah, I can fix her right up," Maeve says tersely. "Unfortunately, she might be in handcuffs tomorrow if we don't figure out what to do with this car."

Cassius ignores her attitude and turns to me. "The answer is simple. I drive the Maserati into the caverns under your house."

Maeve shakes her head. "The FBI has cameras on the property. They'll see you."

"Do you have a photograph of the attacker?" Cassius asks.

I pull out my phone and Google Jared Denardi, then show the resulting picture to him. Seconds later, a man who looks surprisingly like Jared climbs into the Maserati and starts the engine.

I punch the button to open my garage, and a disguised Cassius backs down the driveway. As far as the FBI is concerned, Jared has left the building.

Maeve opens the door to the house. "Come on. Cassius is right. We need to get you healed up."

AFTER EVERYTHING, we all decide it's not safe for me to stay at Harcourt Manor. If someone comes looking for Jared, either another Denardi or Agent Fuller, I might not make it to the auction. The madams only come up from

Night Haven for new blood once a month. I can't miss this one.

Damien has been down there far too long as it is. Although I believe he's alive because I can still feel the bond between us, it's like someone has lodged a pebble in a chamber of my heart. It will never beat the same until the day he's free. I'm done waiting. I'm done begging for help. Tonight I go after Damien myself.

After I pack a single bag made up of tactical gear, courtesy of Cassius, along with a few regular outfits, I give Maeve the tightest hug I can. Then Cassius and I climb into my Jeep, Phantom curled in the back, and we leave Harcourt Manor. He drives until the sun threatens a silvery glow on the horizon, when I take the wheel and he recedes into the shadows of the back seat. He has a friend, someone in the Lamia coven's network, with an apartment in the Dakota building in Manhattan.

We spend the day there. At twilight, we take a cab to a nightclub called Wicked Divine.

"How exactly will this work?" I ask as the cab comes to a stop in front of the club. I'm feeling jittery. "You called it an auction. Am I going to be led out on a stage and bid on like a piece of furniture?"

Cassius helps me out of the car and leads me inside. "That's happened in the past, but for you, no. You're not being sold into the life. You're going in voluntarily. I'll take you to a party. You'll introduce yourself to the madams. If they like you, they'll offer you a position."

"So it's like a job interview. Should I have dressed up?" I'm wearing jeans and an emerald-green sweater. Nothing embarrassing but not an outfit I'd wear to impress someone.

"No one will care what you're wearing." His eyes darken. "All they'll care about is the scent of your blood and your ability to be agreeable. You *can* pretend to be agreeable, right?" He grins.

I feign offense. "When have I ever not been agreeable?"

He chuckles. "Tony and Jared Denardi might remember a time had they lived to tell the tale."

I shrug a shoulder and smile wider. "You mess with the bull, you get the horns."

We exchange smiles. He guides me to the lower level, sticking to the shadows before stopping outside a conference room. "This is where I leave you." I can't hide my surprise or disappointment. I thought he'd escort me inside. "I'm not supposed to be in this territory."

I blink back the sting of tears. "Of course. You've risked enough." I give him a swift hug and close my eyes when he hugs me back. "Thank you, Cassius, for everything."

"I hope to see you again soon and with Damien at your side, but if not, then later when we meet in the Darklands."

"What are the Darklands?"

He glances down at his toes and then gives me a sad smile. "That is the name we call the place shades go in the afterlife."

He means if I die. I force a smile at the sober thought. "But I'm not a shade."

His eyes crinkle at the corners. "In Tenebris, we worship a group of gods and goddesses. The goddess of death is called Thanesia. It is said she favors brave warriors and loyal mates. As you are both, I must believe she'd welcome you with open arms."

I sigh. "I hope not to give her the chance."

He nods and takes my pale hand in his dark one. "One more thing, Eloise. If you have the option, choose Marabella's. She treats her wards well, and the brothel is the closest to the palace. It will give you the greatest opportunity to serve members of the royal court and learn when you might find an audience with the queen."

I swallow hard and nod. "Marabella's."

With one more bow, he breaks apart into shadow and slips from my fingers.

And then I'm alone.

23

THE RED DOOR

ELOISE

The voices that filter into the hall from the meeting room don't sound afraid or depressed; they sound excited. As I pull open the door and enter the brightly lit room, I'm surprised to find servers mingling among the participants with trays of canapés and champagne. Men and women are gathered around small tables, caught up in animated conversations with people holding clip-boards. I assume those are the madams. I pause in the entryway, wondering which table is Marabella's.

"It's strange how you can see it," a woman beside me says. Dressed in a white sundress with tiny red flowers, the petite blonde seems better suited for Sunday brunch than an interview for a blood brothel.

"See what?"

An eerie intensity slips into her expression. "The thirst for death. You don't choose this unless some part of you longs for the end."

I gulp. I'm here for Damien, but she's right that I'm willing to die rather than let him go. What has happened to her to bring her to this point? I force a shallow smile. "Well, my Grams always said the end of one thing is usually the beginning of something else. Maybe for some of us this isn't about longing for death but for change."

She shrugs. "What is change but a sort of death?"

I lick my lips. "Nothing to be afraid of then. I've been through my fair share of change."

Now she gives me a certain nod. "I'm Olivia."

"Eloise."

She turns back toward the heart of the room. "I hope to see you on the other side of the red door, Eloise."

She drifts off toward the crowd. I watch her go, noticing how people rotate from one table to another. Speed dating for blood brothels. I take a deep breath and choose.

At the first table I try, an older woman with the lanky build and perfect posture of a former ballerina speaks in a heavy German accent. She addresses a man in line ahead of me. "Tell me why you want to work in Night Haven."

The man scratches his scruff of a beard. Tattoos cover both his exposed arms, extend under his black T-shirt and up the left side of his neck. He's thin with dark shadows under his eyes and a few tracks on the inside of his arm that look like they might be infected.

"No place for me topside anymore. Served my time, but no one will hire me," he says.

"What were you in for?"

"Robbery and involuntary manslaughter," he mumbles.

I think back to what Olivia said, that everyone here is

seeking death. Maybe she's right. This guy looks like he's seen better days.

"And what is your tolerance for pain?" the madam asks him.

The question causes me to stiffen. Why is *that* a necessary question?

He offers her a shaky smile. "As high as it needs to be."

Without warning, the madam snatches the man's hand off the table and holds his arm over the candle at its center. He doesn't even flinch. Doesn't try to pull away. Just stares at her with dead eyes as the smell of burning hair and flesh blossoms around us. That has to hurt. Fuck, she's burning him alive.

My stomach clenches.

My eyes dart between him and the madam, growing wider as the torture goes on and on.

A noise of disgust in my throat causes her to cast a reproachful glance in my direction.

She releases him just as his skin starts to blister.

"Harissa's will have you." She flips through her clipboard and writes his name on her roster. "Take your things and go wait by the red door."

He slings a duffel over his shoulder and heads toward the back of the room where others wait with their bags. The madam raises her eyes to me, but I just shake my head and move toward the next table. Jesus, what have I gotten myself into? Am I going to be burned or otherwise tortured before I find a way to get to Damien?

I steady my breath. No, Cassius would have warned me if that were the case. I lift my chin and focus again on Damien. He's probably being tortured right now because he refuses to give up my name. I have to be brave. Cassius said to try for Marabella's. Which table is Marabella's?

I stroll through the room, listening as I pass each table. I pause when a heavyset woman with the voice of a drill sergeant announces, "Be aware, Marabella's only has two openings this time around, and we already have over twenty interested candidates."

A few people leave the line to take their chances with another house. I get into line.

The madam of Marabella's is an older brunette, mid-forties, with an ample bosom and a hearty laugh. Dressed in a plaid shirt and black leggings with her curls sloppily clipped behind her head, she looks more like a neighborhood mom than the manager of a blood brothel. I watch her quickly dismiss the five women in front of me one by one. At least she isn't burning anyone. But I swallow down nerves anyway. I need Marabella's. I have to get to Night Haven. I can't wait another month.

"Next!" She flips the paper on her clipboard.

My palms are sweating. She *has* to choose me. Somehow I need to make it through that red door, and I trust Cassius that Marabella's will make my mission easier. I step up to the table.

"Name?" She scans my hair, my face, then shifts so she can see my body behind the table. She didn't do that with the others. Will she weigh me and check my teeth too?

"Eloise Harcourt," I say.

"Marabella," she says by way of introduction. "Have you been a donor before?"

"Only for my boyfriend."

She looks up at me, narrowing her eyes. "We can't have

jealous vampires storming our doors all hours of the night."

Fuck. Why did I say my boyfriend? She's going to dismiss me. "You won't. He's… no more." I swallow.

"Met the sun, eh?"

"Yes."

"But before, when you were together, you had sex with him?"

"Uh, yes." A chill goes through me despite the relative warmth of the room.

"Good." The woman gives a throaty laugh. "We don't require it of our donors, but you'll have the option. It's a benefit that you understand what you're getting yourself into. Vampires aren't known for being soft and sweet with their meals."

My time with Damien flashes through my head. I will never agree to sex with anyone else, but she doesn't need to know that. "No. Definitely not."

"All right. You can go. I'll let you know when I make my decision." She turns her attention to the woman waiting behind me.

I clear my throat. "One more thing," I blurt. I have to make her choose me. "My blood is special."

Marabella turns her attention back to me slowly, her lip curled in annoyance. "Is that what he told you, sweetheart? Everyone's blood is special when one of 'em wants at your neck." She gestures for me to step aside.

I lower my voice. "Um, no. I mean I met a vampire when I was in Chicago named Cassius. He's the one who told me."

Now I have her attention. Cassius didn't give me permission to use his name, but I assume his recommendation of Marabella's was based on personal experience, and no woman would easily forget a man like him. "You've known Cassius, have you?" She gives me another once-over.

I nod. "He's a friend. Actually, he's the reason I'm here. He said Marabella's was the best and I should seek you out personally."

She taps her clipboard. "And he told you to tell me your blood was special?"

"Yes. Unusual. Rare, he said."

With a lick of her bottom lip, she motions to a bored-looking man standing in the corner. As soon as he moves, I know he's a vampire. He's too quick to be human.

"We're in need of a taster, Perceval. If you please." She motions to me.

I hold my arm out toward the vampire, wrist up. His oversized amber eyes spark with a sudden curiosity, and he lowers his nose to my vein. I feel air brush my wrist as he inhales. I'm careful not to flinch when he strikes. The bite isn't deep. Just a nip *at first*. But as the first drops hit his tongue, I feel his fangs drive deeper and his mouth seal over the wound. I can't restrain my gasp no matter how much I want to appear an experienced donor in front of Marabella. Perceval is taking a lot of blood, *fast*. He draws my arm closer to him, cradling it from wrist to elbow. I have no choice but to stumble forward until I'm flush against his side.

A silver blade sings through the air and presses into Perceval's throat with a sizzle. A bead of blood forms on its edge.

"Let her go," Marabella demands.

The vampire stops drinking and seals the wound with

one last languid lick. The silver has left a burn under his Adam's apple, but he does not release his hold on my arm.

Marabella grips the handle of the blade tighter. "I said a taste, Perceval. If you ever want to grace my halls again, you'll leave it at that."

He reaches out and brushes a strand of my hair out of my eyes. "I'll buy her," he declares. "I want her for myself. I'll pay you anything you ask."

Marabella grabs my hand and pulls me behind her, that heady laugh filling the air. "Buzz off. You don't have the coin for what she's worth. If you want another go at her, you'll need to wait until she starts work."

My heart leaps in my chest, pounding hopefully at the promise in her words. Perceval backs away, but not before I notice the bulge in his jeans. He's hard and still looking at me like he might consider murdering Marabella to get to me.

The madam scowls, her eyes flicking from his crotch to his still-extended fangs. The silver blade is still in her hand, and she doesn't lower it. Another vampire moves in from a neighboring table and stares Perceval down. He slinks back to his corner.

Marabella turns to me, her face transforming to pure happiness as she tucks the knife away. "Eloise, I'm pleased to offer you a position at Marabella's, effective immediately."

"I accept." I have to stop myself from squealing.

The next girl in line releases a disappointed grunt, but Marabella ignores her. "Grab your bag and wait over there. She points to the queue forming at the back of the room near the red door. I roll my little bag to the back of the line, feeling Perceval's gaze on me. Every time I glance his way, he's still staring.

"Damn, your blood must be the bomb." Olivia steps into line behind me.

I shrug, not wanting to draw attention to myself. "I guess."

"No, really. The vampires they choose as tasters are known for their control. They have to be, or a lot of girls could end up dead. He's so enamored he can't take his eyes off you. If Marabella wasn't such a badass and the other taster hadn't moved in to back her up, I think he might have thrown you on the floor and had his way with you."

A shiver travels through me again. Is this what waits for me on the other side of the door? Will any vampire who tastes my blood try to rape me if I don't have a blade pressed to his throat? And if something awful happens to me in my quest to get closer to the queen, will Damien forgive me?

"Don't look so worried," Olivia says through a crooked grin. "The madams don't allow them to have sex with you unless you're willing. Some of the donors are in their sixties and seventies. They say they have the purest blood. The houses protect the blood. Sex is never demanded."

I release a breath I don't remember holding, and a tension in my shoulders eases.

"Anyway, most vampires find taking blood far more intimate than sex."

"Seems like you know a lot about vampires," I mumble, growing more anxious as the people in the room that weren't chosen for a brothel are dismissed. This is really happening.

She laughs. "Yeah. This is my second time."

I do a double take. "You've been a donor before?"

"Three years ago. I thought I wanted something else, but there are definitely benefits to this life. You'll see. The rush you get when they bite is addictive. Your living expenses are completely covered, and if you manage to find a patron, the perks are amazing. Where did you end up?"

"Marabella's," I say.

She grins. "That's both of us then. Best house in the city."

Perceval claps his hands at the front of the group. "All those with house contracts, follow me. Stay with the group. If you fall behind, I can't guarantee your safety."

He turns, and I see the blood lock on the door. Pressing his thumb to the pad, he opens it, and the people in front of me begin to file through.

"Once we pass through that door, our lives are going to change forever," Olivia murmurs.

Don't I know it. I roll my bag over the threshold and follow the others into a dark passageway.

24

MARABELLA'S

Now I understand why Sabrina didn't want to antagonize Queen Valeska. Night Haven is enormous. The subterranean world on the other side of the door goes on and on. For a vampire, the distance is probably nothing, but my Apple Watch says we've walked two miles by the time we reach a train that Perceval declares will take us to our houses. To my disappointment, there are no seats. But then everything here is designed for creatures that don't get tired or need to sit down. Olivia and I cling to a metal pole on one end of the car while Marabella chats with another madam at the far end. Four other donors shift nervously near a pole at the center of the car.

Phantom is curled in the corner, although no one can see him but me. I'm relieved. Everything about this journey makes me desperate for the familiarity of my family's presence. I hold on to the thread that binds us like a child clinging to their teddy bear as the train lurches into motion.

Night Haven, I learn from Olivia, isn't just one coven, it's twelve. Valeska has conquered the masters of a dozen covens along the northern half of the Eastern Seaboard.

"That's why they call it a hive instead of a coven. The queen lords over multiple distinct communities," Olivia says.

"Which one are we in?" I ask.

"We'll be in the capital city, the original Night Haven. Right next to the palace."

"Like New York, New York," I muse.

She chuckles. "It's a good comparison. And just as wild." She flashes a lopsided grin. "Hey, if you can make it here, you can make it anywhere."

We both laugh. The train slows to a stop, and a half dozen new donors and their madam exit one of the other cars.

"Reveria coven," Olivia whispers. "They have a high turnover, and between you and me, fewer people leave than come in. I shudder to think of all the bodies buried around that place."

I shiver, focusing on Olivia's perfect Barbie waves to keep myself from panicking. "Since you've done this before, do you have any advice for a newbie? It's all over-whelming."

She lowers her chin and looks at me through fluttering lashes. "Men are men, Eloise. These ones are just stronger. You deal with them the same as you would any man."

I chew my lip. "I haven't had the best track record when it comes to men."

She sighs. "I have three rules. One: never promise

anything you don't plan to deliver. You absolutely cannot change your mind with a vampire. Two: make everything about them. Don't say, 'If you don't stop, I'll die.' Say, 'If you kill me, you won't be able to feed from me again.' And three: if it gets too bad and you have to fight back, play dead first. If you struggle, it turns them on. But if you go limp, they loosen up. Makes kneeing them in the balls far more effective."

A wave of anxiety causes my stomach to clench. Great. I survived Tony to put myself in a position where every client I serve is a potential Tony. "Thanks. I appreciate the tips."

"Us girls need to stick together," she says. "Oh, one more thing." Her face turns grave. "I wish someone would have told me when I was new that it's the female vampires you should fear. The males are not unlike human men. They can be reasoned with or manipulated, but the females... They'll rip your heart out of your chest just to watch you bleed. Good news is that they don't use blood brothels often. Tend to get it for free topside. But if one does come to see you, mind yourself."

In the corner, I see Phantom lift their head and meet my eyes. My plan is to face off against the strongest, most vicious female vampire in this hive. Not for the first time, I wonder how I'll survive.

HOURS LATER, WE REACH THE CAPITAL AND ARE THE LAST TO disembark. Marabella leads us through a vibrant market-place where the scent of spiced meats combines with the aggressive solicitation of vendors selling everything from silks to furniture. At first I'm confused why a vampire hive would need food vendors, but when we reach Marabella's, I get it. The house is enormous. It's simple really. Vampires feed on humans and all those humans need to be fed. Unlike Lamia coven, I don't see a single blood bag among them.

"We have thirty rooms," Marabella says as we approach a mansion worthy of an emperor. "You'll notice everything is in the Japanese style with sliding doors and tatami mats. That's by design. The original owner was a geisha who was brought here from Japan by a soldier turned vampire in 1944."

"Is that a cherry tree?" I murmur as I follow her through the two-story foyer, past the front desk, and into the house proper. Two enormous, heavily muscled vampires guard the juncture between the waiting room and what I presume are the bedrooms. The tree takes up an entire corner, decorated with an explosion of fragrant pink blossoms. Behind it, a waterfall flows down a stone wall, giving the room the feeling of a high-end spa. A vampire waiting on one of the black leather sofas eyes us both as we pass, his eyebrow peaking when he sees Olivia. I try not to make eye contact.

"It is," Marabella answers. "Charmed to be forever in bloom. A gift from a friend topside."

"Marabella has friends in magical places," Olivia adds.

"I thought witches were forbidden in Night Haven." I instantly regret mentioning magic. Nothing good can come from me talking about it here. But Marabella only smiles and says, "Witches aren't welcome, but no one's ever complained about the charm. I think the vampires enjoy it." She stops at a door with a brass plaque that reads Room 101. "Eloise, you'll be here."

It's the closest room to the front desk, but I don't have time to think too hard about why that might be. She opens the door and leads me inside. The nondescript space might be any hotel room in America, but my eye falls on the bed. A black silk kimono lies on the spread, a cherry tree airbrushed on the back.

"When you're working, you wear the robe," Marabella says. She tips her head as she takes in my outfit. "*Only* the robe. You'll donate every third day unless there are complications."

"Complications?"

"If one of 'em takes too much and the doctor says your blood count's too low." Marabella frowns. "Our clientele is asked to show restraint or we charge extra. Most girls can eventually donate to more than one vampire a day. However…" She lifts her chin and stares down her nose at me. "After Perceval's reaction, we'll start you off with one. If you have any trouble, you pull that cord." She points to a red tasseled rope hanging from the wall next to the bed.

I look again at the robe, and my pulse pounds. I'll be practically naked when they feed from me. I close my eyes for a beat and remind myself of my purpose. I can do this. I walk deeper into the room and park my bag.

Marabella nods. "Dinner will be delivered at six, and you'll take your first client tomorrow." She moves to close the door, and I notice the lock. It's the type that takes a key to open from both sides.

"Excuse me." I catch the edge of the door before she can close it. "Can I have the key?"

Marabella smiles, and this time it holds an edge.

"Eventually. Don't worry, we'll bring you everything you need."

"What? Are you saying I'm not allowed to leave? Ever?" I pull harder on the door, but she pushes my hand aside.

"You'll be able to leave the moment you pay your fees."

I claw at the door again, and she shoves me harder into the room. "What fees?"

"It costs money to bring you here. To feed you and house you. Until your expenses are paid, you'll stay here. You'll find all the details of your contract on the desk." She gestures toward a manila folder. "This was the deal you made, Eloise, when you stepped through the red door. Welcome to Marabella's."

I'm trembling now, realizing the madam blocking my door isn't a friend. Neither is the woman behind her. Olivia smiles a crazy, Harley Quinn smile at me, her hands clasped on the handle of her bag. She gives a beauty queen wave as the door closes between us and the lock grinds into place.

25

MY DEBT

ELOISE

I lower myself onto the desk chair and look down at the paper inside the folder. "New donors are subject to the following fee schedule. Finder's fee: $1,000. Food: $150 per day. Lodging: $200 per day. Clothing, incidentals, and healthcare costs as incurred." I turn the page over. "Donor portion of service fees. The following amounts will be credited against the donor's debt as follows. Blood donation: $100–$300, blood donation with full body massage: $200–$500, blood donation with oral sex—"

I slam the paper down on the desk, nauseated at the tabulation of sexual acts and their fees. It doesn't take an accountant to figure out the system is rigged against me. Without performing sexual acts, I'll never pay off my debt. I lean my elbows on my knees and bury my face in my hands.

"You know, we could unlock the door with a little magic," Phantom says.

I peek through my fingers to find Phantom's emerald eyes twinkling at me. The thread between us snaps into place like a steel cable and I stand, hands balling into fists.

"Or we could blast through the door with a little more magic." Phantom trots into place beside me, excited at the thought.

The buzz of power grows within me, and the door starts to rattle in its frame. I'm tempted to knock it down and storm out, daggers in hand.

But then a vision of Damien's parched body baking in that silo flashes through my mind. I draw the power back into myself. "And then what?"

Phantom sits and turns his pointed nose to look up at me. "We charge into the palace and challenge the queen."

I snort. "I don't even know where the palace is. And if I could find it, I wouldn't know how to gain access to the queen. The guards at the front of Marabella's will surely overpower me even with magic and my daggers. I'm not good enough to take on two oversized vampires. If I survived, what next?"

I walk to the one and only window in my room. It's barred and looks out over a walkway lit by streetlamps. Vampires stroll past the house in both directions. "The queen has an entire army. I'd never reach her alive."

"You should wait and go during the day when the vampires are sleeping," Phantom suggests. It's a good idea until I remember why that hasn't worked for Damien.

"The palace is guarded around the clock by witches and humans. It's too risky."

"Then what are you going to do?"

Chewing my lip, I sink back into the chair and pick up the list of fees and services. Maybe I could refuse some meals in order to lower my debt. This time I read every word on both pages. In small print on the second page, it says, "Tips paid directly to donor can be applied dollar for dollar against debt."

Phantom gives a laugh that sounds like a fox's bark. "All you need is a few generous benefactors."

"Do you know any spells to make vampires feel more generous?"

The fox stares off into space for a moment, nose twitching. I picture my grandmother interviewing the rest of my ancestors for the spell. When Phantom's eyes meet mine again, his fox mouth sags. "Not without a host of herbs and a cauldron."

I take a deep breath. "Well then, I'll just have to trust that my blood is special enough to do the trick all on its own."

"You're going to go through with it, darling?"

I lean back in my chair, resigned. "I have to."

I TAKE MY FIRST CLIENT THE NEXT MORNING AFTER breakfast. At least I can say the food at Marabella's is good. I enjoy poached eggs on toast with a side of coffee and cream, delivered by a terse but polite female vampire in a kimono. Once she's cleared away the tray, I have twenty minutes to ready myself before the lock on my door turns and the vampire lets himself in. That's a surprise. No knock. No warning. I'm not allowed to have a key to my own room but they freely give one to the vampire who will feed from me. It hangs, gold and glinting, from a red velvet tassel nestled in his fingers.

He wears a uniform, red and black with a braided gold cord across the front of his tunic. Although he appears about thirty, I presume he's far older. Attractive, I suppose, objectively, although all I feel is dread at the idea of him touching me. The robe I wear covers me but feels far too much like lingerie.

I force a shallow smile. "Hello."

"You're new," he drawls, nostrils flaring.

I have no idea how this usually goes. What am I supposed to say? "I am."

His gaze rakes over me. "Marabella tells me your services are limited to blood donation."

"That is correct." My tone is matter-of-fact with no room for negotiation.

He sniffs as if he's disappointed I didn't take one look at him and change my mind. This vampire has an ego. He carries himself like someone important. Maybe someone from the palace? A frisson of hope cascades through me. If he likes me, maybe he'll give me information about the palace.

"Do you have a name?" he asks.

"Eloise."

He takes another step closer. "I'm Marcel."

In hindsight, maybe I should have used a fake name. Then again, if it mattered, if the queen knew who I was, she wouldn't be looking for me here. "I like your uniform, Marcel. Do you work at the palace?"

Another step closer. He runs a featherlight touch along my outer arm, and I try not to cringe away. "I'm the commander of her majesty's guard."

"Commander?" I have to catch my breath and am relieved when he preens, clearly thinking I'm impressed when in fact I'm terrified. I'm standing before the vampire who would, no doubt, be sent to kill me if Valeska knew who I was. "Have you ever met the queen?"

"Many times." He reaches for one of the curls resting on my shoulder and rubs it between his fingers. "Red. We don't see it often in our kind. It tends to fade toward brown after we're turned. Green eyes too. Lovely."

Marcel is dark-haired and dark-eyed with a silver ridge around his iris. While they cast their own light, they are nothing like Damien's. I try not to cringe when he bends his head and his lips brush the side of my neck. This is, after all, what he paid for.

I swallow hard. I'm ready.

He strikes, and for a moment I'm confused. There's no pain. Complete euphoria bubbles through my body. It's both similar to feeding Damien and completely different, like the difference between lust and love. With Damien, I've always felt both. This feels shallow, uncomfortable. My pulse pounds and my cheeks flush. If I'm honest, a dull but persistent throb begins between my legs. Biological responses to the venom in his bite, I recognize. My conscious mind wrestles against the feelings, rejects them, holds them at a distance.

Vampires are death. They hold death's seductive draw.

His swallowing becomes rhythmic, peppered by his moans of pleasure. I sag in his arms, weakening from loss of blood. "You've taken enough." My eyes flick to the red cord, so far out of my reach. "Stop. It's too much."

"Mmmm," he groans, drawing back slightly, then seeming to change his mind and sinking back into my throat. *Fuck.* Behind him, Phantom forms, teeth bared. But my training with Cassius kicks in before any magical remedy is required. I reach down to the split of the silky robe below my waist and palm the dagger holstered on my upper thigh. Just as Cassius taught me, I arc the blade between our bodies and press the edge into his throat, hard. The blade sizzles against his skin. That's a surprise. The blades must contain silver, like Marabella's.

"Stop. Now!" I command.

He releases me with a final flick of his tongue to close the wound. I half expect him to thrust the blade away. He's bigger and stronger. He could try to overpower me. But he looks at me with reverence as his long, tapered fingers rise to touch his lips. When I see he has himself under control, I lower the blade but keep it in my hand.

He clears his throat. "I'm usually known for my restraint." His bushy brown eyebrows bunch together over his hooked nose. "Your blood is… indescribable." He swallows again and again. "It's perfect. It's…"

I don't have to be a mind reader to know what my blood is doing to him. Beneath his pants, his hard length nudges my hip through my robe, and although he's just fed, his expression holds a different sort of hunger.

My stomach turns queasy at the thought. I slip the blade back into its holster and force myself to sound sweet as I say, "I hope you'll come see me again. I can donate every three days, although…" I look down at my coupled fingers, trying my best to look forlorn. "Marabella tells me my schedule is filling up fast. Maybe I could move things around to make room for you if you'd help relieve some of my debt."

I've never been much of an actress. When it comes to

the arts, my talents lay with painting rather than drama, but with my blood running through his veins, I can see he's impressionable, and I plan to make the most of it. I remember then, remember the fear in Damien's eyes when he found out I had magic in my blood. Fear of being blood bound. By feeding Marcel my blood, might I move his heart by magic instead of emotion?

Commander Marcel reaches into his pocket, pulls out his wallet, and hands me every dollar in it. His lids flutter as if he's confused by his own actions.

I fold the bills without counting them and slip them into the silky pocket of my robe. "Thank you."

He moves like he might leave but then turns back to me, moving so fast I have no time to protest. His lips slam down on mine with a passionate, although completely one-sided, kiss. I hold very still, teeth clenched, until he finishes. His eyes are sparkling when he pulls away.

"See you in three days." He winks, then unlocks the door and slips out.

Feeling woozy, I sink onto the edge of the bed. Only then do I reach into my pocket and count the money. Over six hundred dollars.

Phantom forms from the void again, eyeing the wad of dough. "I don't like to see them touch you," the fox says in my Grams's voice. "He came far too close to draining you dry."

Strangely elated, I hold up the wad of cash. "I don't like it either, but tips like this are going to get us out of here."

26

MARABELLA'S SECRET

ELOISE

Marabella's secret, I learn, is a shake that all the donors are given to drink with lunch. The girl who delivers it tells me it's charmed to help replenish my blood supply. The drink tastes like berries but revives me better than any espresso.

"Marabella is incredibly pleased," the girl says through a smile. "Apparently Commander Marcel was particularly taken with you—even offered to buy you. She refused, of course. She's anxious to introduce you to other clients and wants to keep you strong."

"Introduce me?" I scoff. "Is that what she calls giving my room key to anyone willing to pay?"

The girl offers a conciliatory smile. "We all knew what we were in for when we signed up for this."

I school my features. This unassuming young woman in a kimono is currently my only access to another human being and the outside world. I need a friend right now, and complaining isn't going to earn me one. "You're right. Sorry for the negativity. I'm Eloise. I should have introduced myself this morning, but I was too…"

"Nervous?" she asks. "We all are at the start."

"Oh, then you've been a donor before?"

"Still am. I'm Ren." She offers her hand.

I shake it and give her my first genuine smile of the day. "So you're a donor *and* you deliver food?"

She nods. "Yes, all of us who deliver trays are also donors. We do this on our days off. It's a way to earn money when we can't give blood." Her eyes shift to the door. "If they ever offer you a position, you should take it. It helps toward your debt and allows you to meet the other girls. You know, get outside your room."

"How long have you been here?"

"Three years. I'm one good tip away from buying my freedom though."

"Three years!" The schedules of income and expenses are unbalanced, but certainly a beautiful woman like Ren would make enough tips to make it out quicker than that. Unless I'm missing something.

She holds up a hand. "When I came here, I had a health condition that Marabella cured. My debt started out higher than yours."

"You're better now?" It would be rude to ask what was wrong with her, but I'm painfully curious.

She nods. "Three years sober."

Oh. I look her over again. She's the picture of health with dewy skin, clear eyes, and straight white teeth. "The past three years seem to have agreed with you."

She nods. "It was the right choice for me."

I take another bite of food. "Thanks for staying with

me while I eat. I think I'm going to go crazy in here for three days with nothing to do and no one to talk to. I tried to call my friend last night and couldn't get any reception."

"We're too far underground." She reaches into her kimono and pulls out a paperback novel. "Something to help pass the time."

I look down at the shirtless man with a sword on the cover. "Thanks for this." I have books on my phone I can read without a connection, but there's nothing like the feel of a paperback.

"Anytime. Oh, and it might not be three full days. They'll check you tomorrow, and if the shake works, you'll get another client the next day. Some girls take up to three a day, but Marcel told Marabella he took too much from you for you to see anyone else today. Wild that he admitted that."

"Yeah. Wild." I finish off my shake. "Um, is he really commander of the guard?"

"Sure is. Most of the girls in here would give their left tit to donate to that guy. Attractive, wealthy, and power-ful. You got hella lucky to have him be your first."

I eat the last bite on my plate.

Ren picks up the tray, looking disappointed. "I guess I should get back to work. Don't take this the wrong way, Eloise, but once they start letting you out more, be care-ful. Let's just say you are the nicest person working here right now."

I laugh. "You've known me for like five minutes."

"You can learn a lot about someone in five minutes." She's halfway out the door when I realize I'm allowing a wealth of information to slip through my fingers. "Oh,

Ren, can I ask you since you've been here for a while, do you know if the queen ever makes public appearances?"

She squints over her shoulder at me. "Why do you want to know?"

I shrug. "I've never seen a queen before, human or otherwise. Call it a dream."

Ren's brows lift. "When you put it in human terms like that, I guess it makes sense, but Valeska isn't that kind of queen. I've heard she comes out when they have military parades in her honor, and sometimes she visits the masters of the different covens to solidify support, but I've never seen her in person myself. Honestly, if you have your heart set on it, you might be disappointed. She rarely bothers with anyone but the elite. Well, unless you're chosen as one of her personal blood donors, and I don't envy anyone in that position."

"Why not?"

She sniffs. "Because in the three years I've been here, I've known a lot of girls who were sent to the palace. None of them ever came out again."

A WOMAN NAMED HOLLY VISITS THE FOLLOWING MORNING, dressed in a lab coat. She draws my blood. I must pass whatever test they run, because Ren tells me at dinner I'll have a client the following day. On schedule, a key slides into my lock and another vampire enters my room.

This one isn't in uniform like the commander. He's dressed in a bespoke suit tailored in a fabric that drapes elegantly over his tall, distinguished form. A diamond-encrusted watch glints from his wrist, and a gold ring sparkles on his finger. He's brunette like Marcel, but his eyes are lighter, almost golden.

I check the position of my daggers under the guise of straightening my robe and make sure my belt is tied tight. I might have to wear the robe, but I'm wearing it in the most conservative way possible. "Hello. I'm Eloise."

His eyes flick over me. "Marabella tells me you're the best she has."

Despite my desire to please this vampire and earn an enormous tip, I can't help but take offense. "I'm not sure what that means. We're women, not bottles of wine."

He offers me a charming smile, seemingly entertained by my response. "You only say that because you're human. If you were a vampire, you would understand that blood varies from human to human, usually based on their health or where they were raised. It's hard to find pure blood anymore. Harder still to find something new. Marabella tells me you're different."

I lick my lips and swallow. "You'll have to judge for yourself. I wouldn't know." I brush my hair to the side. "What's your name?"

He moves in closer, lowering his face toward my throat. He's taller than Marcel but narrower. He has to bend his knees to be on my level. His breath brushes my skin as he inhales over my jugular. "Everald," he finally answers.

My lips part to say something trite like it's nice to meet him, but I don't get a chance. He strikes. This time I'm more prepared. I stare at a spot on the wall, allowing my mind to drift as he drinks and drinks and drinks.

I'm about to command him to stop when he draws

back and seals the wound of his own accord. He wipes under his full lower lip with his thumb.

"I'm not disappointed." He sounds almost surprised.

"In that case, a tip would be greatly appreciated," I say. "I'm trying to pay off a large debt—"

"I'll pay it off. Whatever it is." He points at the door. "Let me negotiate with Marabella. I'll have you out of here by morning. You can come home with me."

I look down at my fingers, knotted in front of my hips. "She'll never sell me, but with a tip, I can make sure there's room for you on my schedule." I press a hand to my heart. "Please. If you can give me anything… whatever you have on you."

His eyes glaze as I speak, and he pulls his wallet from his pocket, handing me two thousand dollars from within its folds. I've never seen anyone carry that much cash. Not even Tony. "What exactly do you do for Night Haven, Everald?" I ask as I slide the significant wad into my pocket.

He sways on his feet like he's buzzed, a goofy smile on his face. "I own the marketplace."

"You… *own* it. Like a few of the shops or something?"

He shakes his head. "No. I own the entire thing. I rent the stalls to the shop owners. Nothing comes into Night Haven without going through me." He leans forward and whispers in my ear. "I'm a very powerful vampire, Eloise. I can get you anything you want. Anything you ask for."

I help steady him when he almost falls into me and find myself giving a genuine laugh at his confused expression. Everald is not a vampire used to tipping his hand, and right now he's not only showing me his cards, he's telling me how to play mine. He offers me a wild grin.

"Oh? Can you introduce me to the queen?" I say with a sassily raised chin.

His smile dissolves. "Don't joke about that, Eloise. The last place for you is with the queen. If I have anything to do with it, you'll never be within a mile of her." He slides the key into the lock and then he's gone.

"YOU DID IT AGAIN," REN SAYS, LEANING HER BACK AGAINST the door while she watches me eat. "Marabella told me to wait in here and make sure you eat every bite and drink your entire shake to replenish your blood. Apparently it's more valuable than gold. Everald absolutely begged her to sell you to him, and that vampire is not used to being told no."

I return the book she lent me and smile when she pulls the sequel out like she had it at the ready. "Thanks, Ren. These are keeping me sane."

"I'll bring you more if you tell me how you do it. Marabella is charging $500 a slot for you already. You're the highest-priced girl in the house, and you've served two vampires. Tell me the truth, are you taking it up the ass?"

I toss my spoon at her. "No! I only offer blood. That's it."

She looks at me skeptically and tips her head. "Seriously?"

I have to tell her something to appease her curiosity. She's studying me like the mystery might keep her up at night. "I grew up in a little town in Virginia with super-clean air and water and never went anywhere. I guess my blood has less pollutants or something."

She snorts. "Damn it. So it's nothing I can change about myself."

I frown. "You don't need to change anything about yourself, Ren. You're beautiful and the kindest person I've met since I arrived."

Her laugh lights up the room. "I'm the only person you've met since you've arrived."

Our laughter dies slowly, and I toy with the fork on my plate. "How long do you think before I can leave this room?"

She scratches behind her ear. "I don't know, El. Normally a couple of weeks, but the way Marabella talks about you... It's like she's found her golden goose. I think she's going to be damned careful before she lets you out of your cage."

27

OLD FRIEND

DAMIEN

I pace the confines of Valeska's room, breaking into shadow and testing every corner. There is no escape. I'm a prisoner here, as certainly as when I was surrounded by sunlight. Only a few days ago, I was ready to die, secure in the promise of one day being reunited with Eloise in the Darklands. Now my fate is far worse. Only with careful and clever distraction have I been able to evade Valeska's questions about Eloise. I suspect the only reason she hasn't forced the name out of me is that she wants me to give it to her freely, wants me to accept culpability in my mate's death so that I'll be more pliable once I'm hers.

That will never happen. I will never give it willingly. But how long can I deny her? With her poisonous blood in my veins, she will compel it from me eventually.

Unless I can find a way to dilute her influence.

A knock comes on the door and I break into shadow,

hiding in the darkness behind the bureau. A human meal is delivered to me once per day, a necessity for a shade. Only now am I strong enough to consider how to use the regularity of its delivery to my advantage. If I can find an alternate source of nourishment, I can purge Valeska's blood from my system. I might even be able to hasten the process by bleeding myself just short of death and then replacing what I've lost with a clean donor, preferably human.

Yes. The plan forms in my head. I will pounce upon the deliverer of my food, knock them unconscious, then drain my own blood before replenishing it. If all goes well, I'll be free of this room before Valeska returns.

I hear the door open. The wheels of the cart squeak into the room. The door closes again. The serving cart rolls across the wood floors into view. I hover like a storm cloud over the dark-hooded servant's robe, ready to descend with a violent blow. But pale, knotted fingers pull back the hood, and my plan is shot to hell.

I coalesce in front of the ancient scribe in my corse form. "Lazarus."

"Oh, Damien, gods it is good to see you alive." The scribe spreads his arms, and despite my disappointment at not being able to enact my plan, I embrace him. He is a true friend. I know that now more than ever.

"You've put yourself at risk coming here, old friend," I whisper, glancing toward the door.

He sighs. "It was necessary. I mean to warn you—you must not drink her blood. She's spelled it using a potion to bind you."

My shoulder's sink. "It's too late, I'm afraid. I don't suppose you have the antidote."

He frowns. "There is none. You must wait until the blood leaves your system."

It's a disappointing realization, but I'm suddenly distracted by the scent of the food. Hunger pangs cut through me, and I pull the dome off the tray. Chicken. Roast vegetables. After tearing the leg off the bird, I swallow it whole, bones and all.

"Oh dear. She's been starving you then?"

"Until recently," I admit. "I am only allowed to drink from her and supplement with these human meals, so of course I've taken as little blood as possible. The lack of nourishment has slowed my recovery."

He groans. "Then her blood is concentrated inside you. I fear it will be some time until we can break her hold. But this should help." He uncovers a goblet and hands it to me. It's full of blood.

"Lazarus, you brilliant male." I drain the cup dry, then tear into the chicken again.

"Had to compel the human servant to donate and allow me to serve you. I'm not sure I can do it again. It cost me. I'll need to visit Marabella's soon."

"I thank you, my friend. I will not forget this."

He studies me for a moment. "You truly will not give up her name?"

"I love her, Lazarus. She is more than my mate. She is the other half of my soul. I will not give her up. I would rather cut out my own tongue."

Lazarus nods. "I can smell it on you. Your mating scent even overpowers the scent of the queen's blood in your veins."

I finish the last of the chicken and start in on the

vegetables. "You've already done so much for me, but I must ask one more favor."

"Anything, Damien." The scribe's bulbous eyes shift.

"Find Cassius. Ask him to get a message to my mate that she's in danger. He'll know how to find her."

Lazarus frowns. "Cassius knows who she is then."

I nod once. "He does. He'll hide her. He'll protect her." I swallow hard. "I'm unsure if I can anymore. If Valeska commands me…"

"Say no more. I will do it at my earliest opportunity to leave Night Haven undetected."

"Thank you, my friend. I will not forget this."

The scribe bows his head, contemplative. "I never thought I'd see the day when I'd actively work against the wishes of the queen, but what she's done to you is wrong. The old laws are very clear that mating bonds are to be respected. Few in this coven are old enough to remember the old laws, but they still stand, enforced by our forebears. What Valeska is doing goes against everything our kind was founded on."

"I doubt Valeska understands the old laws or the consequences of breaking them. And I doubt even less that she cares. No one here has seen the forebears in decades. And I wager if they did come to enforce their laws, Valeska's power would render them impotent."

With a shake of his head, Lazarus disagrees. "The old law isn't words on paper, Damien. It's binding magic woven from the same stuff that animates us as vampires. She can never overrule it. That magic is why she can't take you as her mate while your true mate lives! She's a fool to ignore the law as she has."

I glance down at the empty tray. "You should go before she returns. I don't want you to garner her attention."

Lazarus gives a shallow bow and then grabs the handle of the cart. "I will seek out Cassius. Good luck, my friend. Remember what I said. The bond you share with your mate is blessed. Valeska has no idea the forces she is tampering with. The gods will not be pleased with her behavior."

I don't know what to say to that. Vampire gods are not shade gods, and I've never been an overly religious sort. As the scribe maneuvers the cart out the door, his age shows in his struggle. He's sacrificed too much to help me. "Feed, Lazarus. Before you go to Cassius. You look pale."

He gives me a nod of agreement, and then he's gone.

It isn't long before Valeska returns, followed into the room by a troop of servants and blood donors. The sun is rising. I can feel the fatigue in my bones.

"You look well, Damien. Stronger. That's good." She eyes me like one might a prized steer.

I say nothing. She begins to undress, her lady's maids removing her corset and the silver gown underneath. I avert my eyes.

"Damien, look at me," she says through her teeth.

I keep my eyes focused on the wall until my head starts to throb, tremors shake my limbs, and my blood burns in my veins. Slowly I turn my head and the pain abates. She's naked, making no moves to cover herself. I stare at her, completely uninterested.

Her gaze travels the length of my body, searching for some evidence of a physical response, but there is none. There will never be one. All I feel for Valeska is loathing.

When she realizes the truth, she snaps her fingers and one of her attendants brings her a red silk nightgown. The two humans help her into it. With a bend of her fingers, she summons one, tips the woman's head to the side, and sinks her fangs into her. Valeska never takes her eyes off mine as she drinks and drinks and drinks. I'm relieved when her command wears off and I'm able to look away.

"Soon your blood will be strong enough for me to feed from you," she says. "Once we've regularly taken each other's blood, our bond will be unparalleled."

I say nothing.

"You will be mine, Damien. You're only prolonging the inevitable by fighting it."

I don't hear her move, but suddenly her hand is on my chest and her lips are dangerously close to mine. I cringe away from her touch, breaking into shadow and moving to the other side of the bed. It's the wrong thing to do.

Her lips draw back from her teeth. "You dare reject my touch?"

"My biology precludes me from mating another," I say for the umpteenth time. "Enough of this. Release me, Valeska. Every day you spend with me is a day you could spend finding a true mate. Perhaps one of the coven masters or a captain of one of the guards. I am useless to you."

She growls, the feral growl of an enraged vampire. The two human servants take a step toward the door. She can no longer hurt me as she once could when I was mortal in the silo, but I can't hurt her either. She's commanded me not to.

"Enough games," she says through her teeth. She's

around the bed and in front of me in the blink of an eye. "Don't. Move."

My stomach fills with dread as her hand shoots out and grips me by the jaw, her claws digging into my cheeks. My growl matches her own.

"Tell me her name."

"Angelica." It's the name of her lady's maid. She didn't specify which *her*.

"Tell me the name of your mate."

"Little Dragon."

She squeezes harder, and I see drops of my blood fall to the floor from the place her nails dig in.

"Fucking bastard." Her eyes lift to the ceiling. "Tell me the legal human name of the woman you are mated to."

Fuck. No, no, no, no no! I try to fight it. I close my eyes and grit my teeth, then go for my own throat, meaning to rip out my voice box.

"You will not hurt yourself. You will tell me the answer now."

The words come up my throat like cut glass. "Eloise Harcourt."

Her eyes brighten and she releases me. I explode from her grip, breaking into shadow with a howl and tearing through the room. Blood sprays as I slice open her two humans. I paint the walls with blood. The bed. Her. I slice open the mattress. Wreck the lamp, the chair.

Only when I go for her closet does she say, "Enough! You will damage no more of my things! Form again now."

Reluctantly I do, but my rage and hatred for her cause my entire body to shake.

She picks up her phone and dials a number. "Yes. I need a crew in here to clean my chambers immediately."

Once she hangs up, she steps over the remains of her humans and heads for the door.

"Where are you going?" I ask through my teeth.

She laughs. "To talk to the commander of the guard, of course. He needs to find Eloise Harcourt."

I swallow, desperation burning like acid through me. "Don't kill her, Valeska. I'll do anything you ask. Anything you want if you leave her alone."

Her answering laugh is darkly wicked. "Oh, I'm not going to kill her, Damien. I'm going to have her brought here. And then I'm going to command you to do it."

She turns on her heel and leaves as I break apart on an endless scream.

28

DEAL WITH THE DEVIL

ELOISE

The third vampire I'm scheduled to feed isn't anything like the first two. He's short, balding, with a portly belly that precedes him into the room. He's Danny DeVito. The neighborhood plumber. Your best friend's dad.

"So you're the new gal," he says, a Boston accent creeping in.

"I'm Eloise."

"Name's George. Welcome to the *hive*." He shakes his outstretched fingers as he says *hive*, like I should be afraid.

"Uh, thanks?"

"Ahhh, I don't mean to scare ya or anything. It's just, you know, this is a new world we're all livin' in with multiple covens under one queen. I'm sure most of your visitors will be the type to kiss the ring. You might as well know I'm not really a fan of this new arrangement. But then, my coven was one of the last to be incorporated."

"You're the first to openly complain about it, but your secret's safe with me. It's not like I'm going to tell anyone. They haven't even let me out of this room." We both burst into laughter. I actually like this vampire. Bonus points that he hasn't looked at my boobs even once.

"I bet you're wonderin' how someone like me ends up master of the Liberty coven." He places both hands on his belly and shakes.

I stop completely. "Wait, you're master of the coven in Boston. When you say your coven was incorporated, you meant YOUR coven."

His lips draw thin and he nods. "Yepperooni. I know I'm not the type. Truth is, my maker was this really beautiful woman vampire who invested in a fuckin' money pit. I fixed some things for her. She liked my work. Decided to turn me for the free labor. Imagine my surprise when she got herself burned at the stake during the Salem witch trials and I inherited the coven." He smacks his lips. "Anywho, I still like to fix things, but as you might imagine, I'm not exactly the type to find easy donors."

I shrug. "I don't know why not, George. I think lots of human girls like a man who can fix things."

He waves a hand dismissively. "Ahh, stop. You're makin' me blush. Anyway, I come here when I'm in town. Marabella is a doll, you know. Always hooks me up with the nicest girls."

He takes a step closer, and I realize we have a problem. He's shorter than me. There's no way he's reaching my neck without standing on a box, but if I sit down, this robe is going to ride up and show my daggers. Not that George seems like the type to care. My instincts tell me he's trustworthy and only after blood.

"So, how do you like to take it?" I ask, shooting a quick glance toward the chair. He's not stupid. He knows what I'm asking.

"The wrist is fine," he rumbles.

I offer him mine and he brushes his nose across the vein. I hear him inhale, and then he bites. I feel the rush of venom, but it's far less personal than my other donations. I have no trouble blocking out the strange chemical reaction that inevitably happens.

George draws back earlier than either of my previous donors and politely closes the wound without being weird about it. "Yeah, you're delicious. I'm guessing Marabella is gonna have you booked into next year." He laughs.

"It's good to keep busy," I say because "I don't plan to be here that long" doesn't seem appropriate.

Without me asking, he pulls out his wallet and tips me five hundred dollars. "That's for you."

I stare down at the money. I should just say thank you.

"George, do you think anyone can stop the queen?"

He frowns. "You're brave to ask that question. Maybe don't be so brave with anyone else. But since you did ask, I'll be brave enough to answer. I thought there was one person who could stop her. Strongest motherfucker I ever met in my life. And right now she's got him jailed in that dungeon of hers. If she can take that guy down, I'm not sure anyone else is capable of unseating her. Especially if she wins him to her side. If she does that, our fates are sealed."

Damien. He's talking about Damien. As he pulls the key to my room from his pocket and exits with a quick goodbye, I know in my gut I don't have much time.

I'VE BEEN AT MARABELLA'S THREE WEEKS BEFORE I'M allowed to leave my room. By that time I've collected enough tips to pay off my debt and then some, but I hold it back. I know the location of the palace now thanks to Marcel, and I could ask Everald for a disguise if I needed one, but until I have a solid plan for gaining an audience with the queen, I need Marabella's protection.

I'm relieved to be wearing some of the clothing I brought from home after so much time in the silky robe uniform. An actual bra along with my jeans and T-shirt. I'm thankful for the opportunity to stretch my legs. I've kept myself strong with yoga and the exercises Cassius taught me, but I am woefully tired of the same four walls.

The guard who escorts me, a vampire named Samuel, leads me out the back door for what I'm told is a prescribed walk. As he opens the door for me, my jaw slackens at what is behind it. After the blooming cherry tree in the foyer, I didn't think anything else about Marabella's could surprise me, but I was mistaken.

A Japanese garden unfolds before me within the confines of a towering stone wall. A trail of raked pebbles beckons us to flow forward into the quiet space, the path edged by a lush jungle of carefully pruned azaleas, camellias, and mums set among squat stone lanterns. The hollow sound of bamboo water features tipping on their axis as they fill and empty welcomes me forward. It's irresistible. I step onto the stony path.

Only when I'm a few yards into the garden do I notice that Samuel is no longer beside me. I glance back to see him standing guard in the shadow of the doorway. Bright light drenches my skin. But we're still underground. When I look up, if I squint, I can make out the ceiling of this subterranean world. Maybe the vampires just don't like how intense the artificial light is. Fine with me.

I stride forward, following the bend of the path around a lone maple standing sentinel, its crimson leaves a riot of red against the muted tones of weathered rock and raked gravel. Beyond, a small wooden bridge rises from mossy outcroppings over a babbling creek. I'm delighted to find the flowing water populated by koi fish, living brushstrokes of orange and white darting beneath the rippling surface. The water winds to a small forest of dwarf pines that buffer the base of the stone barrier. Is it there to keep me in or them out?

"Ingenious, wouldn't you say?" Marabella rounds the corner and flashes a cultivated smile in my direction. Dark brown hair gathers in loose curls atop her head, and her ample figure fills the elegant lavender cashmere sweater and wide-legged pants in ivory silk she's wearing. Gone is the suburban housewife who ushered me through the red door, replaced by a shrewd businesswoman who owns every inch of her space. "When Sakura's lover built this place for her, she was wise enough to insist on a sunlit garden. I imagine her relaxing here when Night Haven became too much for her."

"Is it a charm like the cherry tree?"

She sighs. "No. Full-spectrum grow lights. Not strong enough to kill a vampire intruder as the sun would but strong enough to make them sorry for trying."

Ingenious indeed. No human could possibly climb out. No vampire would risk climbing in.

She leans her elbows on the railing of the bridge, staring out over the water that flows beneath us. I wonder why she's here. No way is it a coincidence that we are standing on this bridge at precisely the same moment, but the longer she remains silent, the more I wonder at her purpose.

"You never explained about the fees," I finally say. There's no emotion in my voice. I simply state the obvious to break the silence.

"We tell the donors who are smart enough to ask." She stands up straight and turns toward me, her legs crossing at the ankle. "Anyway, I doubt it would have changed your mind had you known. Your reasons for wanting to be here are your own, but I'm guessing money isn't the primary one."

I say nothing. It isn't a question anyway, and even if it were, I couldn't share the answer without putting myself at risk.

"People come here for all sorts of reasons. Some to get clean or sober. Some to lose weight. Some to escape abuse or neglect, homelessness, poverty, a life of crime. Others, like your friend Olivia, hope to convince a patron to turn them, give them immortal life."

"Olivia wants to be turned?"

"She didn't tell you?" Marabella gives an uneven smile. "Oh yes, she has her mind set on it. I seriously doubt she'll find a vampire willing to do it though. Few would risk it."

"Why? I'd think vampires would want to make more vampires."

She snorts. "No more than humans want children. Most who do understand it's an enormous responsibility. A maker is responsible for training his progeny and keeping her within the old law until she learns. And that's if both human and vampire survive the turning. To do it, the vampire must bite the human. Vampire venom is a must. Then the vampire must feed the human an uncomfortably large portion of their own blood, enough that it weakens them. And then they have to have the balls to kill the human."

"Kill them, as in fully dead and gone?"

"As a doornail. Once they've turned, it's very possible the new vampire will be stronger than the old, their body having their own blood to feed on. It's not uncommon for the newly turned to kill their maker. Valeska killed hers. Olivia seems like the type who wouldn't hesitate to do the same."

"I had no idea." No wonder the vampire population is far less than the human one. Procreating is a huge risk for them.

"But back to you." She studies me, drumming her fingers on the railing. "Since your arrival, you've donated to three vampires exactly three times each. Every single one has offered to buy you outright. They've all made me offers. Did you know that?"

Ren did tell me as much, but I shake my head. I want to hear her version of it.

"When I told him you were too valuable to sell, Commander Marcel paid a premium to book a regular spot with you until the end of the year. He's a handsome vampire. Usually chooses a donor who allows sex or goes topside to enchant a human into getting it for free. You seem to be his catnip, Eloise."

I shrug. "I told you Cassius said my blood was special."

"Everald is the very definition of suave and sophisticated. He's been around a long, long time, Eloise. I've never seen him shaken the way he was when he left your room the first time."

"I wouldn't know," I say, playing dumb.

"Even George was a bit flustered. George, who has been in love with me for years, barely remembers to flirt with me after visiting your room."

"George is in love with you?"

"I feed him myself sometimes for free." She quirks a smile. "What can I say? I'm a sucker for a kind heart."

I laugh. "He feeds from the wrist if it makes you feel any better."

She tips her face toward the light. "Interesting though, every vampire who has visited your room mentions you asking about the palace and the queen. That's a strange obsession for a new donor. Some would say a deadly one."

A chill runs through me. Does she suspect my true intentions? How much does she know about Damien?

I brace my hands on the railing, concentrating on the koi while I formulate a lie. "I am obsessed. With all royalty if you must know, even the human variety. It would be a dream to see an actual queen in person."

Her eyes narrow slightly. She's not buying it. "Why did you become a donor, Eloise?"

"I told you. Cassius said my blood was special."

She sniffs. "Yet you decided to come here and not stay with him. He'd have been a fine patron."

"I wanted to see Night Haven. I'd heard about it and it seemed adventurous."

She nods once. "I believe that's a partial truth. But I'm going to have to ask you to stop the bullshit. No one leaves their family and friends topside to live among vampires unless they have a death wish. And absolutely no human with half a brain cell wants an audience with a vampire queen unless they wish for death. So, maybe I need to be more direct about it. Why do you want to die, Eloise?"

What does she want from me? I scrutinize her, her manner of dress so different than the night I first met her. Everything about her screams shrewd and cunning. Cutthroat businesswoman. A woman who understands how to spot a lie.

She knows I am lying and wants the truth.

So I give it to her. "The man I love went missing," I start. "And I have reason to believe he might be living as a vampire within the palace walls, working for the queen."

She inhales sharply. "Turned?"

I nod, afraid my voice might betray my lie.

She frowns and looks back toward the creek. "You are too valuable. I won't sell you to the palace."

My blood heats with anger. "I never asked you to sell me. I only want access to the palace to find my lover."

"If you get within sniffing distance of the queen, she'll demand you. She'll want to taste you, and once she does, I'll never have you back."

I slide my hands into the back pockets of my jeans. "I can pay my debt. I'll buy my freedom and go myself."

Her expression morphs into a sneer, and I can almost see her brain calculating the money she's going to lose if I go. When she speaks again, her voice is low and placating. "I'll make you a deal, Eloise. I will get you safely into the palace to look for your turned boyfriend if, and only if—"

"Yes?"

"You agree to work for me for three more months no

matter what. Lord knows I'll never succeed in holding you longer than that anyway. I believe you could buy your freedom today, but don't think for a second you'll survive navigating that palace without my help."

My heart leaps. I can't believe my luck. If Marabella can get me safely into the palace, surely I can challenge Valeska, and once I do that, I won't have to comply with our deal. I'll either be dead or gone with Damien. I have nothing to lose.

"Deal," I say.

She pumps my hand once, twice. "Enjoy the garden, but not too long. You need your rest, sugarplum. For the next three months, your sweetness is mine."

29

SAFE PASSAGE

ELOISE

Marabella slips inside my door a few days later with an enchanted shake in hand. "He's here."

"Who's here?"

"The safe passage I promised you." Her brows lift as I take the shake. "We have a regular client who has certain privileges inside the palace. He's agreed to escort you."

"Great." My heart kick-starts into a trot. "I need to change. I can't go like this."

Marabella holds up one hand. "There will be time for that. First I need you to sign our agreement. Three months. Then you can go." She draws the contract out of the inside pocket of her blazer and hands it to me.

I flip through the pages and then look at her in disgust. "This says that you keep one hundred percent of my portion of services rendered to be paid back when the three months are up. You plan to not even pay me the portion I'm owed until the agreement is fulfilled?"

She shrugs. "I need assurance you won't leave early."

"What happens if I die?"

Her head tilts in annoyance. "I have no provision for that, but I don't think you will. The man whose care I'm placing you in is highly reliable."

I try to focus on the rest of the language, but it's not like I'm in a place to negotiate. I grab a pen off my desk and sign it. Marabella gives me a broad grin and tucks the contract away.

"Can I get dressed now?" I ask.

"Not yet. You will feed him first."

I stand, thrusting my fists toward my sides. "I've already fed Marcel today. If he takes much more, I'm going to pass out."

Marabella rolls her eyes. "That's why I brought you an extra shake."

I grab the glass off the desk and start sucking it down. They really do help with fatigue and recovery. "What's in these anyway?"

She waves a hand dismissively. "They're a concoction of vitamins and herbs developed by our on-site doctor. She goes topside every now and then for ingredients. Whatever's in it is supposed to increase your red blood cell count."

I stop drinking and narrow my eyes at her. "Is that healthy? These aren't going to give me cancer or something, are they?"

"Hasn't happened yet, and we've had people who have worked here for fifty years and counting and have never missed a shake."

"Fifty years!"

She sighs as if I'm the most exasperating person she's

ever encountered. I finish the shake, deciding that facing Valeska is a more immediate threat than the health of my liver, and hand the glass back to her.

"I'll send him right in."

I duck into the bathroom to wash my hands and freshen up. "Do you even know what you just signed?" Phantom asks, following me into the bathroom.

"I skimmed it," I say to the fox. "It wasn't exactly like I had room to negotiate."

"What 'services' did you agree to provide over the next three months?"

I frown. I thought the terms were the same, but the truth is I didn't read every word. "It's the same. At least I think it's the same."

"Oh, Eloise."

I rub Phantom's fuzzy head. "I need to get inside the palace. I'll never be able to challenge the queen from this room."

The key jingles in the lock. "Hide. He's here."

The fox dissolves into nothing. I check that my daggers are in place before charging from the bathroom to stand where I usually do. I adjust my robe, tying the belt tighter. Standing is the best position to greet my guests. If I sit, the robe rides up. Eyes wander. Ideas are had. I never want to give the wrong impression. I fold my arms over my chest and wait for my palace tour guide to enter.

The vampire who walks through the door is older with skin like parchment and large, bulbous eyes that make him look like a nocturnal animal. His hair is thin, and he's wearing a red hooded robe similar to a priest's. He stops inside the door and stares at me awkwardly.

"Hi, I'm Eloise. What's your name?"

He takes a step toward me, nostrils flaring. "Lazarus." He draws out his name absently, studying me with a furrowed brow like he's never seen a human before. He looks ancient. Maybe he can scent my special blood already.

"Well, Lazarus, Marabella says you can get me into the palace to search for my boyfriend after I feed you. Is that true?"

"Er, uh, yes. I'm a scribe in the palace library. I have unparalleled access and knowledge of every palace room." The words tumble distractedly from his lips as he tips his head in contemplation of me. I'm not sure what's bothering him, and I don't care. I want to get this over with so we can find Damien.

I hold out my wrist to him. "I hope you don't mind the wrist. My neck has had it for today."

He takes my arm and runs his nose along it, then drops his hold on me, absolutely horrified. He staggers back a step.

"Do you want to feed first or not? We can get Marabella back in here. If you want someone else, it's fine. I can get dressed and we can go when you're done. You have the key, just go back to the front desk."

The man doesn't move, just stares at me, dumbfounded.

"You know what? Never mind, I can call for help." I move to reach across the bed and tug the velvet cord.

"You're her," he says, stopping me in my tracks. I turn back toward him, a chill traveling through me.

"Excuse me?"

He takes a step toward me, those enormous eyes

holding wonder and fear and something I might guess was disapproval. "I can smell him on you. You're Damien's mate."

My hand lowers to trace the hilt of my dagger under the silk robe. "I don't know what you're talking about." My voice cracks. A muscle in my jaw twitches. I feel the connection between Phantom and me snap into place. If I have to, I will burn this vampire to ash. I will cut off his head, steal the key, and take my chances in the streets of Night Haven.

But he holds up both hands. "You're right to be wary. No one else would know, you understand. It's only he's my best friend, and I'm an old vampire with a highly developed sense of smell. Shades have a distinct odor compared to vampires. It's there, in your blood." He coughs. "Under all the other scents."

That disapproving look is back, and I get it now. This is Damien's friend, and he's probably appalled to see me working here. Tears come to my eyes at the hope that it's true, that it might be possible that this vampire is on Damien's side. On our side.

"I had to get into Night Haven," I say, voice cracking.

"Oh dear, don't cry. He wouldn't want you to cry. Your secret is safe with me, only I wouldn't put your trust in anyone else. You've taken a terrible risk coming here. There's a price on your head." He tugs a Kleenex out of the box on my desk and hands it to me, and just like that, I decide I have to trust him. I have to know what he knows.

"Is Damien still alive? Do you know where he is?"

Lazarus's wrinkled face turns serious. "He's alive, but—"

"Take me to him," I say excitedly.

But he shakes his head. "She's cursed him with a blood bond. If she doesn't kill you herself, she'll order him to do it, and he won't be able to refuse her. Oh, he told me he'd been fighting her, distracting her to avoid giving up your name. If she knew you were here, right next to the palace, I hate to think of the diabolical things she'd do to you or to him."

Crushing despair makes it hard to breathe. A blood bond with Valeska? She must have forced him to take her blood. Who knows what else she's forced him to do? And what has Damien done to distract her from me? I swallow down bile as my stomach churns at the thought of her hands on him. I squeeze my eyes closed. I can forgive whatever he's done. We can put it behind us. But now that I know he's bonded to her, it's not enough for me to challenge her. I also need to break that bond.

"How do I break the blood bond?"

Lazarus coughs. "Her blood must be purged from his system."

"I'm not talking to you, Lazarus," I say softly, looking at Phantom.

The scribe jumps when he sees the fox standing behind him, his hands flying to his chest although I'm sure it's been centuries since a heart beat there.

"What is that?" he hisses.

I'm not sure how to describe Phantom except to say, "He's my familiar."

"Then you're a witch?" Lazarus whispers. "You don't smell like a witch."

I shake my head. "No. I'm not a witch."

"But—"

I hold up a finger to Lazarus as Phantom answers my

question. "They say that if I feed Damien my blood, it will break her spell on him." I raise my eyes to the old man who is gaping at the fox. "When he was held by the candle, I used fire, but that was a cursed object, and this time it's his blood that's cursed."

He tucks his chin, looking positively aghast. "You broke the Gowdies' spell on him?"

I nod.

His face lights up as if he's just discovered the answer to an alchemical equation. "You are the bearer of the sigil. You are the key, forged of dragon's blood."

How does he know about my sigil? Damien must have told him, which means Damien trusts him. I turn my back to Lazarus and lower the robe to show him my tattoo. Behind me, I hear him inhale sharply at the sight.

"Centuries I've lived, and after all this time to be surprised, to find something new." His voice is breathy and filled with awe.

I straighten the robe, making sure everything is covered before I turn back around. "You might as well know I've come to challenge Valeska for Damien. Provocationem Ad Mortem."

His jaw slackens. "Oh dear, that is old law. I'd forgotten it existed until now. No one has invoked the challenge in centuries. How on earth did you ever learn of it?"

I swallow. "A friend of a friend." Mentioning Sabrina doesn't seem like a good idea. Not when she's the one who inspired the plan that brought me here.

His gnarled fingers lift to his lips. "We will need to find the box. We must take care to understand the rules before she does. Knowledge is far more powerful than might in these situations."

I interrupt him before he can say anything more. "You have to take me to Damien right away, Lazarus. I'm sure what you're saying is important, but our first priority has to be breaking the blood bond. If he takes my blood and breaks her bond, we can leave here without me challenging her at all. All you have to do is take me to him when he's alone."

The ancient scribe toys with the neck of his robe, silent for a moment. He nods to himself as if setting his mind to something. "I know just what to do."

30

THE PALACE

DAMIEN

My meal is late. Has Valeska decided she will no longer feed me? Or has she gone to retrieve Eloise now that she's forced me to give up her identity? There is no end to the woman's cruelty. I would not put it beyond her to not only force me to kill my mate but then to have her roasted and fed to me.

I retch at the thought and then make a decision, one I should have made days ago. When my meal is delivered, I will use the knife that often accompanies the meat. I will take the blade, wait until Valeska's order not to hurt myself wears off, and slit my own throat. It will be difficult to kill myself in this state. Almost impossible without sunlight. But I must try.

I will kill myself before I can be forced to kill Eloise.

Nothing can save my mate now. Valeska will have her by the time the sun rises. But if I am dead, we will meet again in the Darklands. We will be together in the next life. The thought makes me smile. The vampire queen has taken everything from me, but she can't take this.

Perched on the edge of the bed, I meditate, preparing myself for what I have to do. When the click of the key turning in the lock comes, I stand, relieved when I see it's not Lazarus wheeling the cart. My friend would likely try to talk me out of what I plan to do. This scribe is slight, almost womanly under the robes. I wonder if the vampire is new. It's odd for a scribe to serve meals, unless of course Lazarus sent them.

I spot the knife next to the domed tray. "You can go," I tell the scribe.

"I'd rather stay." The voice from beneath the hood is one I never thought I'd hear again. Delicate hands reach up and draw the cloth back from her face. I stumble backward.

"Eloise. How? Am I asleep? Is this another dream?"

She turns gravely serious. "You have to drink my blood, Damien. It will break the bond Valeska has over you."

She approaches me, but I back away, lifting a hand. "Wait… wait…"

"We don't have much time. Lazarus says that Valeska could return within the hour."

"You've met Lazarus?"

She nods. "Yes. Now do as I say and take my blood." She pulls her hair to the side. "Then we can get out of here."

I shake my head. "I won't take it from your throat. I don't trust myself. Eloise, she means to have me kill you.

She's ordered me to do as much. Sometimes she commands me in my sleep. What if I start and I can't stop?"

She hikes up the robes she's wearing and draws a dagger from a sheath strapped to her thigh. "Take from my wrist. If you take too much, I'll stab you somewhere that will heal."

Charging toward me again, she thrusts her left wrist toward my mouth, a familiar dagger held firmly in her right.

"That's Cassius's dagger."

"Yes. He gave it to me after he trained me to use it."

"Trained you to use it but didn't come himself?" I take her hand, so soft in my own, my eyes falling on the flutter beneath the skin of her wrist. Guilt and anxiety claw at my lungs and throat. What if I hurt her? Will this even work? I had her blood when I was bound to the candle, and it didn't break the curse. Although she did break it with fire. She has the power.

She's here at great personal risk to help me. Me, the person who betrayed her.

"Damien, we don't have much time. What's wrong? You're trembling."

"I can't do this. Not without you knowing the truth." I lower her wrist.

Her brow furrows. "Whatever happened, we can talk about it once we're out of here." She thrusts her wrist back toward me. She's right, of course. I'm not making sense. But accepting the gift of her blood when I betrayed her seems wrong.

"I gave up your name." My neck heats with the shame

of it. "I tried everything to avoid it. I'd hoped to die before…"

She's staring at me, tears in her eyes, the dagger gripped in her hand. "Drink, Damien. I forgive you. Valeska forced a blood bond on you, and whatever happened, I forgive you, but as your mate, if you don't drink my blood in the next fifteen seconds, I'm going to fucking lose it."

Hearing the command in her voice spurs me into motion. I strike, and the taste of her blood is like lightning flowing over my tongue. Heat travels down my throat, through my veins. I'm hard in an instant. It takes all my willpower to break from her wrist and close the wound with a flick of my tongue. I pull her against my body and bury my face in her neck.

"Did it work? Can you tell if the bond is broken?"

I draw back, my muscles tensing. "I smell another vampire on you. More than one."

"It's a long story," she says, taking my hand and sheathing her blade. "Let's try the door. Lazarus says she contained you to this room, right? So if you can leave, we know it worked."

She leads me toward the exit, but the barrage of scents haunts me. Vampires. On her neck. In her hair. "How did you get into Night Haven, little bird?"

She doesn't have a chance to answer me.

The door swings open and Valeska, flanked by her lady's maids, enters, wearing the same smug smile she's worn since the day she captured me. I tug Eloise behind me, but there's no hiding her. The queen's smile fades as her gaze traces over my mate's borrowed scribe robes, her face, her hair, and then our coupled hands.

"Who is this?" she hisses through her teeth, but when her nostrils flare, her yellow eyes spark with recognition and she bares her teeth. "Kill her, Damien."

Her command is direct, and I wait for the burning to start. Wait for the compulsion. It doesn't come. Eloise's blood has broken her hold on me.

"No." Our eyes meet and hold.

Then she moves. Fangs and talons bared, we collide. She tries to knock me aside to get to Eloise, but my hand closes around her throat and what do you know, I can squeeze.

The problem is I'm still recovering, and Valeska is as strong as she is wicked. She claws my hands off her throat and attacks. I avoid the stab of her talons by breaking into shadow and retaliate with a jab to her jaw that knocks her back a step. My shadows rush her, piercing her flesh like needles, but she heals almost immediately, and when she retaliates, she goes straight for Eloise. In shadow form, I whirl between them and stop the queen just in time, my hand gripping her throat.

But her lady's maids are screaming, and palace security pours into the room. The queen has backed us into a corner. Eloise is behind me, her dagger raised bravely toward the queen, but there's nowhere for us to go. A half dozen guards stand between us and the door. If I break apart to kill them, I have to release the queen to do it. And if I do that, she'll kill Eloise. I squeeze harder, but she's strong. Her talons dig into my hands. As a vampire, she doesn't need to breathe. I'm going to have to take her head off to end her. I raise a taloned hand.

Valeska's eyes shift to the side, no doubt hearing the guards move in behind her, and she grins. Grins like she knows she's already won. If I behead the queen, the arrows fly and Eloise is dead. If I break apart to take out the guards, Valeska kills Eloise.

My mind races. There must be a way.

Foolishly, Eloise moves out from behind me. What is she doing? Does she plan to get herself killed?

The air crackles with her ire as she says in the old language of the vampires, *"Valeska, I challenge you for Damien, my mate, under the law of Provocationem Ad Mortem."*

A thrum of power pulses through the room. It blows my hair forward and causes the guards to stumble back from us. Valeska uses the distraction to break from my grip long enough to claw at Eloise's face. Power like I've never experienced blasts the queen into the air. She crashes into the wall, denting the stone and sending rocks cascading to the floor. I look back at Eloise and then at Valeska, who is already climbing to her feet, albeit slowly.

Eloise sheathes her blade. "I'll save you some time while you come up to speed, Valeska. You can't hurt me, and you can't have someone else hurt me. And the same goes for Damien. I'll see you at the first trial." She takes my hand and pulls me toward the door.

"What have you done?" I whisper.

"Stop!" the queen hisses from behind me. "You will *not* go with her."

Without a glance in Valeska's direction, I follow Eloise, even when the queen's wails of outrage send her guards scurrying after us. An arrow flies, and I whirl to block it with my body. But it hits an invisible barrier and crumples like crushed paper. This is old magic. This is powerful magic.

"Come on." Eloise yanks me toward the hall.

Behind us, I hear the queen scream. "Call the scribes. No one sleeps until I know everything there is to know about *Provocationem Ad Mortem.*"

31
CONTRACTS & PROVISOS

DAMIEN

I've never even heard of Provocationem Ad Mortem. Shades have no such magic in Tenebris. "Explain, little bird."

"Each participant completes three trials." She looks over her shoulder as we wind our way through the halls toward the exit. She has her hood up, and she's taking me through the scribes' passages. Lazarus must have shown her this. "The trials will be chosen for us by rolling dice. There's a box. Sabrina showed it to me, and I thought I understood, but Lazarus told me more."

"Sabrina?"

"The master of the Lamia coven. I went to Chicago after you gave me Cassius's address."

"For you to see Cassius, not visit with a vampire master." My protective instincts are working at a fever pitch, but the blood pounding in my ears is my mating instinct obsessing over the vampire stench on her.

"The full moon's light shines on these octagonal silver disks that open the way for each trial. We'll be in two different trials based on our abilities. We won't fight each other. The winner is decided by magic and displayed in a mirror on the lid of the box. The winner of two out of three trials wins you as their mate."

"What happens to the loser?"

"The loser is executed at the discretion and in the manner the victor sees fit."

Rage and fear battle for dominance within me. "And you knew all this before you challenged her?" I grit out.

She looks my way, her face a bit paler than before. "I didn't know the trials were once a month. I thought they were like three days in a row. And I didn't know that if I lose, Valeska can choose to torture me or something. But I understood the rest of it."

"Gods. How could you take such a risk?" I drop her hand. "A human with a few magical abilities is no match for a vampire queen. Do you even realize the mess you've gotten yourself into?"

She stops short. We're just inside a stained-glass door that leads to the stacks and a rear exit close to the market-place. The light from the next room paints her mouth in reds and purples and sends a dark shadow across her eyes.

"Do you even realize the mess I've gotten us out of?" she snaps, planting her hands on her hips. "The last time I saw you, she was torturing you. You were ready to die. I was not going to let that happen. The plan was to break her blood bond and sneak you out of there, but that option went up in smoke when the queen returned early. And well, we were not getting out of that room alive without me using this magic."

The fire in her voice burns me. I am torn between blessed relief to see her again and horror that she must fight for us, fight to the death. It should be *me* fighting. It should be me, not her, in the trials.

Eloise releases a deeply held breath. "Until such time as a winner is declared, no harm can come to either challenger or the mate in question. We can be together for the length of the challenge, and she can't do anything about it."

She throws open the door, and we walk through the stacks. Once she's checked we're alone, she sheds the red robe, folds it, and leaves it behind a shelf of books.

"The full moon is in *three days*." My stomach sinks.

"Yes. That's the first trial. Lazarus says the challenge will take place in the silo where the moonlight can reach the disks. Until then, we're both safe."

"Safe?" Is she joking? Three days. Three fucking days.

We're on the move again, and this time we don't stop until we're outside the palace grounds on the edge of the marketplace. She finds a sheltered corner behind two tents and draws me into it, away from the crowds. Bending over, she braces herself on her knees and draws in a deep, shaky breath, as if the events of the day are finally sinking in. All the rage swirling in me about Valeska, our situation, the risks she's taken, the fucking scent of other vampires on her skin, it all dissolves at the sight of her mounting panic.

I force my voice softer but can't completely strip the embers of anger from it. "My little bird." I hook my knuckle under her chin, lift her face to look at me.

Her eyes are red and lined with silver. I draw her into my arms. Gods, I never thought I'd feel her against me again, the heat of her, the soft touch of her skin, the scent of her hair. I capture her lips with mine, and we kiss as if the answer to everything lies within each other. Maybe it does. Maybe the entire universe revolves around this connection between us. It certainly feels that way.

She breaks into frantic sobs, her fingers exploring my face, my chest, my shoulders, as if she can't quite believe she's actually touching me. When we finally break apart, she can't speak fast enough.

"Oh my God. Oh my God, Damien. I... I hoped. I prayed. But I wasn't sure—"

I smooth back her hair. "How did you even get down here?"

"I... I..." Her eyes dart over my shoulder, and she frowns.

I'm suddenly aware of onlookers. Of course our voices would carry to vampire ears. I grab her hand and lead her through the crowd that's formed at the entrance to our hiding place and through the sea of gossipy whispers. Word has come down from the palace. The words *challenged the queen* and *old law* lift above the unintelligible din.

"We'll go back to my place. It's not far. It's not as grand as Harcourt, but I'll be able to keep you comfortable during the trial."

But she's shaking her head, staring at something in the crowd now, and her face is not just pale but ghostly. I follow her line of sight to find Marabella walking toward us through the throng with a wicked smile on her face. I look between Eloise and Marabella, a deep dread balling in the pit of my stomach.

"How did you find safe passage into Night Haven, Eloise?" I demand, fury rising in my veins again.

Marabella appears beside us and takes Eloise's hand. "Damien, it is a pleasure to see you again. And this, I hear, is a happy, if not a bit scandalous, reunion." She smiles wider. "I'm afraid, though, we must be going. Eloise is contracted to house Marabella for another three months, and as she'll be taking the full moon off for each of them, we need to rework her schedule."

"No." I stare down at Eloise, thinking it can't be true, but the steady flow of tears drenching her shoulders tells me I'm wrong. The stench of other vampires on her skin punches me in the chest.

Her voice is small and broken as she admits it. "This is how I got into Night Haven. I've been working for Marabella and I traded three months for safe passage into the palace to find you. Marabella fulfilled her end of the deal. I owe her."

I am a man made of shadows but the darkness that coalesces in me is on a whole other level. I am barely contained violence. I am death with a heartbeat. I turn to Marabella. "I will pay you twice her debt. Release her now."

She scoffs. "That's not how this works, Damien. Her contract is for time served, not dollars. And now I think many vampires would pay all they had for a taste of the challenger's blood."

Beside her, Eloise's eyes are trained on the street, her cheeks flushed with embarrassment and dread.

"Marabella," I say through my teeth, "I will book every slot with her for the next three months."

The madam raises an eyebrow. "Come to the manor and I'll see what I can do. But you do understand that a donor with blood like Eloise's already has a full stable of regulars. Still, I'm sure we can fit you in," she says, wrinkling her nose.

She tugs on Eloise's hand, and they move away from me toward Marabella's, Eloise shuffling behind the madam like a child reluctant to go home. My teeth grind. Is the contract still binding if Marabella is dead?

"Don't do it, my friend," Lazarus whispers from beside me. Where did he come from? "Eloise needs all the support she can get right now, and if you kill Marabella, the backlash will be as much risk to her as the trials."

"You helped her do this?" I turn on the scribe, my growl drawing unwanted attention.

With a knowing tilt of his head, he says in a voice loud enough for anyone to hear, "Oh, Damien, you know as well as any that I never leave the stacks. Your mate stole those robes from the laundry. I had nothing to do with it. Why, there are six scribes who will confirm I was working in the library at the time she entered Valeska's room."

I grab his wrist and pull him close. "Tell me one thing, old man. Did you taste her blood?"

He snorts. "She offered. I could have, you understand. But I didn't. Chalk it up to knowing the consequences I would face if her plan worked out. You'd do well to remember, old friend, that Valeska had her name. If she hadn't done what she did, she might be roasting over a spit right now."

I close my eyes and release a breath, hearing the truth

in his words. He knows better than anyone. I release him. "I'm sorry. Thank you, Lazarus, for everything."

He gives me a firm nod. "If you need me, I'll be in the chapel, praying she can win."

I watch him stride toward the palace, and then I break into shadow and race toward Marabella's.

32

CONFESSIONS OF A BLOOD WHORE

ELOISE

"Three months? You knew. Somehow you knew what I was here to do." I point an accusing finger at Marabella, my eyes stinging with tears.

She shakes her head. "I didn't know the specifics. I certainly didn't know you were Damien's mate! Congratulations on landing that fish, by the way, and you'd best know you have made no female friends today." She winks at me.

I wipe beneath my eyes, my face feeling swollen. "Why three months if you didn't know?"

"Because, Eloise, no one who looks like you with blood like yours sells themselves to a blood brothel without an ulterior motive. You were obsessed with the palace. I suspected you were up to something with someone of means. If I'm going to lose you, I'm going to have three months of top earnings for my trouble."

I follow her up the steps and back into Marabella's, through a packed waiting area. I feel a dozen eyes track me through the room. "Please," I say as she lets me back into my room, "Just Damien. He'll pay you anything you want. I'm sure he will."

She sighs. "Look, I like Damien. He was once a very good customer. I'm sure he'll be visiting me with an offer. But you have three slots a week to fill, honey, and he only needs one of them."

I shake my head. "I won't do it."

She comes into my room and closes the door behind her. "Have you bothered to stop and consider I've done you a favor?"

"What the fuck are you talking about?"

She tips her head. "I sent you the best of the best, Eloise. Marcel—the commander of the guard—if he gives the word, the entire army will bow down to you. Everald —a vampire so wealthy he controls the marketplace. He can get you any weapon, anything you need. And George —did he tell you he's the master of the Liberty coven? They were forced into this hive because they didn't have the numbers to fight her, but he's no fan of Valeska's, I'll tell you that."

"Are you actually trying to convince me you sent those vampires to me out of the goodness of your heart?"

She scoffs. "Certainly not. I did it for money like I do everything." She says it flippantly, and I get the strongest sensation that she's... lying. But why would she? "I'm just trying to help you see what's right in front of you. These are powerful men, Eloise. Powerful allies to have in your corner. And they are bonded to that strange and luscious blood of yours. You should be thanking me for holding you to this contract. It gives you an excuse to maintain those connections. They just might prove useful."

"I'm mated to Damien. He will never allow another to feed from me."

She narrows her eyes and approaches me. "Then it's up to you to convince him he must."

I roll my eyes in frustration.

"You haven't been in Night Haven long, so let me tell you how this will work. In three days' time, you will meet Valeska in that silo, and all the elites of Night Haven will gather to watch. They'll take bets. They'll cheer on their favored competitor. Do you seriously want everyone in that room betting on Valeska? Or would you rather have some of the most powerful vampires in her coven shouting your name?"

I'm speechless. A deep pit in my stomach tells me she's right. Marabella isn't my friend, but she does have an interest in keeping me alive. I suddenly realize how valuable that is. I give her a silent nod.

Unspoken questions hang between us, details of my contract, of what she'll expect of me. But I'm struck silent by her sharp, unwavering scrutiny. Marabella has questions too, ones she's deciding not to ask. Finally she leaves, the lock clicking into place behind her.

I throw myself onto the bed, burying my face in the nest of my arms as the tears flow. The way Damien looked at me, like I'd betrayed him by donating my blood to a vampire, tells me everything I need to know. He was so concerned with me forgiving him for telling Valeska my name. Who knows what else he did with her under her influence? I forgave him instantly. I understood it wasn't his fault. But when it was time for him to forgive me, to understand what I had to do to save him…

My heart aches as if it's tearing down the middle. What if I win Damien only to find out he can't look at me? Can't forgive me? What if he hates me?

I inhale sharply when I feel a hand stroke down my spine. I lunge away from the touch. Has Marabella given someone my key so soon?

But it's Damien's hand that reaches toward me. Damien who sits on the side of my bed. I'm not sure how I can possibly have any more tears to cry, but I do, sliding my hand into his and allowing him to pull me into his lap. He rocks me gently, holding me firm as I fall to pieces in his arms. My monster. My shadow. My mate.

"She can refuse to allow me to pay your debts, but she can't stop me from using the shadows to be with you," he says softly.

"I thought you were angry. I thought you couldn't stand what I'd done."

Damien's expression sobers. "As I thought you would detest what I had done in your absence, how I'd taken Valeska's blood, allowed her to touch me, bent to her will and betrayed your name. You should hate me, little bird. I would not blame you for shrinking from my touch." His voice is barely a rumble but carries so much emotion. Shame. Anger. Frustration. Resolve.

"You had no control over any of it, Damien. I saw the way she tortured you. You would've died—"

"I tried to die. I would have preferred to die."

I shake my head vigorously. "No. No. Don't say that."

"There was a time I thought it was my best option."

Silence unravels between us. Nothing said, yet so much hanging in the air around us. "Did she force herself on you? I mean, did you have sex with her?"

Now he cracks a smile. "No." His attention shifts to the wall, to somewhere distant. "But she touched me, every-where, with her fingers, with her mouth."

I have to grit my teeth to keep from reacting to that confession.

"She wanted to force herself on me further. She tried. Only my mating bond made it impossible. I thank the gods for that."

I swallow hard, knowing in my heart that plenty of damage can be done by touching alone. Valeska violated him. My strong, virile warrior mate might not want to admit it, but a violation like that leaves wounds. Wounds that, if we survive this, will have to be healed.

He strokes my hair, his lips pressing to my temple. "Will you tell me, Eloise?" His voice is so low it seems to rumble in my bones. "How you came to be here. How you learned about the challenge. How many vampires you've fed. Let us have no secrets between us."

I adjust myself, straightening in his lap until we're face-to-face. And then I tell him everything, about Morpheus and Cassius and Sabrina and Tobias—how his brother Nathaniel's blood runs in my veins. About how it was Sabrina's idea for me to use the blood brothels to get into Night Haven and how she told me about the chal-lenge. I tell him about training with Maeve and then with Cassius. Even though it's hard, I tell him everything about my time here too. About the vampires who've visited me and why I signed the agreement with Marabella. And then, finally, about Phantom. The fox appears at the sound of their name and strides toward us, their bushy red tail wrapping around their feet as they come to sit and stare up at me.

When I'm through, he just stares at me like he's seeing me for the first time.

"Say something, Damien. Can you accept what I had to do to get here?"

His eyes crinkle at the corners. "The night we met, you trembled like a sparrow caught in the first freeze of winter. A true damsel in distress. I wanted to save you then. I could have saved you— killed Tony, and ended your nightmare."

"Sometimes I think I should have let you."

"But look at you now. A true warrior with magic at her fingertips and a familiar by her side."

I give a hard laugh. "I'm not sure about the warrior part. I can handle a blade though. It's saved me on a few occasions."

He frowns.

"And Phantom is my anchor and my ancestors. But I suppose you could call them my familiar. I have for simplicity. But my magic isn't like Maeve's magic. I'm limited when it comes to what I can do without a spell."

A hint of a smile turns his lips. "Anyone who claims you have limits is a fool. You can win this, Eloise." His gaze traces every part of my face, and his eyes sparkle. When he speaks again, his voice is heavy with emotion. "You *must* win this."

My heart swells. Damien believes in me. As much as he wants to protect me from all this, he believes I can win.

And that means everything. "I will. Sabrina told me that the magic makes the challenges fair. It won't give me a challenge I can't best. The question is if Valeska can complete hers faster and better."

He nods slowly, his face turning grave. After a few long moments, he says, "I asked you to share everything with me, and now I'll do the same. I believe you can win, but if the worst happens—"

"It won't."

He tucks my hair behind my ear, his fingers hovering near my temple. His lips part, but the words seem to catch in his throat. "If you..." He shakes his head. I can guess what he means to say—if I lose the challenge and forfeit my life. "I will end myself, Eloise. I cannot be mated to her, not only because she is vile and revolting, but because she will use me as a weapon for an eternity. That existence would corrode my soul, a slow, bitter murder of not only my will to live but of everything I am. I can't let it happen. Better I join you in the Darklands."

I swallow and press my forehead to his. My instinct is to fight him on this, to tell him to go on without me. But what he says is true. There isn't a life on the other side of this challenge for him if I lose. It would be a prison. I kiss him fiercely, communicating my acceptance of his decision even as tears sting my eyes again. He holds me until the noise filtering in from the street outside quiets.

"The sun is rising," he says, although the light doesn't change in this subterranean world. He just knows. He feels it.

I stand from his lap, resting my hands on his shoulders. "Will you stay the day with me?"

His silver eyes lift with one crooked corner of his

mouth. He brushes his knuckles over the curve of my cheek, his voice a low growl as he says, "Oh yes, little bird. You summoned me and struck your bargain, mated me, and came for me. Now that I'm free and we're together, you must know I've spent every moment since we parted, waking and otherwise, thinking of you."

"Every moment?" I flash a teasing smile.

He answers with a kiss. Damien's kisses are always intoxicating, but this one is positively silken. His lips dance with mine, and the heat of his tongue is the lick of a flame. It's hot and deep and just a bit sharp as his fangs get in on the action. I tap the tip of my tongue to one as he draws back.

My entire body feels flushed. It's been so long. Too long. The throb between my legs takes on an ache only he can quench. His hands land on the waist of my tunic, then drift down to grip its edge. He smoothly lifts it up and over my head and tosses it aside, leaving me standing in front of him in my bra and leggings, my daggers strapped to my thighs. He stares up at me through his lashes, and my heart flutters, my breath coming in pants at the longing in his eyes.

He draws the dagger from my left sheath and presses the cold side of the blade to my belly. "Did Cassius tell you that these daggers came from Tenebris?"

"No." My voice sails on a breathy and uneven exhales, as the cold edge of the blade barely traces up my skin toward my left breast. My daggers are insanely sharp, but I trust him even when he presses the point right under my pebbled nipple. The lace of my bra is no barrier, and I feel the icy bite, just on the edge of pain. Oddly, as cold as the steel is, only heat rushes to my core. Wetness pools between my legs. I straighten, my breath coming faster with my excitement.

"Oh yes. These are Stygian blades, forged by Stygarde's renowned blacksmiths in the belly of Mount Damocles. Warrior blades. Perfectly balanced. Made of the sharpest metal our world has to offer. It's a silver alloy, effective against vampires and shades alike." He uses the blade to cut the lace beside my nipple. Although I feel the edge, he doesn't so much as scratch my skin. My breast spills from its containment, the tip straining toward his mouth.

He pauses, simply staring, as if the sight of my breast is too beautiful, too distracting, to even remember to breathe. The adoration in his eyes sends a rush of heat through me. My breath stutters. He hears it and flashes me a wicked smile before removing the blade and replacing it with the curl of his tongue. He sucks the tip between his fangs. The scrape of his teeth against my skin is an exquisite fuel for the combustion happening low within me. I gasp and bury my fingers in his hair. The rumble of his growl tickles my flesh as he draws back and uses the dagger to cut through the other cup of my bra. I squirm as he suckles my breast, until I think I might die of wanting him.

The entire time, his eyes are on me, worshipping, hungry.

"You owe me a bra." I slant him a grin, then snatch my other dagger from its holster, bringing it to the collar of his shirt. I grip the cloth with my opposite hand and cut it off him, throwing the garment aside.

"The shirt makes us even."

I trace my hand over the smooth expanse of his broad chest, hard bands of muscle leading my touch south. I point the tip of my blade toward the tent in the front of his pants. "Will you remove those, or do I have to do it for you?"

His eyes dart from the blade to my face. "I think I'll do the honors." Tossing the blade in his hand aside, he stands from the bed, forcing me to take a step back as he toes off his boots and strips off his pants and everything underneath. I release the blade in my hand, and it clatters to the floor.

A naked Damien is an overwhelming sight. For a moment I'm left breathless. My gaze roves over the rippled landscape of his abs, thinner now after his time in the silo but as tantalizing as ever, up to the blocky structure of his chest and shoulders, then to his neck. His dark waves are longer now, down to his shoulders, but his face is exactly as it was the night we met. Strong jaw, full lips, hollow cheeks that hold a hint of hunger, and ice-blue diamond eyes that cut right through to my soul.

His lids sink low until he's looking at me through his lashes.

"Do you know what it does to me to see you like this?" His erection, thick and long, juts from between his legs, and I lick my lips, my body throbbing with need. "You're larger than life. You're like a god."

His eyes close as if the compliment causes him physical pain. I remember then what he's been through, what the queen did to him. I can't smell her on him the way he could smell vampires on me, but I make a silent vow that by the time this day is over, the only scent on either of us will be each other.

I fist his hips and turn him as I kneel on the bed, his intimidatingly large length swollen between us. Lifting my eyes to meet his, I load mine with all the love and longing I've felt these past months. His cock twitches at the feel of my breath, sending a jolt of need through me. Our gazes locked, I flatten my tongue against his shaft and lick him base to tip.

He moans, his hands finding my hair and digging in. I circle the head of his cock with my tongue, humming at the salty bead of moisture I find in its crease. He tastes incredible, and I wonder if this is something that comes with our mating bond or if it's just him. I can't get enough. I suck his balls into my mouth until he growls, then lick his full length again, savoring the moment as I swirl my tongue over the tip.

"Gods, Eloise…" His chest rises and falls like he's in a full-out battle.

I stop, smile up at him, and then suck him deep, opening my throat to allow him even deeper. He's too big to fit, but I take as much as I can, stretching my mouth wide.

He growls, his expression somewhere between ecstasy and awe. It kindles the fire within me. I squeeze my thighs together as I wrap a hand around the base of him and fall into a rhythm, sucking and stroking until his fingers in my hair grow more urgent, cupping the back of my head as his thrusts increase in intensity.

"Mmmm." I hum my pleasure, feeling him harden and lengthen.

He finds his release on a silent, shuddering scream. I swallow everything he gives me, our mating scent filling the room like the best musky cologne. When his body finally relaxes, I sit back on my heels and offer him a slow, sinful smile.

He cradles my jaw in his enormous hand, beholding me with a possessive and singular focus. "What a good little bird." In a flash, he scoops me off the bed and sets me on my feet in front of him. With a firm grip on my hair, he leans down to whisper in my ear. "How shall I reward you?"

Neither of his hands move, but cool fingers trace up my thighs. I glance down to see his shadows coil up my legs and around my waist. Air caresses my skin as I'm stripped of my pants and currents of darkness lick up my legs like a growing fire. I feel them along the backs of my knees, between my thighs, rounding over my hips, exploring my ribs. They sweep under my breasts, then tease my nipples like a breeze against naked flesh.

"Damien please." The ache between my legs is almost painful.

The shadows tease their way lower, fill my navel with silken darkness before slithering south to circle the swollen bud between my legs.

I moan, unable to contain the pleasure I'd forgotten my body was capable of. Damien kisses the sound away, his tongue claiming my mouth like an unexplored land. His fang knicks something, his lip or mine I have no idea, but the slight taste of blood flavors the kiss. It must be his. I feel no pain, only a building ecstasy. Desperate for more, I thrust my hips, seeking friction, wanting the shadows to press harder, faster.

I tremble with need.

"Do you know what I thought about every day I was a prisoner in that fucking tower?"

I shake my head as the shadows lick between the

mounds of my ass, teasing my back entrance, up my sides. It's like a thousand tongues flicking along my skin.

"When the pain was too much and I thought about giving up, I thought about you and how if I could just be in your arms one more time and have you look at me like you're looking at me now, it would be worth every moment I spent burning in that hell."

I reach up and dig my fingers in his hair, the shadows up to my shoulders now, like I'm surrounded by a million beating butterfly wings. I tip my head back, groaning as one parts my folds and enters me, stroking deep and leaving me breathless.

With my hands on his chest, I gasp. "Please, Damien, I need you inside me. I've waited so long."

With a growl, he lifts me, and I wrap my legs around him. He kneels on the bed so that I'm straddling his hips, then positions himself against my entrance. His cock teases my opening. As wet and ready as I am, my body invites him inside and I lower myself slowly onto him. He stretches me to my limit, working himself in and out. I breathe deeply. He's enormous, and it's been months. It feels like the first time. He slows until my body acclimates to the sheer size of him.

His nails scrape gently along my spine, tracing the length of my tattoo. I arch against his touch, and then I start to move.

"I told you not to risk your life for me," he says with a deep, punishing thrust.

I moan, the pain giving way to the most intense pleasure. "And I told *you* I wouldn't let you die in there."

"You should have kept yourself safe."

"Safety is death if it means living without you. I

promised I'd come for you. And I did." I drag my parted lips along his neck to kiss behind his ear.

"I guess you fucking did."

Our mouths meet in a wild tangle of teeth and tongues. It's like he's trying to touch all of me at once. His hands are everywhere. I'm wrapped in his shadows. He's in me and around me. A second skin. A shield for my flesh. Intense but protective.

Our lovemaking has never been like this. It's always been hot and it's always been passionate, but this time he makes love to me like it could be our last time. It's slow and hard and deep. His teeth are sharp, and he's strong enough to snap my bones, but his eyes and his touch are tender. He gently lowers me onto my back and melts into me, so deep it feels like he's trying to possess me. He slows, breathing me in, our hearts beating in time, our skin flushed with exertion.

Every second I only want him closer.

His enormous hand strokes up my side, over my armpit, along the soft underside of my elbow to thread his fingers into mine above my head. He moves over me, picking up speed like a gathering storm.

He hovers. He strikes.

Heat branches through my body, my climax rolling through me until I throw my head back, lost in a cascade of showering light. This is more than an orgasm. As Damien follows me over the edge, it feels like a missing part of myself snaps into place. Like I was walking around with half my soul gone and didn't know it until this very moment. Now, finally whole, it's not just pleasure I feel but joy. Pure elation. Connection.

He meets my eyes and he's trembling. No. It's not him.

It's me. I'm shaking, our arms locked around each other, breathing each other's air.

Only then do I realize he hasn't taken my blood. I tip my head to the side, offering my neck.

"I don't think you have any extra to give." He looks at me sadly. "Although I'll do my best to change that as soon as the sun sets. Marabella can be bought, but if I can't find the right price, I won't hesitate to pay a visit to the vampires on your schedule and show them what it feels like to donate blood."

His building anger turns his skin cold, and he rolls off me.

I snuggle into his side, stroking his chest. "I don't think you should," I say softly.

He scowls at me, flashing fang.

"I have to believe that part of these trials is mental, Damien. Valeska has an entire hive cheering her on. I know this is hard for you to hear, but the men who have fed from me act as if they're bonded. One of them is the commander of the guard. I don't know what's going to happen, but it seems wise to keep someone like that in my corner. Keep a bond like that in my back pocket."

A low growl rumbles in Damien's chest, and he stares up at the ceiling. "I hate this idea."

I sigh. "I don't like it either, but I've come to realize lately that sometimes getting what we want in life requires doing a great deal of things we don't want to do. The magic of this challenge means you can't leave Night Haven. If you're not feeding from me, you're going to have to feed from someone else. Is it so much worse for me to donate blood to someone else than for you to take it?"

He doesn't answer my question but presses his lips to my temple and sighs deeply. "Sleep now, little bird." He pulls the blankets over us both.

Only then do I realize just how tired I am. I close my eyes, thinking about how far I've come for Damien and just how far I'll go. My mind still hasn't settled on a limit when I finally drift to sleep.

33

GATHERING ALLIES

ELOISE

I'm sitting on the green velvet sofa in the parlor of Harcourt Manor, a cup of hot tea in my hand and a book in my lap. My grandmother is singing in the kitchen, the smell of her favorite grilled cheese wafting from the hallway. The grandfather clock ticks from the corner of the room beside a cozy fire.

For a few beautiful moments, it feels real, but then Phantom is there, curled near my feet. The fox wouldn't be in the house if my grandmother was still alive. I'm dreaming. Still, when I sip the tea, it's my favorite flavor, peach.

"Oh, thank the goddess!" Maeve stands in the center of the room, looking like she was dropped unwittingly into my dream. She's wearing a set of Evil Queen pajamas, and her hair is wrapped in a messy bun. "You are a difficult person to catch dreaming."

"Maeve?" I squint in her direction.

She nods. "It's me. I mean the real me. I used your parents' Hitch and Cast spell to enter your dreams. Not an easy feat for an animator, I might add. This type of magic is like using my left hand to write. I can do it, but it's fucking draining and inefficient. I'm just relieved it finally worked."

My best friend is really standing in front of me! I bound off the couch and yank her into a tight hug.

"Yeah, yeah. I love you too," she says, hugging me back. "So you're still alive. That's good news."

I straighten and lift my chin. "I am. At least for now. I rescued Damien and challenged the queen. My first trial is the day after tomorrow."

Maeve blows out a full breath. "Goddess protect you, Eloise."

I nod, refusing to give my anxieties a voice. Damien and I are together now. After last night, I'm more convinced than ever that we're meant to be. Nothing can stop us. "I will compete. I will win. Valeska will rue the day she took Damien from me."

Her eyes glisten as she says, "That's exactly what's going to happen."

"Thank you for risking the spell. It means everything to me to see you today."

Maeve frowns. "Unfortunately, there's something else I need to tell you."

"Oh?" Shit. Of course there is. And it must be important for her to risk walking into my dreams.

"If... I mean *when* you win, you can't come straight home to Harcourt Manor."

"Why not?"

"The FBI found Jared's car in the caverns under your

house. They've been searching for you for weeks. They've sent certified letters. They've visited my office on more than one occasion. I told them the truth, that I didn't know where you were. It's *good* that I don't know your exact location, El. Makes my story more believable. They've been asking about you all over Echo Mills though. And as of yesterday, you're officially a missing person."

I sigh. "Great. I'll have to come up with one hell of an explanation when I get home."

"There's more."

I frown.

"The Denardis know Jared's dead. His body was never found, but he never checked in. Nick Denardi visited my office. He's less convinced I'm telling the truth about not knowing where you are. In any case, he's been asking around Echo Mills for you as well."

"Both the FBI and the mob? I'm a popular lady."

She gives a maniacal laugh. "You don't know the half of it."

"There's more?"

"Vampires. The woods around your place are crawling with them."

I wave a hand through the air. "Valeska knows who I am. She compelled Damien to reveal my name before I challenged her. I'm sure she sent vampires to kill me before I showed up right in front of her."

Maeve massages her eyes under her glasses. "I don't think she's called them off though, hon. Some of these hired guns are paid in advance, and they don't stop until the job is done."

"Oh. So what you're saying is, on top of the FBI

wanting to question me and the mob wanting to torture me to find out what happened to Jared… and then likely *finish the job of trying to kill* me that Jared started, vampire assassins might be waiting in the wings even if Valeska is dead?"

She nods. "That's why I'm here. If you… I mean when you win, come to my apartment, not Harcourt. We'll figure out a plan together."

I sip my tea. I know it's a dream, but it feels warm and comforting going down. "Thank you for letting me know," I say toward the flames.

"I'm so sorry, Eloise. I know it's a lot—"

I whirl back to her. "No, really, thank you. When it's done, I'll call you first before I come home."

She blows out a breath. "Exactly."

The clock ticks louder. "What did you use as your anchor anyway?"

She points at the tea set on the coffee table. "My grandmother's."

I look down at the floral cup I've been drinking out of and recognize the set as Maeve's. The cup is almost empty, although I only remember drinking a little. "We don't have much time, do we?"

"No."

I take her hand in mine and squeeze. "No matter what happens, Maeve, you are the best friend I've ever had, and I appreciate everything you've done for me and Damien."

"Stop." She shakes her head, tears streaming now. "You're going to win. You'll be back. We'll work it all out."

I kiss her on the cheek. "Of course."

"See you soon," she says. And then Maeve and the tea are gone.

I wake at twilight, the streetlights outside Marabella's growing brighter and the sound of voices in the marketplace filling the room. I stretch long in my bed, turning over to kiss Damien good morning.

But he's gone.

"I cannot bear it." Damien's outline comes apart at the edges with his anger. The moment the sun set, he visited Marabella and tried to buy out all my available donation slots. But as I suspected, the three vampires I've fed, some of the wealthiest and most powerful of their kind, Marcel, Everald, and George, had booked out months in advance. They could not be persuaded to reschedule with someone else, and Marabella refused to deny them. It didn't hurt that they were paying three times the regular price for my blood.

"I told you, Damien, it's in our best interest to have supporters. These are powerful males. It will be better if there are voices in the crowd cheering me on even if that cheer is a whisper."

He growls. "These males want you for themselves. They don't want you to die, but they don't want you mated to me."

I sigh and take his hands in my own. "They don't have a choice. I'm only offering blood."

A growl percolates in his chest as he glares down at me. A knock comes at the door. "That'll be breakfast. My first appointment will follow."

Damien's lips twitch. The key turns in the lock, and the door begins to open. He shakes his head, his eyes closing tight for a moment. When he opens them again, he doesn't look at me. "So be it."

He shatters into a confetti of shadows that dart from the room. It's for the best that he's gone. He needs to stay far from here while I do what I have to do. Ren enters with a tray almost overflowing with food, coffee, and Marabella's special charmed shake. She set's it down on the desk.

"Are you alone?" she asks. "I thought I heard a man's voice."

"I'm alone." I feel alone, all the way to my bones. Damien can't be in the room when I donate. As a mated shade, he'd likely rip any vampire who touched me in half. But the way he left leaves me feeling empty.

"You must be the bravest woman who ever worked here, Eloise," Ren says, handing me another book. I take it and give her back the last one I borrowed.

"Not brave. Desperate."

She gives a sad laugh. "I was desperate once. I took pills. I didn't feel desperate afterward. I didn't feel anything. You… you challenged the *queen*. That's fucking brave, Eloise."

I blow out a deep breath. "Yeah, maybe it is. Brave or stupid."

"I think the same thing about my decision to come here and get sober."

Our eyes meet and hold and then she slips out my door.

MARCEL ENTERS MY ROOM LATER THAT DAY IN FULL uniform. It's the first time he's visited since I challenged Valeska, and I brace myself, prepared for anything. Will he feel betrayed that I didn't tell him the truth about my identity? Will he try to hurt me out of loyalty to the queen? The magic of the challenge provides me some protection, but it doesn't do much to ease my fears when he walks into my room, looking deeply disturbed. I'm more thankful than ever for the daggers strapped to my thighs.

"Eloise, thank the gods you're all right." His face softens, his gaze traveling over me.

"You must have heard."

His eyes narrow. "She commanded me to kill you."

I take a step back, my hand dropping within easy reach of the hilt of my dagger.

He holds up both hands. "I didn't know it was you. I knew your name was Eloise but not that you were the Eloise Harcourt who stood between her and the shade she was so intent on mating."

"His name is Damien."

Marcel backs up a step, leaning against the door. "I know your mate well. He isn't happy about me feeding from you. I can't say I blame him." Longing flits through his expression. He catches himself and replaces it with an impassive mask.

"I make my own choices."

"Right." He takes a step toward me. "I've called off the men who were tracking you topside. Now that you've challenged the queen, there's no reason for it."

"Thank you." A small but real sense of relief comes over me.

"The rules of the challenge are clear. She will not harm you while you compete." His tone sounds protective. Marcel isn't going to hurt me. I know it in my bones.

"Are you upset that I challenged your queen?"

His lids lower until he's looking at me through his lashes. "No. I'll be upset if you lose. She'd lock me in the tower until I met the sun if she heard me say it, but it's true."

"You're unhappy with her rule?"

He scowls. "I will speak no more on this topic."

I nod and offer him my wrist. At first I think he might reject it, might ask to feed from my neck again, but instead, he lowers himself to his knees in front of me. My eyes widen as he takes what I offer more gently than any vampire has ever taken my vein. And when I tell him to stop, he does.

He bows before letting himself out my door.

Afterward, I pace my room, then try to distract myself with the book Ren left me. I hoped Damien would return before dawn, but he doesn't. I take a long shower before crawling into bed and crying myself to sleep.

When I wake, Damien is lying beside me, holding me. "You came back."

He kisses me breathless, long and slow. When he finally pulls back, he says, "There will never be a day when I can watch another male feed from you and not destroy everything within reach. I had to go, or there would have been violence. But I'll always come back, little bird. Always."

"You've fed," I say. Not a question. The wrinkles around his eyes are smoother, and his cheeks and lips are full and pink.

"As you wished." His voice holds an uncomfortable edge.

"I do wish," I say, smoothing my hands up his chest. "I don't want to know the details, but I'm glad you have more blood in your system that's not hers."

He strokes a hand along the outside of my arm and then my side. "I had blood bags at my apartment for an emergency. If I eat well—human food—I won't need to feed again for several weeks."

"Oh." I wrap my arms around his neck and pull myself flush against him. "But…" I sigh. "We've come too far for petty jealousies, Damien. What would we do in your world if I was also a shade? I'd have to watch you eat, and you'd have to watch me."

He caresses my shoulder, his touch trailing down my spine. The corner of his mouth quirks into a crooked smile. "We'd hunt together. My mother and father often roamed the woods behind the castle, hunting for mountain sheep. There are no humans on Tenebris to feed on. We eat only animals."

"I thought you said there were witches? Wild ones who lived in the outlands or something."

He nods. "It's true they look human, but no shade would ever try to feed on one. Not anyone who valued their life. The elves look human as well, but their blood is toxic. We don't even drink it on the battlefield."

"Cassius told me that one of the witches helped you with your mission to recover your father."

He sits up, smiling. "He did?" He tucks in his chin as if truly surprised. "He told you that story?"

"When he explained his scar and the one on Morpheus's face."

He trails kisses along my neck to my ear. "Sometimes I miss those days."

I take his hand. "I'm off until tomorrow. Last day before the full moon. How do you want to spend it?"

He kisses me again, until I'm certain we'll spend the rest of the night in this bed. But when he draws back, his face turns serious. He lifts from the bed as if the laws of gravity don't apply to him and holds out a hand to help me up. "Get your daggers. We're going to train."

34

THE SERPENT & THE GARDEN

ELOISE

The night of the full moon brings a trio of red-robed scribes to Marabella's to usher me to the palace. I'm nervous but as ready as I can be. After I trained with Damien, Marabella supplied me with not one but two of her recovery shakes. I'm as strong as I've ever been.

The scribes form a triangle around me as we parade through the marketplace toward the challenge. I have flashbacks to that episode of *Game of Thrones* when Cersei has to walk naked through town, but no one screams profanities at me or throws rotten vegetables. No one rings a bell and announces SHAME repeatedly at my side. Surprisingly, the many vampires and the rarer human companions who watch my procession wear a mixture of curiosity and cynicism in their expressions. I'm not sure what that means.

Damien follows behind us in his monster form. Maybe his considerable presence is the cause of the silence. No one in their right mind would ever voluntarily piss him off.

At the scribe's direction, I navigate a series of halls to reach the silo. It's exactly as I remember it from my dream, only without the walls of sunlight or my mate huddled in the center like a boulder. Instead, Lazarus stands at a small podium with an ornately decorated box that looks similar but not identical to the one Sabrina showed me. The octagonal mirrors are placed on the floor on either side of him, spaced about eight feet to his left and right. He gestures for Damien to join him, and my mate takes a spot next to the scribe.

As if on cue, Valeska enters, similarly escorted by three scribes in red robes. I silently laugh to myself. Oh, how the mighty have fallen. She no longer looks like a queen but a competitor. No fanfare. No elaborate dress. In fact, she's dressed similarly to me. I'm in the fighting gear that Cassius obtained for me—black tactical pants and a long-sleeved T-shirt. Her pants are leather but her black mock turtleneck gives the same general affect. We both have daggers strapped to our thighs. Her black hair is in a ponytail. Mine is braided and bright red. We might be dressed the same, but we are very, very different, and I'm not stupid enough to underestimate how deadly she is.

"It's worth it just to see her like that," a man behind me whispers.

I pretend to scratch my cheek with my shoulder and catch him rapidly exchanging money for tiny slips of paper, some white, some blue. They're betting on this trial. I don't know which color paper represents me, but there are plenty of both colors gripped in people's fingers, which means Valeska, at least in these vampires' minds, isn't foreseen to be the clear winner. I hold on to that thought like a talisman as a radiant yellow moon rises over the edge of the silo on a path toward its apex.

"Challengers, step forward," Lazarus announces as he opens an enormous tome to the place where it's marked with a red silk ribbon. "Eloise, as the challenger and Damien's current mate, you will roll the position dice first. The highest number wins."

I step to the box, and he hands me a six-sided die that appears to be made from scored bone. I toss it into the cloth-lined box.

"Make a note that Eloise Harcourt has rolled a four," Lazarus says to the scribe who sits at a small table near the wall, scribbling furiously. "Now you, Valeska."

The vampire queen does not look at me as she takes the die and rolls it. She hisses when it lands.

"Note that Valeska has rolled a two," Lazarus says. "Eloise, you will roll for the challenge and be the first to choose a doorway."

I nod.

Lazarus turns to the crowd that has lined the walls three rows deep and raises his red-robed arms. "Provocationem Ad Mortem is a game fueled by ancient magic, designed to protect our most sacrosanct bond, the one between mates. As such, each challenger will be required to prove their worthiness of the bond. The magic will harvest challenges based on Damien's own memories. The competitors will solve the challenge and return through the archway. A winner will be named based on their individual performances." He gestures toward the large rectangular mirror on the top of the box.

The harvest moon rises a bit higher, and moonlight

falls on the two octagonal mirrors. A blinding flash sends a murmur through the crowd, and then two identical archways stand where the mirrors once were. Lazarus mumbles something that sounds like a curse.

Each is made of ancient, worn stone, chiseled with barely recognizable arcane symbols. The tattoo on my back tingles with awareness as if the symbols that make up my sigil recognize the power of those chiseled in the archway. I try to make out the specific designs, but the ravages of time have left the grooves shallow. The sides rise like pillars toward a gentle arch with a square keystone at its apex. One such stone bears a symbol like a star, the other a crescent moon. Rippling darkness fills each archway like two oil-slicked pools.

"Eloise, if you will do the honors."

I take two dice from Lazarus's hand. These are also made of bone but look more like Dungeons & Dragons dice than anything that might belong in a casino. The sides are not numbered but bear a series of sigils the likes of which I'm not familiar. Anxious to get this over with, I toss the dice.

They land with a red *x* and purple fish facing up. I have no idea what that means, but the large mirror at the back of the box turns smoky. When the white haze parts, a woman in a gown and elaborate pearl earrings is running through a forest, laughing. She looks over her shoulder, and I get a clear view of her face. This is Damien's mother. I've never met her. Never seen a picture. But I just know it's her. The resemblance is striking. She smiles, and one of her earrings drops from her ear. A close-up of the earring fills the mirror and then vanishes.

Valeska growls. "So we are to recover this… this woman's earring?" She flicks her red nails at the looking glass.

Lazarus frowns. "I'm afraid I cannot provide assistance to you, my queen."

Is it possible that Valeska didn't notice Damien's likeness in the woman's dark hair and diamond-colored eyes? That is Nyxadora, I'm sure of it, although I suppose it could also be his sister Karyl. No. Not with that dress and that crown. That was the queen. I close my eyes and picture the pearl earring, made from a dozen blue pearls strung together into a geometric pattern. Damien said his mother and father used to hunt behind their castle. It did look like a forest behind her where it fell off.

"Eloise, you are the first to choose."

I look at the moon archway. Where before there was only rippling darkness, now lies a dark green forest with what could be snow on the ground. The queen was running in a forest, but I'm sure Tenebris has many wooded areas. I don't think this is the same one. The way Damien speaks about his world, snow is limited to the mountains. I don't remember seeing any snow behind Nyxadora in the scene the mirror played for us. Furthermore, wouldn't someone as important as the queen hunt close to home, especially since the kingdom was at war? I'm presuming a lot, but what other way might I make a decision?

I turn my attention to my other option. Under the star archway, it's also green but there's no snow. A path and a lone purple rose are visible within. I take a deep breath. I remember purple roses from Damien's dream of the castle garden. If I end up near the castle, I should be able to find the forest where the queen most likely lost her earring.

Fisting my hands, I choose the star archway and its purple rose. As I approach the arch, I notice the octagonal mirror is gone, replaced by a stone threshold with characters I recognize as vampiric Romanian. I can't read what it says, but I can only imagine it is some terrible warning. I take a deep, fortifying breath and then step over them, ready for wherever this challenge takes me.

The stone of the silo's floor gives way to an artfully designed pathway that leads into a garden. I walk toward the purple rose and then look back toward the archway. It's gone. The only thing in that direction is a steep garden wall. For three solid seconds, I worry that something went wrong. How will I get back? And then common sense kicks in. If the archway opened magically when I rolled the dice, it will most certainly open for me again when I find the earring.

I continue along the winding path, walls of trellised flowers and vines making me feel like I'm in a labyrinth, until the space opens up to what I was hoping to find. The castle from Damien's dream rises beside a garden of strange foliage and purple flowers. I will never forget this place. I smile at the bench where we made love, the place where he showed me the moon. Just as he promised, it looms large and dark yellow on the horizon and lights up the garden like a muted sun.

"Phantom?" I reach out with my power, and the fox appears in front of me, my connection to it snapping into place like a dull buzz.

"Darling, what can we help you with?"

"Is there anyone who knows a spell to find an object?"

The fox stares off into the distance for a moment, emerald eyes glowing. "Yes, but you'll need a pendulum."

A pendulum… I need a string and a weight. I quickly search the garden, but can't find anything of use. I turn my attention to what I'm wearing. My boots have laces, but I'm not sure how long I'll need to walk to find the earring. I'll need well-fitting shoes. I might be able to use my hair. I draw one of my daggers, fully prepared to cut a chunk of my red locks out to braid into rope, but as I do, my fingers brush a decorative orange zipper pull on one of my pockets. I grab it and inspect it more closely. "Thank you, Cassius."

Cassius chose these pants for me. I've never worn tactical gear before, but the many pockets and the fabric's moisture wicking properties seemed like a wise choice. Now I appreciate them on a whole new level. I unclasp the end of the pull and unbraid the cord. When I'm done, I'm left with three feet of line. I snatch a stone from the walkway and tie it to the end.

"Ready," I say to Phantom.

"Hold it out in front of you, darling, and picture the earring clearly in your mind. Pour some energy into it," Phantom says in my grandmother's stop-messing-around voice. "Aunt Sara is going to help you."

Red haze filters through the darkness, bringing with it a light shower of ash and the scent of smoke. I feel a tug on the bond. All at once, I regret not practicing my magic the past few weeks. Our connection feels heavy, like I'm bench-pressing my own weight. I grunt as a woman I've never met before emerges from Phantom's body in all her translucent, black-and-white glory. Her dress has lace-tied sleeves and an apron, reminiscent of a renaissance fair. I can only imagine how far back our blood ties go. There are definitely no pictures of Aunt Sara on our gallery wall. Pins and needles strike through my hand as she merges into me from the elbow down, but the effect is immediate. The stone tugs me left. I take off across a dark field as Sara sinks back into Phantom.

The grass here is strange. It feels like I'm running on kitchen sponges. My boots squelch and spring off the strange mounds of green. With my Aunt Sara back inside Phantom, the heaviness I experienced before is gone, and I'm able to pick up speed, my energy returning. The stone guides me to the edge of a lake, pulling toward the water. It's too dark to see anything beneath the surface even at the edge. For all I can tell, this water could be clean and clear or the color of mud.

"Um, what now?" I glance toward Phantom. "Do we have a spell to summon it from the bottom?"

Phantom paces again and then shakes their head. "Not without a drawn sigil. We don't think you'll have time for that, darling. Valeska is fast and doesn't have to breathe. She doesn't have the magic you have to find the earring, but she can cover more ground and has unparalleled senses."

Anxiety shoots through me again, and I toe off my shoes and socks. When my bare feet hit the curled grass, I shudder at the feeling. "I'll just have to wade in. If it's on the bottom, maybe I'll feel it with my toes."

"That's the spirit," Phantom says encouragingly.

The last thing I want to do is plod into the mysterious depths in front of me, but Phantom is right, I have to assume Valeska is moving faster. I can't stall. I dip my toe under the surface of the water, expecting it to be cold. "It's warm as a bath but more viscous than water. Almost like soup." I step forward. "The bottom is smooth but striated, kind of like I'm walking on fallen branches. It's not bad."

"Follow the stone," Phantom reminds me.

I watch the pendulum and move in the direction the stone points. The bank angles deeper, the water coming to my knees and then my waist and then my chest. The slick black fluid is more buoyant than regular water. My guess is it has a higher salt content based on the scent. It smells like I'm standing next to the ocean.

When the water comes up to my chin, I regret not having stripped out of my clothes. I'm going to have to swim. A few experimental positions and I figure out that the easiest way to follow the stone's direction is if I float on my back. I kick in the direction it pulls me. A few minutes later, the pendulum goes lax, the stone hanging straight down toward my chest. A smile spreads across my face. The earring is directly under me.

I allow my feet to sink under the water and am surprised that although I'm in the center of the small lake, I touch the bottom. I start searching with my toes again. It's smooth here, almost slimy. I tuck the pendulum into one of my pockets so that I can use my arms to guide me as I feel around with my toes for the earring. My foot hits a stony outcropping. I feel my way around it to another section, similarly slimy. This part dips when I put my weight on it. Then the entire bottom shifts beneath my feet.

"What the hell?" I look down but see nothing but black.

I glance back at Phantom. Maybe we can illuminate the water. But before I can speak, something clamps around my middle. I have a half second to gulp air before whatever it is pulls me under.

Eyes closed under the inky water, I twist and turn, reaching for my dagger. I'm tossed about like a rag doll. Water streams over my skin, growing colder, heavier around me.

We're moving quickly, diving deeper.

I give in and open my eyes but can't see anything in the dark depths. I can feel it though. I'm held by a creature with the flesh of a fish and a mouth big enough to span from my bottom rib to mid-thigh. My lungs burn for air as I place my hand on top of what I assume is its head and start punching. My fist lands in something soft—an eye, I hope. It releases me. I grab for my dagger and have just enough time for my fingers to graze the hilt before I'm captured again.

I bend, impaling the back of my thigh on what I assume is a tooth, but I get hold of the knife and drive it home. Am I stabbing its neck? Its ear? Its head? I have no idea, but I stab again and again and again.

It releases me and I swim to the surface, drawing a loud, gasping breath into my lungs. Water rushes by me and then curls, a ripple bending along the surface as the creature turns and heads straight for me. I raise my dagger and plunge it into the ripple. Resistance as the blade sinks deep. I try to pull it out for another stab, but it's stuck in the creature's leathery hide. The thing passes me, pulls me along behind it at a frightening speed. I tug and tug again.

"Fuck!" Another quick breath. It dives. I refuse to lose my dagger. I need it. This is only the first trial! I hold the hilt in a death grip—one I hope won't be my literal death

—as I slide the second dagger from its holster. Bracing my feet on the creature, I stab and rip. Stab and rip. Stab and rip. The creature thrashes and then slows. We're sinking but not as quickly. The thing twitches erratically, swimming in a circle.

I look up toward the surface, seeing the moon's glow. I need to breathe, but I can't let whatever this thing is out of my reach. The stone pointed toward it. What if the earring is in its stomach?

I reach for my bond with Phantom and feel a familiar buzz start. It's heavy—so, so heavy—but the water moves, pushing me, lifting me and the beast toward the surface. I cough and sputter as my face breaks free of the water, my hands holding the hilts of my daggers with everything I have left. My magic moves the water, pushing me and the creature toward shore. A yard, two yards. This is nothing like making a wave lap in a bowl. This feels like I'm dragging the entire lake. I fix my eyes on Phantom's glowing green stare, my mother's witchy energy buzzing down my side.

My teeth grit against the agony of the effort. I push and push and push until the current I've created washes me and the beast held in my daggers onto the rocky beach. We wash up next to Phantom, and I roll off the thing, flopping onto my back and heaving air into my lungs in great hungry gulps. I close my eyes for a second, but Phantom is there, licking my face.

"Get up now, Eloise. Now!" my Grams's voice snaps.

I obey, but it's difficult. My ribs hurt, and I'm bleeding from the back of the leg. Something hot oozes over my chin, and I wipe my mouth with the back of my hand. Blood. My nose is bleeding. I've overused my magic. That explains the dark spots circling in my vision.

Fighting the urge to lie back down, I lean over the thing that attacked me, bracing myself on its side. The closest to anything from earth I can compare it to is a salamander if salamanders grew as large as whales. Two tusks protrude from its lower jaw. That must be what impaled the back of my leg.

I plunge my dagger into its belly, praying that I'm right and the earring is inside the beast and not on the floor of the lake under where I met this thing. Guts pour out around my feet. Quickly I open the creature's stomach.

The earring washes across the stones in a burst of fluid.

I slide both my daggers back into their sheaths and snatch it from the rocks. The dark spots swirling in my vision grow larger. I sway on my feet.

"Hurry, darling!" Phantom urges.

The star archway forms only a few feet away from me, and the fox tugs me by the pant leg toward it. On wobbling legs, I sway toward the opening and launch myself over the threshold.

Back in the silo, there's a collective gasp from the observers when they see me. I toss the earring into the box in front of Lazarus. I don't see Valeska.

"Did I win?"

The floor bends up to slap my cheek, and then everything goes dark.

35

HEART OF DARKNESS

DAMIEN

I smell the blood before I see it. Eloise stumbles through the archway and tosses my mother's earring in the box. She's beaten Valeska back to the silo, but something's wrong. Blood streams from her nose, and her face is white as ash. More blood pools around her bare feet. Where are her boots? Why is she soaking wet? And where is all that blood coming from?

She collapses to the stone just as her name appears on the mirror, declaring her the winner.

As the vampires who've bet on her howl in victory, I break apart and re-form by her side. "Eloise? *Eloise?*" She's too pale. There's so much blood.

She doesn't respond, but she's still breathing, thank the gods. I move to pick her up, and the hand I scoop under her knees meets gushing blood. With some repositioning, I locate the source—a puncture wound in the back of her left thigh—and set her down again. Tearing a strip off the bottom of my shirt, I make a tourniquet for the wound. Thank fuck her nose seems to have stopped bleeding on its own. Another bloody spot under her rib reveals itself to be from an abrasion and not an open wound.

Lazarus's already-wide eyes seem to pop out of his head as he leans over us both. "She needs a healer, Damien!" he whispers.

"Where?" Night Haven's healers practice vampiric medicine. She needs a human doctor. But according to the old law, we're not allowed to leave Night Haven.

Lazarus shakes his head. Panic flares behind my breastbone. It can't end this way. I can't lose her like this.

Marabella appears in front of me and shakes me by the shoulders. "Get her back to the house. Now!"

"She's hurt. She needs a doctor," I growl.

The madam rolls her eyes. "There's one at the house, Damien. How do you think we care for forty human women down here?"

The second archway flashes and Valeska steps through, grinning with the earring in hand. I don't wait around for what happens when she finds out she's lost. I take off for Marabella's, flying through the palace, through the marketplace, and up the stairs into the house.

"The doctor," I scream at the woman manning the front desk.

Alarm sparks in her eyes when she sees Eloise, and she points to a plain white door at the end of the hall behind her. I hug my mate to me and carry her through a waiting room of vampires whose fangs drop and nostrils flare at the scent of her blood. When I reach the unmarked door, it's locked. I move to kick it down, but Front Desk Girl runs up behind me with her badge.

"Sorry." She opens the door for us, and we all go through. "Dr. Everline! There's an emergency!"

A squat human woman in a lab coat saunters around the corner, takes one look at Eloise, and thrusts her coffee into Front Desk Girl's hands. "In here, man." She gestures wildly at an examination table through a set of automatic doors.

I place Eloise's limp body on it. Everline smacks a red button on the wall, and an alarm sounds.

Two nurses run in, nudging me aside to work on Eloise. One seems to be attaching her to an EKG while the other pushes me out of the way to gain access to her arm to start an IV.

The doctor clicks on an overhead lamp.

"Eloise?" I say frantically from the head of the table, her face cupped in my hands.

"You should go to the waiting room. There will be blood," Everline says.

"I'm not going anywhere." I growl and bare a little fang. "I'm her mate!"

"I know who you are, shade. Everyone in Night Haven knows who you are."

"I'm not going anywhere."

Everline sneers and grabs a pair of shears from her lab coat. "Let's take a look at this wound."

She cuts away her clothing neatly and efficiently and hands it to me along with her daggers, still in their sheaths. I hate the sight of my mate lying naked and wounded on the table. She looks too small, too pale, too unconscious. I'm oddly relieved when Everline partially covers her with a thin white sheet.

The doctor turns her on her side, inspecting the

deeper wound on the back of her leg that is now free from my binding. "This is a puncture wound. Do you know what bit her, Damien?"

"Bit her?" My heart beats faster. From my place next to Lazarus, I couldn't see the details of the challenge or what Eloise saw in the archway before she stepped through. Valeska mentioned an earring. What exactly did Eloise face tonight?

The doctor grabs an instrument from a rolling table and scrapes inside the wound, holding up the result. Her brown eyes shift to mine. The ooze that covers the instrument is silver and viscous. *Earring. Oh no.*

A rush of fear courses through me. I lift her clothing to my nose, the brackish mildew scent of Stygarde's Black Lake filling my nose. I draw one of her daggers. It's still stained with black blood, and when I smell the blade, my memories are transported to Tenebris. I will never forget that smell. This is the blood of a creature that almost killed me as a child. A creature whose bite caused my brother to languish in bed with fever for a week.

"She was bitten by a Black Lake salamander," I say, feeling like I've been punched in the stomach.

The doctor arches an eyebrow at me. "The pattern of this bite runs from below her ribs to her thighs. No salamander could do this."

"It's from my world. Not from earth. They're the size of your sharks and venomous."

Dr. Everline and her nurse exchange glances. Everline nods and the nurse scurries off, returning seconds later with a bag of blood. "Now, I understand she's your mate, Damien, but she's running out of time. I'm going to have to do surgery to repair this wound. You're an infection risk. I can't start until you leave."

I'm about to argue, but a hand lands on my arm.

It's Marabella, and her face is grave. "Every minute you stand here, Damien, is a minute Dr. Everline can't do her job and a minute closer to death for Eloise. Come walk with me. She's in good hands."

I press a kiss to Eloise's cold, pale forehead and then force myself to follow Marabella from the infirmary. The door clicks closed behind us, and it's all I can do not to slide back under the door in my shadow form. But Marabella urges me toward the back door where she nods at a guard and then types a code into a pad on the wall. When it opens, I find myself in a carefully manicured Japanese garden.

"Do the grow lights bother you? I can have them lowered."

I test my abilities in the light, and while the brightness isn't exactly comfortable, my shadows are still under my command. This garden is brightly lit, but the light isn't painful. I'm not mortal. It's not sunlight.

"They're fine. How good is Dr. Everline?" I grumble.

Marabella starts walking. I fall in beside her.

"With humans? The best. Between you and me, she has connections among witches and has a stockpile of healing herbs and spells to enhance her medical practice. We regularly use her enchantments to improve the girls' recovery time. I told her to spare no expense on Eloise."

"Thank you."

She smiles wickedly. "Oh, I can't claim to be doing it out of the goodness of my heart. Your mate's welfare is extremely important to me."

"You bet on her today, didn't you?"

"I did."

"Why?"

"Why not?" Marabella stops on the apex of a small wooden bridge over a creek filled with colorful koi fish. I study her, trying to deconstruct her motivations. The madam is an unrepentant capitalist. It doesn't make sense.

"She's human," I say, "pitted against the deadliest vampire queen of the last five generations. Why would you expect her to win?"

A slow grin spreads across her face, the type that's condescending in its smugness. "When she showed up at Wicked Divine with Cassius's name on her lips, I knew she was no blood whore. Despite her wild red hair, Eloise is possibly the sweetest thing that has ever entered this city. Truly a kind heart. Not a mark on that creamy skin of hers. No addictions. As pretty as a doll. But that wasn't why I chose her."

"Then why did you?"

"She enchanted my taster."

"Perceval?" I sneer, wanting to slit the vampire's throat.

"That's the one. One sip of her blood and if she'd have asked him, he would have knelt and licked her boots. I knew then that her blood was not entirely human."

I turn to watch the water babbling beneath the bridge. "You're wrong. She is human."

"What she is, is rare," Marabella snaps. "Call it a hunch." She leans her elbows against the railing. "And I have excellent intuition. I heard rumors that the queen was keeping you prisoner in the palace. The girls hear everything, you know, and the guards couldn't stop talking about how you'd ripped a donor's bones from their flesh to fight your way out of the silo. I thought to myself, why would Cassius send this woman with the strange blood to me? Why was she so desperate to become a blood donor at my house? Unless… No one knew your mate's name. The queen would have done anything for her identity. You've been one of my best customers over the years. I know enough about you to make some assumptions about the type of woman you'd choose, and Eloise fit the bill." She laughs to herself. "So yeah, I put my money on Eloise, and I will do it again."

"She's a regular ATM for you," I say through my teeth. "Between forcing her to sell her blood for three months and gambling on her welfare."

"And saving her life. And getting her into the palace to save yours. You should be thanking me."

"Don't hold your breath."

"Have you even paused to consider why I introduced her to the clients I did? The commander of the guard. The master of Liberty coven. The wealthiest merchant in Night Haven."

"Eloise told me you convinced her she needed a cheering section."

"And you couldn't see through that?"

I stare at her, waiting for an explanation.

She scoffs. "Damien, Valeska mating you would be the worst thing to ever happen to Marabella's. The queen has forcibly incorporated sixteen covens into her hive since she took power. If she manages to mate you, no coven will be safe. No coven in America. No coven in the world. And with that kind of power, why pay human blood donors? This hive would be strong enough to enslave all the humans they wanted. So while Valeska does have her supporters, I'm not one of them, and neither are the three vampires I arranged to take Eloise's blood. Your mate is a godsend. I want Eloise to win this thing as much as you do. So when I tell you that her blood has enchanted the most powerful vampires in Night Haven, please know that it is no coincidence that they found their way to her room."

The pieces fall into place, and it all makes sense. "This isn't just about money for you. You're hoping the queen loses. You and your friends want an end to the hive."

She folds her arms, drumming her fingers on her cashmere-clad biceps. "Oh, Damien, money is always the priority with me, but in this case, overthrowing the queen is a close and very sweet second."

36

A LIGHT IN THE SHADOWS

ELOISE

Everything is white. Are the walls of the silo made of sunlight again? I take a deep breath, smoothing my hands across soft cotton sheets. A bed. I blink and the room comes into focus. I'm facing a wall of glass, looking out onto the Japanese garden at Marabella's. My head is up. I'm in a hospital bed. An IV runs from my arm to a dark bag dangling from a pole, and the stiff edge of a bandage pokes above my bottom rib. A tube runs along my cheek to my nose.

"Finally!" A woman in blue scrubs comes in, smiling in my direction. "You're awake." She starts hastily taking my vitals.

My mouth is dry, my throat thick from lack of use. I clear it with a cough. "Did I win?"

Her bright red lips spread into a smile that twinkles in her large blue eyes. "Yes, you won. Valeska was mightily pissed about it too."

My lips feel like they might crack, but I manage a shallow smile. "Are you a doctor?"

"Nurse. I'm Karen."

"Eloise. Nice to meet you."

She laughs. "Oh, I know who you are. Everyone knows who you are." She gestures behind her to where a table is overflowing with flowers, stuffed animals, and balloons.

I shake my head. "Who… did this?"

She tucks a strand of her blond hair back into her bun. "Who didn't send something? Marabella told me to tell you that Commander Marcel, Everald, and Master George all sent well-wishes along with flowers and gifts, but there are also ones that came without a card—"

"What about…?" *Damien. Where's Damien?*

"Damien? No flowers from him, but to be fair he's hardly left your room." She points to the corner. I have to crane my neck to see him sleeping in the chair there. "It's noon topside, and he's barely slept since your surgery. He's going to be out for a few more hours."

Noon. It was still night when I came back through the archway. "How long have I been out?"

Her face falls, and her hand finds mine before she says, "It's been six days."

"Six days!"

Over the next few minutes, Karen removes all the tubes but the IV from my body, helps me to the bathroom, and orders me food. I'm in remarkably good shape for someone who's been unconscious for six days, but I'm told it's because Dr. Everline used magic as well as human medicine. I eat some soup and drink a protein shake.

And when Damien finally wakes, I'm standing next to the bed. "Hey, sleepyhead," I say lightly.

A cloud of darkness swirls around me, spiraling in a ticklish rush that takes my breath away until Damien forms with me in his arms. He hugs me gently, his breath brushing the side of my neck.

"I'm okay," I say softly, kissing the edge of his ear. "Feeling better by the minute."

He draws back, taking my face in his hands.

"I won, Damien," I say excitedly. "I only have to win one more challenge and we're free."

He licks his lips. All at once he looks gaunt, and I remember how Cassius said he could hide his scar but at a huge personal cost. Damien is desperately trying to mask his condition, and that mask is slipping. Has he eaten anything the past six days? Has he taken any blood?

"You can't go back through that archway," he says in a voice that is more grit than words.

I shake my head, searching his face for any hint that he's joking. He's not. "You know I can't just quit. That's not how this works. Sabrina told me the challenge is a magical contract."

He swallows. "The magic is strong. I tried to travel, to consult with Cassius and his coven master about how to break free of this challenge. I was not able to leave. The spell is binding."

"Right." I lay my hands on the sides of his handsome face. His cheeks are unusually hollow, and his eyes are icy without the hint of blue I often see when he's content. "So... you know then I have to go through again. I have to compete in the second trial."

"You could have died."

"I didn't."

He helps me back into bed and takes one of my hands

between his own. "That thing you faced is called a Black Lake salamander," he mumbles.

My eyes widen in surprise. How could he possibly know what my challenge entailed? "Could you see what was happening to me from the silo?"

"No. The venom was in your leg, and I smelled its blood on your daggers."

"Oh."

"Tell me what happened."

With the light from the garden shining through the window behind him, his face is cloaked in shadow, but when he sits on the edge of the bed, his shoulders slump like he's exhausted. "I'm not sure that's a good idea."

"Tell me," he grits out.

"It's over, Damien. I think you should eat."

He closes his eyes for a beat. "Tell me. Please."

I reposition myself in bed, a twinge of pain flaring in the back of my leg. "I chose the star archway because I could see a purple rose and thought it would lead to the garden in your dream. You said your mom used to hunt behind the castle. I figured that was what she was doing when she lost her earring."

"Smart."

"I used a locator spell to find the earring. The spell led me out to the center of the lake, and I realized quickly it was actually in the belly of the salamander. Well, not quickly enough. Only after it tried to eat me and tore into my leg. I killed it and used magic to get it to shore. A little too much magic. But I was right. The earring was in its stomach."

"I had no idea the challenges would be about me."

"Of course it's about you. We're fighting for the privilege of being your mate." I try not to sound bitter saying those words, but Damien is already my mate. How unfair is it that I have to risk my life to have what's already mine?

"What I mean is I had no idea the challenges themselves would be drawn from my personal history and take place on my world, or else an echo of it."

Our eyes meet, and the meaning behind his words clicks. "Are you saying that challenge wasn't just about finding your mother's earring, it was related to something that happened to you personally?"

He nods slowly. "I was twelve, my brother was ten, my sister six. Babies by shade standards. Our parents took us hunting in Stygarde Forest. It borders the Black Lake. My mother lost her earring and didn't notice until we were home."

"Why was she wearing earrings to hunt?" I ask. "And for that matter, her gown and crown?"

A wistful smile curls his lips. "My mother owned no other clothing but dresses and at the time almost never wore the same one twice. Besides, to a shade the type of hunting we were doing was an easy stroll in the woods. She was barely at risk of breaking a nail."

I try to get my mind around that. I suppose when you can easily run as fast as any stag and are as strong as a bear, dealing with a gown isn't exactly an issue. "How did the earring end up in the lake?"

"Mother had an event that night, and she lamented that she didn't have the earring. The set had been a gift from my father. So I volunteered to go back into the woods to find it for her. It didn't take me long. As you saw, the blue pearls glowed in the moonlight, and it stood out on the forest floor. But before I could return it to my mother, Brahm snatched it from my hand. I hadn't even known he'd followed me into the woods, but he was always up to mischief, and that day was no different. I chased him, trying to get it back, but he darted through the woods and to the shore of the Black Lake, taunting me to follow. I didn't want to go there. Our parents had always told us to avoid the lake for fear of the monsters that lived in it. It's said the bottom is covered in bones."

I think back to the feel of the bottom under my feet. I'd thought I was walking on branches, stripped of their bark and smoothed over time. Bones, though, in retrospect, make more sense. I shudder.

He takes a deep breath and blows it out. "In any case, Brahm walked out onto an outcropping and held the earring over the water, daring me, through an ornery smile, to take it from him before he dropped it in the lake. I thought about taking on my battle form or tangling with his shadows but then decided he wasn't worth the effort. Brahm would return with the earring and take credit for finding it himself, and that was fine with me. But before I could leave, a Black Lake salamander, presumably the one you killed, leaped from the water and tore Brahm's arm off, earring and all."

"Jesus Christ! He lost an arm to that thing?"

Damien pushes off the window and comes to my side. "The salamander's silver venom is toxic even to us. The sight of Brahm screaming as his body bled, his shadows swirling around him, is something I will never forget. We can transform into shadow, but if we do so with an injury like that, it can become permanent. So I told him not to shift and carried him back to the castle where he had immediate care by the best doctors in Stygarde. It still took over a week for his body to rid itself of the toxin and for his arm to regenerate."

"That must've been terrifying for both of you. Thank fuck he was able to regenerate at all!"

Damien takes my hand, rubbing his thumb over the back of it. "You are lucky to be alive with all your limbs attached, Eloise. It's a miracle you survived."

I flinch at his words, and at first I'm not sure why. There's nothing uncaring about them or callous. But then it dawns on me. "It wasn't a miracle, Damien. It was me. My magic. The box didn't give me more than I could handle. Yes, I was injured, but I still won. And I'll win again."

"Maybe." He frowns.

"I need to know you still believe in me. You of all people have to believe I can do this."

He takes a deep breath. "I believe you can do it."

"Good."

"I also believe you shouldn't have to."

I lean my head back and look at the ceiling. "That ship has sailed."

He grunts in disapproval, but I soldier on. "Look on the bright side, now that we know the nature of the challenges, you can greatly improve my odds of success by telling me more about yourself."

A low chuckle rumbles in his chest. "How can I do that when my life didn't start until you summoned me?" We both groan and then laugh together. "I will do as you wish, little bird, as I have always done. But I loathe the thought of you going back through that archway. I'd bargain my soul to get you out of it."

I shake my head. "Don't you dare. No more bargains. No more deals. Our debt to this world ends here."

He gives me a slow, almost reluctant nod, then leans forward to kiss me, saying without words that his only true bargain is with me. A bargain for forever. A bargain to be mates.

When he draws back again, he straightens my blankets. "Now that we know the challenges come from my memories, you have one clear advantage. I plan to share as many of them as possible, only with you."

I scoot over to make room and he slides into bed next to me. Damien spends that night and every night of my recovery telling me stories about his world and drawing me maps of Tenebris. He describes in detail the kingdom of the dark elves in Willowgulch to the north, Stygarde to the south. The forest between, which he explains is a major source of contention, and the river of magma that runs from the mountains along the western border of the witch kingdom of Dimhollow. He tells me about the independent coastal territory of Aendor and the way merchant boats carry goods from the other side of their world to Stygarde's shores and Dimhollow's, and how pirates steal goods for the benefit of the dark elves of Willowgulch.

I try my best to commit everything to memory even when it all starts to run together.

After a week, Marabella clears me to go back to my room and back to my scheduled donations.

Much to Damien's growling disappointment.

37

UNEXPECTED GUESTS

ELOISE

With only a week until the full moon, the key turns in my lock and Everald is there. Once again, he's the picture of sophistication, his long, lean frame dressed in a waistcoat of amethyst velvet. A diamond earring winks from his lobe under perfectly coiffed hair. But it's the shopping bags weighing down his leather-gloved hands that catch my attention.

"You're already paying for my blood, Everald. You know you don't have to bring me gifts."

"You'll thank me for these," he says through a fang-filled smile.

I adjust the neck of my robe to cover more of my chest, then flip a hand over in his direction. "It's just, you know now that I'm mated, right? Accepting all this under the circumstances isn't appropriate."

He pulls a set of boots from one of the bags. They're a higher-end version of what I left beside the lake during the first trial. "I couldn't help but notice you came back through the archway barefoot."

I can't restrain my excitement as I take the boots and quickly try them on. "They're a perfect fit!"

"Marabella helped me with your sizes." He opens the second bag and hands me new tactical pants and a few different T-shirts and jackets. "I heard Everline had to cut yours off you when she did surgery. I told you I can get anything."

I hug the clothes to my chest. "I'm not sure what I would have done—" Before I can consider the consequences, I deliver a peck to his cheek. It's meant as a friendly gesture of thanks, but his eyes lock on me and his nostrils flare. Everald isn't human, and I've made a grave mistake treating him like one.

I back up a few steps, lifting my chin and offering an even, restrained smile. "Excuse me. That was, uh, I don't know what came over me. Um, the clothing is perfect. I will wear them in the next trial."

He holds up a hand. "Relax, Eloise. I wouldn't dream of trying anything with someone else's mate. I'm here for blood, that's all."

I blow out a held breath. "Thank you for understanding and for this very thoughtful gift."

He plants his hands on his hips. "I'm only going to say this once. You can thank me by winning this challenge. My money is on you, kid."

He's outfitting me because he wants me to win. This isn't because of my blood. He wants Valeska dead. "You want me to win."

"I do."

I'm about to ask why when his eyes narrow. "This isn't

a conversation we should have, Eloise. Suffice it to say that I am passionate about a free market, and nothing that exists under Valeska's rule is free. Now promise me you'll win, and let's move on." He tugs the velvet cuff of his jacket.

"I plan on it." The tension in my shoulders eases a notch. "So if you don't mind…" I offer my wrist.

He tips his head. "Of course."

Everald does not fall to his knees as Marcel did. He raises my wrist to his mouth and strikes. He drinks his fill slowly, just to the point where I feel woozy. When he draws back and seals the wound, he smiles a blood-tinged smile, his gaze focused over my shoulder toward the window.

I turn around to find Damien standing there, glaring at Everald like he's picturing his head on a pike. The vampire pulls my key from his pocket and leaves without another word.

"Don't let him get to you—"

My back thuds against the wall, my robe spread wide, Damien's hips pressed between my thighs.

"Damien—" I want to reassure him that the donation means nothing to me, that Everald is just the type of man who enjoys being seen as one of the haves. Someone with access to something that others can't have. I want to tell Damien that I'm his and only his. But he cuts me off with a deep kiss.

In a feat of strength that would be impossible for a human, he holds me up with one arm and works my robe open with the other. And shifts out of his clothes. His hands slide down to my knees and spread me open as wide as I'll go. And then he's in me. In one slick thrust, he buries himself all the way to the hilt, filling every part of me.

"You're mine, little bird," he rumbles, stretching me to my limit. *"Mine."*

"I love you, Damien." I dig my fingers into the silky waves of his dark hair, completely his. Supported against the wall, I'm at his mercy as he starts to move, and there is no place I'd rather be.

"I love you, my mate." His thrusts come harder, faster, deeper. He fucks me senseless like he's trying to merge our bodies. Sweat breaks out across my skin even as his shadows wrap me in their cool embrace. His illusion slips, and his horns and wings break through. My monster. My mate.

I reach over his shoulders and stroke the inner webbing of his wings. It seems to turn him on, because he growls and picks up the pace. My back thumps against the wall as he unleashes himself. This time my climax doesn't roll in like a gentle storm, it tears through me like a lightning strike. I scream loud enough they can probably hear me in the waiting room. Damien revels in it. He watches me come apart with a satisfied grin even as he swells inside me and finds his own release. I wrap my arms and legs tighter around him, taking everything he has to give.

"Mine, Eloise. Only mine," he repeats into my neck. "Always."

As the time for the second challenge closes in, Damien stays with me every day and trains me during my time off at night. We've started practicing my magic again too. Lighting and extinguishing a candle, making water form into salamanders that crawl the sides of the tub in my bathroom, creating a breeze strong enough to blow the covers off my bed. I'm getting stronger.

Physically, I'm in the best shape of my life. I've done more push-ups, lunges, and squats in this room than a fitness guru. And the witchy shakes Marabella has been feeding me make my recovery from my donations faster than ever. I need all the help I can get. I must win this second trial. Damien and I deserve better than this. It's time we put it behind us.

A knock comes on the door. I stiffen as the key turns in the lock. I'm not due to donate until after the next challenge. It's not time for a meal, and Damien never uses the door.

When it swings open, I see a face I haven't seen since the day I came to Marabella's.

"Olivia? How did you get my key?" I smile brightly, although the last time I saw her, she withheld vital information from me. We'd bonded during the auction and the train ride over, and at first I thought of her as a potential friend. But looking back, she'd worked at Marabella's before and knew about the outrageous expenses donors are charged that can keep them indebted to the house for years. She knew how difficult it would be for me to buy my freedom without having sex with my clients, but instead of warning me when the topic of sex came up, she comforted me with Marabella's strictly enforced rules. If I ever met a potential donor, the expense schedule would be the *first* thing I'd mention. Anyone with half a heart would do the same. Olivia didn't. I don't hate her. After all, nothing would have kept me from coming here. But I don't trust her.

"I wanted you to be the first to know." She widens her smile under those same doll-like features I found so arresting the day we met, and I see fangs. "I no longer work at Marabella's. I'm a client now."

I hold my smile, although if she suggests I feed her, I'm diving across the bed for the rope. This is my day off, and I don't want to feed a brand-new vampire whose restraint, I assume, is questionable. "You found someone to change you?"

She nods enthusiastically. "Finally met a vampire willing to do it."

Olivia struck me as perfect when I met her, but now I notice some enhancements. Her skin is smooth as marble. Her straight-backed posture is effortless. And her big blue eyes put off their own light. "I'm glad you got what you wanted."

She sighs. "Me too. Finally." She brushes nonexistent wrinkles from her dress. "I just wanted to say goodbye. I'm no use to Marabella anymore, so she's letting me go."

"Congratulations. So you'll be living here now, as part of the coven?"

She nods excitedly. "I was approved to stay, and my sire is taking me in. We're… involved."

"So, uh, good to see you, and good luck with every-thing." It's as close to *see you later* as I can get. "It's my day off, so I'm trying to prepare for tomorrow."

She sniffs, grinning as if I've said something funny. "Uh, right." She stands as if to leave. "I thought I might get a taste of your blood, but Marabella says all your slots are booked. I guess this challenge has made you, like, a famous donor or something." She rolls her eyes.

I lift my chin. "Not for too much longer now. With any luck, I'll win the next trial and Damien and I will be free of this place."

Olivia unlocks the door. "True. It will all be over for you soon, one way or another." She stares at me, a smirk plastered on her face, as the door slowly closes between us.

By the time the lock finally engages, I'm not surprised to find my hand on the hilt of my dagger.

38

THE SECOND TRIAL

ELOISE

I t's louder in the silo the night the scribes escort me to the second challenge. Thanks to Everald, I'm more prepared than ever in the state-of-the-art tactical gear he brought me. I find him leaning against the wall and give him a nod of thanks. From his spot beside Lazarus, I see Damien roll his eyes.

As the moon climbs, I spot Olivia against the wall with a familiar vampire at her side. I can't place where I've seen him before, but he's wearing a palace uniform—not in the military style like Marcel's, but similar to the ones vampires in administrative roles wear, those who work directly for the queen. Olivia's hand is coupled with his. So this is her sire.

My eyes snap back to the podium and box as Lazarus starts to speak. "Challengers, step forward." We do, and I can't help but notice that Valeska looks smug. I narrow my eyes and study the bitch. She has something up her sleeve. I can feel it.

"Valeska, because Eloise rolled for the first challenge, you will roll today."

Valeska tosses the dice. They bounce around the box until they land on three wavy lines and a blue circle. We both stare at the mirror in anticipation as it fills with white smoke. And then a set of eyes the color of melted chocolate come into view, fringed with thick lashes. The view pans back, and I see a gorgeous woman in a purple cloak with a silver crescent moon hanging around her neck. Her red lips move. A few seconds later, as if I'm watching an old film and the sound isn't properly synced, I hear, *say my name* as if it were whispered in my ear. Damien's eyes meet mine. He can't see what I see from his place next to Lazarus, but he gives me an encouraging nod.

I look again. Clearly my task is to find this woman and ask her her name, then return to the silo to announce it to the box. But where do I start? She doesn't resemble Damien at all. I don't think she's family.

Feathers and crystals adorn her hair, and when she twists her hand, magic erupts in her palm.

I chew my lip. She must be a witch. I shuffle through all the stories Damien shared with me. He only ever mentioned one witch and not by name. I'm guessing she's the one who helped Damien get his father back. The one from Dimhollow, the wild lands perched between the sea and the volcanic mountains that border Willowgulch. I picture the place Damien described in my head, hoping it will help me.

"Valeska, choose an archway," Lazarus commands.

I know which one I would pick. The moon archway shows a beach of red sand lapped by dark, rippling water. A boat waits ashore in the distance. The topography looks nothing like where the witch in the mirror is standing. In contrast, the star archway shows a dark forest, similar to the one in the mirror.

My heart beats harder as Valeska chooses the star archway and the forest within. I rush for the moon archway and leap across the threshold. Once my feet land on the red sand beach, I have to smile. Blood Beach is the seaport of Aendor, the coastal territory of Stygarde. If I row the boat around the stone wall sheltering the harbor, I can go ashore on the edge of Dimhollow which lies on the other side. Valeska might be closer, depending on which part of the forest she was transported to. But with any luck, she ended up on the other side of the volcanic river. She'll have to search for the witch. I know exactly where I'm going. I can win this.

"Don't get cocky, Eloise," Phantom says, jumping into the boat with me, their dainty paws landing cleanly on the wooden seat. "Remember, Valeska is faster than you. She may not have a map like you do, but she can cover ground ten times as fast. And if she gets lucky, she might be able to make it through the Dark Forest and over the river and mountain before we can get around the seawall buffering the harbor."

I pull up anchor and man the oars. "It doesn't look that far, but you're right. Do you think I should use magic to help push the boat?"

Phantom seems to consider it. "No. It's tempting, but we can't risk overusing your magic. The last trial came terrifyingly close to killing you. Save your power in case the witch won't give you what you want."

I throw my back into it the old-fashioned way. Pretty soon it's just me vs. an ocean that seems to go on forever. I hug the bank and fall into a rhythm. "Did you notice that smile Valeska gave me? Smug, right? What was that all about?"

"Don't let her get in your head, darling," Phantom says. "Who knows why someone like that does anything?"

I nod. "Only, she lost the first challenge. Why wouldn't she be more nervous about this one? Her entire disposition just seemed odd. It's like when Tony would try to gaslight me. Same expression."

The fox stares off into the distance with its glowing green eyes. "What could it be though? It's not as if she can cheat. You're not even in the same world."

"What do you mean?"

"During the first trial, based on the times you returned through the archway and the fact that both of you obtained the same earring, we know that there were two versions of the same test. Mirror worlds. Somehow the magic is plucking these scenarios out of Damien's head and creating all this, balancing the odds with your abilities. This is ancient, deep magic, Eloise. We can feel it like a dull vibration in the air."

I can't feel anything, but I'll take their word for it. I row steadily until we round the wall of the harbor. Instantly, waves barrel into me, rocking my little boat and making it harder to row. Phantom has to stand to keep their balance.

"How far?" I ask the fox.

"About a thousand yards I'd say."

"Fuck." My hands have started to blister, and as I look over my shoulder, the tip of the forest we're aiming for feels like it's getting farther away.

Phantom does a little dance when another wave plows into us and says, "Perhaps a little magic?"

The bond between us rises like a slack rope going taut, and I reach again for the magic my mother showed me how to call. Racking the oars, I feel the boat take off toward our destination, the water itself pushing us along. It's easier this time. All the practice I put in during my recovery has paid off. I'm not even winded as we slide into shore. The beach here is rocky, and I hug myself against a sudden chill.

"Does it seem colder here to you than on the boat?" I whisper.

"At least ten degrees. More, we think."

"Weird." I know better than to let it slow me down. All I need to do is get the witch's name and I'll be snuggled up to Damien in no time. Thankfully, the tactical jacket from Everald is appropriate for this weather. I pull on a skull cap and dark gloves from the pockets, then stride quickly toward the dense woods bordering the beach. If I understand correctly, this is Dimhollow. I just need to find the witches and then the witch in question.

As I enter the forest, I almost hit my head on a bundle of sticks and bones hanging from a tree branch. I step around it. We continue along a winding path, walking faster until I break into a jog.

"We have a… feeling," Phantom whispers. "Careful."

I check that both my daggers are sheathed at my thighs where I left them. "What's going to happen to me that hasn't already?" I say softly. "Giant spider? Bear? Can't be worse than the salamander." Up ahead, a pile of pine needles swirls like it's caught in its own mini tornado. Above it, another bundle hangs from a tree branch—this one cloth and fur and leaves. Past that, I see a pile of stones under another one: bones and hair and something smeared black. As I pass it, the stones topple.

Phantom stops, the hair along their back standing on end. "We don't like this, Eloise."

"What is it?"

As if in answer, a hand pops out of the ground beside the rocks and slaps the soil, palm flat on the forest floor. Behind it, a head and then a dirt-covered body rise from the earth in a way that reminds me of a swimmer exiting the side of a pool.

"Shiiiiit," I hiss, and then we run. We don't get far. Another hand breaks through the dirt in front of us, the body of a man rising up from below. This one is dressed in animal skins, wearing a headdress that appears like a wolf's skull with horns.

I stumble back and spin around to return the way we came, only to find three women waiting behind me, brushing dirt from their shoulders. I'm surrounded.

I touch the hilt of one of my daggers.

One of the women bares her teeth.

I leave it where it is.

They're not attacking me, but they're closing in. Studying me.

I clear my throat. "Can you take me to the leader of your coven?" I ask. "I need help."

They circle me, studying me, their paths growing tighter and tighter, closing in. I try not to panic. "Phantom, do you know what these things are?"

"Wraiths, darling. Like us."

"Like you?" My voice rises in disbelief.

"They are dead witches possessed by witch spirits."

"Zombies.

"No. Zombies are animated corpses. These are spirits. Thinking, intelligent spirits that have manifested using the dead. Just like us."

"Please," I say to the wraiths. "If I could just talk to the witch who helped Damien… It will only take a moment."

They act like they can't hear me. They close in.

"These are spirits, Eloise," Phantom says again. "You can command them. You have spirit magic."

"How?"

"Believe you can and you will." The fox steps into me until the soft fur of their side is brushing my leg.

I stand taller, lift my chin, and search deep inside myself for any magic that might connect me to these wraiths. I feel something, but I'm not sure exactly what it is. I've never used this part of myself.

"Stop!" I command, leaning my energy into a tingle I feel between my eyes.

The wraiths stumble to a halt. I want to ask where to find the witch in question, but without her name, I have no idea what to ask for. In the end, I simply say, "Show me to the witches of Dimhollow."

All four of them step around me and start walking deeper into the woods. I turn on my heel and follow.

"Good work," Phantom says.

"Let's not count our witches before they're hatched," I mumble. "This is heavy magic."

"Hang in there, darling. All you need is a name."

I get the very real perception that we are navigating a

labyrinth of trees. The way the path winds and folds in on itself disorients me, and I know without a doubt that I'd be lost if not for our ghostly guides. But every step comes at a cost. By the time we reach a large clearing between a neighborhood of quaint cottages made of stone and thatched roofs, I'm seeing spots and sniffing back the threat of a bloody nose. I'm also so cold I can't feel my fingers.

Weighed down by fatigue, my hold on the dead slips. The relief is instant, like I've been carrying five-hundred-pounds on my shoulders and just dropped it into the dirt. But the moment I release the spirits, they turn on me.

I bend myself protectively over Phantom as their screeches pain my ears and their icy claws scrape my back. The cuts are cold, then turn hot once they're open. I howl in pain. Tears form unbidden in the corners of my eyes. It hurts so bad I shake.

"Please!" I scream, curled into a ball around Phantom. "Does anyone here know Damien?"

"Let her go," a woman's voice says.

The clawing stops. Although my entire back feels stripped of skin and I cry out as a straighten, I turn toward the voice. It's her, just as the mirror portrayed her. Thank God it's her.

"I need to know your name," I force out.

She scoffs through perfect, full lips. "I'm not telling a fellow witch my name without knowing hers first."

"I'm Eloise, and I'm not..." Humans don't exist on this world, and I'm not going to win her trust by claiming not to be a witch.

"You're not what?"

"I'm not going to hurt you."

"Come inside. I'll treat those wounds before the death sinks in."

I don't like the sound of that. Pain steals my breath as I drag myself after her, Phantom hugging closely to my side. The witch pulls out a chair and guides me into it, then tears open the back of my shirt. I cry out as pain shoots along my spine and ribs like someone is electrocuting my bones.

"Ooh, ooh, ooh, they got you good. You protected your anchor though. Smart witch." She points her chin at Phantom, who is sitting near the door, foxy features striking a cunning profile as they watch the witch.

She grabs a clay pot from her rustic kitchen counter and starts smoothing a salve over my wounds. The pain abates immediately.

"That feels incredible."

"Start talking. Don't make me regret saving you."

"I'm sorry to barge into your coven like this, but I need your help. Damien is in trouble, and I need your name to free him."

Her eyes narrow. "Damien knows my name, girl, and I doubt he'd send an inexperienced witch like you here to obtain it for him if he didn't. Names hold power. But then you wouldn't be here if you didn't know that. Sorry, but I don't give mine out freely to anyone who asks."

"Just tell her the truth," Phantom says.

The witch drums her natural, unpolished nails on the table. "Listen to your familiar, Eloise. Tell me the truth."

"You can understand them?" I say, surprised.

"I speak many languages, girl. The one of the dead is a bit of a specialty."

My stomach drops as I think about the clock ticking

down. I need her name, and I need it five minutes ago. I give her a very quick recap of what I'm doing here, ending with, "I challenged the vampire queen for Damien. If I don't return with your name, I'll lose the second trial and risk losing him as my mate. I can't let that happen. Please, please help me."

She studies me for a few long heartbeats and then grabs my wrist and pulls my palm to her, inspecting the lines there. "You *are* Damien's mate."

"For now, but if I don't return with your name—"

"I never thought I'd see the day—"

"Please, if I could just—"

"Where is he? He disappeared centuries ago."

"He was pulled through a rift to my planet, Earth."

"Earth." She frowns. "But you can bring him back here. I sense the power in you."

"I can eventually, but—"

"You must." She grows agitated, squeezing my hand harder. "You have no idea the evil things that have transpired in Stygarde since he was lost. The kingdom needs him now more than ever."

I squeeze my eyes shut. Any other time, I'd love to hear everything, but the clock is ticking and Valeska is so fast. "Please. Without your name, Damien will remain a prisoner of the vampire queen on my planet forever, and I will be dead."

My hand is still resting in hers when I see an idea flash in her dark eyes. She moves to a cabinet pushed against the far wall and returns with a set of tarot cards. She starts flipping them on the table in front of me. I don't know anything about tarot, but I recoil when the death card is the last to flop.

Her dark eyes meet mine, and her lips draw into a wide grin. "You hold a secret in your blood."

My dragon blood. "Yes."

She lifts her chin and places her hands on her hips. "I will tell you my name if you swear to bring Damien back here after you've freed him. This world needs him as much as you do."

I stand from the chair. "I swear it." I've always planned to eventually return here with Damien anyway, when we're both ready.

She leans forward and whispers the name in my ear.

I bolt for the door and see the arch rise in the central space. I race for it, my back throbbing with the movement, and leap across the threshold. I have a second to register that Valeska is already there. Her mouth forms the word before I can part my lips.

"Aurora," she says, so fast I can hardly understand it. But the vampires can. I'm too late. I've missed winning by a fraction of a second. I grab my pounding head as Valeska's name flashes across the mirror. The crowd goes wild, exchanging money among the sound of curses and howls of excitement. I catch Marabella's eye, and she turns away with a shake of her head like she can't even look at me. George is at her side. He doesn't look at me either.

Someone touches my shoulder, and I jump back.

"Little bird?" Damien's voice sounds like it was conjured from cinders. I throw myself into his arms and weep. He picks me up and carries me back to Marabella's through a crowd of hissing vampires.

39
RICOCHET

DAMIEN

"Back so soon?" Dr. Everline asks as I sit Eloise on the examination table. I haven't inspected her wounds, but her clothes are soaked in blood… again. I'd do anything to save her from this, anything to protect her from the next challenge. Truly, I must have offended the gods. This helplessness is my worst nightmare. It's like having a slowly tightening noose around my mortal neck.

"Believe me, if I had a choice, I wouldn't be bothering you again," Eloise says with her usual cheerfulness. Even covered in blood, she's concerned with putting the people around her at ease.

But there is no comfort for the two of us. She's right that she doesn't have a choice. I've tried everything. I've had Lazarus scour every manuscript in the stacks and turn over every magical stone. We're not getting out of this until she faces that last trial. The trial that will either free me or doom us both.

"Hmm," Everline says from behind her. She's spread the pieces of Eloise's bloody shirt. "Can you explain how your clothes are bloody and shredded but your back is completely healed?"

My mate looks over her shoulder at the doctor. "Aurora—the witch we had to find—healed me with some salve while I was inside the challenge."

One of Everline's eyebrows lifts into her hairline. "Magical salve inside the challenge? Stars above, that's some damn powerful magic." She does a quick assessment. "You've lost a lot of blood. We'll give you an infusion along with a potion to speed healing and watch you overnight. You should be good as new by morning."

The good doctor vacates the room, leaving me alone with Eloise.

"Are you well, truly?"

She takes my face in her hands. "Truly."

"By the gods, I'm not sure I can endure seeing you walk out of that archway bloody again."

She sighs and touches her forehead to mine. "Sad. I'm really enjoying myself."

I give a low chuckle. "Little bird, if you weren't in need of medical care, I'd show you what to do with that smart mouth."

She puts her hands on my shoulders and pushes gently. I give her some space. "Damien, there's something I have to tell you. Something happened during my challenge. Something I think you should know."

"Tell me."

"Aurora asked me to promise I'd bring you back to Tenebris if I won the challenge. She said bad things have happened since you've been gone and that Stygarde needs you."

My inner shadows churn, going cold within my torso. "Did she give you any specifics?"

She shakes her head.

Eloise would never lie to me, but the Aurora she met in the challenge wasn't the actual Aurora. These challenges are simulations, mirror realities. They might be an accurate portrayal of what my world is like today or they might be a simulation based on my memories.

"When you win," I say carefully, "we will decide together what we'll do next. But nothing has changed for me. I will stay here as long as you wish to stay."

She leans into me, and I pull her into a tight embrace. "As long as I'm with you, the geography doesn't feel quite as important as it once did."

"Rest now. All you should be worrying about is winning the next challenge. Did the map I drew for you help at all?"

"Yes. My archway led to the Blood Beach in Aendor. I found Aurora's house quickly enough. I thought I had it. Valeska must have gotten really lucky."

My eyes narrow. The place where Valeska entered the forest was near the castle. Even with her advanced speed, it should have taken her longer to find the witch village. She would have had to search an entire forest and cross a mountain. Unless she somehow guessed correctly and went straight there.

The door opens and a nurse enters with a bag and IV supplies. "Hi, Eloise. Oh hi, Damien." She looks between the two of us and smiles warmly. "I'm here to start your

IV. Don't worry, I'm new but I've been practicing. You're my third one today."

"I believe in you, Ren," Eloise says kindly. "I didn't know you were working down here though. Is this new?"

"I took over for Olivia." She swabs a vein and prepares to insert the needle.

"I didn't know Olivia was working as a nurse for Dr. Everline."

Ren's eyes flick up to Eloise's and she frowns. "You don't remember? I think she was your nurse the last time you were injured. I saw her standing outside your room for what seemed like an hour. I thought she was waiting for you to finish with Damien before bringing you your meds or something."

Dark suspicion flits across Eloise's features as she meets my eyes again and holds an intense stare. Ren finishes hanging the bag, hugs Eloise, and leaves. Once we're alone, Eloise grabs my arm. "Olivia stopped by my room yesterday. Marabella told me she only returned to Night Haven to be a donor again because she wanted to find someone to turn her into a vampire. She came by to show me her fangs."

"A recent development, I assume?"

"Yep. I saw her at the trial tonight with her sire."

"What did he look like?"

"Palace uniform. Not a soldier. Short, slight frame."

"Fuck. That's Galloway, Valeska's personal assistant."

Eloise gapes, her eyes narrowing in disgust as she draws the connection I've already worked out. "Do you think Olivia spied on us and exchanged the map of Tenebris for becoming a vampire?"

I growl. "I think it explains how Valeska performed that trial like she had directions."

She squeezes her eyes shut and fists her hands. "That fucking bitch. And now I have no advantage going into the last challenge."

Rage burns in my blood, but I try to remain calm for her. "I must go. The night grows late and I have not fed."

Her brows dip in disappointment, but she nods, clearly more concerned with my welfare than her comfort. Typical Eloise. "All right. Will you spend the day with me after?"

"Eloise…" I cup her chin, using my thumbs under her jaw to tip her head and kiss her in a way that will last until I return. She wants me to stay, but there's something I need to do for her. Something that can't wait. "I wouldn't miss it, little bird."

I stride from the infirmary and break into shadow.

OUTSIDE GALLOWAY'S HOME, I LURK IN THE SHADOWS, waiting for dawn. By Night Haven standards, it's a mansion. The place has to have fifteen rooms, and the front yard's landscaped stone and statuary are worth hundreds of thousands of dollars. The massive fountain out front features the three graces, the figures circling a central pedestal, hands linked and backs to the column. The water that arcs over their heads is dyed red to resemble blood.

So fucking pretentious.

Why didn't Valeska choose Galloway as her mate? The little pissant would have happily licked her boots. As it is, his nose is permanently brown from kissing her ass. Obsequious little shit.

The streets have grown quiet by the time he arrives with a blond vampire on his arm. Something about her reminds me of Valeska—the type of woman who wears her beauty like armor and whose eyes betray no compassion or empathy. Shark eyes. This woman was a monster before she ever became a vampire.

I step out onto the walkway, blocking their path. "Olivia?"

"What do *you* want?" she asks, folding her arms. She's not afraid of me. She should be.

Such a new vampire.

Galloway's eyes shift from me to her, and he steps away from Olivia. Does she even realize that her sire has no interest in protecting her? They aren't mates. She's a plaything to him, nothing more.

He holds up his hands. "Damien, you know I only do what she tells me to do."

Olivia scowls. "You don't owe him an explanation, Galloway. He'll be Valeska's dog soon enough."

I chuckle to myself as Galloway takes another step away from her.

"Can we talk about this?" he asks, but the question is half-hearted. He knows what's about to go down, and he's not going to do a thing about it.

"Hmmm. No." I move closer to Olivia, staring her deep in the eyes. Compelling a vampire is harder than compelling a human but not impossible. "Did Valeska ask you to spy on Eloise or did you do it on your own?"

Her eyes go dull, and the corner of her mouth curls. I'm inside her mind but not in control. Still, I feel her desire to confess. Her mind is begging for her to spill what she believes is a cunning act of ingenuity. She's proud of what she's done.

"It was my idea. I heard everything you told Eloise and relayed it to Valeska once she agreed to have me turned." She lifts her chin defiantly. "And now I have immortality."

My lips curl, but it is no smile. "Is that what you think?" I strike before Olivia knows what's coming. She struggles. I taste the fear in her blood when she realizes vampire strength is nothing compared to the strength of a shade.

Galloway slides his hands into his pockets as I drain her dry, feeding my hunger and my need for revenge. "Try not to get blood on the stone, Damien. It's imported."

I retract my fangs. She's desiccated but not dead yet. I dig my fingers beneath her jaw and tear her head from her body. Both head and body burst into flames and settle to the stone, nothing but a pile of ash. I reach down and grab a fistful, my narrowed eyes trained on Galloway.

"Don't look at me like that, Damien. You know Valeska ordered me to turn her. I had no idea what agreement she struck with the queen."

"Right. It's never your fault, is it Galloway?"

He snorts, shakes his head. "She'll never win anyway. You know that, right?"

A growl rumbles through me. I'm too full to drain him… tonight. "My mate was strong enough to win the first challenge and threatening enough for Valeska to resort to cheating on the second. Eloise will win the third trial, and when the queen falls, you'll be lucky to survive the transition in leadership."

For a full breath, I enjoy the flash of fear that colors his features. Then I break apart and return to Eloise.

40
DISAPPOINTMENT

ELOISE

I've barely settled into a new room in the infirmary when Marabella storms in without knocking. Her strides are quick, her arms stiff with her agitation.

I lean my head back against the pillow and stare out at the garden beyond the window. "Relax. The doctor says I'll be good to go tomorrow. You won't have to reschedule any donation sessions."

"Is that what you think this is about, Eloise? Donation sessions?"

I turn my head slightly so that I can examine her face. "Don't tell me you've started to actually care about me."

She turns around, pokes her head out the door and looks both ways, then locks us both inside the room.

"Why are you locking the door?"

"Because we need to talk." She strides back toward me and pulls a chair up to the bed. "Today's loss cost us all."

"Is this about money? Did you lose something betting on me? I can't be responsible—"

"It's not about money," she retorts. "The resistance is losing hope."

"The resistance?"

"Haven't you put it together yet, girl?"

I shake my head. "I don't know what you're talking about."

She frowns. "You need to know what's at stake for the entire vampire species if you don't win the next trial. Most of the masters whose covens make up this hive never agreed to be a part of it, Eloise. Valeska conquered them one by one. She's already so powerful that there are rumors that even the forebears—the most powerful of their species—won't be strong enough to stop her with Damien at her side."

I groan and look at the ceiling. How many times have I heard that dire warning? "Obviously I'm doing everything I can to keep that from happening. In fact, I've almost died twice trying to prevent it. In case you can't tell from the safety of the observation area, I'm doing the best I can."

She meets the sharp glare I send her way and holds her ground. Blowing out a held breath, she takes my hand in hers with a tenderness I doubt she feels. "The day you challenged Valeska, people were afraid to dream that you might be the answer to our prayers. But when you won the first challenge, everyone in the resistance celebrated. You proved you were capable of winning this thing, and we dared to hope. You are the first real hope we've had of stopping her. Abolishing the hive in favor of independent covens is what's best for everyone, and you can be the catalyst to make that happen."

I snatch my hand away. "If you think I need more pressure to succeed, let me set you straight. I'm at capacity. None of this is helping. But yeah, if it will make you feel better, I'll keep in mind the future of the vampire species when I'm wrestling a shadow bear or swimming a river of lava next trial."

Marabella turns away with a huff of exasperation. She paces toward the window, looking out over the Japanese garden. "You're strong, Eloise. Much stronger than I ever expected. If you believe you can win the next challenge, you *will* win."

"I think I can win," I say. "I won't know until I see what—"

"No." She slashes a hand through the air. "You *will* win. You were strong the day you came here. I've made you stronger every day since."

Something in her voice gives me pause. "How exactly? Providing me with powerful allies is great, but they aren't in the challenges with me, Marabella."

"The charmed shakes, Eloise. The herbs, the enchantments, the blood that flows into you now from that bag in your arm. You had magic the day you came here. Everything I've given you since has been to make you stronger and more resilient."

The shakes definitely helped me recover faster, but did they make me more resilient during the challenges? I don't think so. I owe most of my survival to training with Cassius and Maeve and help from Phantom.

I close my eyes, suddenly exhausted. "As soon as I'm able,

I'll train with Damien again between my donations. The only reason Valeska won this time was because Olivia spied on us and gave her the map of Tenebris that Damien gave me."

"Olivia spied on you?" Marabella's voice drops in disgust, then her eyes widen as she puts it all together. "She exchanged the map for her turning. That bitch!" She points a finger at me. "She and that slimy sire of hers are officially banned from Marabella's for life."

I nod. "Thanks. It isn't the end. The map might benefit Valeska again, but I'll make sure I know everything there is to know about Damien before I step through that archway."

Marabella folds her arms over her chest, chin lifting. "You are officially off the schedule for now, although I insist on one more donation for George. I will clear out a room for you down here, and you will have guards. I should have suspected Olivia. That snake has always had her eye on the prize of immortality. This time no one disturbs you without being cleared by me first."

My lashes flutter in surprise. This is very unlike Marabella. "That will be helpful."

She waves a hand dismissively. "The only way I want you to thank me is by winning the next trial and…"

"And?"

Marabella approaches my bed again and looks me directly in the eyes. I get the sense that this entire conversation is really about this, what she's about to tell me. The air between us suddenly grows thick and heavy. "If you kill her, you will be queen, Eloise. You will have the right to take her place. No human has ever been a master before, let alone a queen, but Lazarus tells me that technically you earn the title if you kill her."

"I don't want it."

She breathes out a sigh of relief. "Then you will have no problem doing the right thing and rejecting it. Once you reject it, you must do three things. First, order Marcel to dismantle the troops and split the soldiers among the separate covens. Second, order Lazarus to transform the palace into a library for all covens, and third, tell Everald to sell Valeska's personal wealth to fund the transition of power. The covens will need capital and goods to make the transition to self-sustaining units successfully. Everald is in the best position to lead that transition. George will use his position as master to help other covens peacefully make the break."

"You've planned this from the beginning. You made sure that three powerful vampires had my blood. Lots of my blood. You made sure they were blood bonded to me so they must obey me."

She nods once. "I took a chance, you understand."

"Because I might lose?"

She snorts. "You won't lose. Despite that awful performance today, you want him more than she does. You know him better than she does."

"Let's hope you're right about that."

"No, I took a chance that you wouldn't want Valeska's power for yourself. That you wouldn't want to be queen of Night Haven."

"I'm human. I can't lead a vampire coven."

"You say that now, but you'll be tempted."

I shake my head. "Not for every dollar that's ever been printed, mama."

She laughs. "Good. Then we have an understanding."

I send her an exaggerated smile. "That depends."

Her eyes narrow. "On what?"

"Technically I owe you another month of service after the challenge. If I win…"

She rolls her eyes. "If you win, I will ride with both of you to the surface and throw confetti as you walk through the doorway. Time served."

"Time served *and* with my cut of the money I've earned for you. I'm done being taken advantage of."

Marabella taps her foot, considering. "Deal."

We shake on it and say our goodbyes. The lock clicks as she lets herself out of my room.

A few hours later, Ren comes back and removes my IV. "You're good at that, you know. I didn't even feel it going in."

Her cheeks pinken. "I think, maybe, when I leave here, I want to do this. Be a nurse, I mean."

"You'd be great at it."

She holds pressure on a piece of gauze over the tiny hole in my arm. "I've paid my debt. Technically I could leave, but…"

"But?"

She shrugs one shoulder. "I want to, but I'm afraid. No one is waiting for me up there. I'm sure everyone thinks I'm dead. And I deserve that. The drugs were a problem. I'm lucky, really, that Marabella fished me out of the gutter. But now when I go back, I'll be starting over from scratch. I'll have no support system. No friends. No lover. I'll be alone. Really, truly alone."

I frown and place my hand on hers. "You're a beautiful person, Ren, and I don't just mean how you look. You're kind and a hard worker. I'm willing to bet you won't be alone for long."

She tips her head. "I'm not so sure about that. It's a big world out there, and we're all just running around loose in it, trying our best to carve out an existence."

"Running loose is better than being held captive. The pro and the con are identical in this situation. Nothing will happen to you if you stay here. Then again, *nothing* will happen to you if you stay here."

She looks at me and smiles. "I wish I were as brave as you, Eloise."

"You think I'm brave?"

"You challenged the queen. It's like you're not afraid to die."

I scoff, but the truth of it settles in quickly. I knew I'd probably die if I came here. I did it anyway. "I am afraid to die. I'm just more afraid to live without Damien. If we're lucky, we find someone worth dying for. I hope that you meet someone someday who inspires you to be brave. But I don't think that's going to happen if you allow fear to keep you here."

"You're right. I know you're right." She takes a deep breath and blows it out.

"You're strong and you're smart, Ren. You'll meet people, good people. Besides, what good is reading all those romance novels if you never get to live your own story?"

"You're a good friend, Eloise." She stares at me for a heartbeat, then hugs me in my hospital bed. "Oh God, I hope you survive this."

I laugh to keep from crying. "Me too, sister."

I'M IN DEEP SLEEP WHEN FOOTSTEPS IN MY ROOM WAKE ME. Damien stands next to the bed, his expression dark. He extends his fist and drops a handful of ash onto my hospital tray.

I rub my eyes. "What's that?"

"Olivia's head. Well, part of her head. It was hard to determine how much of her remains constituted her head."

I try to process what he's saying as I stare at the tiny pyramid of dust.

"You should know I killed her," he adds in a voice that's all grit and cinder without a hint of remorse.

I push myself up in bed. "You murdered Olivia and brought me her head?"

He nods slowly.

How do I feel about that? I try to find some empathy for the woman who betrayed me, but I can't. I'm too tired. The old me might have challenged him, encouraged him to find a way without using violence. That girl is dead. I've endured too much. There's too much riding on this next challenge for me to waste a single moment fretting about Damien being Damien.

Olivia had it coming, and the fact that he took her life so effortlessly is a reminder of the power of my mate. This is why Valeska wants him so badly. It's also why his kingdom needs him. Damien is wired to be loyal. To be loved by him is to exist in the shelter of that love. This challenge has left him feeling helpless, like a cat without his claws. And good for him for finding an appropriate scratching post. I refuse to mourn a woman who traded my best hope of survival for a chance to become a vampire and then came to my room and rubbed it in my face. I refuse to mourn fake friends when true love is standing right in front of me.

The way he's looking at me is halfway between patient and defiant. He did what he felt he had to do, and now he's waiting for me to fight him on it.

I flop back on the mattress and smile lazily up at him. "Wash your hands before you come to bed. I don't want her ashes in the sheets."

The smile he rewards me with is lined with relief. He rolls the tray away from the bed, then strips off his clothes, never breaking eye contact. Brazenly, he walks into the attached bathroom, leaving the door open as he steps into the shower. Thank God I'm not hooked up to a heart monitor, because my pulse flutters as the water slithers along the moguls of his hard, toned flesh. Soap dribbles down the groove of his spine, disappearing in the valley between the two perfect mounds of his ass. I have half a mind to drag myself in there so we can take turns getting dirty and then clean again, but when I pull back the covers, the wave of fatigue that hits me warns me I'm not completely recovered. Not even close.

I don't even pretend like I'm not ogling every part of him as he steps from the shower, dries himself off, and then climbs into bed beside me.

"Better?" He lifts a teasing brow. He knows he's hot as fuck and just teased my still-injured ass into a puddle of lust.

I run my nails down his chest and lick over one of his nipples. His breath draws in on a hiss. I raise my gaze to his. "Thank you for defending me."

His hand digs into my hair, his eyes taking on that blue-tinged intensity they do when he's exceptionally passionate. "I'd turn this entire hive to ash and every vampire in it to be with you, Eloise. I'd burn this world down to protect you."

I throw one knee over his hips and slide on top of him, brushing my lips against his. "I know. I hope you don't have to, but I know."

Our soft kiss grows deeper, his hands stroking down the open back of my hospital gown and cupping my ass, the tips of his fingers sending heat between my parted legs. As worn out as I am, I'm already wet for him. But there's one more thing I need to know before I lose myself in him.

I draw back, my face close to his. "You didn't tell me about the resistance."

He nibbles my bottom lip. "I didn't want to put you under more pressure."

Unlike Marabella, who heaped it on like a scoop of mashed potatoes.

"You, your kingdom, my own life… What's one more reason I have to win this?"

"I should have told you." He's quiet for a moment. "I realized something tonight when I was removing Olivia's head from her body."

I suppress a shiver. "What's that?"

"From the beginning, I keep making the foolish mistake of underestimating you, my little dragon. You are no rabbit of a woman in need of my protection from the prowling lion. You are a fierce thing with sharp claws and teeth. And you've become quite good at cheating death." He strokes my spine from the ends of my hair to the backs of my thighs. "Someday, when you are ready, I want to take you to my kingdom and make you my princess."

I beam down at him. "Your princess, huh? I don't know. Would I have to live in the castle and wear gorgeous dresses and a crown like your mother's?"

He chuckles. "That wasn't even her crown. It was just a tiara for casual use."

I laugh so hard we shake the bed. "For casual use. Washing-dishes tiara. Mowing-the-lawn tiara."

"Would you like to see the crown jewels reserved for my princess?"

"I think it's important for me to make an informed decision."

He holds out his hand, and shadows coalesce to form what appears to be a crown of black ice with sharp spires that rise higher in the front than in the back. "This doesn't do it justice of course. It's composed of black diamonds and carbon steel, befitting shade royalty. It will look radiant against your red hair." With a turn of his hand, the image is gone.

"Do you think your family will accept me? A human?" A family of shades inviting a mere human into their royal ranks would be like a royal family of orcas inviting a seal.

He presses a kiss to my nose. "They will if they want their eldest son back."

"But Damien, we can't force—"

"Shhh. Enough for now. We will discuss it when the time comes." His hands begin to stroke me again, down my back, over my hips, fingertips brushing along my slit.

The room grows quiet except for the sound of our breathing. I meet his eyes again, thinking about his kingdom and the crown he showed me.

"I used to think I lost myself when I married Tony, that the abuse turned me into a shell of who I really was.

When he died, when I helped to kill him, it felt like waking up in many ways. But now I understand more and more that I never actually knew who I was before you, Damien, before I was forced to grow taller to reach what I wanted. When this is over, I will never take that for granted. Someday, when we're ready, I will accept that crown."

"It will be yours," he growls. He fists my hips, lifting me onto the head of his cock. I sink onto him, my body singing at the invasion. Damien knows this body better than anyone, and I see the concern in his eyes that I'm not fully recovered. He gently turns us over, supporting his weight on his elbows as he rocks into me over and over. Tenderly, he kisses my throat, my breasts, his shadows caressing places his lips can't reach.

My climax snowballs slowly from a deep wave of pleasure to an elaborate and spectacular release that drags him over the edge with me. Afterward, he cleans me up and I nestle into his side. Content and safe, I drift off to thoughts of castles, crowns, and Damien.

41

THE THIRD TRIAL

ELOISE

Marabella is true to her word. I train in a converted room in the infirmary, practicing both my magic and fighting skills until exhaustion each day. The protein shakes keep coming. By the end of the second week, my endurance is noticeably improved in both departments. Everald supplies me with another set of new gear but doesn't ask me for blood. In fact, I'm not required to donate to anyone.

Until George.

The night before the full moon, the master of the Liberty coven appears in my room, escorted in by Marabella's guards. Then I remember I promised to feed him one more time before my trial.

"Marabella didn't tell me you were coming tonight." I gesture toward the yoga pants and T-shirt I've been practicing in. "I'm supposed to wear the robe."

"Never mind the robe. This won't take long, and I won't take much. You'll barely notice."

The guards leave us.

I step forward, offering my wrist.

He holds up a hand. "We'll get to that." He waddles over to the window and looks out on the garden. "Some view you got here. Fancy. Bright as fuck, but nice to see flowers down here." He backs away from the glass, stepping out of the rectangle of light and blinking his eyes.

"I'm looking forward to going home. My grandmother has a garden where I live. Not like this. I mean, not a Japanese garden. Roses and rhododendrons mostly. She had a green thumb."

"She's not around anymore?"

My gaze drifts to where I last saw Phantom. "She's always with me in one way or another."

He slumps against the wall. "You gotta win tomorrow, Eloise."

"I'll do my best," I say. "I've been practicing. I'm better than before."

He rubs his sagging jowls. "The woman who sired me, she was like Valeska in many ways. Centuries old. Vicious. They say we're immortal, but I don't think that's the right word for it. We do age in a way. The bodies we inhabit become worn over centuries. And although we won't ever meet a natural death, we can be killed. The oldest ones spend their years sleeping, bored of this world, desperate to preserve what's left of their bodies and always looking over their shoulder, paranoid that a younger vampire wants what's theirs."

"That doesn't sound like an enviable position," I say softly.

"It ain't. Life, whether it lasts fifty years or one thousand and fifty, is only good so long as you have purpose. That's what my maker never understood. She turned me because she needed someone. I thought she did it for someone to maintain her house, but what she really wanted was love and friendship. And I wasn't the person to love her. I resented her for keeping me there like some kind of pet."

"You couldn't leave?"

"When a vampire sires you, they have a strong influence over you. They can compel you to do things. Victoria compelled me to stay with her because her sire bond made me the only one she could trust in the Liberty coven. Everyone else wanted her dead. I did too, but it's a complex relationship a new vampire has with their sire. I couldn't kill her. Didn't have the guts for it. Anyway, I hated her for turning me. Hated her so much that I made her life hell for years. She released me from our sire bond just before she took her own life."

"I'm sorry. That sounds horrible, George. But why are you telling me this?"

"Let's just say I wanted to give you something to focus on. Whatever comes tomorrow, you're mated. You've got love. And that's worth living and dying for. So just know you have something that Valeska has never had. She tried to steal Damien because she has no one to love her like he loves you. She hates you for it because she's jealous, but even if she wins, she'll never have him like you have him."

Wow. Who knew that George the vampire plumber could be so deep?

"Now feed me some blood and I'll see you after you kick her ass in trial number three."

I laugh and hold out my wrist. I feel the now-familiar rush of vampire venom when he strikes, and all my insides go bubbly. He only takes a few sips, and then he seals the wound.

"Good luck tomorrow, sweetheart," he says, turning for the door.

"George, did you ever find a mate?"

He grins. "Maybe she's runnin' this place. How about that?"

"I can see it." I smile as he leaves without another word.

THE FOLLOWING NIGHT I'M ESCORTED TO THE SILO LIKE every time before, only there's something different in the air. As I walk through the marketplace, people have T-shirts with my face on them. They have signs wishing me well. Someone even has a giant foam finger. I see Everald and know who's responsible. It definitely lifts my spirits.

The silo is packed, and Valeska is already there, surrounded by her admirers, that same smug smile on her face. She's confident she's going to win. But I hear the sounds of people betting on our lives behind me. One of the bookies tells a vampire that the odds are slightly in Valeska's favor. Slightly. People believe in me. People want me to win.

My heart swells as I acknowledge that the most important people want me to win. Damien, for one. I spot him behind the box, next to Lazarus, who gives me a reassuring nod. As I turn slowly, scanning the crowd, I spot Marcel strategically at the very center. He bows his head to me when our eyes meet. George and Marabella are directly behind me and also smile encouragingly. Everald salutes me from his place near the wall.

When I turn back toward my mate, Damien's eyes are only on me. Valeska and I are about sixteen feet apart, each standing in front of one of the archways. There's no disguising the way Damien's head is turned to face me. Our connection is a palpable thing. It must infuriate Valeska. That vain, narcissistic psychopath wants to believe that somewhere, deep down, Damien is attracted to her. That some part of him wants her to win. Anyone with half a brain knows the idea is ludicrous. She tortured him and assaulted him. He can't wait to see her dead.

I imagine it driving her insane inside that pretty, dark head of hers, and the thought makes me happier than it should.

"Eloise, it's your turn to roll," Lazarus says as the moon reaches its peak.

I take a second to appreciate how beautiful the moon is, how much I want to have a life under it with Damien. A rush of adrenaline makes my hand tremble as I pick up the dice and throw them into the box.

I've become so much stronger these past four weeks that they ricochet around several times before coming to rest on a carving of a diamond and a swirling blue symbol. White fog bleeds into the mirror at the back of the box, clouding out the silver. I stare intently, waiting for our mission.

A single word fades into the center of the mirror. CHOOSE.

Choose? Choose what? I step back, and the portals within the archways go wavy, and then I see something that makes my heart leap. Under the moon arch is the crown of black diamonds that Damien showed me when he told me he would one day make me his princess. Under the star arch is the casual tiara his mother wore during the first trial.

I already know I'm going to choose the crown that represents the promise Damien made to me. But the mirror smokes over again. Another word. WIN.

We wait, but there are no further messages.

Lazarus prompts me to choose first. It's my turn.

I race for the black diamond crown and leap over the threshold. My right hand palms the hilt of my dagger. All is dark. The sensation of falling goes on and on, and I brace myself for impact. Have I unwittingly launched myself off the side of the castle? Am I being dropped into a lion's cage at the center of a deadly labyrinth? It doesn't matter. I'm ready for anything. I will do anything to be with Damien.

My feet hit stone, and it doesn't feel like I'm landing at all, only like I've taken one giant step. But what's in front of me makes no sense. I'm back in the silo. The two crowns are suspended in the air above my head. I glance toward Damien. He and Lazarus look completely befuddled.

I look back at the crown. Clearly my challenge is to jump for it. It's high but not impossibly so. But before I have a chance, the crowd rumbles and I look to my side. Valeska steps out of her archway. She's as bewildered as I was until she sees that there's no barrier between us.

Damien moves for me and slaps an invisible wall. The impact ignites a honeycomb of purple cells that stretch in a dome over me and the queen, a force field between us and everyone else in this silo. It's just us in here. Me and her. No one can interfere.

And then I understand.

The goal is the crown of our choosing.

I'll have to go through her to get it.

And she'll have to go through me.

Win, the mirror had said.

For a split second, I'm terrified. This was never supposed to happen. Sabrina swore to me that the magic of the box kept the challenges even and fair. I was never supposed to have to face her directly.

It's so unfair.

How am I supposed to—

I stop my thoughts right there and unsheathe my second dagger, raising both of them between us. This bitch does not get to win. She does not get Damien. The bond between Phantom and me wrenches taut as I sink low into a fighting stance, echoing the chilling smile she sends me. Magic buzzes in my torso.

Valeska's pretty face morphs into a sardonic grin, her eyes going full black as her fangs extend. She eyes my fighting stance and laughs, hers remaining upright and casual. She's confident that she can beat me in a one-on-one fight. "No separate challenge to save you. No help from your blood-whore friends. I'm going to enjoy killing you, human filth. Slowly and with pain."

A chant rises in the crowd. "Va-les-ka. Va-les-ka." No one here thinks I can win *this* trial.

I lift my chin. No one but me.

Without breaking eye contact, I extend my upward-facing palm, open and curl my fingers around the hilt of my dagger, beckoning her to me. Once. Twice.

She attacks.

Six months ago, this fight would be over in seconds. Valeska is the strongest and fastest opponent I have ever faced, and that includes Damien and Cassius. But I'm different now. I'm stronger. Months of practicing my magic and ingesting the healing herbs from Marabella pay off.

Her claws come at me at superspeed, and I weave and dodge with perfect clarity, my daggers sweeping ever closer to her face, her limbs, her gut. Her foot kicks toward my middle, but I turn to the side, sweeping my dagger up as I whirl around her back. I nick her cheekbone.

The crowd goes wild.

She pauses to wipe the blood, surprise ricocheting through her expression. She sucks the bead of red off her thumb.

The next time she attacks, she's nothing but a blur. Only my hold on Phantom keeps my head attached to my shoulders. Bending backward until I'm parallel to the floor, I narrowly avoid Valeska's clawed fingers as they pass right over my nose. I flop on my back, shoot my legs out between hers, and roll, taking her down to the floor with me. It's an ugly, unrefined move, but it catches her off guard. She doesn't expect me to be this fast.

That's when I understand. The magic of the box ensures that these trials are fair. Sabrina said I'd never have to face Valeska because she was so much stronger than I was, thus the previous parallel challenges. But as Valeska's fist narrowly misses my head and connects with the stone beside my ear, I sink my dagger into her kidney and realize why this is happening.

I am stronger now.

I am as strong as Valeska.

And I can win this thing.

I roll out from under her, tearing my blade from her side. It spurts maroon blood across the floor but heals quickly. Back on my feet, I go on the offensive. Closing the distance between us, I move inside her next blow and sweep my blade up. I aim for her throat, but she moves toward me so fast my blade lands under her bottom rib. I hear her flesh sizzle and know the Stygian blades are doing their dirty work. The angle of my blade means I must be close to her black heart. She catches my wrist, tries to pull it out, but I hold firm. I'm so close I imagine the tip scraping the useless organ.

She shifts and a vise closes around my throat—her opposite hand. I stab my other dagger through her wrist and try to use the blade as a lever to pry the hand off my throat.

Neither of us yields.

"Have you learned nothing about vampires, you human cunt?" Valeska spits in my face. "Our hearts don't beat." She releases my wrist. My dagger slices through her bones and lands in her heart. Gritting her teeth, she grabs my neck with both hands. Using all my strength, I drag the dagger up through her ribs, her lungs, her heart, splitting open her chest before tearing it sideways from her torso.

It's a move that would be impossible with human weapons, but my blades are not of this planet.

Blood spurts from Valeska's lips, and her grip on my throat eases just long enough for me to pull free.

"Your heart may not beat, but you do bleed," I rasp through my recovering airway.

"Fucking cunt!" she gurgles. She shoves me with a strength I don't see coming. I fly across the dome, my back slamming into the barrier with enough force I almost black out. I hear Phantom whimper inside my head. Our connection goes slack. My daggers clatter to the stone. My body crumples between them.

I can't breathe. I can't move. Black dots circle in my vision. I've never been hit by a car, but I have to believe this is what it feels like. Not a car, a truck. Not just a truck, a semi.

Precious minutes pass before I manage to draw a tiny sip of air into my lungs, and it burns.

Above me, Damien is in his monster form. and he's slamming the heels of his paws against the dome, yelling for me to get up. I try. My arm bends. One knee. I spot a dagger and reach for it.

A chant grows in the silo. "EL-O-ISE, EL-O-ISE." They're chanting *my* name now. The corner of my mouth twitches.

I'm on my side. My searching hand finds the dagger, and I dare a glance toward Valeska. Inside a puddle of her own blood, she's closed the wound I opened in her torso and is tucking all her parts inside. She's managed to tear her shirt off and tie it around her chest like a tourniquet.

She's hurt but she's standing.

And she's fucking angry.

Cassius taught me the only way to kill a vampire, short of direct sun, is to cut off their head.

I make it to my hands and knees.

I crawl for my second dagger.

Air finally fills my lungs. It's a small mercy.

Everything hurts.

Somehow, drawing on every ounce of magic I can pull from Phantom, I stumble to my feet. I am a tower of torn and broken things, but I face the monster I came to slay. Can she see it in my eyes? That I have become an even darker monster? Can she see the promise I have for her in the glint of my blades? Can she see how love has made me hard as stone and sharp as broken glass?

I bare my teeth.

I taste blood.

She comes for me.

I let her.

She reaches for my head.

I sweep the dagger between our bodies, aiming for her throat.

A loud snap rings through my ears.

42

THE END OF EVERYTHING

DAMIEN

The sound of my mate's neck snapping is a gong that drowns out every other noise in the room. Eloise drops like a sandbag, her beautiful green eyes staring sightlessly in my direction. A few strands of her hair have come free from her ponytail, and the bright red curls stick to the sweat on her fair skin. Her hair is the color of blood, although I'm spared the sight and scent of the actual thing. Valeska broke her neck. She's otherwise intact.

All color and life drains from the world. I drop to my knees. "Eloise! My little dragon. My fallen bird." I sob openly, not caring about the shame it brings me as a warrior. Not caring about anything but the shattering of my soul as I stare at my fallen mate. My hands beat against the barrier between us, morphing from enormous, black-taloned paws to my corse form, the form that fits with hers, the form in which I will die.

Through the deep, wrenching agony of our severing bond, our time together flashes through my mind. The night she summoned me. Her smile. Her laugh. The way she held herself like she was larger than a grizzly bear when she was feeling brave. I see her in the tiny dress she wore to Bad Witches' Club that brought me to my knees. I see her kneeling on her grandmother's grave. I see her trembling, covered in her assailant's blood. This woman was my goddess, my lighthouse, my freedom, my sanctuary. I cannot bear a world without her in it.

I glance toward Lazarus, who is beside me now, hand on my shoulder. "Do it. You must do it," I tell him. He knows what I want. We spoke of it for hours before this night.

My pleas are swallowed by the roar of the crowd. Some are chanting Valeska's name. Others are wailing at the loss of their wagers. Still others, like Marabella, who appears at the edge of my vision, stand in silent vigil to the death of my mate.

"Now Lazarus. You must decapitate me before Valeska can reach me." I grab the scribe's hand and beg. It is no bother. I am already on my knees.

"She hasn't been declared the winner," Lazarus hisses. "The mirror remains occluded."

I raise my eyes to find Valeska still struggling to grasp my mother's crown. My little dragon has gutted her, and without blood to heal herself, she's weakening. She bares her fangs and leaps, but her fingers just miss the gold edge. A small thrill goes through me as I watch her struggle.

But then my gaze drops to Eloise again. A fly lands on her face, crawls across her open eye. Any pleasure I've gained that the crown remains out of Valeska's reach is dashed at the sight of Eloise's motionless body.

Valeska *will* win.

There can be no other outcome.

Eloise is dead.

I turn toward Lazarus. "You must do it. I cannot go on without her, old friend. Please."

The scribe draws the Stygian-steel dagger I gave him from the folds of his robes.

I lower my face closer to Eloise's, nothing but the barrier between us. I bare the back of my neck to Lazarus. It will be easier if he severs my spine with one quick blow.

"Don't be a fool," Marabella says, suddenly beside us.

I glance up to find her hand on Lazarus's wrist, keeping him from delivering the killing blow.

"Have mercy," I say to her. "I cannot bear to live without her."

But Marabella's eyes are focused on Eloise, her slightly open mouth set within a drawn face as if she's bet on a horse she believes is about to break from the pack and cross the finish. I can't make sense of the expression. Marabella is no fool.

"What secrets have you kept from me?" I grit out.

Her gaze drops to mine. "Do you think we'd leave the future of Night Haven in the hands of a human?"

I do a double take when I swear I see one of Eloise's fingers twitch.

"What have you done?" I pound on the dome again, terrified that Eloise is dead. Terrified that she's not.

Valeska continues to leap for the crown, now using the wall of the dome to help her.

She's distracted.

She does not see Eloise's leg straighten or her arm bend or her eyes blink.

She does not see her fingers slip around the hilt of her dagger.

She does not see my mate sit up.

"All she needed was a vampire to kill her to complete the turning," Marabella whispers.

Eloise's lips peel back from her fangs.

43

KINGDOM COME

ELOISE

I must have passed out after I stabbed Valeska because I wake from a dreamless sleep to find myself bent uncomfortably on the stone, my daggers scattered to my right and left. I experiment with moving my limbs, straightening the leg that's bent under me and curling one arm. Ah, that's better. Quickly I assess my injuries, cracking my neck and testing the movement of my limbs. I blink and blink again. My vision adjusts to the lighting in the room. It's so much brighter now. I can't figure out why. The moon is as full as before above the silo. It looks no bigger, but it beams like a floodlight through the dome.

So beautiful.

The sound of feet hitting stone brings me back into the moment. I sit up. Valeska is jumping for the queen's crown, but I've injured her enough that she's struggling. Her fingertips just brush the gold base, but it remains stubbornly out of her reach. I lean over and wrap my hand around one of my daggers. As quietly as possible, I climb to my feet.

Miraculously, I feel good. Healed.

I creep over to my second dagger. Pick it up. The crowd has started to murmur. Some of them are even trying to alert Valeska that I'm awake. She doesn't notice. She grunts as she again tries to catapult her weakened body toward the crown. She's so close. I don't have much time to stop her.

Out of the corner of my eye, I see Phantom, his glowing green eyes trained on me. My body feels different, almost buoyant, but my mouth hurts. I rub the side of my jaw and then over my lips. Yep, my teeth hurt. Hurt like hell. But I narrow my focus back on Valeska. If I don't take her out, I'll have a lot more to worry about than some dental work.

Steadying myself, I rush Valeska from behind with unprecedented speed. This time I go straight for her throat. At the last second, she whirls to face me, her gaze widening as I smack into her. Oddly, she doesn't even try to fight me. Her entire body goes slack. She simply gives up.

"I am forsaken," she says through dry, pale lips.

I clutch the top of her head and slit her throat. Blood drenches my arms, my torso. It splashes over my boots. I don't stop there. Cassius taught me too well for that. I press harder, completely severing her head from her body. I stare into Valeska's lightless, dead eyes as her body flops to the stone. There's a chiff, and then the head and the rest of her go up in spontaneous flames. I release her hair before it can burn my fingers and back up a step from her remains. Seconds later, she's nothing but ash.

I sheathe my daggers and brush my hands together, only narrowly aware that the silo is wild with unrest. But I haven't finished this challenge yet. I pivot to face the two crowns, still hovering about six feet above my head. I don't know how I'm going to reach either of them, especially if Valeska couldn't do it, but I have to try. Taking a few running steps, I leap for the one Damien promised me, the one that looks like it was carved from black diamonds. Not his mother's crown, but the one that pairs with his own. The magic of the challenge must be lifting me, because I easily snag it out of the air. I land softly with a proud smile stretching my mouth.

On impulse, I turn to face the box and Damien standing behind it. Our eyes meet and hold. His are red, his hair ruffled, but his smile is true as I lift the crown and place it atop my head. The silo goes eerily quiet as the smoky surface of the rectangular mirror clears and Eloise Harcourt scrawls across the silver.

I've won!

Damien is mine.

My mate.

We are free.

It feels like Damien and I are the only people in the room as the dome slowly dismantles itself, falling to the stone like purple stardust. The archways collapse into mirrors again that float through the air of their own volition and plop down into their storage spaces inside the box. The mirror goes blank. The box closes and locks itself.

And then even the weight on my head disappears. I run a hand through my hair, noticing the crown is gone. Everything is as it was before. The challenge is over.

In the next heartbeat, Damien has me in his arms. His thumbs are on my cheeks, his fingers in my hair. And then his lips are on mine.

The silo erupts in cheers, whoops, hollers of laughter. I hear the shuffling of money, the excited voices of the vampires I just made rich, and the lower groans and growls of the vampires who put their money on Valeska.

I draw back when intense hunger storms through me. Hunger for him. Hunger for food. Hunger for more. With a force I'm surprised to find remaining in my limbs, I drag Damien to me and kiss him once more, until a soft but persistent tap on my elbow demands my attention.

"Eloise, remember our agreement. Please," Marabella says. George is at her side. Both of them have happy tears in their eyes. "You must do it now."

George takes my elbow in that fatherly way of his and says, "Go ahead, sweetheart."

Slowly, I turn to face the audience of vampires. They've gone eerily quiet. It's so quiet I can hear mice scratching inside the walls. One by one, every vampire kneels.

"My queen," Marcel says.

I see the way they're looking at me. According to the old law, I could slide into Valeska's position. With Damien by my side, I could rule with an iron fist. I could have power over everything. I could make this hive like the Lamia coven, a fair and just vampire community where hurting humans was punishable by death. I can eliminate how humans are used by houses like Marabella's, save people like Ren and others in desperate situations. I could use vampires to fix problems in the human world.

Damien's fingers thread into mine at my side.

Fuck no. If I'm ever going to rule a kingdom, it will be his. All I want to do is go home.

"I will not be your queen," I say as loudly and clearly as I can. "No one will." An excited murmur flows through the crowd.

Galloway's head rises, his teeth bared. "If you do this, the palace will fall!"

I ignore him.

"All my authority as regent shall be deposed and returned to the masters of the individual covens. Marcel will lead this effort, including assignment of all military resources to the covens based on their relative size. I give him full authority to do so. Everald has agreed to provide goods and services to aid in the transition. The covens will need money initially to replace what the monarchy stole. To fund this endeavor, George and Everald will lead the liquidation of all palace art, furniture, and decor. The palace itself will remain but be transformed into a public library, open to everyone and led by Lazarus."

Vampires are rising now and rushing out the door. Some are ecstatic, like they've just been freed from their cages and have to scream it to the world. Others look like they just want to scream. The latter group seems disappointed and nervous, and I can only assume they fear their previous support of Valeska might be a death sentence.

I'm not interested in killing anyone.

I only want one thing—Damien.

But when I turn around, Marcel is there. He bows low. "Congratulations, Eloise. It was a sincere pleasure to witness you win and emancipate Night Haven."

Everald slaps me on the back. "I knew you could do it. Way to go, kid."

George grins at me and says, "You're free, sweetheart. Get the hell out of here and go live your best life."

By his side, Marabella holds out her hand to me. "Thank you," she says, beaming. "You've made the right choice. Come back to the house and Dr. Everline will help you… adjust. You're going to need a donation."

Damien grabs Marabella's arm and whispers something in her ear.

The madam nods and offers us both a smile. "Anything she wants," she says softly and then strides toward the door.

I watch her leave and then turn back to Damien. "What was that all about? What did she mean? I do feel strange. Maybe I should see Dr. Everline for another infusion." I look down at myself. I'm covered in blood. "I don't know how much of this is mine. I lost consciousness and — God, I just want to go home. And I want to eat. I'm… hungry. Fuck, I'm so hungry, Damien."

"Eloise." Damien runs his thumb along my cheekbone. His voice is strained. "There's something—"

A jolt rings through me like I've had one of those dreams where I'm falling. I wobble on my feet, and for some strange reason, I look up. The slightest wash of silver signals the coming dawn. It's so bright it burns my eyes, and I shade them with my cupped hand.

"I feel like I'm going to throw up. I think there's something wrong with me." My head throbs, and I grab it with both hands. "Owww. Fuck. Maybe I have a concussion."

I can't hold myself up any longer. Thank fuck Damien catches me, holding me against his chest as he strides out from under the brightening sky. I'm barely aware of anything but my pounding head as he makes his way through the palace, but when we reach the marketplace, people are waiting for us there. And they're cheering my name.

"Thank you, Eloise!" a woman cries.

I'm too weak to do anything but give a wave. There is definitely something wrong with me, and when Damien doesn't make the turn toward Marabella's I become worried. "I need the doctor. Damien, take me to Everline."

His warm kiss lands on my head. "Close your eyes, little dragon. I'll take care of you. I have everything you need at my apartment."

His apartment. I've wanted to see where he lives since we met. I try to fight the exhaustion. If I have a concussion, I should definitely not sleep. But the second I close my eyes, I surrender to a darkness as thick as death.

44
CHANGES

When I open my eyes again, I'm surrounded by Damien's scent. The bed I'm in is small but comfortable with a plush comforter in deep evergreen. I snuggle in closer to his warmth, my ear against his heartbeat, and take in the dark wood furniture. The room is almost austere in its tidy composure. Aside from some clothes folded on the dresser, there's not a thing on any surface.

Not even a lamp.

I search the room for the source of light. Maybe a window or a bulb in the ceiling, but we're underground. The room is completely dark. Why then can I see as clear as day?

I sit up and swing my legs over the side of the bed. The movement is quick, unnaturally so. I search for my bond with Phantom, wondering if it's magic.

Damien's oversized hand lands on my back, and then a

cloud of black smoke coalesces beside me and he's sitting next to me.

"It's twilight."

I turn to face him, utterly confused. "I can see in the dark."

He nods, his eyes wide and somewhat sad. "You can."

"What happened to me, Damien?"

His fingers slide into mine. "They weren't protein shakes, my little dragon. Everline never gave you any herbs."

"What are you talking about?"

"It was blood. Vampire blood. Yours contained George's blood."

I shake my head. "Why would Marabella feed me vampire blood? Why would George?"

He runs his tongue along his bottom lip. "It has a strengthening effect on humans. Makes them heal faster. All the things she said the herbs did, vampire blood can do."

"So why didn't she tell me it was vampire blood?"

"Because you might have stopped drinking it. You might reject it. And that was unacceptable to her. She was desperate for you to win. The blood was her insurance policy."

I fight back tears as my mind offers up what he's trying to tell me. I can't accept it. I won't. A fist-sized lump forms in my throat, and I swallow it down. "We should have breakfast. I'm starving."

I start to stand, but he gently holds my arm.

"Vampires turn humans into vampires by first drinking their blood and then replacing the blood they've drained with their own. You had vampire venom in your system from donating and vampire blood in your system from the shakes and the infusions. The only thing that was missing to change you was the final step in the process."

I think back to Olivia, how she couldn't find a vampire who had the guts to change her. How excited she'd been to tell me about her change. I should have asked more questions. I should have known what was going into my body.

"I don't want to talk about this now," I squeak. "I'm so tired. I just want this nightmare to be over. I want to go home."

"Valeska killed you in that dome, Eloise. She broke your neck. That's the last step—a vampire has to kill you. Valeska had no idea that Marabella had primed you to turn. When you awoke, you awoke… You are… a vampire. That's why you can see in the dark and why you can feel the dawn coming. It's also why you're hungry. You need blood."

Hot tears run down my cheeks. "I don't want to be a vampire."

He wipes my tears away with his thumbs. "I know. I didn't want this for you either. Not like this. As much as I wanted you to be with me forever, I didn't want it to happen like this."

"Forever…"

"You're immortal now. As immortal as I am."

I stand, realizing I'm completely naked. I spread my hands and look down at myself.

"Your clothes were torn and soaked with blood. I retrieved your clean things from Marabella's while you were sleeping." He points to the stack on top of the dresser.

My brain circles around the truth that's impossible to deny. I am a vampire. I stretch my fingers, my toes. Pressing a palm to my chest, I feel nothing. My heart isn't beating. Panic rises in me at the thought. I did not consent to being turned, and the idea that I am now the same species as Valeska turns my stomach. Or maybe that feeling is the endless hunger that's seemed to gnaw at me since the challenge.

Do I want to be a vampire?

I move across the room with a grace that isn't mine. It's like I'm inhabiting someone else's skin. My movements are too fast, too certain. I realize the green light cast across the clothing on the dresser comes from my own eyes.

I'll never see the sun again. I'll have to survive by drinking blood.

I frown, wondering if the process could be reversed if that was my choice. But when I turn to ask Damien as much, his words sink in. I am now immortal, Damien's true equal. I've always planned to eventually return to Tenebris with him. Now we have nothing but time, and his night world will suit me perfectly. When I came here to free Damien, I was ready to die for him. I guess I did. How lucky is it for both of us that it wasn't the end? My stomach growls loud enough for Damien to hear.

"You're hungry because you need to feed," he says softly.

And then I remember something. "George is my sire? Does that mean he can compel me?"

"He freed you from the sire bond. Remember? After

you refused the crown, he told you you were free. The sire bond was their backup plan, just in case you decided you wanted to take over where Valeska left off."

"Oh my God." I grab my head as pain slices through it. My hands start to shake. I'm weak, hungry. I need to feed. "I… don't think I can use a donor." My voice cracks. "The idea of biting a human, especially after working at Marabella's… I don't think I can make myself do it. It's too intimate." My words choke off, and I shake my head.

He crosses to me and takes my hands in his. I meet his eyes and remember why I chose this path. I love Damien. With him standing naked before me, I get the full sense of him even in his humanlike form. Desire rushes through me. Only it doesn't come with the usual quickening of my pulse. Instead, my fangs elongate and throb with need. I raise a hand to cover my mouth, embarrassed.

Gently, he guides it away again. "It's nothing to be embarrassed about, but if you do not feed, you will eventually die."

I nod. "Maybe an animal. You said I could survive on deer?"

"You will feed from me, little bird," he says, as if the idea I'd take blood from anyone or anything else is preposterous.

My mind quiets. "What?"

"I have never offered my blood to another. What Valeska took was not freely given. But I offer it to you. My blood as a shade can sustain you. More than sustain you. My blood is stronger than human blood."

My fangs throb. My stomach clenches. Thirst, like fire, blazes in my throat. My eyes settle on the subtle pulse of the vein in his neck.

"I am told that this first feeding is the most important for you, that it completes your transition. I want it to be me, Eloise. We are already bound by heart and soul, why not blood?"

I open my mouth to say something, but my throat is too dry. All my thoughts fade away, replaced by a single focus, the *lub dub* of his heart and the scent of the blood it pumps through his veins.

He takes me by the hand and leads me to the bed, sitting on the edge so that we're face-to-face. "It will be easiest for you to hit the vein if you straddle me."

He pulls me toward him, and I do as he suggests, planting a knee on each side of his hips.

"You're so warm," I rasp. My voice is shot. My throat too dry to say much. My other senses though are sharper than ever. I close my eyes at the pleasure of the skin-to-skin contact. Touching him is like stroking sun-warmed velvet.

He chuckles, and the rumble travels through my own chest. "You're ice-cold because you haven't fed." He tips his head. "Please, my little dragon."

"You're sure this is okay after..." My words are breathy and weak through my parched throat, but I have to be sure. After what Valeska did to him...

His large hand strokes up my spine and massages the base of my skull. His lips brush the shell of my ear and his baritone rumbles, "Do you think I'd let my mate feed from any other man? You're mine, little bird. You'll feed from me and only me."

His words are slathered with heat and need. The smoky scent of him is more complex to me now. More unique. He's leather and spring rain, oak and something uniquely him, uniquely male. It smells delicious, and I can deny my hunger no longer. Instinct guides me. I strike, my teeth piercing the pulse at his throat. Hot deliciousness pours over my tongue. It's the best thing I've ever tasted, like someone translated an orgasm into a flavor. I moan as it fills me, my mouth, my stomach. It warms me to my fingertips and toes and then drives heat between my legs.

My nipples pearl against his chest, and I grind my hips, desperate for sensation. He hardens under me, his full, thick shaft parting my folds. God, this is heaven, but when he moans, I'm afraid I've taken too much. With all the restraint I can muster, I draw back and lick his neck, closing the wound as I've seen others do. I've had my fill, but the taste of his skin is decadent. I lick again and again, molding to his body and nibbling his earlobe, content as a cat.

He reaches around me, stroking along the crack of my ass, circling my tight entrance before continuing all the way to my hungry pussy. "You're so wet," he says, nuzzling my cheek. "Is this what my blood does to you?"

I reposition my hips until he slides into me, hard and fast. I moan, tipping my head back. In this position, he's almost painfully deep, but I love it. We fit. We've always fit.

"Are you well, little bird? Am I hurting you?" He stops the movement of his hips and meets my eyes, tucking a wild red strand of my hair behind my ear.

I offer an easy smile. Wrapping my arms around his neck, I raise and lower my hips ever so slowly. "You're not hurting me. I was just thinking how amazing it is that we come from two different worlds a universe apart and somehow you found your way to me. Somehow my soul found its other half. And right now, with you in me, your blood coursing through my veins, it's like finally feeling whole again, even in a different skin."

He runs his hands down my hair, my outer arms. He fists my hips. "It's your skin, Eloise," he whispers against my throat. "It's just less fragile."

I lick along the seam of his lips. "Show me."

Damien starts to move. I ride him, the movements slow and gentle at first. He fills every inch of me as I explore his chest with my touch, tease his nipples with my teeth. A current flows through me, a dark electricity, tangling into a storm of energy and need. I come down harder, and he meets me thrust for thrust. He's pounding into me now, his fists gripping my hips, moving my body in time with his. He's so deep I can feel each surge of his body through my torso and into my throat. This sex is almost punishing. Almost. In this new body, it doesn't hurt. It's not too much.

My breasts sway as we connect again and again. Bending his head, he captures one of my nipples in his mouth and flicks his tongue across the sensitive tip. The sensation feeds something wild in me, and I move faster, ride him harder.

Smooth as silk, he lifts me and turns me around, setting me back on his cock with my back to him. The feeling is so different this way. So much fuller. He reaches around my hip and rubs circles over my clit as we start to move again. His other hand captures my breast, rolling my nipple between his fingers.

Pressure builds, drawing me closer to a cliff that might be higher than I've ever flown over before. Everything is just so raw. The way he stretches me to the limit, his adroit fingers between my legs.

His hand slides from my breast, down my side, and then I hear him lick his fingers. Warm wet pressure teases my back entrance and pushes inside. The pressure, the fullness. My climax barrels into me, and it's so much stronger than when I was human. It feels like I've broken the restraints of my body entirely and am nothing but expanding energy. I cry out, arching my back, as he follows me over the edge.

He fills me, his shadows coiling around me. His growl of ecstasy is almost a purr against the side of my neck. We stay that way for a long while, until I remember something. Damien can survive on vampire blood as well.

"You can take from me if you need it."

His kiss lands where my pulse once was. "I am well fed, and right now you need to keep your blood. Your body needs it to transition."

"Then I have a request." Slowly I climb from his lap, feeling satiated and truly happy for the first time in months. I also feel strong. Damien's blood has healed whatever was still broken in me. I cup his chin. "Damien, please take me home. I don't want to be in Night Haven any longer. This place holds too many painful memories."

He kisses my palm. "I couldn't agree more."

45

HOME AGAIN

ELOISE

"I did it. She's dead. She'll never hurt anyone again."

Maeve squeals on the other end of our call. "You won! You beat the vampire queen! Goddess, I thought you could do it, El. I did. But hearing your voice… Praise the goddess."

There's a pause while she processes it all.

"But… if you killed her, who is ruling Night Haven?"

"I released all her power back to the individual coven masters."

"I bet the vampires at Bad Witches' Club are shitting their pants right now. Huge changes coming their way. I'm sure my phone will be blowing up with the news as soon as it reaches the witch community."

"It's so good to hear your voice. Listen, I'll tell you everything when I see you, but right now I need to go home."

"Not Harcourt, El. You can't. It's not safe."

"The vampires are gone. I'll be fine."

She hesitates, and I picture her chewing her lip on the other end of our connection. "It's not just the vampires. The FBI is up the Denardis' asses over this Gold Weaver thing, but they haven't had enough evidence to nail them. You know too much, El. There's still a price on your head."

I sigh. "I'm going home. Damien's with me, and I'm…" I hesitate. I don't want to tell her that I'm a vampire. Not over the phone. "I'm stronger now. I proved as much by my victory over Valeska."

"Okay," she says softly. "I'll see you there."

"Wait, Maeve—" I try to tell her that she shouldn't risk herself for me, but she's already hung up.

We arrive at Harcourt after midnight to find Maeve waiting for us. A sob breaks from her throat as she embraces me. "Goddess, El. I love you, girlie. I'm so happy you're home."

"I love you too," I say through a laugh, careful not to squeeze her too hard. "And I couldn't agree more."

Her nose twitches as her senses tell her something's not right with me. With her hands still gripping my shoulders, she takes me in, that witchy part of her bubbling to the surface and surrounding us with an aura of magic. How had I gone so long not knowing what she was?

Behind her square-framed glasses, her eyes narrow. I can almost hear her working it out in her head. "Oh, Eloise…"

"It wasn't my choice," I say softly. "But it is the way I was able to win."

She refuses to let me go and pulls me into an even harder squeeze. She's still wearing her coat. It's early spring, and the weather is cold and rainy, but I can't feel it. This new body of mine is extremely resilient to changes in temperature. The royal-blue trench coat I'm wearing and Damien's dark gray wool one are just for show, just to help us look more human.

All at once, I remember that she *is* still human. I catch the scent of her blood, hear her heart beat faster, smell her adrenaline spike.

"Can I take your coat?" I ask, trying to act human as best I can. *I'm the same as before. Relax.* "Are you hungry? We could order something. I could make tea." I point toward the kitchen.

Emotions flit through her expression so quickly I can't interpret them all, but a few of them come through clear as day. She knows I'm a vampire. She knows I no longer eat like she does. She still loves me, but things are different. Different in ways she's not sure how exactly to deal with. I see all these things in her eyes and can relate to each one because I feel them too.

"I'll hold on to my coat if it's all the same. It's freezing in here." She hugs herself. "And I'm fine, thanks. It's late for me. I've already eaten."

Of course she has. "I'll turn on the heat for you." I move for the hall and the thermostat, careful to slow my steps, move as a human would, to put Maeve at ease. Technically the heat has been on, but it's turned down to fifty-five, just enough to keep the pipes from freezing. I bump it up by ten degrees. Then glance back at her and nudge it to seventy-two. The heat kicks on with a click, and I feel warm air blow into the room.

When I release the dial, I wipe my fingers on my coat. Everything is covered in a thin film of dust, including the top of the thermostat. Even the wood floors are badly in need of a sweep. It's been months since I was in this house. Truth be told, I was not a stellar housekeeper even before I left, but the ghosts of my ancestors always took care of things when I lived here. Unfortunately, I took them with me when I left for Night Haven. Which means…

I wander into the kitchen and see that the spider plant hanging over the sink, the one that has grown there for as long as I've been alive, is dead. I reach up and take a crispy leaf between my fingers. Pieces crumble and float to the floor.

"I should have had someone water that. I forgot it was in here," Maeve says. "After the threats, I—"

"You did your best," I say, holding up a hand. "It's just a plant. Thank you for paying the bills and managing all the crap with Tony's estate and everything."

She slides her hands into her pockets. "About that, if you stay here tonight, you should expect to have visitors tomorrow. Nothing has changed since I visited you in your dream. Agent Fuller still wants to talk to you. They found the Maserati and Jared's body. He's going to want to know where you've been. He'll have questions."

Damien gives a low growl. Of the two of us, he's the only one who could so much as answer the door. The light would kill me.

"We'll figure something out," I tell her.

She hugs herself and shivers. I'm not sure if it's from the drafty house or the situation. It can't be easy learning your best friend is a vampire, especially considering vampires and witches haven't often been allies.

"The heat in here always did take a minute. Let me light a fire for you."

I march into the parlor and reach for the tin of matches on the mantel.

"Really, you don't have to do that," she says, striding in behind me. She goes straight for the lamp next to the sofa and clicks it on. I don't need it anymore.

Damien appears beside me, his hand fitting into the small of my back. I might be stronger than ever, but I melt into that touch, melt into his side. This house isn't just dusty; it feels dead. Soulless. Cold. The scent of my grandmother's perfume is long gone. No sounds or smells of cooking come from the kitchen. The pictures of my ancestors on the walls feel distant and disconnected from me.

I try to push the feeling aside as I squat down to stack a few logs and attempt to light them using magic. It doesn't work, and I end up grabbing the tin of matches and doing it the nonmagical way. As the fire catches, I can't shake that something has changed.

"Something feels wrong." I say to Damien.

"You're adjusting to the transition. It's going to take time." We stand together, and he crosses the room to reposition a pillow on the green velvet sofa. "I remember the day you summoned me to this room... naked." He offers a wolfish smile and cocks an eyebrow. It's an obvious ploy to lighten the mood, take my mind off what's bothering me.

Maeve laughs. "I don't want to hear about it."

"Why? It was your idea, witch." Damien's eyes crinkle at the corners, and I wonder if he'll ever forgive Maeve for the part she played in his captivity, or if she's still alive for my sake. Because he'd never hurt someone I loved.

I think back to that night. To that spell.

Maeve's footsteps on the wood floor echo in the room when she stops in front of the fire. My gaze drifts to the corner where the grandfather clock stands. Silence.

"Eloise, are you okay?" Maeve asks.

"The clock has stopped."

Maeve shrugs. "It probably just needs to be wound. Don't these things usually have a crank or something?" She walks over to it and sticks her nail in the lock that holds the cabinet shut. "Your ancestors probably did it before, just like watering the plant."

I move closer to it and raise a hand to the clock face. Maeve is probably right, but it feels so much bigger than just a clock in need of maintenance. A heaviness forms deep inside me, like I've lost something precious that I didn't even know I had.

Phantom appears next to the clock, eyes flashing green. Their mouth moves, but I can't make out my grandmother's voice. I can't hear them at all. But then, I haven't heard the fox speak on behalf of my ancestors since my transformation. I thought it was simply because I couldn't yet feel the buzz inside this new, strange body, but now I wonder. I search for the connection between us and—

Pop! A clink comes from the front window, and a piece of the mantel bursts into shards.

Maeve draws a breath into her lungs like she's about to scream.

Some deep instinct has me throwing myself in front of her. *Pop, pop, pop.* Glass rains across the sofa, the rug.

Damien forms behind me, shielding me. "We've got visitors, little dragon."

A bullet passes through his side and wedges in mine with a dull pinch. I look around Damien to see men in my front yard. Six men in dark suits who all look too much like Tony to not be Denardis. They walk toward us, guns raised.

"How many cousins does the bastard have?" I ask no one in particular.

The clink of metal hitting the floor draws my attention to the bloody bullet my body has just expelled. Maeve stares at it, her face ashen. She's a powerful witch, but she isn't bulletproof.

"The attic. Let's go!" I move Maeve, shielding her as I lift and carry her to the base of the stairs.

The second I set her down, she sprints toward the second floor.

I whirl to find Damien staring through the broken window. Bullet holes riddle his white shirt and jeans as well as the sides of his long, dark wool coat. His eyes, diamond blue and hard as ice, meet mine.

"We need to talk, Eloise," one of the men says in that patronizing way Tony and Jared spoke to me. "Come out and no one needs to get hurt."

"You don't want to do this," I call back. "The FBI is watching the house. They can see everything you're doing."

The man snorts. "We've taken care of the cameras. Next we're gonna take care of you if you don't cooperate."

I see red. I've had enough of the Denardis. This is supposed to be my homecoming, my safe space, my rest. I refuse to entertain these fuckers for one more second.

"You don't need to be afraid anymore, little bird." Damien holds out his hand. "Shall we?"

I flip my bright red curls over my shoulder and give a low, deep chuckle. "Oh, we shall."

Together, hand in hand, we step up onto the couch and out the broken picture window. Our boots land in the front lawn. We get one more step in before bullets shower from their guns. Damien moves in front of me, taking shots to the chest, the stomach, the legs. One slides past him and lodges in my biceps. It hurts but not too bad. I take one to the cheekbone, which stings.

When the bullets finally stop, Damien flashes me a flirty smile and reaches out to wipe the blood from my already-healing wound. "He'll pay for that."

We both turn our attention to the men who are only now realizing there's something not human about the two of us. I glare at the Denardi who stands at the center, the one who appears to be their leader, and raise an eyebrow. "This is going to hurt."

Damien breaks apart into a dozen streams of shadow that drive like dark needles through the men. Their voices ring out as their slow human minds try to understand what's happening to them. My vampire senses catch it all —the spout of blood that erupts from a lung, a throat, a wrist. The guns go flying, some with hands still attached.

It seems like an incredibly long time before the men's screams rend the night, their senses finally catching up to ours. My mind moves so much faster now. My senses are so much keener. They turn and try to flee. In their long gray coats, they scatter like pigeons across my lawn. Pigeons hit with scattershot, bleeding to death as they run.

Damien catches up to two of them in the time it takes me to decide what to do next. His shadows toy with them, slowly draining their life as they beg for their lives. I spot another one running down the drive. He's almost reached the road. That won't do. No one can leave this place. I want to send the Denardis a message. Anyone they send to kill me is never coming back.

I catch up with the man easily and kick the side of his knee. The bone breaks with a resounding crack. His shriek as he crumples to the pavement is chilling.

"Why did you come here to kill me?" I ask the man as he crab walks backward, trying to get away from me. I know why, but I want to hear him admit it.

"Fuck off, cunt!"

I grab him by the front of the shirt. He punches me with everything he's got, his fist slamming into my jaw. I barely feel it, as if I've been batted by a kitten's paw. "Why. Are. You. Here?"

He stops breathing, his pupils dilating with fear. "Hail Mary, full of grace…" His mumbled prayer drifts over me and into the night.

"Hmph. Something tells me Jesus, Mary, and Joseph aren't too thrilled that you came here to murder an innocent young woman whose abusive ex-husband tried to frame her for his crimes."

His eyes narrow to slits. "You're a loose end. You know too much." He whimpers. "All you had to do was follow directions and the family would've let you live."

"Directions?" My brows lift, and I laugh as he flails in my grip. "Is that all I had to do? Maybe what I needed was a demonstration. Do you know how to follow directions?"

He says nothing.

I reach into his pocket and extract his wallet, checking the ID. "Following your directions isn't going to work for me, Nick. But how about you follow mine?"

He sneers and tries to break my hold again.

"I'll give you an easy one." I draw his face closer. "All you have to do is lie here and die." I slam the back of his head against the driveway hard enough to crack his skull, then with the stomp of my heel, I break his other leg. He passes out, but I can still hear his heart beating as his blood pools beneath his skull.

I stride back toward Damien, leaving Nick there to bleed out. A part of me recognizes that I'm not this person. Eloise Harcourt doesn't hurt people, not intentionally. I'm not a killer. But right now my humanity feels like a distant memory. Just like this house, this property. It all feels like something from a different life. A different time.

But no matter how different it might be now, the Denardis can't have any of it.

46

NIGHT BIRD

DAMIEN

She has no idea how beautiful she is. Eloise strides toward me, the deep red curls of her hair a stark contrast against the bright blue trench. Her skin is flawlessly pale. Her lips full and red from my blood. And those eyes… her green eyes cast their own light now, just like mine.

But I lament the grief I see flash in them. The mourning for her old self.

Part of being a warrior is learning how to live with the consequences of your actions. I remember my first kill, a dark elf who'd entered our territory with murderous intent, armed to the teeth. Killing Tony and Valeska has changed her, made her harder in ways she likely didn't see coming.

She broke the bones of the man in the driveway and left him there to die. He was sent to kill her, and she is justified in taking his life. But I still see a glimmer of the girl I met almost six months ago as she walks toward me, a woman who is second-guessing herself. A woman who senses she should be compassionate, even now, even after these men have wronged her over and over.

Her body is stronger.

She's harder to kill.

But she's still vulnerable. A warrior who gave all of herself to protect the people she loved most. A warrior who saved me. A woman who now must make sense of it all.

It pains me to see her like this, still fighting for the scraps of her humanity that remain. She deserves so much more.

I would kill a legion of men if I thought it would make a difference for her.

And our trouble is just beginning. My little bird is now a night bird. The human authorities will come, and she will not be able to answer the door. She will not be able to discuss the case over tea. My night bird cannot return to her human life no matter how much she wishes to go home. Her old nest was built out in the open, in the sunlight, designed for fair weather. The storm is upon us now.

"I need to go tell Maeve it's safe. She must be so frightened." She sounds tired. Exhausted. Her eyes sweep over the dead, her bloodied lawn.

I take her face in my hands and kiss her until the tension bleeds from her shoulders. "Go. Be with Maeve. I will take care of this and join you in a moment."

She nods, looking relieved. I watch her go inside, and then I get to work.

It doesn't take me long to collect the bodies and feed them to the river. I finish off the man in the drive before I throw him over to join his brethren. At this point, the fish of the Rappahannock must have a taste for Denardi flesh. I clean the blood from the lawn with a hose from the side of the house. There's no car in the drive. Where did they come from?

A mile or so up the road, I find a van. No plates. I leave it there.

When I'm finished, I stand in the yard, staring up at the light in the attic. Everything in me longs to take Eloise back to Stygarde. After what she told me following the second trial, I'm more curious than ever about what has become of my kingdom. Even though the trials took place in a mirror world, Aurora's magic is unparalleled, and I wonder if there is any truth to her warning. Besides, I want to see that crown Eloise won on her head. But I can't ask her to leave a life she's not ready to leave. I can't ask her to leave Maeve, who is as close to family as she has left, or this house and property that contains her ancestors' bones.

I promised her I'd wait until she is ready, and I will never go against that promise. My home, my kingdom, will always—first and foremost—be with her.

But I see what's ahead for her here. Neither of us has a coven. Night Haven holds too much trauma for either of us to return to. We might find refuge with Cassius. The Lamia coven would take us in. Yes, that is surely the answer.

Only, what will become of Harcourt Manor? Her heart has always been here. After all, she summoned me, willing to risk everything, to save it from Tony's clutches.

And will I ever be able to convince her to leave it behind?

47

THE RAREST TREASURE

ELOISE

"I never meant to put you in harm's way by coming here," I say to Maeve.

She frowns. "Of course you didn't. None of this is your fault."

"But it is problematic." I watch as a tear traces her cheek.

"You're a vampire, Eloise. How is that going to work? After tonight, the FBI is going to have even more questions. There is Denardi DNA everywhere. I'm good, but I'm not this good. I can't clean up this mess. And you can't be in the sunlight. You need a safe place to sleep during the day, and it's not here."

I stare out the window, at Damien hosing down my front lawn. "I won't go back to Night Haven. Neither will Damien."

"What about the coven in Chicago? Maybe you could both take refuge there?"

She's right. We could go to Chicago, but if I'm willing to uproot myself and move across the country, there is somewhere else I'd rather be. I look around the attic, my parents' books, their herbs and magical accouterments, the outline of the spell I drew on the floor to send Damien home, and the answer clicks. I've been fighting it, but it's the only way this all works, and remarkably, when I consider it, I feel nothing but peace.

"I love you, Maeve, and I'm so glad I got to see you again."

"But?"

"But I think I have to go with Damien, back to his world."

A sob breaks her throat. "I thought you might say that."

"It's just the fair thing to do. His kingdom needs him. He never intended to leave. And now, being what I am, there's no place for me here anymore."

She nods. "I hate it so much, but I think you're right."

I feel a fat tear break the dam of my lower lid. "You are the best friend I've ever had, and the sister I've always wanted. It kills me to consider leaving you."

"I feel the same way." She sniffs. "But Eloise, you have a man down there who loves you the way you deserve to be loved. And you love him enough to die for him. Your home is with him."

"My home is with him." I nod, my tears joining hers in solidarity.

"Do you think the Hitch and Cast spell works between worlds?"

I shrug. "I'm the key. If I can go there using a symbol, I can come for a visit using one. Phantom can teach me."

She huffs and then pulls me into a tight hug. "I'm going to miss you."

"There's just one more favor I have to ask of you."

"Anything," she says.

"This house can't fall into the wrong hands. My family is buried here. I want you to have it. I want to gift you the house."

She nods. "I'll take care of everything." With a snap of her fingers, papers appear on the worktable. "Sign here and it's done. I'm still not sure how I'm going to explain all this, but where there's a will and magic, there's a way."

I scribble my name at the bottom of the page. And then I hug her for the last time.

DAMIEN

I SURF THE SHADOWS INTO THE HOUSE AND UP THE STAIRS to the threshold of the attic. I'm surprised when I easily move through the open door. Before, the room was guarded by a ward that Eloise had to pull me through. I don't know if the ward is gone or if it simply remembers me.

The scent of tears immediately reaches my nose. Eloise and Maeve hold an embrace, weeping in each other's arms. It's physically painful for me to see my mate cry, but her scent tells me these tears aren't completely born of sadness. Something else is going on here.

I wait silently in the shadows, watching over them both.

Eloise breaks away first, clearing her throat. Maeve draws some papers from the table and holds them while she kisses Eloise on the cheek. Then she turns to me. "Goodbye, Advocate. And thank you for your service." She slides from the room and descends the stairs.

"What was that all about?"

Eloise turns to me. "We need to talk."

I raise a brow and swagger closer to her, wiping away her tears. "I'm listening."

"We can't stay here," she says, although I can see by her trembling lip that admitting it almost destroys her. "Maeve helped me to see that. The people of Echo Mills know me and my family too well. They've already been reaching out to Maeve, asking when I'll be back. I can't be back and not see them in the sunlight, and that's not even considering the legal trouble I'm in."

I nod. "I'm sorry, little bird. This isn't the fate I wanted for you."

Her eyes sweep up to mine. "But maybe it is the fate that was meant for me. Maybe this was all meant to be." She sighs. "The clock is no longer my anchor, and all the books in this attic are contained in Phantom." She points toward the fox, who watches us from the corner of the attic. "Everything here feels disconnected. This new body… I'm not even connected to Phantom as I once was. Wherever I am, wherever I go next, I'm starting at the beginning when it comes to my magic."

Absently, I work my finger into the coil of one of her soft red curls. "It's wise of you to acknowledge this. Change is inevitable. And when you're immortal, it's the only certainty in life. In my experience, the ones who cause the greatest suffering are those who refuse to accept it."

"Right." She looks down at her toes between us. "So we can't stay here. Not long term."

I wonder if she's come to the same conclusion I have, that the Lamia coven is probably the only place on earth that's safe for us now. I place my bent knuckle under her chin and lift. "Where would you like to go? Say the word and I will make it so."

Her trembling lips spread into a smile. "Stygarde."

My heart leaps, and I grip her chin between my thumb and forefinger. "Do not tease me with this unless you are decided on the matter. To do otherwise would be cruel."

She shakes her head. "I'm ready. I want to go to your world. I want to be your princess. I'll have Phantom with me, and if I need help with my parents' magic or to visit Maeve, I will. But I think it's time for us to have a real home, and that home is your home. There's nothing left for me here, and there's so much for us to discover there. You were brought to this world against your will, and you've suffered here, first because you had no choice and now for me. Because you love me. Well, I love you, Damien. I want to see your face when you finally return to the home you left behind.

Besides, what if there's a kernel of truth to what Aurora said to me during the second trial? I know she was just a mirror version of reality, but don't we have an obligation to return to your kingdom if it needs you?" She takes my face in her hands. "There's nothing left for me here, Damien. Take me home to Stygarde."

There isn't a word for the amount of joy that fills me

in that moment. This outcome is exactly what I wanted and the thing I thought I'd have to wait a short eternity for.

"Yes, little bird." I hold out my hand to her. "My world will be your world. My life will be your life. Open the way."

48

LOST THINGS

ELOISE

I turn to the sigil on the floor of my parents' ritual room, the one I drew months ago to send Damien back to his world, and know I'm doing the right thing. Since the moment I woke up in Damien's room and realized what I was, what I had become, I knew this world would never feel like home to me again. It just took some time to admit it to myself.

But as I reach out to Phantom and the fox forms in the corner of the attic, I doubt my abilities. I no longer feel the familiar buzz of our connection. I still see the fox. When I call, my ancestors answer. But it's like trying to read the lips of an actor through bad television reception. Our connection is staticky, distant.

Will my magic alone be enough to carry Damien and me home to his world? Just in case, I grab my parents' grimoire and hold the giant tome close to my chest. If something goes wrong, at least I'll have their spells to guide me.

"It will have to be your blood," I say to him, stepping inside the symbol. "You are the only one who has actually been there. In theory, I am the key. I can open the portal. But only you can direct us where we need to go."

He steps in behind me, his front pressing into my back, and extends one hand over the edge of the sigil. Using a talon from his partially shifted opposite hand, he moves to slice his palm.

"Wait!" I pat my thighs. "Phantom, come!"

The fox runs and jumps into my arms. I rub my cheek against their soft head. I'm not sure yet how to fully open the channel between us again, but I need my ancestors with me, wherever we're going.

"Ready?" Damien asks.

"Ready," I say, smiling over my shoulder at him.

He makes the cut, and it's almost exactly the same way I opened mine over the candle to summon him to me. It's a cut just deep enough for blood to pool in the cup of his palm. He wraps his other arm around Phantom and me, holding us close as if he's afraid we might get separated during the journey. Slowly he extends his hand out toward the edge.

"Think of the garden, Eloise," he says softly, in that voice of his that reminds me of the sound of warm skin against velvet.

I close my eyes and picture the moon, the purple roses, the castle, the stone benches. It's so clear in my mind, not just from his dream but from my time there in the mirror world during the first challenge. I nod my head, open my eyes, and he tips his palm.

Blood drips onto the symbol. Nothing happens. It's just blood hitting chalk. My heart sinks.

Then my vision changes. The chalk lifts off the floor, becoming like a billion twinkling stars around our feet. The floor opens and we drop.

I'm more than thankful for Damien's arm around me as we hurtle through absolute darkness before landing in the red, ashy fields of the underworld. Harcourt Manor rises in the distance, beyond a field of narcissus. The river of lava surges behind our backs.

Unlike my visit before though, none of my ancestors are here. Phantom licks my face, and I realize why. They're all here. All with me now.

In the next breath, we shoot up a straw, straight into the sky, into the darkness. I lose all sense of what is up or down, right or left. My entire body tenses. I forget to breathe. I squeeze my eyes shut and think of the purple roses, the moon, the garden. I anchor myself to Damien's arm around me.

My feet collide with stone hard enough that my knees give out and I'm thrown from Damien's grasp. Head spinning, I find myself on all fours, cool stone beneath my hands and knees. Eventually I open my eyes, and the first thing I see is the fist-sized bloom of a purple rose.

Slowly, carefully, I stand on shaky legs, the grimoire still clutched to my chest, and turn to find Damien watching me with a weightless smile I've never seen on his face before. It's the smile of a child at Christmas. It's the smile of someone who has never known pain. I follow his line of sight to the castle behind me. It's still there, and by the well-maintained grounds around us, it appears his kingdom is still standing as well.

"Welcome to Stygarde, Princess Eloise." He holds out his hand to me.

I reach for him, noticing for the first time what's missing.

"Phantom?" I look around the garden. I reach for the bond between us... and can't find it. "Phantom!" I call again.

But Phantom and my connection to my ancestors are gone. I close my eyes and search for the staticky connection I felt when we left the attic. It's there, I think, but faint, and when I attempt to tug on it, I feel only exhaustion.

I hug the book to my chest. Learning my magic took time when I was human, and will take more time in this body. But if my magic brought us here, it still exists, which means Phantom isn't really missing. My connection to him is probably just... recovering. I take a deep breath. It's going to be okay.

I slip my fingers into Damien's.

"Should we keep looking, little bird?" he asks.

"No," I say quickly, not wanting to worry him. "Phantom is never lost. I think I'm just tired. I'm sure once I've recovered, the bond will return and so will the fox."

"Then come," he says, gesturing toward the castle. "I can't wait to introduce you to my family."

The End—for now.

THANK YOU FOR READING BATTLE FOR THE SHADOW Prince. If you enjoyed this title, please leave a review wherever you buy books. Want more? Sign up here to read the exclusive Battle for the Shadow Prince bonus scene!

Damian is relieved to find the kingdom of Stygarde at peace, even if he's surprised by who is sitting on the throne. He vows to make the best of it. After all, he owes Eloise a proper courtship. Hell, he owes her everything and hopes he can be the mate she deserves after the sacrifice she's made for him.

Eloise wants to enjoy her time with Damien but she struggles to reconnect with her spirit magic. The grief and loss she's feeling over losing her family all over again make it hard to enjoy anything at all.

Until Eloise disappears and Damien learns the one thing that changes everything.

Preorder BARTERED BY THE SHADOW PRINCE today!

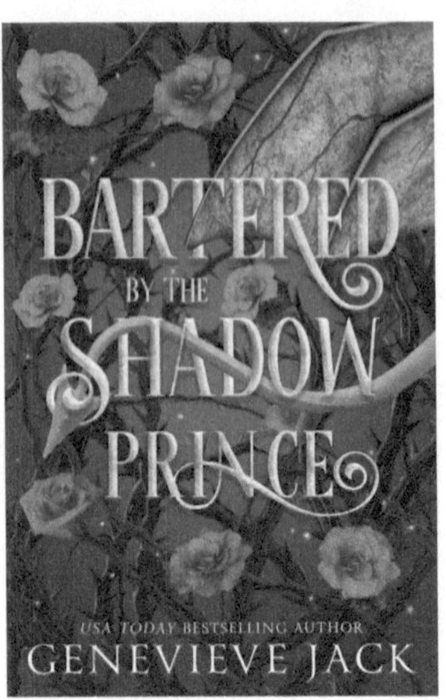

Acknowledgments

Battle for the Shadow Prince was a monster romance that was a monster to write. The length and complexity of this story meant I needed all the help I could get. Thankfully, I found it in Tiffany Mills who provided an initial read and some sharp suggestions for improvement. After wrangling Battle into submission once again, Anne Victory, my long-time editor, worked her magic. I couldn't have finished this one without her. My deepest, most sincere thanks to both of you for your talent, ongoing support, and encouragement. My thanks also goes out to all the readers who are giving the A Bargain with the Shadow Prince series a chance.

MEET GENEVIEVE JACK

USA Today bestselling and multi-award winning author Genevieve Jack writes wild, witty, and wicked-hot paranormal romance and romantic fantasy. She believes there's magic in every breath we take and probably something supernatural living in most dark basements. You can summon her with coffee, wine, and books, but she sticks around for dogs and chocolate. Her novels feature badass heroines, fiercely loyal heroes, and fantasy elements that will fill you with wonder. Learn more at GenevieveJack.com.

Do you know Jack? Keep in touch to stay in the know about new releases, sales, and giveaways.

MORE FROM GENEVIEVE JACK!

A Bargain with the Shadow Prince Series

A Bargain With The Shadow Prince

Battle for the Shadow Prince

Bartered by the Shadow Prince

Bride of the Shadow King

The Treasure of Paragon

The Dragon of New Orleans, Book 1

Windy City Dragon, Book 2,

Manhattan Dragon, Book 3

The Dragon of Sedona, Book 4

The Dragon of Cecil Court, Book 5

Highland Dragon, Book 6

Hidden Dragon, Book 7

The Dragons of Paragon, Book 8

The Last Dragon, Book 9

The Angel of Paragon, Book 10

The Three Sisters Trilogy

The Tanglewood Witches

Tanglewood Magic

Tanglewood Legacy

His Dark Charms Duet

Lucky Me

Lucky Us

Knight Games

The Ghost and The Graveyard, Book 1

Kick the Candle, Book 2

Queen of the Hill, Book 3

Mother May I, Book 4

Logan (companion novel)

The Wolves of Fireborn Pack Trilogy

Fated Bonds

Feral Instincts

Forever Mated

www.ingramcontent.com/pod-product-compliance
Lightning Source LLC
Chambersburg PA
CBHW061105310726
48974CB00002B/397